"At last New Hampshire has her ░░░░░░░░░░░░ ░░░ turbing novel chronicles the hards░░ ░░ ░░░░░░░░░ ░░░ and their colorful, compelling neighbors. Here's a tale of betrayal and loss, ignorance and poverty. Merle Drown knows that what's important is the exploration of the human heart in conflict with itself."   —John Dufresne, author of *Love Warps the Mind a Little*

"Drown knows the language of despair and deploys it with blistering acuity, ingenious turns of phrase and colloquial metaphors . . . [the family's] lives are vividly depicted."   —*Newsday*

"[The] characters are captivating in all their human frailty."
          —*Library Journal*

"A tense blend of hilarity and savagery . . . Lots of edgy, quick humor."
          —*Kirkus Reviews*

"Brutal and hilarious . . . a mini-masterpiece of Southern Gothic gone north."   —*Gallery*

"Drown clearly has affection for his cast, and he isn't slumming: he knows what a motel housekeeper's job entails, how a trailer's plumbing system works."   —*The Boston Book Review*

"Drown's earthy, graceful, hilarious prose explores love and marriage, friendship, the power of money and poverty, middle-aged regret, and other baggage of life. As funny as it is poignant . . . as fine a piece of literature as it is a provocative story."
          —*Portsmouth (NH) Herald Sunday*

"Drown has created a dead-on community of characters where *The Beans of Egypt, Maine* meets *Tobacco Road* in a trailer park in Penacook County, N.H. Hold on to your pickup; it's quite a ride."
          —*Roanoke (VA) Times & World-News*

continued . . .

"Exploring the violence-tangled love that runs in families, with a saving grace of down-east black humor, Merle Drown achieves compelling mastery in this riveting, eloquent novel."

—Richard Rhodes, Pulitzer Prize winner

"Chaucer would weep a little, laugh a lot, and inquire if Mr. Drown might not like to sit on the tailgate and split a twelve-pack of Stroh's. A gritty, funny book." —Theodore Weesner, author of *Novemberfest*

"Reminds me of Anne Tyler's *The Accidental Tourist* . . . frequently very funny . . . Drown creates vivid characters, even in such supporting players as town cop BB Eyes and Fesmire, the backwoods Bartleby who would prefer not to do anything." —*Milwaukee Journal Sentinel*

"Biting, ribald . . . engaging characters . . . What gives *The Suburbs of Heaven* much of its charm are the voices of its narrators, the five Hutchinses. Each of them is endowed with a similar blunt and idiosyncratic eloquence." —*The New York Times Book Review*

THE Suburbs of Heaven

MERLE DROWN

Merle Drown

BERKLEY BOOKS, NEW YORK

A Berkley Book
Published by The Berkley Publishing Group
A division of Penguin Putnam Inc.
375 Hudson Street
New York, New York 10014

THE SUBURBS OF HEAVEN

This is a work of fiction. Names, characters, places, and incidents either are
the product of the author's imagination or are used fictitiously, and any
resemblance to actual persons, living or dead, business establishments,
events, or locales is entirely coincidental.

Copyright © 2000 by Merle Drown.

Published by arrangement with Soho Press, Inc.

All rights reserved.
This book, or parts thereof, may not be reproduced in any form without permission.
BERKLEY and the "B" design are trademarks belonging to Penguin Putnam Inc.

PRINTING HISTORY
Soho Press, Inc., hardcover edition / February 2000
Berkley trade paperback edition / November 2001

Berkley trade paperback ISBN: 0-425-18156-1

Visit our website at
www.penguinputnam.com

This book has been catalogued with the Library of Congress.

PRINTED IN THE UNITED STATES OF AMERICA

10 9 8 7 6 5 4 3 2 1

For Pat, my lovely Owl

one

Penacook County, New Hampshire, 199-

Here I am, Jim Hutchins, fifty years old, holding a shotgun so long tendinitis is tearing right into my elbow like a starving dog after raw meat. I feel like I've crept along on dark ground far enough to wear out both knees. I'd rather tell a joke or swallow a forbidden beer with my enemy than be standing here ready to shoot, because killing just ain't in my nature. But when it comes down to it, there ain't no enemy like your own, especially when you find them right in the family. Only when you got the round chambered and the hammer cocked will you find out what you'll do. Course it ain't usual you can get your sworn enemy in your sights. Most of the time you can go along and be satisfied cursing the tire that blew on the road. But one day I woke up and said I ain't living in most of the time anymore. I've got a sworn enemy to kill. And that's when I grabbed a gun.

Life makes you eat the thorns. Smell the roses if you can, but don't forget, you're going to eat the thorns. Course I ain't so smart. If I were smart, I'd've hunted up a pistol, then my elbow wouldn't hurt so.

❧

JIM

Call me a dreamer, but walking along my old familiar road helps me to think and sort things out. I'm walking a good clip. In my lifetime I been up and down this road enough times to wear out my feet about halfway to the knees. Long ago Emory Holler and I used to skip school and trot out here and down Two Captains Road to the river. Never thought we'd be living out here. Course, he married my sister Helen, got rich, and bought a house. Me, I quit school after eighth grade and ended up in a trailer. But I don't hold that against nobody. Just the way things worked out.

It's a fine summer's day, with the sun high and proud as a boy with a new truck, the only sound a strong V-8 somewhere behind me. I'm burping the sandwich I wolfed into me, sweet burps, flavored with gherkins. If I could get Pauline to see daylight, get my kids settled, and pay off my debts, why, we could be living in the suburbs of heaven.

Up on me comes Emory's blue, one-ton Ford with a light rack big enough to illuminate airplane runways. High in the cab he sits, with no more smile to him than there is on a hammer. His right wheel carries my name. His air horns blat. Then I'm rolling in the ditch feeling a spray of gravel from his rear tire. When I stand, my left thigh stabs me right back to earth. Emory skids the truck to a halt and laughs.

"Come on," he yells. "I'll give you a ride."

When I hobble up the ditch, he pulls ahead a few yards and laughs again. "You got to move faster than that if we're going to make any money in Florida," he says. Off across the field in an old pine tree a crow caws. I pick up a stone and wing it, not at the crow, but at Emory's prize blue Ford. It dings off that fender like a perfect metal chord.

"You like to make enemies, don't you, Jim," he says. He's a solid six-footer, with long black hair, who likes to talk tough. "You know man was put on this earth for just one reason, to pull his own weight. Lately you ain't pulling enough to start one of those talking dolls."

A man can't take care of his family, what's he worth? I've asked myself that question every night. "Running me down on the open road ain't going to improve my earning power."

"Don't you carry life insurance?" he asks, and like a fool I start to answer him before I catch the smile behind his whiskers. "Maybe you're trying too hard. No one wins races by running all the time." Emory wants me to fly down to Florida and earn a lot of money roofing. I tell him that nobody goes to Florida to work. "Exactly my point," he says. "People'll throw money at you." He claims in a month I can earn enough money to pay maybe half what I owe. "I'll take good care of Pauline while you're gone."

"It ain't everything money can buy, Emory." Since Helen died, Emory can't get it up. That's what he told me.

"If sticking your dick in a woman would keep them happy," he says, "there wouldn't be a smileless female walking the face of the earth. There ain't ever been a shortage of dicks."

"Keeps me happy, Emory," I say, and head back to my trailer.

If Emory did kill Helen, like some say he did, it wa'n't with kindness.

I'm wearing debts like a second skin. I may have to turn snake to get shut of them. Dust rises under my feet, and every blade of weed in New Hampshire casts a shadow across my path. Even without wind I keep seeing movement out the corners of my eyes, like something's creeping up on me. Emory, a man with a savings account, says it's the damn $6.99 reading glasses I bought at the discount. He's always saying he wouldn't need any glasses at all to enjoy the sight of beauty I got sitting across from my breakfast every morning. Pauline—she's the beauty I've sat across from every morning for twenty-five years—says Emory's a joker.

Two years ago, Pauline wouldn't go anywhere except up to the graveyard every day. Emory, he could cheer her up. Now she's seen trees blossom twice, she has her happy days, but mostly she worries. I know she worries I'll die and leave her stranded in a trailer owing three years' back taxes. It ain't only gravity holding me down.

I don't set both feet inside my trailer before the telephone starts ringing its head off. That right there is the curse of modern man. An electric wire reaches right into your home and grabs you by the throat anytime it wants.

"Mr. Hutchins," a woman says.

"Ain't no handle on my name," I tell her. "I answer to Jim."

"Mr. Hutchins, this is Agent Roberta Emerson of the Internal Revenue Service."

"Hey, I ain't no stranger down there, you know. We used to be on a first-name basis." They garnisheed my pay a few years back, and I want to tell you it hurt, first name or no first name. They were snatching the meat from our plates before we could even set a fork to our food. Those people down to that office put me in mind of my son-in-law, Fesmire, in his younger, grabbier days.

"You owe us two hundred dollars," Agent Emerson says, like she might just be telling me the special of the day. "Now to correct your mistake, we want you to mail us a check."

"I can do that." I want Roberta Emerson to know I'm an agreeable kind of guy. "I can write a check for two hundred dollars and send it, but it'll bounce back so fast you might not get to see if I've spelled your name right."

Course I didn't make a mistake on my taxes. I just didn't have two hundred dollars. The calculator my daughter Lisa loaned me couldn't turn those numbers into cash money, any more than I can write a check right now. Just for starters, I don't have a checking account. Maybe Agent Emerson thinks she can attach my bank account.

With one son near to jail, and the other closing in on the asylum, a daughter keeping the gossips away from their TV shows, and poor Pauline so deep in grief the only things she cares about are the kids' troubles and Emory Holler ('cause she says he understands mourning), I speak right up to Ms. Roberta Emerson. "Now you've hassled me and threatened me and attached my wages, and it's not getting us anywhere. Now, what I'd like to do is pay by the month. Stores let you pay by the month. Could be time for you people to catch up with us working people."

"You send us a check for one hundred dollars next week," she says. "If you don't, we can come and put you in jail."

"For one hundred dollars you'll put me in jail?" I'm shouting loud enough for the Glebes across the street to call out the army to handle the riot in my trailer. "Ms. Emerson, you don't understand, you're talking to a loser." I laugh. "For one hundred dollars you'll feed me and clothe me and house me. From where I'm sitting, that looks like the wheel stopped at my number."

"You send us fifty dollars, Mr. Hutchins."

"Don't answer that phone," I tell Pauline. "We've had a nice fish supper, and we're going to take a walk. Bad news can wait." I shake a Camel from the pack while Pauline eyes the phone as if she can read its crying message.

"It's probably somebody selling something," she says in a kind of surrender.

Me at fifty, her at forty-five, we might make life a little easier if we step right into the sunshiny evening and for a few minutes allow a warm yellow hope that things will get back to normal. Walking keeps Pauline's legs and back limber. Still, limber or not, she tells me to slow down. "I'm not some young heifer you're hurrying home to the barn."

"You're young enough for any practical purpose," I say, running my fingers down her spine and letting them linger slyly below the small of her back. If the phone hadn't stopped, Pauline would have run right back across the yard, scattering peacock and guinea fowl on her way. She must know the caller wasn't one of the kids. They never hang up so soon.

Patting my lean stomach, I ponder the fine fish dinner, haddock with a dusting of olive oil and bread crumbs, that Bernice Hurd showed me how to fix. "A supper like that takes a gunnysackful of woe off my back," I say. I pick up the pace a little until we get past the Glebe farm. No need for Pauline to go tight-faced with tragedy tonight.

Fifty feet beyond the Glebe place, the road curves broadly to the right. I slow to the stroll I know Pauline prefers. She takes my hand, making me wonder how much is thanks for getting her past the Glebe's pond and how much is for the pleasure the two of us used to take in touch. We stroll along the road edge, heading for summer's late sunset.

I tell Pauline about Florida. At first Emory laid it out like we'd be starting a reconstruction business, with him, his boy Scooter, and my boys replacing roofs and what not and me keeping the vehicles and engines in good shape. When I asked him about permits and licenses and all, he told me I would go down there first and set it up.

"Six hundred a week, Jim. Aren't you interested?" she asks.

"I ain't ever bid on a job," I says. "Nor has Emory."

"It'd give the boys a chance to work together. I hope you're not refusing this because it was Emory offered it."

"It wouldn't matter if Mr. Goodwrench offered it," I says. "Besides, Emory ain't an enemy of mine." I never hanker after enemies the way some people do, as if having an enemy caulks cracks in their soul seams. I just let the wind blow through mine.

Don't talk to me about Mother, Gregory, my oldest, told me last week. She's my sworn enemy. It's getting so that having a sworn enemy is one of life's necessities, though I'm confounded to see why a twenty-eight-year-old guy like Gregory should lose the fit in his soul seams. If I thought going to Florida would seal him tight again, I'd jump on the first flight south.

Another turn in the road brings us to a meadow where town people pasture their horses for the summer, just like they send their kids to camp. A pair of chestnut mares walk from the watering trough to the rough stone wall by the road. I hold Pauline's hand to steady her footing as she reaches out to rub the horses' heads.

"Here comes our little friend," Pauline says, showing her heart's affection for anything young or small.

The gray, spotted pony sidles shyly beside the mares. Pauline holds out to the pony the sugar cube she brought from home. When the pony lips the sugar from her palm, she smiles as if she herself tastes the sudden sweetness.

I have to agree with Emory. Pauline is a beautiful woman. Her skin keeps the creamy glow of her young days while her gray eyes have widened, as if she sees more of the world. Sometimes at the Shaw's supermarket up in the city, I'll spot some man, often a younger guy, giving Pauline a smile that lingers beyond "hello." A beautiful woman she is and blown by with grief.

"Come along, now," I tease, "or we'll go soft in the legs from lack of exercise."

Pauline answers right back. "You think I'm an old field horse. I'm lucky you haven't hitched a plow onto me."

"I don't own a plow."

We return to our "ramble," as Pauline calls it, a mile and a half out, a mile and a half back. "You're a pretty woman, Pauline," I tell her.

"I'm sweaty as a racehorse."

I wonder why women see themselves only in the right now but men see themselves in some forever place, either handsome or ordinary. I notice she compared herself to a racehorse this time. Not a field horse. At the big curve, we turn onto the nameless dirt road, strewn with rocks as big as your hand, that becomes soft, rutted grass. We follow the path to the clearing that looks out over meanders in the river. Swallows fly in and out of their nesting holes, so busy, they might be human.

The sinking sun sends violet rays across the sky, improving my health more than walking. I lay my arm across Pauline's back, careful not to put weight on her bad shoulder. To the west violet deepens to red. Down in the valley, where the cut bank has made a beach, people come out of the water to put on shirts and jeans.

Pauline says, "What are you going to tell Emory?"

I strain my focus to the beach where a woman standing by a black four-by-four is pulling off her bathing-suit bottom. Half-hidden by the truck's open door, she tugs a long T-shirt below her hips, steps out of a bikini, and slips on a pair of shorts, pulling them up over the round curve of her behind. My groin begins to blossom like those slow-motion films of desert flowers. The woman is Kari Reed, my boss's twenty-five-year-old daughter. I recognize the truck. I recognize more of Kari than I should.

Hitching my jeans and resettling my crowded crotch, I say, "I'll smash Emory if he ever tries to run me over again."

When I make threats, Pauline usually sputters at me like a cold chain saw's first start. This time, she squeezes the corners of her mouth and turns her eyes to the ground. She is too worried to scold me, worried about the children, like we might step on one right here in the matted grass, like at any moment another one will stop walking the face of the earth. Though I'm a miserable bastard for thinking it, I'm hoping she'll quit her worry so we can cap the evening with romance. As it sinks, the sun bands the sky scarlet. There is nothing grieving about its beauty.

Walking back, Pauline talks about her day at work, talk I favor to keep her mind from skidding into the ditch of worry. Pauline works as a housekeeper at a motel twenty minutes south on the interstate.

"Elaine's finding it too hard to bend to make the beds," she tells me. "Pretty soon she'll be sitting to home waiting for her new baby. Lucky for me because with tourist season near over they'd've cut back our hours."

I say, "I'm glad you'll keep that job awhile longer. I don't long to move to the village of hunger and starvation."

"Making up beds starts my shoulder to aching," Pauline says.

We grip hands and swing our arms playfully as we walk back on Two Captains Road. "If she'd move me to laundry permanently, I could manage, but there's not that much business."

As we walk into our half-dark yard, the motion-detector light switches on, flooding my pickup, her Tempo, and the trailer door-way with a quick shot of daytime. Inside, the telephone rings again. I jump in to answer it myself. I guess it's Tommy, our youngest, who causes more trouble than a loose pair of billy goats.

"Hello?" I say. "Hello?" I hang up.

Disappointment on her face like spoiled milk, she says, "Maybe it's the underwear thief, seeing if anybody's home."

"We could take the phone off the hook."

"I pay for that phone," Pauline says, "and I want it working."

She drapes the parakeet cage to set the bird sleeping while I lock the door, something I used to do only when we left the trailer. That was before this guy started stealing women's under-wear all over town. Down the hall we walk, past the bathroom and the locked door of Elizabeth's room, to our bedroom. In our old place we had no bedroom. The four kids slept in the two bed-rooms, and we used the couch.

Privacy aids what I call the good sense of an old dog. I keep a package of rubbers right on the built-in bureau under the VFW hat I never wear. Neither me nor Pauline being fixed, I say the old dog knows when to stop breeding pups, though at the rate we're going lately, this box will last me a couple of lifetimes. "Old dog!" Pauline says. "Old dog! If you're an old dog, what does that make me?"

"Safe."

In the soft grip of our embraces, we swim under the sheet and light blanket. Pauline starts a silky moaning, a sound like croon-ing. Crooning and swimming, the soft taste of her breast, the pushing, stiff, giving nipple against my tongue, giving little, then no thought to the telephone or the weirdo underwear thief or heart-snatching grief.

It's been so long, it seems new.

Linked, we move against each other, our sweat easing our way. Somewhere in the woods behind the trailer a little screech owl sets up his soft and rhythmic call like our soft and rhythmic rocking. Warmth and sweat glide between us. I reach back to toss the blanket and top sheet off us. In the glow of the dresser lamp moisture shines at Pauline's temples and on her upper lip. As she opens her eyes, their stunning gray holds a joy as old and wild as wet stones. I kiss her lips, tongues slithering. We rock each other. Pounding, reaching then falling into a gliding place that passes peacefully into sleep.

The telephone rings. I, without a watch to my name, know it's two o'clock. Out of habit I check the kitchen clock; I'm congratulating myself on being right about the time, and the phone's still ringing.

"Who was it?" Pauline asks.

It was BB Eyes, the local cop. He said our younger boy, Tommy, and his girlfriend, Penny, are in a hell of a fight. Pauline says, "I've got to work in the morning."

Of course I know Pauline can't bear to hear Penny—Squatty Body I calls her—curse Tommy when they're in a row.

In a row they are. When I get to their apartment building, Tommy has Squatty Body by the ankles, dangling her out the third-story window. Even drunk, Tommy's got the strength of a wild horse, but BB Eyes is worried he'll drop her and Cream of Wheat her brains in the parking lot. BB Eyes, he's moving around the parking lot like he's afraid she'll land on *his* head. I tell BB Eyes that Tommy won't drop her, not accidentally anyway. With her dark, curly hair hanging and her shirt fallen past her breasts, she looks like upside-down broccoli.

"Crawl back up the cunt that spit you out!" she screams at Tommy. "Get a life, you goddamned half-footer!"

"*Now* we best worry about Tommy letting go of her," I tell BB Eyes. "Tommy!"

Not words, but growls and roars come from Tommy's throat. I tell BB Eyes to call the fire department to bring the life net. He laughs and says they haven't had one of those in twenty years.

"I called them for a ladder," he says, "but it's damn hard to sneak up on someone with a ladder."

I start up the stairs. Even inside the building I can hear Penny screaming, like rasping a file on sheet metal. To be honest I like it better than hearing her words. Tommy's still roaring. I unlock the apartment door with the key Frank was smart enough to give me back when he rented the place to Tommy. A storm has crashed through this room, tossing chairs and table and ashtrays, leaving upright only the couch like a raggedy old man in the corner.

"Tommy," I say, just loud enough to carry over his bellowing. "Tommy, hear your name for Christ sakes!" His growls shift up an octave, giving me hope he'll start talking. "You don't want to go to jail for her."

"Fucking bitch." Words start spilling out his mouth, but I don't ponder what he says. I bear-hug him and grapple her legs just beyond his hands. Thank God they're skinnier than the rest of her. Then I fall over backward, pulling Tommy and Penny right on top of me.

From the ground, BB Eyes says, it looked like Penny disappeared up into the air. "I thought maybe she'd flown off to heaven."

"Ain't likely," I tell him.

At the station BB Eyes puts Tommy under restraint from going near Penny. "Domestic violence gets you ninety-six hours restraint automatically," BB Eyes says when I take Tommy out to the truck. "You see you stay away from Penny and the apartment."

"Why don't you call it four days," Tommy says, "or didn't anybody teach you numbers?"

Back at the trailer Pauline says, "That's why BB Eyes always picks on Tommy, because the boy is smarter than he is."

"Tommy don't always have to point it out to him," I say.

"Penny frightened Tommy. I know that with a mother's certainty."

"Frightened!" I say. "Blind, mad, roaring drunk is more like it." I look to him for an answer, but he's passed out on the sofa.

"Emory called while you were gone," says Pauline. "Said if you needed help to call him."

She's trying to calm me, I suppose, but this is just poking me in the armpit. "How'd he know about it?"

"Scanner," she says. "He'll put Tommy up if you want."

"Maybe he ought to take Tommy to Florida."

GREGORY

It was hot that day, June 20, two years back. I wonder why I always remember the weather. Momma remembers that the week before the twentieth, Elizabeth had turned woman. Elizabeth, smart as always, figured that things might have changed since Momma had become a woman, so she called our sister, Lisa. Or called the store up there and had them go get Lisa, because her husband, Fesmire, had ripped the phone out of the wall. He said he wasn't going to make it easier for Lisa to talk to her boyfriends. I don't remember the weather the day Lisa came, but I remember the weather on the twentieth. A Fesmire kind of day, so warm that when I saw Fesmire himself at the hospital the evening of the twentieth, he was stripped to just a T-shirt. At noon I'd bought a six-pack of Coke, and we sat outside in the shade drinking out of the cans like cannibals, Momma, Father, Elizabeth, and me. It was past black-fly season, and the mosquitoes hadn't swarmed yet, so it was nice out there. Elizabeth in her jeans and new shirt looked like a teenager the way she tilted back that Coke and swallowed big gulps. Of course she wa'n't a teenager, only just turned eleven. She hogged that Coke down before the rest of us had half finished ours. Then with a "Look, Momma," she grabbed her baton, which always seemed to be near her like a dog hanging around a kid, and jumped onto the grass in front of us. After three years of baton lessons she'd learned to show off.

Elizabeth pranced around the yard, twirling and tossing that baton until she set Buffy to barking and drove the guinea hens to roost in the trees and start their calling. Right in the middle of all that noise, she was the happiest child you might hope to see. Lime dust coated my hands chalky and off-flavored the Coke so I might've thought Tommy had slipped booze in my can if he were around, which he wa'n't. Funny how I can remember the heat and the bitter tang lent to the Coke without remembering where Tommy was. I know he wa'n't in school. He was long past when school would allow him inside. In those days the snake hadn't hatched in my head. I was happier. I could remember more things, though I didn't know as much. Now I know everything. I think the hateful snake sneaks hatfuls of wisdom into my brain.

Those little slow kids from over to the Glebes' place came across the field and hollered for Elizabeth to play with them. I guess only one of them is real slow, though I can never tell which one it is. They were little, only one started school. The Glebe kids, both blond, wore their hair so that from the distance of our yard, they looked like big flowers. When Elizabeth joined them, she became a bigger flower, the three of them a bouquet moving through the weeds to the old cow pond across the Glebes' field. Hot as it was, the rains had fallen steady the week before, brimming up the cow pond, which would have been handy had the Glebes owned cows or even leased out the land for grazing. No cows grazed or lapped water or stood in their stupid way waving flies away with their tails. Instead three children walked to the slippery bank of the cow pond to play.

Father and I talked about the land I'd bought from Uncle Emory, a ten-acre plot, some field land and better than half the rest in hardwoods, so firewood wouldn't ever be a problem. And, Father pointed out, I could always sell some of the wood for ready cash. Uncle Emory had let me have it for five hundred dollars down. Emory Holler, my sworn enemy. Not then. Then I trusted him like the heft of a good ax.

Momma had just said, "I'm glad you're not moving far away," when we heard the children. At first not a one of us so much as turned a head because the squeaks sounded like the jolts little voices give to air for no reason other than they're there. Then, when Momma told me, "I couldn't bear to lose track of you," we all turned our heads, and Father and I stood because the children had walked clear back across the field. Their near voices blatted loud like crows, blatting sounds I couldn't turn into words, nor could Father until Momma said, "Where's Elizabeth?"

"Jesus Christ," Father said. Only the two Glebe children stood there, still cawing.

As we ran across the road, their words came together into human talk. Now, ahead of Father in the field, I could hear him panting and praying, "Jesus Christ, oh, Jesus, oh, no, Jesus."

At the pond's edge was nothing. The sun beat down hot on the raspy grass and the drying mud as if to preserve this empty time, like drying meat. No towel, no shoes, no clothes. Just that wide cow pond, rippleless under the hot, old sun. Then Father, still panting, arrived, and quickly I put my hand on his arm and squeezed hard and reminded him he couldn't swim.

"Here," he said as he pointed. He was so glad to do something, he almost smiled. He pointed to a wide, wet trough in the steep bank's mud showing where she'd slid in.

How long can you hold your breath? I thought, kicking off my boots and ripping off my shirt. The sun suddenly hot on my bare back, I wondered, how long can you hold your breath? I tried to walk into the water, but the slippery bank gave way so steeply I had to dive out to keep from falling. I couldn't tell how deep the pond was. I didn't know. How long can you hold your breath? The water was warm and dark. When I dove under, I couldn't see except for a little light at the surface and the tiny pieces of dirt floating in front of my eyes. How long can you hold your breath? I kicked straight down until I reached the bottom, mucky and still slanting toward the center, like a bowl. I followed the curve, moving my hands through the mud, cooler here than on the top. How long can you? I looked up, but I couldn't see light. Where is she? How long can? I turned to swim along the bottom, back to the shore, but my ears started screaming. How long? I pushed off the bottom, letting dead air out of my mouth as I screamed for the surface. How? Into the air, gasping air, hot air.

"Did you—?"

"No," I told Father, and I dove again.

Down into the dark deep I searched with my chest aching and my mind racing for a clue, a direction. Already she'd been down here three of my breaths plus whatever time it took the Glebe children to cross the field and yell us into the fearful scene. The center of the pond. I swam down. I swam to the center, reaching, always reaching and swimming, while my poor lungs asked their dreadful question. She must be in the center. I knew she was in the center. She had to be in the center. Only she wasn't.

At the surface, I had to turn to find Father. He was pointing back to the road. From there I could hear the sirens. Father pointed down at his feet, so I knew he stood where Elizabeth had gone in. He must have thought I was looking too far away. Again I dove and swam toward him as best I could. When I came up, the divers were sliding into the pond.

Fast, I thought. I wondered if they came from the city or Fish and Game or the State Police. I knew our little rescue squad didn't have trained scuba divers or equipment. Once more I kicked down into the darkness holding my breath against hope. Without knowing where I was, I found Elizabeth, her hair floating between my fingers, but I couldn't close on it. I lost it. Ferns? Pond grass? No, it was her hair. Forcing myself back and waving my arms to catch the hair whose light red I couldn't see, I ran out of air. My lungs emptied. I pulled for the top. Pain in my lungs. Water in my nose. My throat coughing. No light. No light. I broke the surface in a gasp.

"She's under me," I said, but they couldn't understand me. I didn't know I was crying. "She's under me."

A diver swam over and made to pull me out until I swung my fist at him. "Not me. My sister. Under me!" My throat hurt from crying and coughing and screaming. And my lungs.

The diver called the other divers, and they waved me away. I swam to the shore, where Father had to give me a pull to help me crawl up the muddy bank. I gasped and cried. I couldn't stand. They hadn't come up yet. How long can you hold your breath? I coughed sour water. Father grabbed my shoulder and pounded my back. I puked a little more sour water. I stopped crying. The divers, two of them, brought Elizabeth up.

"How long," I started to ask, then coughed up some more sour water, "how long can—"

"It took them a half hour to get here," Father said. "One's Fish and Game, the other's from over to Lake Franklin. They said that's about as fast as they've ever arrived at a scene."

"No. I couldn't have been out there all that time."

"You've been diving and diving," he said. "I thought—"

He stopped. We could see her clearly as the divers handed her up to the paramedics on the bank. She wasn't breathing. She looked shiny, like a fish. Only when Father grabbed my arm did I realize I'd started to go to her. One of the dark-uniformed men said, "CPR." They fitted the oxygen mask to her face, her small face. She was the youngest, the littlest, of us all. "Heartbeat," the guy said, making my heart jump right up and down like it was half fool, like a pleated paper heart they have at Valentine parties. Elizabeth, the party girl, always a costume for school, a Pilgrim, an elf, queen of the May, she marked the holidays and seasons for us so well I scarce can remember her going off to the bus in regular school clothes. There was nothing regular about her.

That's what I said at the hospital. "There was nothing regular about her."

"Shh," said Father. We were in the downstairs lobby, where he could smoke. In those days I didn't smoke. Outside, the dark grew.

"What?" I asked.

He pulled me over to the windows, away from Momma. "You're talking like's she's already died."

It grew darker outside. Shadows swelled among the trees, and the nice old houses. I wondered if they always built hospitals in nice neighborhoods so people would feel safe or comfortable going there. I knew Elizabeth was going to die. I couldn't understand why Father didn't know it too. The shadows along the streets lengthened and lengthened, pulling darkness in long lines into the nice neighborhood. Momma's cheeks turned chafey and red from her crying. She twisted her ring round and round her finger and bit her knuckles until Father stubbed his cigarette and held her hand. I'd never seen him hold her hand before. I used to put Elizabeth in my lap after supper so we could watch a TV animal show together, and while she sat there, she'd wrap her fingers around my hand. Tonight she would die.

The next day my chain saw chewed through a shade tree in the nice neighborhood. I would leave all the houses naked. The raw cut stumps would stand dumb when the next parade came along without Elizabeth twirling her baton, her skinny legs pumping up and down and flashing the sparkling white boots, her face swiveling her smile. But when BB Eyes stopped me, I'd only cut down one tree.

I used to see her in her room practicing her smile in front of the little mirror she'd set on her bureau, standing there and stretching her lips until she could see her gums. The kids from the grade school marched in the Memorial Day parade with the Cub Scouts and the high school bands and only three baton twirlers from the grade school, including Elizabeth. Momma took a whole roll of pictures.

By the third or fourth day her pet turtle started to smell bad enough to send its scent through the closed door of her room. We'd all forgot the turtle Elizabeth changed every other day, a little pond turtle crawling around the sink while she washed out the fishbowl he lived in. She liked to turn him on his back and scrub his yellow belly shell with a toothbrush, tracing the dark lines as if she were drawing a picture. Father cleaned the turtle once. Then, after the funeral, when the smell started again, he took the turtle out to the lake to release it because he'd already put the lock on Elizabeth's bedroom door. He said we'd always be forgetting the little turtle.

Talk. All the talk. Not about her turtle, which she'd brought up from the lake the year before, not about her baton twirling, not even about her smile. Talk about the cow pond, because it was a great mystery that Elizabeth never woke up to explain. "If she even knew the answer herself," Tommy said in his smart-alecky way. I said I'd cuff him if he kept acting smart-alecky. Momma said he wasn't acting smart-alecky. I'd cuffed him before so he got cagey and kept his smart-alecky comments to himself.

We didn't even know how she came to be in the pond. Those Glebe children were too little or too slow to tell us what happened. We all knew the bank was slippery. I heard that word *slippery* so often before the funeral it made me want to throw up. I couldn't eat much anyway, but what I did eat slid down my gullet and turned all wet and slooshy in my insides, making me feel sick even after I ate. Tommy ate okay. Nothing slippery bothered him because he's slippery himself. And Father kept saying, "The thing that gets me is she could swim. Swim better than I ever could."

She had taken swimming lessons at the Parks and Recreation Department pool, much as she had taken baton lessons and joined the Brownies and done all those things Lisa and Tommy and I never did because Elizabeth, once she got to school, always felt part of everything. Momma got out all those little white cards with the red crosses on them that Elizabeth had earned in the swimming program and sat with them in her lap and counted them as if the one that might solve the puzzle must be missing. "She could swim," Momma too said, echoing Father, but with some sense that if she said it often enough, Elizabeth would swim up out of the cow pond and not be dead anymore. And I tried all by myself, speaking so softly no one, not even me, could hear the words, "She could swim," over and over, one hundred times.

Talk. About how slippery were the edges of the pond. How she must have slid in. I pictured her walking the edge of the pond, legs lifted high and arms aiming for the sky as if she were marching in the parade only without her baton, but I didn't say it. I listened. Tommy thought maybe in roughhousing with the Glebe children she'd taken a push or shove and lost her balance. But Momma said those children—she'd seen them a thousand times!—never roughhoused. She thought Elizabeth'd leaned over to get something, maybe something she'd dropped—Father interrupted and said that none of her things were missing.

"Well, maybe it was something she'd just made," Momma said, half-sniffling, half-shouting, "like a flower bracelet or something."

"And hit her head on some rock?" Lisa said. She stayed a couple of days after the funeral, looking for something to do the whole time, making coffee or washing dishes, washing the coffee cups before you'd even taken the last swallow.

"The mucky bottom of the pond sucked her down," I said, "and locked her there in its suction."

"She could swim, though," Momma said, and kept sobbing.

I dreamed of the muck. Every night muck started at my feet, crawling over the sheet, past my ankles and knees, filling in my crotch, crowding my chest and arms, catching my breath and smothering me as it covered my face, warm, dark, slippery-slidey muck. Muck seeped in my ears, up my nose, sluicing into my mouth. All that muck.

And talk. Talk talk. Until I couldn't stand it anymore. With my chain saw dangling from my arm, I took off into the woods, and still above the cracking and snorting of the mufflerless McCulloch and the falling trees, I heard the talk. I would have gone back to the hospital for more trees, but BB Eyes told me he'd have to jail me. I would have gone across the field, but you can't chainsaw a cow pond.

Then came the burial.

Father told me, "At least the grave will be too small to jump into." I knew he had started worrying about what I might want to do. He made like he was talking about Momma or maybe himself, but I knew he meant me. I could hear all the talk.

Momma talked about the tombstone. She wanted it carved in the shape of a doll, a Cabbage Patch doll like Elizabeth loved. Her Cabbage Patch dolls and teddy bears and the long-legged, gangly, striped Yon-ey she used to drag everywhere through the house, all sat on her bedroom shelf along with the stopped pendulum clock Aunt Helen had given her, behind the closed and locked door. The only Cabbage Patch doll of hers anyone would see would be her grave marker.

"It will cost hundreds and hundreds of dollars," Father said to us, to me and Tommy and Lisa, not to Momma. And to me alone he said, "Just meeting the taxes ain't easy."

"Don't be scrinchy, Father," Lisa said. "Momma needs for that stone to be there."

Tommy said, "It don't matter what's there. We know where the grave is, Momma ain't going to see it but about once a week, and Elizabeth ain't ever going to see it." He looked at me real quick, his hand going to the table fast like he might have to hoist himself out of his chair and run out of the trailer. I bore down on him with my eyes to seal and sear and seam his fear up inside him. It kept him watching, like I have to watch.

Earnest money that I'd given Emory for my land I asked back. When I gave it all to Father, he told me it wasn't enough to put that stone doll atop Elizabeth's grave. But Father ordered the doll anyway because Tommy was wrong about how often Momma would visit the grave. Every day Tommy stood, winging stones out in the yard as if he would waste death and grief, and every day Momma got into her little car and drove to the cemetery. Tommy stood, winging stones, not saying that he was wrong, but letting me see, so I unseamed him and let the fear pour out and wrapped my arm around his shoulder so he knew I wouldn't waste him.

I worried that Father would have no money for taxes and not enough for the tombstone, and he'd be evicted and Elizabeth left with a naked grave. Tommy, back to his smart-alecky ways, would be no help because he wouldn't keep a job longer than to earn the price of a drunk. Lisa, living with Fesmire, had no money. Out in the woods on my land I sat sore and sorrowful and couldn't find a plan any more than I could find a platypus.

I drove my truck to Father's friend, Malcolm Hurd.

"It's a terrible thing, Gregory," Malcolm said, talking only about Elizabeth's headstone because I didn't dare go so far as to mention the taxes.

"A dreadful thing, a child's death," Malcolm's wife, Bernice, added. She'd brought out ice tea, which was nice of her except the lemony taste cut out the sweetness most altogether, but I wasn't brought up to complain over what I was given. The glasses themselves amazed me with soft, bubbly bumps all over so your hands didn't feel the cold of the ice tea.

"Your mother's picked out this doll already?" Malcolm asked. His talk bumped over *doll*. He stared away at where his donkeys ate by the fence Father had built for him. I wondered if he was worrying about spending money for a stone doll. Father always said Malcolm had more money than God, but unlike God he worried about the tiny mistakes and not the big sins.

"She's seen a picture of it," I said.

Bernice drank her tea and wiped her lips as if she'd just slugged down a shot of liquor. "It'd be a comfort to the poor woman. Can you think of another?"

"That ain't what's the predicament here," Malcolm Hurd said. "Jim works for me."

I couldn't figure what was fussing him, but I wasn't going to ask him because I could tell that Malcolm was going to give Father the money. "I can show you the picture of the doll," I said.

"No," said Malcolm. He started over to where his dog was running along the chain-link fence Father had set up. "The Legion has got a fund for such a thing. The rest of the money will come from the Legion."

"Jim's not a vet," Bernice said.

"I'm the commander of this post," Malcolm told her, "and it'll be my money anyway."

Knowing the stone doll was coming comforted Momma. She didn't try to jump into Elizabeth's hungry grave. But every night Momma cried. She cried through the service with the minister saying, "Suffer the little children." I thought Elizabeth must have suffered, suffocated in that mucky mud, and now Momma's suffering and her crying crowded me right out of the trailer until I took to sleeping in my truck up to my land so that I wouldn't come to crying like I was touched. I believe Momma was touched.

You go by that stone you know right away a child's buried there because nobody would buy a doll like that for a grown-up. At night when the sky showed clear and moon-bright, that doll smiled smooth and gray. Momma never came at night, as though she feared tempting fate to touch her again. So she missed the talking, all the talking, talk to teach you and make you feel the suffocating mucky mud that filled Elizabeth's mouth. I asked Father if the doctors ever got all the mud out of her, but he just said, "Gregory, don't think of that so much."

I don't have to think about it. I hear that talk most anytime. It's waiting. I waited up to the cemetery until that smooth, gray stone doll spoke without opening her mouth. "Listen," she said, sounding just like Elizabeth.

"Listen," BB Eyes said one night. "You oughtn't come here all the time, Gregory. It ain't good for you."

"Thank you," I told him. I knew what he was up to. He'd driven the cruiser under the arched ironwork of the cemetery entrance, followed the roads around as if he were running a maze, and stared at me sitting in the truck with the door open listening to Elizabeth talk. I'd switched off the dome light, not so he couldn't see me, but so he couldn't hear what Elizabeth said.

She spoke to me so low, so sweet, it was like our own special code, still I didn't want BB Eyes to hear what she said. She told me to watch him, but not to worry about him. I worried about her because I knew she suffered even though she seldom mentioned it. Just every once in a while she'd say, "It isn't right."

None of it was right.

Not every night did I go to the cemetery. Some nights after working all day and laying out my foundation until past dark at my land, I had all I could do to flop into bed and fall asleep. In my dreary dreams Elizabeth would try to talk to me, but the snake stopped her, the snake I couldn't see. It scared the hell out of me.

PAULINE

The system keeps me going today. Without a system, cleaning motel rooms would be like swimming in the dark. And if I didn't have something to concentrate on besides Jim and Tommy, I'd screech myself right out of my skin. I know Tommy's going to need more money for a lawyer, and I just promised Lisa I'd buy the kids' school clothes, because it's a legal guarantee Fesmire won't waste any money on children's clothes. They don't stay sized to them long enough to wear them out, he told me, and as for style, the less a child knows about style, the better off she is. Let them wear hand-me-downs or buy used clothes, he said. That's Fesmire, no sense of looks, no idea of how a touch of beauty can cheer a person up, as if he slept in a vinegar barrel when he was little instead of a crib. Well, not my children, and not my grandchildren, mister, you'd better believe that. There's enough vinegar sprinkled on everyone in this life without looking for more.

I've loaded my cart, and I'm ready to go.

My boss Carol's gone off to visit Elaine, who's home waiting to deliver her baby. After I got past the morning sickness, I enjoyed all four of my pregnancies, even when people would cast cold eyes on my big belly. Jim's sister Helen all but asked me where the money would come from for this new brat. Course Helen only had Scooter, and were she alive, she might cast cold eyes on how he's turned out, though as for money, Emory and Scooter have no problems. Some women just don't receive the warm joy of pregnancy.

Before she left, Carol handed me the holster belt and portable phone like I might forget and reminded me there were twenty units rented last night, though I had the list stuck to my cart.

On the cart the spray bottle of cleaner stares empty at me. I grab the gallon jug of Speedball and gurgle it up to the line on the sprayer. Carol's husband David's got his system too, always a gallon ahead, but no system's going to help me until I can get on full-time hours here this fall. The telephone rings, I can never ignore a telephone.

I click on the cordless, but nothing. I hope it wasn't an emergency. Jim always says if it's an emergency, they'll keep trying or they'll call back. But I imagine someone giving up. Maybe it was Emory. He said he might call to see how things came out with Tommy.

Inside Unit 2 I head right for the bathroom to give the disinfectant spray time to work while I clean up the bedroom. On the way I notice one good thing—they only used one bed, though the bad thing is the tip envelope's empty. It's not even wrinkled, so maybe they didn't see it. Still, only about half the people think to leave the chambermaids a tip. I got twenty dollars from a couple who stayed a week once. And they put it right in my hand, not in the envelope, so Carol told me I didn't have to put it in the tip bucket and share with Elaine. It brought a month's worth of baton lessons for Elizabeth.

I sit on the bed and let the tears come.

The phone brings me back. This time it receives the call loud and clear. The voice asks for David. I say I'm the maid, and the man says good-bye and hangs up. When you say you're the maid, they don't ask anything else because they figure you don't know anything.

These people only slept in one bed, but they wrestled these covers to death. Emory likes to hear funny stories of what I find in the rooms, sexy stories. Some we never figure out.

One woman left behind a satin pillow cover, which she called for. A lot of time they don't call back for clothes they leave behind, socks, underwear, pajamas. I just bag them, label them with name and date, and wait until spring, when we turn them to rags, but this woman paid to have David mail her that satin pillowcase. She must have had skin like yours, Emory said when I told him about it. Thinking about his saying that has confused me so, I've taken a clean set of white sheets off the cart when I know perfectly well the queen-size sheets are all color-coded beige.

I'm always glad when Emory can laugh, just as he says my laughter is better than another woman's touch. Of course we don't touch, not like that. After Helen died, I hugged him. Anybody would. How dreadful for him to remember the crash down the cellar stairs, then his calling her name, over and over. Oh, God, don't I know what that's like, calling until your throat's so raw it feels like another punishment. Except he knew right away that Helen had died, which made a difference in our cases.

She lay on the cellar floor. When I got there, Emory already had his hand on her neck, shaking his head, saying there was nothing. I thought he meant there was nothing wrong. How stupid of me. Then, on the way down, I straightened one of the carpet remnants on the stairs, and he told me not to move things. He said the police wouldn't want anything disturbed.

That's when I hugged him because I could see grief sucking him into himself. He couldn't get down on his hands and knees and kiss her like I knew he wanted to. I tried to pour all the warmth of my heart into him as the cold seeped into his body making him stone inside. I don't remember, but we must have gone upstairs to call 911. I think I hugged him until BB Eyes pulled into the yard. I asked Emory why the police would come, and he said because of the insurance, which was the first I knew he had such a big policy on her.

I get the blanket and top sheet tucked in with nice hospital corners like Carol showed me when I notice the bedspread is stained, so I have to trot back to the laundry room for a fresh one. When I get there, the telephone rings again. Jim would say I'm getting my due today and would be laughing at me right now. He lacks BB Eyes' weight to shake when he laughs, though his freckles dance all over his face. I see them dance on his cheeks and forehead and on the muscles of his arms, whether he's opening a jar for me or just running his fingers through that short, thinning blond hair of his. Barely tall enough to reach the cupboard's top shelf, he's either laughing or moving or standing still strong enough to cause a stir.

It's a message for this older couple who are renting one of the end cottages, that don't have telephones. When I knock on the door, it takes mister a while to answer. I don't know what he was doing, but it sure wasn't dressing because he's as naked as a pane of glass.

And back there on the bed so is she.

"Here," I say, handing him the telephone. "You press the button and say hello."

At least I won't be annoyed with that telephone for a while. The last time Jim and I stayed at a motel was on our honeymoon. Once I thought of bringing Jim down here, for a kind of holiday, but I worried he'd think it was a waste of money.

These people must have been in a hurry this morning because the tray's all messy with the courtesy cups tipped over, sugar and Cremora spilled, and napkins on the floor. I toss the junk in the wastebasket liner and put a new setup on the tray, then I finish up the bathroom and check the bureau drawers and under the bed before I vacuum.

That's when I see them. They're red, and at first I think they're underpants. Then I realize these are running shorts, his I'll guess from the size. In the pocket I find a fifty-dollar bill with Ulysses S. Grant giving me as blank a look as I gave the naked mister. The first thought that comes is, Will he remember? Will he think, I left a fifty-dollar bill in those running shorts?

Will I get caught? They didn't even leave me a tip. I'm not saying that makes it right, but probably he won't miss it. If he goes running with a fifty for pocket change, he won't miss it. What's he expect to do, buy a twenty-five-dollar Coke and a twenty-five-dollar candy bar?

The first words out of BB Eyes' mouth were, I'm sorry. His blue shirt bulging over his wide, black belt, he said it again and how terrible it was. He even put his arm around Emory's shoulders. I thought he was going to cry the way his little eyes scrinched up and his chubby cheeks twitched. He took off his hat, which was the first time I saw he was starting to go bald. Emory was stone cold.

BB Eyes asked when it happened, then he asked how. Emory

told him she must have slipped on the loose carpet remnant. Which one? BB Eyes asked. When we looked down the stairs, not a one of them was out of place, so Emory said I had straightened one of them, out of habit, from years of chambermaid work, and he forced a half smile when he said it. His face didn't look sad or funny, but harsh, the pink smile hiding in the black beard, and I saw BB Eyes staring at Emory. That's right, I said, I did.

What was she going down cellar for? BB Eyes asked.

I don't know, Emory answered him. I was out in the garage with Pauline. We were bringing in groceries.

I had their gift in my arms, a plaque that said TOMORROW WILL BE BETTER that Tommy painted for me. Emory has it mounted up over the kitchen sink now. I started to explain how I'd stopped over with a housewarming present just as they'd gotten back from the supermarket, but BB Eyes cut me off. She wasn't storing potatoes down there, he said more than asked. She must not have been carrying anything because there's nothing on the floor. Unless you cleaned that up too, Pauline? I shook my head. She didn't have a load of clothes because the washer's up here.

Maybe she heard a mouse, Emory said. She's always hearing mice.

BB Eyes looked at him again like he wasn't at all the Emory Holler that BB Eyes had grown up with, but some stranger speaking with an accent BB Eyes couldn't quite understand. What did you hear, Pauline? BB Eyes asked me.

I heard the crash down the stairs or onto the floor, I told him, and Emory—I stopped my mouth. I was going to cry. Helen and I had hard thoughts against each other over the years, but more than once she had been as good to me as if she'd been my own sister and not just sister-in-law.

Emory what? BB Eyes asked me.

And I did cry then, but still I got it out. Emory went into the kitchen and walked down the stairs and found her gone.

BB Eyes said how sorry he was. He said a photographer would come to take pictures before Helen's body was taken away for the autopsy. He said maybe Emory would like to go somewhere while all this business was going on.

I'm going into the living room for a drink, Emory said. How about you two? I refused, but BB Eyes drank a shot down, mostly to keep Emory company, I thought. Why an autopsy? Emory asked.

It's standard procedure in a case like this, BB Eyes said, protects everybody.

A case like what? Emory asked.

That's when I knew I'd have to lie again and keep lying, and I cried, as much with guilt as with sorrow.

I've cleaned ten units, done a half dozen loads of laundry, and my knees and back are talking to me, but not about that fifty-dollar bill, which is folded in the front pocket of my slacks.

My system keeps me going. The disinfectant spray has set in this bathroom, so I wipe out the sink, polish the fixtures, and buff the mirror. I stop moving, hoping the pain from my back and my knees will clog my rotten thinking. When I first went to the doctor about my knees, he asked me what motel I was cleaning. Just like that, he knew. Sometimes I think Jim knows I lied about Emory being in the garage with me. Jim makes me angry knowing more than I want him to, then he really makes me mad not knowing what I want him to.

On my knees I'm wiping the floor tile as I back out of the bathroom. David says there's nothing worse than showing a unit to someone and seeing a big, long hair draped over the sink. I can think of worse things, many of them.

"Aaahh!"

A thrilling, tickling finger runs back up my spine, scaring, exciting, pleasing me all to once. Emory says, "That's the most satisfied scream I've heard in years."

"You joker," I tell him. "I ought to slap you."

He stands above me and leans his gruff, laughing, beardy face down for me to slap. He's wearing a shirt, tie, and a dark suit. I try to joke about not wanting to scratch my hand on his whiskers, but I'm fighting the feeling of funerals—the only time I've seen Emory dressed up is at funerals. Except that today he's wearing the Leather aftershave, and at the funerals he didn't wear any scent. I pull myself up and ask him what he's all decked out for.

"Big deal, real estate deal." He leans down, whiskers brushing my face, and whispers in my ear like there might be a thousand people watching us, hoping to learn our secret. "Wal-Mart."

"What?"

"A fifty-acre parcel out of my land. They'll pay a telephone number, but don't say a word because nothing's signed except some earnest money."

"I never say a word."

He says his land lies close to the interstate exit, which is why Wal-Mart wants it, only there is a problem, which is Gregory's shack, as he calls it. It's in the way of some access roads they'll have to build, and it's an eyesore, a nuisance really, so sometime soon Gregory'll have to get out. The past year while Gregory built the place, Emory never complained because he had no use for the land (and I know he didn't want to upset me in my mourning), but now he had to act because after all business is business, and Gregory has no legal claim to the land he built on.

"You know I gave him his money back," Emory says. "That was a noble thing he did. Just like you standing up for me to BB Eyes."

Right now, thinking of Emory so stone in that kitchen, thinking of him evicting Gregory off his property, I want to ask him straight out if he did push Helen down those stairs so he could collect the two hundred thousand dollars insurance money, because I did hear words snapping between them in the kitchen before she went down, which was why I stayed in the garage an extra minute. And I never could figure out why she would go down cellar right then anyway.

"Emory," I ask him, "what do you mean, 'a telephone number'?"

2

two

GREGORY

Emory Holler's after my house. Emory's after Momma, and she pretends he ain't. Father's not supposed to know about that. I saw Momma's car parked up to Emory's, and sometimes I see Emory's truck parked at the trailer when Father's not there, and I put one and one together. They think they're safe, only I can hear them.

Maybe Emory Holler thinks he can throw me off my land, but he'll find out different. It's my land, and my place is up, framed, and enclosed. Emory'll be picking his chin whiskers out of the grass before Gregory Hutchins'll be moving.

Tell your father, Emory said, tell him you got to get off my land. If you don't tell him, I will.

I said, You're jealous. Envy eats him up like flies. I'll kill Emory if he steps foot across my boundary. They got to leave boundaries alone. It's a federal offense to move a man's boundary marker. You can kill a man for that.

A snake eats his way through my brain crawling and chomping in the soft and tender tissues. I wish I could reach in and snatch him out and stretch him neck from tail until all he's ate of my brain busts from his stretched belly and I can suck it up and let it go back to my head.

At my roadway I unlock the chain that links log-bar to post and swing the log clear so I can drive in. Father says I ought to clip a counterweight to hang from the log so it'll be easier to open. You may have the strength of a come-along in each arm, he said, but I don't. That's all right. Father, when he tools out, or Lisa, they toot their horns, and I come to the gate and help. Anybody else comes, they come of their own accord, so they can lift the log with their own leverage.

Inside my house the Coleman stove throws its blue ring right up righteous, so I know nobody's been messing with it. I set the coffeepot on the flame, and I sit quiet as an ant's breath until my coffee water's ready. I dish in a couple of superspoonfuls of coffee before I pour the water in so that I can stay shiny-eyed awake. The coffee puts the biting snake in my brain to sleep for a while. Symmetrical, like laying brick. I don't do masonry anymore because you may think you're piling brick on brick, but you're actually putting up a wall to wrap around you like a tomb. You could brick yourself up in your own tomb and not even know it.

I'm going to get a gun to protect myself. Father never kept a gun because he thinks he can handle anything. He's not afraid of God on stilts. Father's a modern man with his telephone and his running water and his running after Tommy and jail and Momma and Tommy and jail and Lisa and Fesmire and the children, who are more precious than God himself, on or off stilts. Emory doesn't know I've tailored a trapdoor escape route right under the subfloor. When I test it, I hear them Hollers. Hollering my name like ravens while I run right between trees until I ram into an iron stake too dark to see. I fall. My cut runs over. How can God keep all the names straight in his head?

For sure I'm going to get a gun so I won't have to run. Dog smells danger, but he can't bite two men at once, and they won't attack me one at a time. That's why I only let them in one at a time, or I go to their place. Like Father comes out here alone. Or Lisa, just with the children, but they're angels like Elizabeth, an angel who couldn't speak harm nor hurt, couldn't let the taste of bad words sound in her mouth. But if Momma or Tommy want to visit, I drive to Lisa's to see them because I smell danger from them. Momma's linking up with Emory.

I give Dog his food. I save a little in the can for myself because I'm only a little hungry. You don't have to heat Alpo, which makes it handy. Just spoon some into his dish, then use the same spoon to feed your own face. I've learned a lot since I've lived on my own, stuff you don't learn looking in books.

I'm going to tell Father to keep Momma away from me now that she's my sworn enemy and ask him where I can get a gun. I'll have to withdraw more money from my bank account. I know that. I hope he doesn't try to tell me that. They don't have to tell me. Or pretend to tell me.

So now I drive back down the road, swing open the bar, drive the truck through, close and lock the chain, and chug off to town. No talk or treachery travels in on the radio. Maybe they bought books to tell them how to block and baffle my receiver's reception. I'll get a book too. They can't ban me from buying a book. I finished high school, only one in the family. I may not be smart, but I know how to snare knowledge. It ain't only the panty thief that can be a dangerous man.

TOMMY

"Father turned down that chance to go to Florida," I say. "He'll want to wait until there ain't no chance there."

"You should've waited until you got to the bar before you started drinking," Penny tells me.

She should've shut her mouth last week, then we wouldn't be out celebrating my return from banishment. Seems as though every time I'm right, the explanation runs too long. "BB Eyes ain't turned on his blue lights, yet," I say after checking the rearview.

"Shit, Tom, BB Eyes ain't even got his headlights on! That don't mean he ain't following you. He's sneaky as an owl. And I'm as horny as one." She gets her face into my crotch and turns her mouth to warm, wet jelly.

It's all I can do to keep the car between the trees. BB Eyes'd like nothing better than to catch me drunk and in an accident with my dick out. Jesus, her tongue just ran to my navel the inside way. My balls push my legs apart. I'm stepping on the gas a little, feeling I could stretch my leg forever. As long as BB Eyes keeps those headlights off, he won't try to stop me, and in a minute not even death is going to stop me. Her lips tug me into wildness. I can't step down anymore on the gas. I'm going to close my eyes. Oh, shit, I left that hot radio in the trunk. Anytime he pulls me over, BB Eyes searches the trunk. Not this time because he's not going to stop us. I'm being pulled right out of myself.

Bang! Goddam! Her teeth! I hit the ditch. Shit, we're off the road. Headlights!

BB Eyes' headlights jumped on. My dick feels like somebody took a can opener to it. A big oak crowds me right against the stone wall. BB Eyes' fingers are itching to switch on the blue light.

"Jesus, Tom!" Penny's screaming. "My head!"

"My dick!"

Crack! The stone wall bites the quarter panel. We're bounding over grass, and I see the blue lights. Cutting the wheel tight's I can, I swerve next to this garage and around to the backyard. Right in my headlights stares a Great Dane. He won't fucking move. We're just bearing down on him. I kill the lights and cut the wheel.

Thump! We smash a doghouse and bump over it. I wheel a one-eighty and sneak back the way I came while BB Eyes races down the road, balls to the wall.

"My dick," I say, tucking it back in my pants and hoping the wet I feel is spit.

"My head," Penny says. "I hit the wheel when you ran off the road."

"The dog wouldn't move, froze in the lights like a jacked deer. I couldn't get the lights off fast enough."

"So you smashed up the exhaust." The motor roars through torn pipes. "Where's that money coming from? You should've hit the dog. Meat's softer than wood."

Now I'm in the shit with her, but I wasn't going to run down a helpless dog. "I got that hot radio in the trunk. If—"

"You sold it to your brother, shit-for-brains," Penny says. She fires up a cigarette, not looking at all horny now. "Where do you think we got the money for this adventure?"

At the bar, two beers and she's nearly forgiven me for not killing the dog. She's dropping quarters in the jukebox like feeding crumbs to birds. In the men's room I sneak a slow look at my dick, which is bruised and purple, but not bleeding.

"Ain't a good place to be playing with yourself," says Gary Reed.

Just because my father works for his father this pea brain

thinks he can put me down whenever he wants. "You want a good look at eye level," I tell him, waving it at him. Just when I see his face dip like the sucker he is, I smash him a good one to the side of his nose. Blood starts out between his fingers. I figure he won't be back in the bar telling stories about me and my dick.

Drinking a fresh cold one, I tell Penny I was lucky. She cocks a wink at me via the mirror. "Me too," she says. Sliding her hand up my thigh, she says, "Maybe the swelling will make it better when we get home."

"Your head okay?" I'm thinking something cold would feel a lot better on my dick than the hot, wet, and wild she's got in mind.

"No bump," she says, "not like your 'head.'"

When I reach for my beer, a blue arm snags around me and yanks me right off the barstool. I get in a good swing at his fat gut before my feet fly out from under me. I grab at his belt. I'm kicking. I can't find the other one. I hear Gary Reed laughing, then they get the stick locked across my throat. Smart, I think, they won't leave marks. Then on go the cuffs.

Penny's out of here. She don't even leave a shadow. If she goes to jail, they'll take Aaron. She says she'd kill herself if they took Aaron. Me, I couldn't stand to lose Aaron. Nothing about my losing Aaron bothers BB Eyes.

"Does it, you fat shit!" I scream. Scootching down in the squad car's backseat, I get in some good kicks at the partition to the front. Industrial-strength wire or not, it bends.

JIM

Soon's Pauline's awake enough to hear me say "BB Eyes," she starts defending Tommy.

"Why can't BB Eyes leave the boy alone?" She throws back the covers as if she's stripping a bed at the motel.

I wish she wouldn't go to the station in the middle of the night, with her gray eyes glistening bright as new tenpenny spikes. But there's no telling her to stay home after Tommy leaves his spoor on the countryside.

Having brushed her hair and put on clean slacks and blouse, she looks damn near beautiful. "Do I look decent?" she asks. "I'm not going down there until I look decent."

"BB Eyes is a friend of mine," I say.

"Some friend!"

She says Tommy, her baby since Elizabeth's death, has bad luck, and other people pick on him for it. She works on freeing him from one fracas after another. For me, Tommy's scrapes just make blurry confusion. "He's a prince," Pauline says. He's a prince, all right. At twenty-two, Tommy, rough, rasty, and rambunctious, wears the crown of chaos.

The police aren't letting Tommy come home. They have charged him: DWI, driving after revocation, and assaulting an officer. "Oh, yes," BB Eyes says, "we got to add vandalism to his charges. He kicked through the mesh in the cruiser. You can bail him in the morning."

Pauline insists on seeing Tommy. Other than wearing bleary eyes and tousled hair, he looks his usual five foot ten of rugged nastiness. He asks her to get him some cigarettes because the cops mashed his. "See," Pauline tells me, "see what they do to the boy!" To save argument and a safari to find a cigarette machine after midnight, I give Tommy the half pack of Camels from my own pocket. Tommy says he'll pay me back, though Tommy's promises run as shallow as a roadside ditch.

In the morning Pauline'll hotfoot it right to the bank to take money out for Tommy's bail. She'll forget that two people in this trailer have to eat and pay taxes. Most of the week I work for Frank Reed, who owns a gas station, garage, auto parts store, and three apartment buildings, although I don't work on the buildings. Frank'd have me pulling teeth and showing horses if he thought he could turn a buck on it. Fridays, Saturdays, some Sundays, and more than one evening a week, I work for Malcolm Hurd, a rich man who has more toys and enterprises than he can keep up with. I like working for Malcolm because the days fill with foolishness, which I leave right in his dooryard. I don't need to bring any home. Tommy dumps a bucketloader of trouble to my place at least once a month.

"Once a month!" I say, fixing my coffee. "I'd settle for once a month and take the carrying charges. The boy'd be better off to give up paying rent on his apartment and put a down payment on a jail cell." I push the twin slices of dark bread into the toaster. Malcolm gave me this dark bread because he says white bread fouls up the digestion. I'll try most anything, though I told Malcolm I couldn't see how I'll ever get used to Lisa's wild-blueberry jam on that dark bread.

"You've been down on Tommy ever since they threw him out of school," Pauline says. "And neither you nor your friend Malcolm managed to do much about it either, even knowing the boy was only fifteen. Emory managed to get Scooter back into school. Sometimes I think you'd treat Tommy better if he were a stranger."

"He is a stranger." Strong dark bread with sweet wild-blueberry jam stops my talk while I wait to see if Pauline will rush me back to my own wild days.

"I'll take care of him," Pauline says, as if she's cleaning a kitchen mess.

The crumbs from my toast lie accusingly on the table. Quickly brushing them into my palm, I feel guilty, with an uneasiness I can't locate, an uneasiness that slinks in whenever we talk about Tommy's hell-raising. Hell-raising? The boy has gone beyond hell-raising in this fracas. Now he's bought jail time and needs bail money and lawyer's fee. And I can see the suburbs of heaven moving farther west, like every sunset is dragging them away.

Emory claims only Scooter as kit, and if Scooter stubs his toe in the gutter, Emory talks or pays his way out of it. When they threw Scooter and Tommy out of school, Emory didn't march himself down to the schoolhouse to plead for the boy. He just sent a check for the stuff the boys had swiped.

"Much as I hate to say it," I tell Pauline, "there's something enviable about Emory's life."

Up at Malcolm Hurd's, I sound him out about all this. He says he's solved the whole thing by paying no attention whatsoever to what his wife says, "Bernice can rattle along ten or fifteen miles over the speed limit in her talk," he says, "and I just stay a legal fifty-five in my listening."

"They raised it to sixty-five," I remind him.

"Only on the interstate, which I also avoid."

Not that any of Malcolm's brag fools me because I know how much dark bread I have to eat so he can keep Bernice from screeching at him. And him a man with so much money he don't even buy a Megabucks ticket.

PAULINE

A man always has to envy something, blame something, instead of wiping clean what lies in front of him. Maybe because a man fixes a motor, then doesn't see that car for another year, is why he expects peace and ease to be the usual turn of the world. A woman, though, wipes the table and slides a greasy skillet into the dishwater with the sure knowledge she'll be doing the like same thing tomorrow. I learned early that life means constantly straightening up.

Jim has halfway finished his coffee when I shuffle into the kitchen to set my tea water to boil. A slow waker, I never apologize for taking small bites of the morning. Today, though, Jim won't leave me nibble into the business of life. Right onto Tommy. And envying Emory and throwing up curdling remarks about him, a man who's always doing us a good turn and giving me a laugh. On the edge of saying something else, Jim puts cup or cigarette to his mouth and stares at me while he stifles his speech.

"All right," I say, "what more riling do you want to start before I even get my tea past my lips?"

"Nothing," he lies, his cigarette already halfway to his mouth, "only where are you going to get the money for that bail?"

I let him stew a minute. He could have waited, at least until he watered and fed the birds. He might have said hello to Terry Glebe across the road and talked about the peach tree they pruned, and he could have done it without making me think of Elizabeth's tragedy. He can go easy when he wants to go easy. He manages that real well when he has sex on his mind. But today he has to edge and dance around like a child about to wet his pants.

"Sometimes I think you begrudge Tommy the air he breathes," I say.

"When he takes it out of my mouth, I do. We've got a tax bill to pay, a hefty three hundred sixty-eight dollars and twenty-two cents, in case it slipped your mind."

The notification of foreclosure that I keep in the accordion file flies off the counter in Jim's hand as if he might whip me with it. Inside the file sit the lien for last year's taxes, the lien of the previous year's taxes, and (until Jim removed it) the foreclosure notice.

"Don't be thrashing, mister," I tell him. "I hike down to that town office twice a month to give them their twenty-five dollars."

"When we're having to live out under a pine tree, I'll remember about your trips to the town office." The foreclosure notice sits on top of his ashtray like a dead bird. "We could be out from under this if you didn't squander money on grown kids who ought to be pulling their own weight."

I lift the orange cover from the parakeet cage. "At least Petey can start today happy."

"Not that he'll be singing when we slide him between two pieces of bread because there's nothing else to eat."

"Stop talking so hateful!"

I pour my tea water. The oversized mug I use has a glazed ceramic picture of birds of paradise. (I found it at the motel, so that's not anything he can blame me for squandering money on.) I love colorful birds, and so does Jim, even if he wouldn't admit it this morning.

"Well, there's another thing gone wrong," I say.

"What's the matter now?"

"I'm making tea with no tea. I forgot to put the tea egg in the water."

I don't explain the financial details for Tommy's bail to Jim, any more than I tell him about the fifty dollars I found at the motel. I've heard all the chewing I'm going to this morning. If he can't go to Florida to make big money, I guess I'll keep my banking to myself. In my savings account sits two hundred eighty-three dollars. The motel holds back a week's wages, so that they actually owe me over three hundred dollars if they paid me the whole amount that I've earned. I can ask Carol to give me the money, though she might call it an advance. No one gives you an advance on wages anymore except Malcolm Hurd, who'll give Jim any amount he asks for. Only Jim won't so much as look under the sofa cushions for a nickel to help Tommy. I pull the metal egg out of the water and watch the dark red tea stain the water. A cup of well-steeped tea gladdens the heart. Right now I'm glad to remember that Jim did ask Malcolm for the money to buy this very trailer after the fire ate our house. And I remember how after Tommy saved his sister from the fire, Jim did pat the boy on the back and did tell him he stood taller than any other fifteen-year-old buck he knew.

Often, on workdays, I'll take a shower at the motel, much easier than washing at the trailer where the water pressure can barely push soapsuds off your back. Emory offered to buy a new pump, but Jim ignores or refuses him, as if he's taken a liking to drizzling water and hauling it from the well by the bucketfuls whenever the pump takes a fit. He says he's got to clear his debts, not add new ones. (Oh, a man holds to his envies and his miseries as dearly as to his heart's desires.) Today, though, I'll wash up here at the trailer so as to be at no disadvantage when I go to the police station.

Kissing Jim good-bye as he leaves for work, I feel his tongue linger on my lips in longing. "We'll have a nice supper," I tell him, "a nice evening."

His smile stymies whatever he was about to say about Tommy or money. After I hear the *chng-chng* of Jim's truck starting, I call work to tell them I'll be in late. Carol always treats me fair, I'd never say otherwise, but Carol's fairness springs from picking through the facts, not from trust, so point by point I have to describe why I need to wait until the bank opens to withdraw cash for bail. Carol won't advance me my week's pay, but she will allow me to come in at noon, though I understand I'll have to stay until I complete the laundry and that I will earn no overtime. I hope Jim will understand that I'll arrive home late, after dark, and there'll be no nice supper, no nice evening.

Tommy wouldn't have half his trouble if he hadn't tangled with that slut Penny, because she's got him so he's running into himself when he turns corners. I'll not have that boy in jail. As a little tyke, Tommy couldn't stand to see so much as a dog chained up and would always set Buffy loose. When he was in jail before, he said he felt just like poor Buffy, just chained all the time.

Why he can't see it's Penny driving him wild, I don't know. There ain't nothing stronger than a bad woman's wildness when it gets under a man's skin, and Tommy ain't more than a few years a man, though God knows he tried early enough. His father had a spell where he couldn't stay sniffing distance away from wild women, and I know something went on between him and that Kari Reed, so he ought to hold some sympathy for the boy. Sometimes I think Jim's so hard on Tommy because he sees his very own self walking in Tommy's boots.

Money can fall like rain on Jim, but he don't think it should get everybody wet. Malcolm Hurd gave him money for this trailer, but Malcolm's just as down on Tommy as Jim is. He wouldn't pay pocket lint to help the boy.

"Emory," I say on the phone, "I need to raise some bail money for Tommy."

"Ah, Sweetness, that boy putting creases on your pretty face again?" he says. "Whatever you need, you can count on me. Course you could count on Jim if he'd take the big bird to Florida."

As the hot water runs in the tub, I strip my clothes off, turning in the mirror to check for sags, bulges, or varicose veins. I'm not skinny, never have been, but I exercise to keep my waist defined and my butt firm. My breasts sag no worse than most women with C cups. Because my back and my knees bother me some, I try to keep my posture healthy. My bad shoulder, loose shoulder— painfully loose, truth be told—is my worst physical problem. If I have to have something wrong, I'm glad it's not something that mars me, because I like pretty things. After the fire, what I could find of pretty—a bird or Elizabeth's smile—kept me going.

Those old times fell hard. Just like now, money was scarce and Tommy was in trouble. Brightest of my four children, why Tommy couldn't behave at school escapes my grasp. Oh, I remember the letter, the Official Notice of Expulsion, headed with the names of men I didn't know. *He can't step foot in the schoolhouse the rest of the year.* That letter should have burned in the fire. What made Tommy save that letter from the fire? And worse, when we stayed in the garage, tack it to the end of a shelf. Strange as he can behave, the light still has not gone out of Tommy's eyes.

Once when an understanding mood took hold of him, Gregory said that moving from eighth grade where Tommy had fifteen in his class down to the regional high with hundreds had bewildered the boy. (Hadn't I worried when Gregory himself started riding the bus down there that he, like me and Jim, would give up school as soon as he saw his sixteenth birthday? Hadn't Lisa quit at seventeen to go to the job-training school?)

Hard times those were, just before the fire. That's when I let Jim take care of Tommy. Malcolm Hurd went with Jim when he paid his visit to the school superintendent because Malcolm, a rich man, sat way up in the VFW. The superintendent said if Jim kept Tommy to home, the school wouldn't press charges for stealing and no one would say a word about Tommy being out of school at fifteen. Tommy, and Emory's boy, Scooter, had stolen from the school as if they planned a career in it—microscopes, televisions, tape recorders. Might as well pound sand in a rat hole as try to get that boy back in school, Malcolm told Jim. They'll have you paying for those things until rust claims them all.

He worries too much about money, I told Jim.

Jesus Christ, Jim said, they stole everything that didn't hold up the building.

Except books, Tommy said. We never took any books.

Come fall, Jim said, you're in the schoolhouse, if it has to be reform school.

Scooter Holler went back to school after Emory paid for the stealing. They said payment or not, Tommy couldn't return because he was the ringleader. If there was only the two of them, how could he be the ringleader?

We lost that one too. The superintendent said they'd expel Tommy permanently in November when he turned sixteen, so I let it go. That superintendent, along with a couple of teachers, had it in for Tommy. I worry that he'll never in all his life learn to sidestep trouble.

Finally, naked and clean, I dry myself and step into the hallway. There stands Emory Holler. Neither towel nor robe to cloak me, I cross my arms under my breasts and let him look.

"Thought you'd be done with your shower by now," he says, chuckling like one kid tickling another. "I brought the bail money with me." Looking me right in the face, he holds out a wad of bills.

"Emory," I say, scolding him a little, "I don't have any pockets."

Taller than Jim, lean, his face marked with that fuzzy dark hair that seems to flow right up to his head, he stares all the way to my feet, his eyes pressing me like hot breaths. "Outfit like that, you don't need pockets."

Behind the closed bedroom door, I wrap my robe around my bare body. "You're turning bold, Emory Holler."

"Yeah, too bad Jim ain't to home. I got to talk to him about Gregory's shack."

Of course, with Jim's truck gone, he knew Jim had left for

work, knew that the minute he pulled into the yard. "Tommy keeps me busy enough," I say.

"Let Jim and me deal with Gregory," he says.

In the narrow trailer hallway we seem to be all bodies, limbs and flesh. As I take the money, his fingers fondle mine. "I'll give you back what I don't need," I say.

He goes out the hall door we never use, lets the screen door slam. "Thanks for the show."

From the kitchen comes Petey's whistling song. "Poor bird," I say aloud. "Here I am neglecting you."

As I wash Petey's porcelain feeding dish, Charley twines around my ankles, his fur rubbing softly against my skin. Feeding him his favorite gourmet cat food reminds me of feeding my babies. I didn't nurse any of them. Lisa nursed all three of hers, but that's the modern way. If I had another child, I'd nurse her. Why do I think of the baby as "her"? To make up for Elizabeth?

I won't think of that now. Emory's visit has rattled my brain. According to Jim, Tommy did that to Penny. Squatty Body, Jim calls her. Grabbed her and shook her enough to addle her brains, Jim said. Penny wouldn't leave Tommy alone until she got pregnant. Now she plagues him with other men. That's what stirs him into acting so ugly. Emory, rough as he looks, would never hurt me. I won't believe he hurt Helen. She fell down the stairs in a freak accident.

Charley licks his paws and rubs his face to clean his whiskers. Petey starts to sing again. Last night I hid my worry, but now I need to think straight. In the bank account sits almost three hundred dollars, saved at the rate of twenty-five dollars a week, deposited from my check. Used to be I'd march myself down to the town hall each Friday morning with twenty dollars to put toward the tax bill, but we never caught up. Sometimes I needed those twenty dollars for something else. Eventually Jim had to ask Malcolm Hurd to help pay the back taxes, or the town would take the place and put us out on the street. Even after Malcolm paid, we are still paying on bills three years back. The $368.22 Jim saw covers only half the year, since the town now bills every six months. They must think we're shut-ins in need of mail. And I need money for children and grandchildren before any damn taxes take it. Emory's wad amounts to five hundred dollars, which I will pay back even if he doesn't care.

How much Tommy's bail will run this time I can't even guess. I ain't going to speculate on that, BB Eyes said last night. Tommy won't even be sober until morning, he said.

Assault on a police officer. Resisting arrest.

Tommy wouldn't fight if they didn't grab him first. Or if Penny hadn't teased him to sit in the barroom half the night drinking beer. And whose fault is that? They put that opportunity in front of the boy like candy to a child, they gladly take his money to ring up in their cash till, but when the liquor drives him to rampage, he might as well be a wild bear just wandered in from the woods. And they tax that beer and make the bar pay for a liquor license, and where does that money go? Right into the pocket of the police, I'm betting, right into BB Eyes' salary. Talk about biting the hand that feeds you.

BB Eyes ought to know by now that latching onto Tommy from behind will make him fight. They could've used other ways. Once a boy like Tommy picks up a reputation in the village, it sticks like grease.

Locking the door as guard against the underwear thief, I shout to Buffy, the half-blind Great Pyrenees, who sits chained near the old pigpen. As a guard dog, he's mean-looking and useless, unable to distinguish friend or foe except for Jim, who feeds him, Gregory, who wrestles with him, or Tommy, who named him, discovered his blindness, and can always calm him from his growling, fang-drooling fits by saying, "Buffy, Buffy, Buffy," in a voice sweet enough to soothe a colicky baby. I pity the dog. Buffy sniffs at me this morning as much as if I were a stranger.

The mist that earlier covered the Glebes' awful pond has lifted, leaving a strange layer of clear air up to about ten feet off the ground. If I had screamed when Emory saw me naked, no one would've heard. I could've danced my naked self for him, and we wouldn't have been embarrassed by the respectable Glebes across the road. Despite their two little retarded children, the Glebes command respect in the village, the respect the village gives to the well-to-do, decent people.

Their retarded children get respect, but for my children every twist or warp gets scrutiny. When I was growing up, town people criticized my own sister Mona, who was not retarded but only slow. Even two years after Elizabeth's death, it's painful to watch those Glebe kids, now big boys with chests swelling their bright colored jerseys, run and shout as they chase each other around the Glebes' yard. I know it's mean, but I think of what was robbed of me, forever.

"I don't know what the chief told you," says Sergeant Dumont, the short, dark policeman at the desk, "except we all go by the same book."

I feel like a fool. "Why didn't BB Eyes tell me I didn't need any money?" I ask.

"You do need money," says the cop, "the bail commissioner's fee, fifteen dollars."

"You think I didn't have fifteen dollars in my wallet last night?" Jim might believe BB Eyes acts as his friend, but I've got a clearer view of what that man intends for Tommy. Pa always went out of his way to stay on the good side of the police, even if he had to pay the man for a few extra holidays and send him an uneasy turkey when it wasn't Thanksgiving. Course Pa could tell a friend better than Jim can.

"The plain and simple fact is," he says, "your son was drunk last night. We don't release drunks."

"My son is not a drunk!" I yell.

"His BAC approached point two oh," says Dumont, arranging papers in front of him. "He couldn't have signed his name last night."

"Tommy is not ignorant, and he's not a drunk."

"You can read the report for yourself, Mrs. Hutchinson." Dumont holds the report close enough to his chest so that I know he doesn't really want me to read it. "Your son couldn't even sign the PR form. We can't release a subject without that. It wouldn't be legal, and it wouldn't be safe."

"What's this PR?"

"Personal recognizance. It's a kind of promissory note." This PR form Dumont does pass over the table for me to read. "By signing the paper Tommy will guarantee his appearance in court a month from now or he will automatically owe the court the sum of five hundred dollars and be subject to arrest."

I count out the fifteen dollars and wait while Dumont writes out my receipt.

"It's Hutchins, not Hutchinson," I tell him.

Dumont takes back the marred receipt, crumples it, and drops it in his wastebasket like a snot-filled tissue. For all his fancy language Dumont could have been born and brought up in a sumac swamp. No wonder they can't catch that underwear thief.

When Tommy emerges from the steel door, he walks slowly on his heels, as much from shame as from hangover, I'll bet. All of them, even BB Eyes, will push Tommy into the shadows.

When Tommy signs the PR form, his steady hand makes those flowing, flowery letters he'd taught himself in grade school, where his art teacher told him he had talent. For a while he made a little money airbrushing names in fancy script on trucks, even decorating Emory's Ford. Then all to once he stopped, like he's punishing himself, so now the only art he allows himself is that elaborate script, that he calls calligraphy.

Out in the car I ask him why he quit airbrushing. "You were getting so good at those scenes," I say, remembering that Tommy paid back the money Jim gave him to buy the airbrushing equipment, "why, you could have made hundreds decorating one truck."

"Swinish," Tommy says. "The scenes people want me to paint are all swinish. Lighthouses, mountaintops, big bucks with antlers, I might just as well have painted Hallmark cards."

"What's wrong with Hallmark cards?"

"Swinish," Tommy tells me, and sets his jaw. "Some scenes they want are funny, but like cartoons. You look at a cartoon, you laugh. Once. Driving around with a big cartoon airbrushed on your truck is like telling the same joke over and over. Swinish.

"When Scooter got me to spray that Ford-eating Chevy on his father's truck, I worried Emory would boot my ass before I even fired up the airbrush, but Emory just said I ought to think if I wanted my name riding all over town under that cartoon."

For a moment Tommy stares at the new houses with their unsown lawns, plywooded porches, new-framed garages, as if one of them might hold some secret to life I've kept from him. Maybe he just envies what we've never had. "Emory'd never hurt you," I tell Tommy.

"Are you nuts? Emory'd kill me if it suited him. Just like he did his wife."

Tommy wouldn't say such meanness if he hadn't just suffered a night under BB Eyes and Dumont.

He has me stop at the 7-Eleven so he can talk with Mary Beth Jewell. He doesn't talk long, but he comes out with a pack of cigarettes.

When I pull into the yard, there stands Gregory holding a car radio in his hand like a dead cat. "I guess you stole this before you sold it to me," he tells Tommy, "and right from the Glebes. I ain't telling the cops, but I guess you'll snake it back. I ain't installing stolen equipment in my vehicle."

"They ain't nothing but flatlanders who'll cheat on their insurance, then they'll buy a better radio with the refund check," Tommy says. "I was doing them a favor, but you're too dumb to understand."

"Cops'd caught me, it'd be me in jail," Gregory says. "I'm not too dumb to figure that out. And I know what you're up to, trying to cancel out the reception of my honest radio with this stolen one, digital or no digital."

I wish Tommy wouldn't call his brother dumb. Nothing makes Gregory feel bad like that.

"I got to stop selling stuff cheap to my brother," Tommy says, and grabs the radio from Gregory. "Trying to help you is like trying to hold piss in your hands."

Quick as that, Gregory muckles right onto Tommy. "You bring disgrace to this family." Gregory is at the boy like a boar hog and has him by the throat and is smooshing his windpipe and cutting off his air. I never thought to see my firstborn tear into such violence. He's killing Tommy. I scream my throat right into a knot before I latch on with both hands to pull him off Tommy. Gregory's arms stay rigid as hate. His eyes sink in his head. I'm screaming. I can't hear Tommy's breath. I cuff Gregory on the ear and cuff him. I'll not lose another child. "Don't you kill him!"

"Kill him? Kill him?" Gregory's eyes blinking, he lets go of Tommy's throat.

I'm shaking so my body aches. I grab my shoulders to keep from shaking apart before I touch Gregory's arm. "We're family," I say.

"I ain't being family with no thief!" he yells.

"Dummy," Tommy says. Then I know I got to take him to his apartment or Gregory will kill him.

I hope Penny won't be home. That girl pushes her mouth into everything as bossy as she pushes her "squatty body" into a group of people. At barely five foot, Penny stands steady no matter how much she's drunk. She holds harm in her hands and carries danger in her pockets. She's always bothering or betraying Tommy, and she upsets me just like Fesmire always torments Jim.

3

three

JIM

He claims Fesmire for a name, though I ain't uncertain that a while back in his family a turnip got over the fence. I've watched Fesmire for some years now, and he's given me a new appreciation for the caginess of turnips. I don't blame him for all my troubles. Trouble's been related to us since long before Fesmire popped out of the knotted ground. A few years back we sent our daughter Lisa to that job-training school in Manchester because she said it was the only place she would finish high school. I was working for the town then, trying to catch up on the taxes for the trailer, and Pauline could only get relief shifts at the nursing home, so it suited me fine to have Lisa fed and housed. "She can't leave the school grounds," Pauline said. "She'll win all A' s and B's." That's what Lisa kept telling us too, right up to February when we got her five-page letter that started out, "Momma, I'm resigning." Then Pauline fretted herself into saying those high grades was all lies.

They wa'n't. When we got up there to bring her home, they showed us her report card, full of A's and B's. I kind of figured she hadn't lied about that. What I hadn't figured or expected was the boy, Fesmire. There he was, standing with her, bundled up ready to go. All lines, he had straight, stringy black hair, a long straight nose like an old man's, though he wa'n't but seventeen, and fingers long enough to steal from the back row. He probably stood about five foot ten, though his long legs made him look like he'd have to duck going through doorways.

Pauline told Lisa we didn't have room for another person in the trailer.

"He can sleep with me, Momma," Lisa says.

"Not in my house, lady," Pauline tells her.

Lisa was smart. She just lifted her things into the trunk along with Fesmire's suitcase. She knew we weren't going to have a fist-fight over it in the middle of Manchester. Down he came. Pauline fixed him a bed on the living room couch, but he was all the time like a weasel without a hole.

Everywhere you looked in the trailer, there was Fesmire, usually stretched out. I came home one day amazed not to find him occupying the couch. The minute I opened my yap, Pauline led me down to our bedroom, where, lo and behold, Fesmire was stretched out on his back between our bed and our bureau. I asked him if he was setting a trap, and he said it was good for his back. Why the living room floor wouldn't have been just as good for his seventeen-year-old back, I couldn't fathom.

Pauline motioned me to go outside so we could talk. "Not a word about him in all that five-page letter."

I watched a peacock go by dragging his tail along the snowy ground. I had to give Fesmire that; with his long underwear and his flannel shirt and down vest and wool coat, he didn't strike no peacock poses. Then too, you couldn't stand too far downwind of him without knowing where he was.

"Pauline," I says, "I guess we know now why she set herself to resigning."

"Well, I'm not resigning," Pauline snaps back. "I catch him once slithering into Lisa's room, he won't want to stand up."

She put our little Elizabeth, who shared the room with Lisa, onto the case. It's always good to have a six-year-old girl looking out for her sister's virginity or whatever might be left of it. Pauline tried to get Tommy to man the night shift, but Tommy'd turned sixteen, and he'd taken to working Fesmire's side of the street—in another town of course—so he wasn't home early enough to take over when Elizabeth fell asleep.

Did you know there are forty-eleven sounds a trailer makes on a cold February night? Only one of them springs from Fesmire sliding off the couch. "There he is," Pauline'd say. "No," I'd say, "thermostat just kicked in." "What's that?" she'd ask about twenty minutes later when the furnace had finished its cycle and I'd about reached dreamland. "That squirrel that scurries across the roof." Then Buffy would grind up against the skirting in his night wanderings and set Pauline into another dither.

One night, long about three o'clock, a couple hours after Tommy had settled in from his ramming, when everything had clamped itself into sleep and silence, I flared right up in bed. "Fesmire," I says without a doubt in my voice, "get back to bed."

"Got to hit the can," he says. "That weak coffee of your wife's goes right through my kidneys."

Then he peed like he held a fireman's hose. Because the supply pipe running back to the toilet had split from freezing, we had to use a bucket to flush. He threw the water into the toilet as if he were quenching a forest fire. There wasn't enough quiet in him then to twitch a cat's whiskers, but, oh, I had to listen close to hear him slide back on that couch and shift those covers over him.

Pauline tugged on my shoulder. "Jim, do I make weak coffee?"

Next evening I came home to see Fesmire up and drinking that weak coffee and chomping a couple of hot dogs to build up an appetite for supper. I says, "I don't care what you do, but I do care what it does to my wife. Now I can put a lock on Lisa's door, or you can stop your night prowling so I can have some peace in my house."

"Lisa's door locks from the inside, doesn't it?" he says, and slipped the last of his hot dog into his mouth. I swear he swallows without chewing.

Another week went by with my identifying all forty-eleven sounds of the trailer. I encouraged Fesmire to pass on the second cup of after-dinner coffee so his kidneys or some part down there don't disturb his sleep. Or mine. The strength Pauline put into her coffee then, a grown man wouldn't need more than one cup a week. Malcolm Hurd says to me, "Why don't you just shoot the son of a bitch?" I says, "Malcolm, I ain't like you. I ain't got the money to hire lawyers, and if I did, I might want to use it for something besides a Fesmire."

I won the battle without firing a shot. Fesmire must have wore that fire hose of his out with peeing because before the next week could finish, he hoisted his suitcase to his shoulder and hitch-hiked north to his folks' place up around Farmingboro. In a while he came back with his father in a big old station wagon and fetched Lisa up there with him. We stopped hearing the fire hose and bucket brigade, but most every night Pauline made that tiny sound that comes when a tear's trying to tumble out of her eye.

She didn't cheer up until we got Lisa's letter announcing her wedding and setting the date for June. About April the town threatened to lay off the whole road crew, leaving me nothing but weekend work with Malcolm Hurd, then we had the washout on the White Road, which runs past the fire station and the Legion Hall, so we were kept on to fix that. That tided us over to snow-fence removal, dismantling snowplows, and filling potholes. I was putting money aside for Lisa's wedding.

The next letter from Lisa announced that she was pregnant and set the wedding up in three days. I told Pauline I wasn't going. I didn't wait for her to ask why but just grabbed hold of the handiest explanation and tossed it to her. "If they'd waited until June like they said they were going to, then I'd've had money saved for this fracas, but this hurry-up-and-get-it-done-with deal ain't for me. You might just as well pour motor oil right on my breakfast."

And I didn't go. I guessed I missed something not seeing Fesmire dressed up, though I've looked at the wedding picture often enough—white suit with the pants wrinkled from knee to heel. When I see he didn't have anything else on except a shirt and tie and a suit jacket, I asked Pauline, "Was he cold? Could you smell him?"

One night I was sitting at the table and watching Pauline at her accounts. She'd started a savings account for Lisa's baby to be. "Two thousand dollars they'll need for that baby come October," Pauline says, "and that hospital won't even let them step foot across the threshold without three hundred because they don't have any insurance."

I tell her she'd better keep quiet about the three hundred she was salting away in the savings account or Fesmire'd have that. He is a regular python, that boy, for swallowing my money, but he don't believe in insurance. Dead set against it, he said. Absolutely poison to him. I says to Pauline, "Your back-tax envelope looks a little thinner than usual." The town clerk had come out to the garage and told me private that Pauline hadn't been dropping by with the payments lately.

"Every letter Lisa writes, she's pleading poverty," Pauline says. "I have to send her a little something."

"Amounts to about fifty dollar a letter, don't it?" I says. "And what's Fesmire doing?"

"Lisa says he figures on fishing. He quit the eighth grade figuring he could get by on fishing the rest of his life."

"What's Fesmire think he's going to catch—goldfish?" I was riled. "Get your car. We're going up there."

Fesmire and Lisa was living in his parents' house, one of those narrow, two-story affairs with a porch for sitting, only you couldn't sit on this one because Fesmire had located his johnboat the length of it. His folks were over to Vermont working at some resort. Lisa, sick to her stomach just like her mother in all her pregnancies, kept to the couch while I talked to Fesmire out in the kitchen.

"You'd better get a paying job or put your wife to work," I says.

"There ain't much work up here," he says, "only a pulp mill the state shuts down about every other day. I'm not going to be employed by nothing illegal."

"You never been too finicky to take any money her mother sent up here," I says, pointing to the living room where Pauline was sharing morning-sickness stories with Lisa.

"Why," Fesmire says, shooting a stream of smoke out his mouth, "she never done nothing illegal to get it, has she?"

"Fesmire." I remind myself this is my son-in-law and the father of my grandchild-to-be. I had to reason with him. "Fesmire, you ain't so numb—"

"I did talk to someone about putting up buildings, but I ain't the carpenter type." He floated a good-size cloud of smoke and kind of inspected it like he might find a fish in the middle of it. "No," he says in no hurry, "I ain't the carpenter type at all. I'm more the mechanic type."

"Mechanic type!" I was bellowing now. "When you were staying at my place, you couldn't screw a spark plug into a donkey's asshole! Now, mister man, if you're the eating type, you'll hum right back and see if they'll still give you that job."

He pulled in close to me. "I ain't got a car."

I let go of him. All I could see was the stink of Fesmire.

I rode Fesmire right over to that construction site. There was as many as four or five lots laid out, enough to give a lifetime of work to a dozen Fesmires. The foreman was in the trailer, and he hired Fesmire on the spot. There, I says to myself, there's one boon I got without even praying.

Come June the seeds were up, the fruit trees blossomed, and Pauline was putting in five nights a week at the nursing home. By the end of the month we'd stuffed that back-tax envelope four times and got nearly two hundred dollars set aside for that first grandchild's birth.

First of July, in the mail right on time, came the letter from Lisa. Fesmire'd quit working the construction job. They'd told him he'd worked there long enough he'd have to join the union, but he wa'n't about to join. Unions were all crooked, he told Lisa. They were dead poison to him. Might just as well give him a gun and tell him to go robbing banks as to ask him to join a union.

Lisa's handwriting wrote the letter, but I smelled Fesmire's voice in every sentence, even the last one, asking Pauline to send up a hundred dollars to tide them over until Fesmire found work.

"Find work!" I says. "If he looked for his dick like he looks for work, Lisa wouldn't be pregnant."

Pauline took a hundred dollars with her when we drove up

there because she wouldn't see Lisa go hungry—carrying a baby and all. She wondered Fesmire's folks didn't help, but I didn't. After all, they knew him; they'd raised him.

When we got there, Pauline says to me, "You wouldn't even know she's pregnant, she's so skinny." She loaded Lisa right into the car and drove her to the supermarket. I sat on the porch with Fesmire. There was room to sit because he'd put his boat in the water.

"How's fishing, Fesmire?" I ask.

"So-so, only you can't eat fish all the time."

"That's so," I says.

"No, Lisa can't keep much fish down. And I can't sell the fish I catch. They tell me that's illegal."

"They do make it hard on a man to live a decent life and support his family at the same time, don't they, Fesmire."

"That's the truth. I shot a few squirrels too, but there ain't enough meat on a squirrel to satisfy a cat."

"Lisa look for work?"

"I don't believe in that, Mr. Hutchins. You can do just as you want, but for me that way just leads right into trouble and danger and immorality." He leaned back and propped his feet onto the porch rail. I saw he was satisfied with that explanation. "Lisa does spend money, though. She likes her liquor. Says it settles her stomach, but I say it's expensive medicine."

"Your mother works, don't she?" I set my feet up too because I knew I had him.

Fesmire stoked his pipe in good stead, the smoke putting up a brave fight against his stench. He was wearing a wool sweater I'd never seen before, and the thermometer was pushing ninety. "She helps Father. It's a partnership deal. There ain't nothing around here like that for Lisa and me. Do you know of a position like that we can get down by your place?"

"Seems a shame for a man to let his wife starve because he can't keep enough squirrel on the table. Maybe she and the baby'd be better off striking off on their own."

Whoosh! His feet slid off that rail, and he stood up so fast the wind he made blew Fesmire stink 'most to the sea. "I know a place, a parts store, at the other end of town. They were looking for someone."

When Pauline drove back with the trunk full of groceries, I— and Fesmire too—carried bags four to a load so we could race right to that parts store. That guy there must have been deficient in the smeller because he hired Fesmire on the spot.

At the end of summer the town cut my hours back to thirty-five a week and talked about laying me off for a month in the fall. That was when Lisa's letter came telling us Fesmire'd quit at the parts store. It seemed they'd wanted him to deliver parts to the local garages every afternoon. Pauline was reading the letter to me, and I leaped right in and told her, "That's simple. Christ, you don't have to join a union to drive a car."

"You have to have a license," Pauline says. Fesmire didn't believe in licenses. They were poison to him. It was a free country, so he ought to be able to drive the roads without any license, particularly a license they were going to charge him for. No, sir, he'd have no part of it. If a free country couldn't let him drive the roads for free, he wouldn't drive at all. He wouldn't go against his principles.

The letter ended with a plea for money. "Don't you do it, Pauline," I says. "We got a pig out there ready for slaughter. You take that up to them." Tommy and I cut up the pig and packaged the pieces so nice you'd thought they were going under a Christmas tree. "There," I says, "that'll keep him away from squirrel and fish for a couple of weeks."

The day Pauline drove up there with those boxes of packaged pork in her trunk was shopping day, and she was going to the supermarket on her way home. I had the animals fed when she pulled in the yard. When I opened the trunk to lug in our groceries, staring me in the face were those boxes of pork. "He told me that they couldn't eat just pork," Pauline says. "And they didn't have all that much room in their refrigerator, so I gave them our grocery money."

I unloaded the pork into our refrigerator, where there was lots of room. "I see he likes some cuts of pork," I tells Pauline. "I see he kept the chops and ham and sent back the liver and ground meat."

"Fesmire says he could make money cutting cordwood if he had a chain saw," Pauline says.

Then I didn't need prayers nor reason either. I just needed a new chain for the old McCulloch that Malcolm Hurd had given me. It had a sixteen-inch blade and a heavy metal case, and though it blatted like a calf being cut, it'd run all day long, just what Fesmire needed to work up a sweat.

I drove that McCulloch with the new chain up to Fesmire the next night. I told him and Lisa that Pauline's hours might be reduced again, so he better get humping. "See," Fesmire says, "that's why you shouldn't get to depending on a woman's earnings."

"Here," I says, "see what you can earn with this McCulloch. If you can't earn a living with it, you can at least cut your throat in style."

Well, there it was out and said, but Lisa wouldn't let me forget it. Or Pauline either. You cursed that boy, each of them told me. The first one was Lisa on the telephone collect from the hospital. Fesmire'd been shot. He'd lost a lot of blood and was in the emergency ward.

I couldn't find Tommy, so we bundled little Elizabeth into the car and drove over to the hospital. Pauline went right in while I sat in the parking lot helping Elizabeth read names on the cars and trucks.

"He's going to live," Pauline says when she came out, "but you cursed him."

"Who shot him?" I ask. "It's not deer season."

"A tree shot him."

I'd be damned, but right in the car I smelled Fesmire himself. "A tree!"

"He was felling a tree in his yard with that McCulloch chain saw you brought up when the chain struck a rifle slug just under the bark. It spun it out and shot him in the foot. Hit an artery."

"Ruined the McCulloch too, probably." Too bad, because I was thinking of driving over to his place and using the McCulloch to slit my own throat. I had to admit it—Fesmire could overcome reason, curse, and I don't know what all. While he was in the hospital, Lisa got a job scanning at the supermarket. Fesmire said he'd make her quit as soon as he got out of the hospital. I wondered how the hospital would get any money out of him. Me, I counted myself lucky he didn't sue me for bringing up the chain saw.

4
four

JIM

I need to leave work about like I need another itch to scratch. But today, with his mother helpless lying back to rug, Tommy's got more rules and regulations than farts at a bean supper. Including, he can't drive the car because his license has moved permanently to the Motor Vehicle Division. When I get to the apartment, I see he hasn't even lifted Pauline onto the couch.

"She might have broke her back," says Tommy. "I wa'n't about to kill her just to get her off the floor."

"How could she break her back fainting, you ninny?" I grind him because Frank Reed told me this trip over here is off the clock. "Your mother's wore out with listening to the telephone sing long before the morning birds start their tunes."

"Jim," Pauline says from the floor.

With the help of Tommy, I get Pauline up on the couch. I ask her how she feels.

"I suddenly felt so tired." She looks around as if she expects to find herself somewhere else. Or hopes to.

On the phone Tommy told me his mother fainted, but Tommy's not contradicting her now. Something's festering between him and Squatty Body, though figuring out what it is would be worse than sticking my hand into a nest of snakes.

"Can you drive yourself home?" I ask. "Because there's probably a run on the bank right now with people withdrawing their money to buy the garage's forty-eight-month batteries by the caseload."

"Mr. Hutchins," Squatty Body says like she wants to sell me something, "can I talk to you a minute?"

We step into the kitchen where the smell of shitty diapers turns my stomach. Back when our kids still shit their pants, we scraped the turds into a toilet, but Squatty Body says disposable diapers are laborsaving devices, so she just wraps the shit right up like a gift for the garbageman.

"Mr. Hutchins," she says again, leaning her back into the counter, "if someone asks for Tommy's address, would you tell them he lives with you?"

"I don't think anybody needs me to tell them where he lives."

She clouds up her face with smoke from her Winston. "See, I can't get my AFDC if they know Tommy lives here," she says flat-out, and leans a little more into the counter.

"He don't have even a hook to hang his coat at my place." Legal trouble like cheating welfare ain't the kind you can avoid by growing up with the local cop. Besides, BB Eyes ain't kindly disposed to either Penny or Tommy.

"He could live at your place," she says. "He could live at your place if I kicked him out—"

"He pays for this place—"

"He pays for the fucking beer," she hisses. "Anyway, my name's on the lease. If you're lucky, you could wind up with him and his baby both at your place to keep you entertained nights."

Pauline's always blamed Squatty Body for Tommy's troubles, but I know she hasn't seen half of the girl's smarts. What I can't tell is how deep her meanness runs. "And I'll tell you something, Penny, the minute that child don't live here, there'll be a telephone ringing at the welfare office."

"Mr. Hutchins, I never supposed you wanted to support Tommy and Aaron all on your own." However lazy or miserable she can turn, Penny's not dumb. She's survived Tommy for over two years and brought him to a whimper more than once. She sidles within breathing distance of me. "We don't have to fight over this, Jim."

"I hate an argument," I say.

"I've always believed that temper of Tommy's sprung from your wife's side."

Penny knows that Pauline don't fight. Not to say Pauline won't stand her ground, because she will and every inch her shadow covers too. Penny stretches the hand holding the cigarette and at the same time rubs her rounded middle with her left hand. Somehow she ends up closer to me.

"Maybe we'd just better hope nobody asks where Tommy lives," I say, and slide back to the living room before Penny can make another move.

Pauline rides me back to work. "What did she want?"

"We were talking about housing."

"I got to work late," she says.

I can see this will be an evening without a romantic walk. I hustle right into the garage and start on the exhaust job for Alice Jewell's Toyota. Frank claims not to understand foreign cars, so he makes me work on them.

"I don't understand Toyotas," says Frank, reasonable as he's ever going to get, "but I pulled the parts for you."

After I've mounted the pipes and wheeled Alice's Toyota out for a road test, the rattling tells me Frank closed both eyes when he pulled the exhaust parts. Back at the garage I call over the intercom for Frank to pull the right part. He sputters at me calling him on the intercom. For some reason he thinks that intercom should only call from whichever end he's operating.

"Gary bought that part from the dealer. It must be the right one." Frank don't like to admit that his boy, Gary, is awful handy at making mistakes and was even before Tommy realigned his nose.

"Now, you can hand Alice the keys to a car with a rattling exhaust if you want," I say. "Myself, I'd rather scrub my balls with Brillo."

"You must have hooked that doughnut wrong onto the bracket."

"What year'd you tell him on Alice's car?" I ask Gary.

" 'Eighty-five," he says, cocksure.

"Hers is an 'eighty-six. Always has been."

Back to the garage, hands on his hips, Frank shifts back and forth like he's holding a turd in his trousers. The pipe's metal has discolored enough so that the Toyota parts man is not going to take it back. Frank says it doesn't look too bad, no dents or scratches, and asks to see the carton. I hadn't flattened it because I like to leave that for Gary. Flattening cardboard about fits what Gary calls his "technical expertise."

Frank gets a smile on him. Out to the store and back again he runs. He hands me a can of aluminum spray paint.

"Take the pipe outside," he says, "so the new paint won't get covered in shop dust."

"You want me to—"

"They'll never know. And don't you think they restock parts like this every day of the week? You hum right along, and we'll still have Alice's car ready for her. I'll send Gary up to swap this for an 'eighty-six. Who the hell would've thought there'd be a goddamn difference." I suppose he feels sorry for Gary because he's sporting a nose that looks like last week's salad. Myself, I think the guy's a screwup with a father to cover for him.

Outside, I shake the hell out of the spray can, put the mixer ball through its paces, and within five minutes I've revirginized that pipe. Course there is a touch of lawbreaking about it, but it ain't like I'm coining money. Anyway, I ain't Fesmire-fussy about lawbreaking.

In and out of some scrub poples flies a red cardinal. When he's joined by a bluejay, the two spray the air with color. I push on to see what's drawing these birds. In a wet spot between the poples and the sumacs lies a pile of grain that's spread out like someone meant to feed the birds. Close up, I see it ain't grain, but wood chips and sawdust with a lot of worms in it calling those birds. I wonder who might've set it out there because neither Frank nor Gary can tell a bird from a winged fart. I slide my foot across the top to raise up some worms, and I uncover a fat, pink one. Another swipe of my boot shows it ain't a worm at all. It's silky cloth.

I know that I've dug up a pair of pink panties, buried here like the idiot tried to compost them.

In the garage I get BB Eyes on the telephone: "You don't need to come over with your gun drawn," I tell him. "I don't think they're going anyplace." Then I hustle outside to gather up the pipe and paint and other evidence of my crime.

"Frank," I call him on the intercom, giving me two up on him today. "Do you own the land all the way to the creek?"

"Yes," he says. "How'd that Toyota part finish up?"

"Sparkles," I say. "You'll want to take a look at what someone buried out back. You're about to become a tourist attraction."

I didn't tell Frank about the pink underwear before I called BB Eyes because I knew he'd want me to move that item to the other side of the creek. Anyway, Frank is outside when BB Eyes wheels around the back of the garage and edges out of the cruiser with a big Polaroid camera and a box of plastic Baggies.

"You're a regular walking crime lab, aren't ya, BB Eyes," I tell him because I'm trying to cheer a little of the sadness out of my system where it's settled like water in a fuel line.

"Pretty sure it'll turn out to be the same as the others," BB Eyes says. "The prosecutors want photos and samples of the environmental materials and, of course, casts if there are any footprints around that aren't Jim's."

"They want the underwear too, don't they?" I ask.

When we get to the site, BB Eyes takes picture after picture until Frank asks him who's paying for the film—the town or the state. There are no footprints, so BB Eyes doesn't have to make any plaster casts. Out of BB Eyes' pocket comes these rubber gloves. He slides into them like he's an honest-to-God practiced professional. "Goddamn fashion statement, those gloves," Frank says.

"Really disgusting," BB Eyes says, "because he always jerks off in 'em before he buries 'em." BB Eyes picks up the underwear and drops it in the Baggie like he was selecting jumbo shrimp at the supermarket. Just looking at it brings me back to sadness. Frank and I help BB Eyes circle the area with that yellow CRIME AREA tape, in case the curious have a hard time finding the place. The stuff reminds me of the plastic pennants they have flapping at used-car lots. Telling Pauline about all this is going to suck the marrow right out of my bones because she'll worry about sex crimes for Lisa and the kids. BB Eyes says that from the size of the underwear and the reports they've had, the perpetrator steals from young women.

Frank's daughter, Kari, is reading through invoices and time cards. She flicks a look at me, which I answer with a quick smile and tell her to go back to business. She winks and blows me a kiss, but even doing that, she won't make a mistake in her accounts. But Frank's son, Gary, he's a one-man Depression when it comes to business. He ain't too far behind Fesmire. I know I'm not the only one with children problems.

I start in on a brake job. Every nut and bolt, even the damn brake line itself, is frozen like it's married to rust, making me wish this wrench had an eight-foot handle.

Gary comes in to return Alice's exhaust pipe and starts commenting. "Too bad Tommy wasn't here, he could chew the nuts off it, he thinks he's so tough."

"Hand me that hacksaw from the bench, would ya?"

"Too tight for my dick," he says, his voice dry and crackly. "Better use yours."

"You know, Gary, I wouldn't have to sucker punch you in the men's room to shut your mouth."

"My old man would be happy to hear how the help treats his son," he says, but out the door he goes with the exhaust pipe under his arm like a slain animal.

With the big open end locked onto the bolt as best as I can, I swing on the other end with the rubber mallet. I feel it slip. No, it turned. It's turning.

I smash it again. The bolt breaks free. A chunk of rust the size of a house cat lands square in my right eye along with a squirt of brake fluid and a coating of solvent.

"Jim. Pauline must have the best body in the state of New Hampshire."

I stumble out from under the car and over to the sink where I rinse my eye as best I can. The stew of lubricating oil and brake fluid stings like someone has started barbecuing in my eye socket.

"Jim."

Funny how a voice will change in the dark. I'm blinded enough so it's all dark to me and confusing me with this half-familiar voice calling my name.

"Jim."

A sharp, slicing voice. I pat my face with a towel and open my eyes, though the light I'm seeing has no more shape than a jelly-fish.

Emory Holler, my sworn enemy, laughs like oil gurgling into a crankcase. If I still held the wrench—but my only weapon to hand is a wadded, wet piece of toweling. "What the hell do you want?"

"Did you try to swing at me?" Emory asks, his voice as fake as diet tonic. My knees buckle from his kick. I'm on the floor, feeling oil and water and the grit of green sweeping compound grind into my palms.

"What are you doing with my wife?" I ask.

"I gave her five hundred for a look at her body."

"You son of a bitch!"

He yanks me to my feet and steps out of reach of my blind punch. "Hey, what damage can I do her?" And his question ain't funny to either one of us. "Seriously, though, we got to talk about Gregory's shack."

While he talks about boundary lines and ancient use, and parcels of land, I get the idea Gregory don't own a square inch of the land he's building his house on. And worse yet, Emory wants him to tear down what he's put up.

"I got a big land deal, Jim, but I'm not at liberty to discuss it."

My eye still hurts from the rust, but my hands are too filthy to rub it, so I yank out my shirttails to daub at the pain. "Gregory wouldn't build in another bird's nest."

"Jesus, Jim, I don't want to take the guy to court. My own nephew, for Christ's sakes." He yells out to Frank to get his workmen's comp files out because he's taking me to the doctor.

I wonder why I fought the rust with that damned open-end wrench. This is no flat-rate shop. I get paid by the hour. I'm just milking the mouse here. I should always take my time. "Milking the mouse, Emory," I tell him, "just milking the mouse."

All the time I'm fighting Emory not to drive me to the doctor because I don't want to pay the doctor to flush rust out of my eye, and he's saying it's important, it's my eyesight. Then he asks why I care since it'll come out of Frank's insurance. And I have to tell him it won't because that ain't how I work for Frank. I'm a private contractor. Then he's mad as hell, but he pays the doctor thirty bucks out of his own pocket.

"You go to Florida and work for me, you won't have any of these problems."

Call me suspicious, but something's up with Emory. Course I'm only speculating here, like I can't tell a foolish thought from a philosophy. Emory runs me off the road, kicks my legs out from under me at the garage, and both times laughs about it. Then right after each time, he comes up with money, for Tommy's bail and for my doctor.

And why is he talking about Pauline's body?

When he gets me back to the trailer, he sits me down at my own table and doles out a bowl of soup like I was a sick kid. I tell him I'm not about to fly to Florida, and he says I'm a fool. By the time I finished up down there, I could be free and clear of debt and disaster. I could start my own business, that steam-cleaning operation I told him about. He tells me you have to grab opportunity by the balls. And here I always thought opportunity was a woman. Well, maybe that's what comes of not being able to get it up, I tell him. Besides, for the steam cleaning I need a helper I can trust and more money than I owe already.

But after all this help and advice, he still won't budge on moving Gregory off his land. Maybe he did kill Helen. Maybe he's going nuts. I know I'm only speculating here, but something ain't lining up. Sometimes I think I ought to head for a state where no letter addressed to Mr. Hutchins, no phone call for Jim, could reach me. Only I know Pauline's set on staying till the kids are settled. If neither fire nor water could drive her away, it'll take more than just my dreams. Or suspicions.

PAULINE

I told Jim if he has big dreams of big money, he should go to Florida by himself because Emory's even offered to pay for his flight down there. It makes no sense for me to go. There are no jobs down there for me. We'd have to rent an apartment instead of a room, like he'll do. It'd give us that much money to save up toward our bills, and I'll still be making money here.

It might do us both good to be away from each other. With all the money problems and the children's problems, he gets fretting and ugly. Half the time he doesn't even want to talk about them. He thinks Gregory's the only one that doesn't do anything wrong because Gregory doesn't drink, but Gregory's changing. He snaps and snarls at everybody, including me. Emory told me the boy tried to pick a fight with him and threatened to come back with a gun.

Jim's mad at Emory because Emory saw me naked in the trailer, as if Jim himself wouldn't have looked, as if he didn't look back in his drinking days, and even after his drinking days if Kari Reed happened to be flaunting her tight little body around. He says I should give that five hundred dollars back to Emory because I already bailed Tommy out of jail, but I'm keeping it awhile. There might be need for lawyers, and Emory said he didn't care. Besides I got a letter to Jim from the Internal Revenue Service. I ain't shown him yet, but I'll bet it's not a refund.

And there's still Gregory to take care of, which I don't know what it'll take, money or what, but I know Emory's not lying about Gregory not owning that land he built his place on. Just as I believe Emory's not lying when he says Helen fell down the stairs, though I hear myself saying "believe" instead of "know."

BB Eyes caught me out in that very same way of speaking when he came to the trailer a week after Helen's funeral. Her death hit Jim hard, his only sister, older than him, always kind of looking out for him, passing him advice or just a shoulder, which he always took. I don't know why he can't see how much I want a shoulder now, how hard it is for me some days just to get out of bed and face the daylight. That first morning after Elizabeth died, I woke and wouldn't open my eyes for the longest time, then I opened them with my face buried in the pillow, but still the filthy light leaked in, and I wondered if I'd ever see anything pretty again.

BB Eyes admired Elizabeth and said, That one will make you proud, because he'd already decided my oldest three children wouldn't. He said Emory'd quit working for the town, what with all Helen's insurance money, gave up that good foreman's job paying him over twenty-five thousand dollars a year, when you counted overtime and all. Which makes me wonder, he said, about Helen's sleeve on her dress being torn like that. You wouldn't think a woman like Helen, neat about her appearance, would have to wear a dress with a torn sleeve. He stopped talking for a minute and ran those little eyes of his over me, not like

Emory does when I'm dancing for him, but just to check that I'm not wearing any torn clothes. He's careful not to insult me.

I believe I noticed that tear too, I told BB Eyes. When I saw her in the garage, I said to myself I should ask her if she knew she had a rip in her dress, out to the supermarket with holey clothes. I tried to laugh a little, but BB Eyes came right on me like he was closing windows to keep a loose canary from flying out of the house.

Believe? he asked. You *believe* you saw that tear, or you know you saw it? Saw it before she fell, because we know that falling down the stairs didn't rip that sleeve. There were no nails or splinters to snag it on.

I'm not talking fancy, BB Eyes, I told him then. I saw the tear in the sleeve when I first saw her in the garage, otherwise I wouldn't've thought about telling her. Sometimes when you're rushing to go somewhere because your husband has thrown on his clothes and doesn't care what he looks like, you don't have time to inspect yourself in a full-length mirror the way you'd like to.

I never knew Emory to go around careless of his appearance, said BB Eyes.

Naturally, I didn't ask what he was after because I knew, just as clear as I remembered seeing that ripped sleeve for the first time when I saw Helen lying on that cellar floor just dead. Even now I can hear their voices raised in arguments before the terrible tumble into the cellar.

I still can't make out what she wanted in that cellar, BB Eyes said.

Nor can I. I know I've stuck with my story long enough so that I'll stick with it. Living with a little lie seems awful easy compared to everything else I have to live with, easier than death, that's for certain. And when it isn't easy, I just tell myself that Emory's been loyal to me, so I can be loyal to him, that's all.

And it hasn't been easy because Carol stopped me right in the laundry room and asked me for that damn fifty-dollar bill. She said the customer had called, identified his unit and his red running shorts, and asked that they be returned to him. He had waited on the telephone until David brought them up from the lost-and-found bin, then he asked if any money was in the pockets. He was quite definite about the fifty, Pauline, Carol said, so now I'm telling you the one thing that'll ruin a motel business faster than anything is a reputation for stealing. David's so concerned, he sent fifty dollars straight out of his own pocket.

I lied right through my teeth. I said I didn't find any money. I didn't even look in the pockets, and I had no idea where the money could have gone. All the time Carol kept giving me hard looks, and all the time I lied and wondered why that rich man's pocket change should bring me to tears and why wasn't I smart enough to throw away those damn red running shorts.

Not so long ago that fifty-dollar bill could have bought me dreams for Elizabeth, but now Jim tells me I need to find other dreams.

I often dream about the old house. Back in the old house, Petey, the first Petey, sat right up in the front window that faced the east and started singing as soon as he caught the morning sun. Everybody liked him, even Tommy, who'd put up with Petey's morning singing when he would otherwise rage at so much as the clatter of a dropped spoon. I wondered some days if Tommy could stay home to listen to Petey instead of going off to that school he hated so, if he wouldn't turn a happier eye on his days. Then he got the chance when the school expelled him.

But I never got to see if my idea would have worked out because Gregory drove all hope of happiness right out of Tommy when he smacked him. It's that same mad that's rising up in Gregory again, only now I don't know where it's coming from. I know it's not Tommy stirring it in him. Poor Tommy, after the school threw him out, he walked around the old place like he didn't know where anything came from, including himself. He'd pace the flatness of our land as if nothing could make him want to lift his eyes, then he'd turn to slinking. Jim could only see another child out of school. Poor Tommy could have been raising the dead, and Jim would still have despised the very air he breathed.

Jim didn't finish school, nor did I, but after Gregory won his diploma, Jim figured they all would. Done once, done forever, he thought. It knocked him right in the ditch when Lisa quit, and then Tommy was expelled. I worried it'd drive Jim back to drink.

Thank God Tommy hadn't touched a drink the day of the fire. He was fifteen, and I told him watching over his sister Elizabeth would rank him high in the human race because from the time she got home on the kindergarten bus at noon to the time Jim walked in at five-thirty, Tommy had full responsibility for her. Gregory told his brother if anything happened to Elizabeth, he'd drive Tommy's nose right through his head. I saw Gregory's threat pushed Tommy's hope of doing a good job right into a dark corner. All Tommy wanted was to do something right, to have someone say, Good job, though I couldn't get Gregory nor Jim either to say more than, He's supposed to do a good job, for Christ's sake.

On that day, I was working at the nursing home, and Tommy was doing a good job, watching TV with Elizabeth in the front room, when he thought to water the sheep. So much the boy, sometimes I think he can't decide when he's awake or when he's dreaming, and it makes him ugly to find out how often he's confused.

With no running water in the house, Tommy had to go out to

the well. How many times I think that if he could have just plunked that galvanized pail right in the sink and drawn water from the tap like we do now, he wouldn't've spotted the fire so soon. And I remember how hard living in the old house was, cramped and cold and grinding, sad as I can feel missing it. Walking back from the well to the sheep's pen, Tommy saw flames shoot out of the ceiling light fixture in the back room. Stock-still he stood, the bucket of sheep's water hanging heavy at the end of his arm, until the window burst, spraying him with broken glass. He got mad as hell, as if someone'd slapped him, and threw that bucket of sheep's water at the fire and ran to haul up another one and threw that one too before he just pitched the pail to the ground.

In the house, screaming so to roust Elizabeth, he scared her so she ran out of the house, across the yard, and right in front of Mrs. Glebe's car. He said the squeal of the brakes brought him to his senses enough so he could dial the 911 for the fire department.

Addled as he was with screaming at his sister and with smoke roaring out of the back room, he grabbed up the photograph albums from under the TV. That snake-strike mind of his told him pictures were about the only things in the house we couldn't replace. I just wish that quick mind could save him from burning himself over and over again with drinking and fighting and Penny, that witch. Sin to say it, but I believe if he were slower like his brother, he'd live easier.

Fire department did what they could, I guess, to save the neighborhood, but my house just disastered. Tommy forgot the framed school pictures on the wall. The fire ate so ferociously all it left were smooth spots on the charred walls, and when Malcolm Hurd came down and bulldozed the ruins, I cried looking at those black walls.

I love pretty things. If I know one thing about myself after forty-something years of walking the earth, it's the joy floods my soul at the sight of a pretty thing. Crossing the yard the day after the fire, I saw the eye of a fallen peacock feather shining purple and green in the dirt. I remember that so well because right then I thought "pretty," even in the dirt, letting purple and green and black fill my mind. For an instant I stopped thinking, stopped thinking at all until I lifted my eyes to the burned-out shell of my house, like a dead beetle someone had crushed. Then all the peacocks that ever lived could die and go to hell, and pretty blew out of my life like a useless, cold ember.

Everywhere fire's dead-ugly smell lingered, as if someone was smothering me with old newspaper ashes. That fire tested me, and I hated it. Hadn't I been tested enough with Lisa and her foolishness? With Jim's drinking and worse? I said, All right, I'll surrender, I'll lay it all down. "Lay it all down" hummed like a tired prayer in my mind. I found it hard to stop that song. I didn't know there'd be more and worse testing in the years ahead because if I had, I would've laid down right there in the ashes of my house.

Fire ruined all the clothes. Even though I washed them, hung them outside, they all carried that burnt stench. On the clothesline hung my white uniforms, new-bought just before the fire, hung there for days like executed criminals. I kept airing them and wearing a different one to work each night, and even though the whole shift long the smell reminded me of my house, I still wouldn't give up those new-bought uniforms.

Jim and Gregory trucked the rest of the clothes to the dump. Some things, Jim said, you have to let stay ruined, no matter how much you cared for them. But he thought I was holding on to the uniforms because they were new-bought, when I was looking just to hold on to something to keep from laying it all down, just like now he doesn't understand what I need.

I thought metal would survive a fire, but that was a lie too because the fire didn't leave me a pot to cook in. I swallowed my pride and asked Jim to call Helen to borrow pots and pans. Thank God she sent down a boxful and an electric oven, which came out of no request, just good and free and unexpected. That oven put a little ease into life, living in the garage like we were.

Living in a garage didn't make bluebirds fly around my head no matter how many times Jim told me it was no worse than living in a cellar hole. "Which lots of people do," he said. It's one thing to thank God you and yours survived, another thing to sing praises about losing everything so you have to huddle up like cave people. I know what to be grateful for and what to get along with, and the difference between the two.

It was only Elizabeth who was so cunning she could make me feel bluebirds singing around my head.

I'd go in the garage and stare at a row of SpaghettiOs, beans, and tomato soup, lined up on the two-by-fours Jim had set at eye level between studs. They were what I hoped to get along with because with pretty Elizabeth I was not laying it down, no matter how loud that ugly hymn played in my brain. I bought cake mixes, which are not luxuries but necessary for the sweetness everybody needs, sweetness as regular as sunshine. And, expensive though it was, I bought food coloring so Elizabeth could make silly frosting—red or green or blue because she did love a pretty cake so. I did everything to let that child swim in pretty.

When Elizabeth had started kindergarten the fall before the fire, she couldn't leave the other children alone because it was the first chance she'd had to be with other children her own age. Jim fretted over it because she wouldn't do her work at school, but after a couple of months she got used to it just as I knew she would. She came to love school, the only one of my children who really took to it. She loved school so much that when she got sick, I had to lie and tell her the school closed for the day, else she'd say, "Pack my medicine, Momma, I'll take it to school."

She liked to dress up for school. First clothes I replaced after the fire were Elizabeth's jumpers and skirts and pretty blouses. I bought them brand-new because Elizabeth was too pretty to hide in hand-me-downs. Just like that old peacock displaying his fan in the yard, Elizabeth liked to parade in the sun. The snub-nosed yellow school bus would pull up, and she'd come skipping across the road, wearing a pale green dress that made her look like a soft new leaf, like green grass coming up after you burn a field. Ain't she cunning? I thought. With this much pretty streaming off that child, how can you think about laying it all down? Which is why I didn't.

And now she's gone too.

5
five

GREGORY

With death and stealing and the panty pervert, I need to get a gun. Emory won't evict me if I have a gun, no matter how much he mauls Momma. They're both my sworn enemies now.

I stop at the 7-Eleven for a big coffee. Scooter Holler's standing over at the refrigerator case, scoping out beer to steal. He'll be back tonight to steal beer out of the rear. MB Jewell's watching me while she ought to be watching Scooter scoping the beer. Tommy told me Scooter's real fussy, will only steal Bud. He's a fanatic when he reads what label's on the swill that gets him drunk. The sugar sliding out of the packets and into my coffee rattles, and the sound hurts my head. Already, I've stood listening to five packets sliding down in a racket MB hears but pretends not to. She's a pretty girl, too pretty to get hurt.

I'll warn MB about Scooter. She's still watching me because of the nasty noise the sugar makes, as if it's my fault they buy noisy sugar. Out of the cooler Scooter pulls a putrid green bottle of tonic. It may be Mountain Dew, I can't tell from here. He's professionally sneaky. He's fooling MB into thinking he don't care about the beer, like he's not picking out exactly, precisely, where the beer he plans to steal stands.

At the counter I motion him ahead of me. He shrugs his shoulders as if it's nothing to him and slides a sweaty dollar bill. "Don't forget about tonight," he says.

MB rings up his money, so sweaty I can smell it, and says, "It's under control." She gives him his change and a smile, though her mouth looks scared.

I guess all the girls are scared after it got out about the stolen and stained underwear. MB is pretty with a square face and fair, smooth skin and big blue eyes. Scummy Scooter would race to rape her. He'd hurt her and not give a care about it at all. If I warn her he's going to steal the beer he's scoped out, it could end up he'll rape her, and it would be my fault. I'll keep my trap shut. It ain't worth risking a woman raped and maybe her killed just to stop Scooter Holler from stealing a case of Budweiser beer. He'll just steal it somewhere else. Tommy says even when Scooter's got money, he steals for fun. Probably rapes like that too. For fun. Did he steal that underwear? Did he stink his seed into them?

If I had my gun, I'd control him. He's my cousin and Emory's my uncle, both of them sworn enemies. When I get my gun, they'll do what I say, or I'll sink them with buckshot.

"You going to drink that coffee or eat it?" MB asks me.

"I could tell you something, but I won't." I give her change for the coffee, coins with no sweat on them. "I'll look out for you because I'm on your side. You don't need to worry about the underwear thief," I tell her so she won't spend the day worrying about Scooter. A shotgun could shoot Scooter right out of his raping rampage and stop Emory from his evil eviction.

"Hey," MB says, "that pervert that's stealing panties ain't got the balls to bother a woman to her face, and he won't have any balls at all if he comes around to bother me."

Out in my truck I get the radio running right away and suck on the coffee as I'm driving out to my place. There's no rain to ruin the reception, so I don't have to follow Scooter to hear him. I just twist the dial between stations until that tough voice of his booms out. "A case of Bud," I hear Scooter say on the radio, so I know he'll be stealing tonight. I listen if he'll say anything about raping MB, but he's cautious. "Blonde," I hear him say. Which could mean MB or some other woman. Looking at Scooter Holler, MB held her face in her hands, like Elizabeth used to. They are alike that way, neither one average or typical looking, but they aren't alike, because Elizabeth's dead.

I could call BB Eyes to tell him Scooter's going to steal at the 7-Eleven tonight. I won't even have to tell BB Eyes who I am because the cops will believe anything bad about Scooter. Or Tommy. He is a thief, drunk, and a fighter, though I wouldn't call BB Eyes on Tommy even if he were burgling with Scooter Holler. I can't call BB Eyes because I don't own a telephone. Electricity but no telephone. I'll use Father's phone.

At the trailer I grab Buffy and wrestle him to the ground. No one else in the world except Tommy can do that without he'd bite right down on their bones. Wrestling Buffy don't worry me at all. I don't want him ever to forget who I am just because I went away and got a new dog. I never named the new dog because I'll never own another dog like Buffy. The whole world can forget me, and it won't matter to me the sweat off a dead tick, but Buffy stays different. Just like Elizabeth.

Then I find Father. He sits on the couch, one eye watching the fish in the tank Malcolm Hurd gave him. He says his eye hurts. He had to take a day off work. He says Emory drove him home.

"He was looking for Momma." I have to help Father see the danger. "He and Scooter are trying to force me off my land."

His eye's all red like he's damned himself with drinking again, but I don't think he's dipped back to that, though Momma worries he'll go wet again, like she wants it to come true. I hear her on my radio. Father says, "I thought you paid Emory for that land."

"Emory's my sworn enemy. He'll lie as easy as he'll sweat." I feel sorry for Father especially because he won't listen to the logic of danger. "You got to tell me where I can buy a gun."

"You'll have to take money out of the bank. You know you hate that."

"You always say just what I know you'll say. No wonder it's so easy for people to fool you."

"What type of gun?" he asks, 'cause he can't argue against me when I'm this right.

"A shotgun, so I won't miss."

"I'd figure on two hundred dollars. You want to put all that money into a shotgun?"

"Scooter's planning to steal beer out of the 7-Eleven tonight."

"You taken to hanging around with Scooter Holler?" Father's rattling the coffeemaker around to rope me into staying. If he was smart, he'd just rear up some instant. It'd entice me just as quick.

"I know."

"You tell BB Eyes about it." Father's pouring the water into the coffeemaker without even looking, like he's so locked onto the right amount he don't have to look.

"He can't even handle Tommy, like you can't handle Emory." The snake's starting in, barking like he could break my braincase right in two. "If you'd watched how you put that water in instead of being so all high-and-mighty, I'd be drinking coffee now."

Father mumbles about the coffeemaker and makes me stare at the fish moving around in the aquarium, like those multicolored fish are going to move me out of my place and purpose. He points out one little striped one, and I dip down into that water with my free hand to snag that striped fish and pop it into my mouth and suck it solid down my gullet. "Now, let's have that fancy coffee of yours so I can go get a gun."

"How may I help you, Gregory?" asks Debra, the bank teller, telling me without her knowing it that she was waiting for me. She's daughter to Malcolm Hurd. If I'd listened to my truck radio on the way from the trailer, I might've heard them talking. I tell her I want to take some money out of the bank. I total about two hundred for shotgun and shells, leaving, say, three hundred in my account to finish fixing up my place.

She says, "You'll have to talk to my father. On withdrawals of that amount, we need approval of a bank officer, like my father."

"Never heard of that."

"It's a new policy," she says, fussing with forms on her side of the counter, "and you don't usually withdraw sums of that size." I don't say anything, then she says, "I think that pervert stole my underwear off my clothesline. Isn't that awful?"

"I'll see Mr. Hurd," I say because I see she wants me to see him, and she's as harmless and helpless as MB. Only Malcolm Hurd's not here at the bank, so I'll have to come back for my money. She shuffles certificates behind the counter until I say not to worry, I'll be back. She has beautiful black hair that even short keeps its beauty.

Outside, I see Tommy coming out of the grocery with a bag in his hand. He sees me too and waves. He wants a ride, but I won't give him one if he's rummed up.

"For Christ's sake, Gregory, it's only beer."

He hops in the truck, and I ride him home to his place on the hill. Then he invites me in, saying Penny's taken Aaron to the doctor's for shots. The snake's biting real bad, barely letting me think, so I go in for a cup of coffee though usually I'd rather step into a coffin than enter Tommy's place. I ask him about guns because I don't know enough about them to fill a hen's pocket.

"What you want the gun for?"

"Uncle Emory's trying to throw me off my land."

Tommy's got a cup of water frying in the microwave and has fished a jar of instant coffee out of the cupboard. "I thought you might be taking up hunting. Back to nature, back to the land." He stirs up the coffee for me and snaps open a beer for himself. "Scooter says the land still belongs to his old man."

"Scooter's a thief," I say, forgetting that he and Tommy steal stuff together. I'm drowning the snake in coffee, but he's swimming to the surface and snapping at my skull. I'll be screaming in a minute, which won't matter because Tommy likes screaming and scratching. I won't scream.

Tommy's talking about thieving. How everybody does it, and a little goes a long way if you linger over your gains. The coffee's soothing the snake. Over the couch is a hole in the plaster where Tommy punched the wall. At least that's what Lisa told Momma. Examining the hole because I'm supposed to patch it, I see what popped it just as easy as if I was watching a movie. Screaming drunk, Tommy's got Penny by the ears, he hammers her head into the wall. Her head will fit the hole in the wall better than his fist will. She knees him in the balls.

I wonder if Tommy's got a brain snake he feeds beer to. He drinks beer while I drink more coffee. Father drinks coffee these days, but he used to drink beer.

"I want the gun for tonight," I say, "but Debra told me I couldn't take out my money until I saw Malcolm Hurd, and he wa'n't there."

"That's bullshit." Tommy's snapped another beer. "You don't need anybody's permission to withdraw your money. Debra, the teller, told you that?"

"Yes."

"Fuck her." He's railing against the teller and the bank, telling me to take my money out and keep it myself, not stopping until I tell him about thieves. "Thieves! Do you think I'd steal from family?"

"Scooter thieves. He's going to thieve tonight."

"Did he fucking tell you that?"

I just shake my head because, brother or not, Tommy could tell about my radio, which Scooter would try to steal as easy as he picks his nose.

"Did you say anything to anyone about stealing?" Tommy asks. He's finishing off this beer quickly too. I wonder how many beers it takes to make him drunk.

"That's why you're not getting your money," Tommy says. "Hurd's friends enough with Father to fool you with some bullshit rigamarole to keep you from buying a gun."

"Who can't get a gun?" Penny asks. Aaron in her arms, she hips the door shut, then spots the six-pack sitting on the counter. "Two beers? Two fucking beers! That's all you left me for sitting a goddamn hour in the doctor's office holding your kid? And he's wet. Don't tell me your brother drank them because I see a cup of coffee in his hand as usual. Say, Gregory, why don't you just break Tommy's neck for me? Do the world a favor."

I say Tommy's a father now, so I can't go hurting him. Momma thought I'd kill him for selling me that stolen radio.

"Beer run later tonight," Tommy says. His mouth twists like a melting candle, too menacing for me to stay. I'd take Aaron with me, only you can't save a child. I know that, just like I know I'm going to get my gun.

six

JIM

Tommy's in jail," I say. I'm getting used to saying it. I'm getting good at saying it. Pauline tells me I'm even getting to like saying it. "Tommy's in jail," I say again, because whether or not Pauline is right, I do enjoy telling the Squatty Body, Penny, her sweetie won't be available for the next brawl she's planned.

Why has Squatty Body called me instead of the police, seeing as how they stick to him like straw to a sweaty neck? "I hate to cut this conversation short, Penny, but I work for a living."

"I'll get back to you."

I'll get back to you. Oh, ain't she the big shot, though the old worry bird sings in my ear that she will get back since she wants money out of me or Tommy. Funny thing about Tommy going to jail, it wasn't BB Eyes who first told me. It was Gregory. And I can't figure out how in the hell he knew.

At least if nothing else I slowed Gregory's buying a gun. Lately, strange has moved in with that boy like a roommate without a job. All the time he talks like he's got ESP, but the only ESP I see in my three kids is a silent agreement to bring grief to my doorstep. What with Pauline messing with Emory to cure her grief, I couldn't bring myself any more problems if I got down on my knees every night and prayed for 'em.

"Better get yourself a gun," Gregory growled on the telephone. "I can't tell you why because they sometimes tap even these public lines."

God knows what trouble Gregory's heading for, but as long as Tommy's in jail, he ain't driving a car drunk or hanging Squatty Body out the window or walking behind the 7-Eleven, casing the joint. Suspicious Behavior, BB Eyes said. Tommy and Scooter. Suspicious Behavior. I suppose it was, even if both of them claimed their kidneys attacked them so bad they had to duck behind the store. Only the cinder blocks wa'n't wet when the squad car lighted them up, and the boys didn't have anything out of their pants, and the back door was unlocked. I'm thinking there's hardly a man in this town ain't guilty of Suspicious Behavior, and that includes Emory, me, and BB Eyes himself.

With all the worry over what happens to the pink underwear, you'd think any two young men could figure out not to prowl after dark. Myself, I try not to go out after dark at all. Hell, they haven't even found all the stolen underwear.

I dream of that silky cloth, lying in the sawdust, fooling me into thinking I was looking at a fat worm. In my dreams it changes to a doll's dish, to a coral bell, to a faded bird. It's never just underwear. Sometimes I think Gregory's all dreams and

Tommy has none. Pauline's gone beyond me, with dreams and nightmares demanding her equal time.

I go to packing the bearings on Alice's truck. I've prised off the hubcap when Frank moves up to me. "Jim," he says, slow and deliberate, "I don't know if I'm going to renew Lisa's lease."

I guess this is his way of telling me he for sure won't renew Squatty Body's lease, even after Gregory patched the hole in the wall Tommy made with her head. "What's the matter with Lisa?" I don't really care if he does put Squatty Body out on the street, but I do care with Lisa, not only because she's my daughter and her children are my grandchildren, but I also know where Lisa and her children will wind up if they don't have an apartment. I ain't stupid.

"Parties," Frank says. I figure the way he's dragging out his talk, he must be paying a hundred dollars or more per word.

"Parties?"

"There's a lot of guys going in and out of her place."

Then I understand it's not that he's paying a hundred dollars a word to tell me my daughter's turned into the town pump, it's more that someone ought to be paying him a hundred dollars a word to say such a thing to a girl's father. He knows. What the hell, he's got a daughter who likes to climb on my wild side. This goddamn cotter pin is as greasy as a lie, and I can't see it halfway properly to grip the son of a bitch with my side cutters and yank it out of that hole.

"That's not my business," I tell Frank, and grit my teeth to let him know who else's business it ain't.

"You want me to help you with those dykes?" he asks, pointing to where my side cutters slip and slide around the miserable end of the cotter pin.

"No." I'll deal with my own corner-creeping visions myself.

He drags a fingernail down across his throat. "The cops are watching her place."

"BB Eyes must have forgot to tell me."

"Guys are coming out of there in a steady stream."

"There's no law against that," I say, "unless she's charging them." Standing there with these side cutters in my hand I must look like I'll slice the tongue right out of Frank if he calls Lisa a whore.

"They suspect there's drug dealing going on."

"She must be giving the profits to the poor."

"Jim, she gets the apartment subsidized. There's lots would jump at the chance—"

"I would myself," I say, getting a purchase on the miserably slippery cotter pin with the side cutters. "Forty bucks a month for durable housing? That's a deal I couldn't pass up." I yank the goddamn cotter pin out of the holes. I turn the castle nut out and remove the washer and outer bearing before I pull the wheel off. "I'll speak to her." I figure out that's what he wants me to say. If the world turned on bearings that I packed, it'd turn a hell of a lot smoother than it does now. The new cotter pin slides right in the hole and waits comfortable for me to slap on the dustcover and hubcap.

On the other wheel the cotter pin slips out as easy as sweat so I don't turn half so philosophical, but when I'm done with the job, I rub degreaser into every crack and crevice of my hands like the stuff's washing away poison. Then I step out into the back for a smoke.

Down by the sumacs bright sunlight glances off the yellow plastic police line that decorates the landscape. In a small town like this, everybody says the panty thief is an outsider, but everybody knows it's one of our own. A rose-breasted grosbeak, his red a bright spot against the black and white feathers of his head and back, hops on a branch. You almost never see more than one or two of them at a time. I think of poor Gregory, keeping to himself, just worn down and dirty.

Another drag on my cigarette shows me the warm wind's blowing the smoke behind me, away from the rose-breasted grosbeak. I follow the yellow line until I reach the stream, slow and quiet running in a kind of midsummer daze suited to the hot, noonday sun. If I could come back after death, I'd come back as a stream. After Elizabeth it's a wonder I can even drink a glass of water, and Pauline shies away from water altogether, but I still like a stream. Grasses grow along the bank and in places right to the edge. Across the stream is nothing. Nor in it. I look in it last, but there's no little girl lying under the surface.

I hope to God it wa'n't Gregory who stole the panties and jerked off in them. I don't believe he's so much as bedded a woman. Now there's a thought to worry you. I mean, if pushing thirty, he's still a virgin, is it because he's looking for weird sex? All that time he worked with sheep, I mean, they make all those jokes, but sheep? No, that's ridiculous. But Gregory a thief? A pervert? I can't even think it.

With a quick, soft hiss, my cigarette floats downstream. Goddamn, if I did come back as a stream, everything from cigarette butts to dead bodies would end up in me. Here I am, messing up my own very idea of heaven with a cigarette butt. With a quick stretch I grab for that nasty bit of white and brown, then my feet give out from under me. I'm flat out. Sudden cold torments me. Gravel mashes my fingers. I can't breathe. Both eyes sting. A mucky weed is in my nose. I can't swim. I'm going to die here.

I push myself up. Snorting, I wipe my eyes. What the hell has tripped me up here? Under my feet, where I hadn't noticed before because I wasn't looking down but up and straight ahead and to both sides, right on the ground the clayey soil is slick and wrinkled. Only one swipe of my boot turns up the pink smeared with gray.

"You all right?" It's Gary Reed, his nose still bandaged from where Tommy lammed him. He's looking at me like I might've just sprouted from the ground.

"More panties here. Unless your father wants to open a lingerie store, I'm just going to leave 'em lay."

Mostly Gary works as a gofer for his old man, running here and there in the Ford pickup truck Frank bought for him, and generally trying to stay smarter than the truck. Like a lot of these young guys, you give Gary four wheels and a set of keys, he figures he's holding the long end of the wishbone.

"How's Gregory?"

"You looking for Gregory?" I didn't know them for running buddies. Running buddies, Gary and Gregory? Neither of them finding women except in the underwear they've stole? Kari did tell me once that her brother was odder than an anteater.

"He's my friend." Gary's voice carries a funny tone, almost an accusation or a whiny plea, I can't tell which.

"He's out to his place." I hope that is where he is.

"Maybe I'll drive over to his place."

"Don't surprise him." In the hot sun his blond hair shines like a crown of innocence. "You surprise him, you might think you're meeting a bear in the woods."

Gary stares as if he's trying to figure out if I'm pulling his leg. Just when I'm about to tell him I'm serious, he says, "Don't worry, Mr. Hutchins, I won't tell my old man you were out here playing in the water." He laughs like he won't ever have to explain anything to anyone.

Long as it's been going on, I still ain't got used to people sticking a handle onto my name. When I was a kid in school, teachers would sling that "Mr." sarcastic onto my name. "Mr. Hutchins, if you are through trying to entertain Mr. Holler, perhaps you could learn something about the principal exports of Portugal." "Cork," said Emory Holler, only with our accents it came out "cock," which turned the teacher's face red. She dropped that "Mr." handle right off my name and Emory's too for most the rest of the week. Then there were all the offices I've sat in, from principals to banks, from welfare to lawyers. I knew the names they were thinking: *back shacker, stump fucker, lowlife*.

I'd guess no one's ever thought those things about Gary Reed because he comes from a family where they paint the house every five years, whether it needs it or not. He even finished school, about the same time as Gregory. All the Reeds finished high school. They wouldn't have it any other way. That's the trouble with your brood, Frank Reed told me after Tommy bloodied Gary's nose. None of them stuck to school.

When I get back to the garage, Frank eyeballs me like me and mine were hatched different from him and his. "Gary says you insulted him."

"I just found another pair of pecker-tracked, pink panties. You don't suppose your boy's our panty pervert?"

"That's stupid, and insulting."

I take Alice's truck out for a quick road test, to make sure the wheels won't fall off. Spinning up the hill by Tommy's place, I see Scooter Holler pulling his truck to the curb. Paying no attention to me, probably because Alice's truck doesn't draw his attention, Scooter walks up to Tommy's apartment building. I wonder why the two of them just didn't go home from jail together.

Over at the cop station BB Eyes sits outside with his hands on his gut like he's holding a hernia.

"You know what," he says. "They tell me I'm too fat for this job. Fat and out of shape. Ain't that a bitch?"

I sit in the truck with the door open. "When did Tommy get out of jail?"

"Unless he walked through that wall, he's still in there." BB Eyes releases his gut. "You ain't going to do anything as foolish as spring him, are you?"

A cough shakes me. Lately, I get this damn morning cough telling me I got to cut back on my smoking. "Let's hope Pauline don't scent him out."

He grabs his gut again like he was hefting it for weight and form. I guess secretly we're all proud of our faults and deficiencies, or in love with them. Else why would we persist in them? "Can you believe they won't be happy until I lose all this."

"Maybe you should let them rub it for luck." I suck down a long drag.

"Those selectmen worry about insurance. One of them's got a relative on the State Police where they train them like they were going to the Olympics. Well, that's fine. Pay me like they pay those Staties, and I'll go into training too."

I want BB Eyes to keep Tommy locked up, but most of the favors he does me I don't have to ask for. "How did Scooter get loose?"

"Emory went his bail." BB Eyes lets go of his gut. "We'll keep Tommy until a smart lawyer comes along."

Even if BB Eyes doesn't give cat shit for the selectmen's rules about his belly, he has come to respect the law since Pauline hired a lawyer last time he took Tommy to court. The lawyer cost five hundred dollars, but Tommy didn't serve any jail time. BB Eyes says that Tommy better stay away from Staties because if he tries his flying-feet trick with them, they'll lay him out and charge him with something that'll stick. Fat as he is, BB Eyes doesn't want to spend the end of his career fighting Tommy Hutchins.

An easy afternoon of fan belts and spark plugs gives me time to wonder why Tommy and Gregory, two boys so different, should both come to grief at the same time. I used to think my children balanced one another. Gregory: slow and moderate; Tommy: quick and hot; Lisa: cagey and independent; Elizabeth: enthusiastic and sociable. Elizabeth's dying is where it all started to fall apart. A family is like one of those little mortarless arch bridges they used to build. You set up a wooden scaffolding, pile the rocks just right, then dismantle the scaffolding, and the stones will interlock. If you pile them right, they'll hold a hundred years or more. But when Elizabeth drowned, it was like the keystone fell out and the stones have all tumbled every which way in the current.

I'm just tightening the alternator after the last fan-belt job when Pauline walks in. "Thank God for Emory because you'd never tell me Tommy was in jail," she says.

"Did you want to lose another day's pay over him?"

"I didn't lose a day's pay," she snaps, "but I had to pay for a collect call Tommy made from the police station to the motel when they let him out."

"He could've called me for a dime. I've been right here turning wrenches all afternoon."

I might just as well have turned on the acetylene torch and scorched her from stem to stern. She says I don't care a thing about Tommy. I could let him rot in jail. I don't love my own child. Nor do I give a care about what anybody thinks, just let the whole town know poor Tommy's in jail again, laughing because he had to use the bathroom late at night. Her accusations swarmed around me like flies at the dump. I'm waiting for Frank to wander in so he can tell her he might be evicting Lisa and for certain will have Tommy out on the street. That'll give her a two-by-four to wham me with.

"Look, Pauline, I didn't hold Tommy down and pour beer into his gullet until he got so desperate to pee he had to duck behind the 7-Eleven. What's more, BB Eyes told me he must have been releasing dehydrated urine. The ground where they stood and the building's walls was all dry."

"And if he was, you'd begrudge him the money to have a doctor check out his kidneys. Besides, how do you know it wasn't coffee he was drinking?"

"That's true. I did see Tommy drink coffee one night, but I forgot to mark it on the calendar, so I can't tell you what year it was."

"The 7-Eleven doesn't have any NO TRESPASSING sign posted out back."

She goes right out through the front and drives home and is still unhappy when I stroll into the trailer, so I go about fixing grilled cheese sandwiches, slicing some of those tasty middle-sized tomatoes to slide between the cheese and the bread, just the way she likes them.

The sandwiches taste just crisp enough without a crumb of black, like I sometimes get on one side, and the cheese has swelled all puffy around the edges. Old Charley's parading the table so that he can snatch a few bites, a favorite of his since Elizabeth used to tear the crusts off her sandwich and drop them on the floor for him. The hot sweet-tartness of tomatoes breaks open in my mouth to remind me I do like this touch of fruit every bit as much as Pauline does, even if I don't clamor for it. When I look across our little table, Pauline's wearing a smile that starts her pretty face to singing. It's a smile that doesn't set wrinkles around her eyes or squeeze them up under her cheeks. It makes me feel so good, I suggest we take one of our nice after-supper walks.

"Then you'll expect to jump right into bed," she says, her smile fading as fast as a burned-out lightbulb. "I suppose you think a grilled cheese sandwich and a walk make up for everything. You're too busy to bother with a table-scraps matter like getting your own son out of jail, but you have all kinds of time to take a walk and look for romance."

"I was busy trying to keep Gregory out of jail." As I tell her about preventing Gregory from buying a gun, piece by piece she tears the edges from her sandwich and drops them on the floor, which draws old Charley right to the on-ramp for cat heaven.

"You should stop interfering with Gregory," she says. "Besides Emory says maybe I should have a gun. To protect myself if that underwear thief tries to break in." She loads the last of her sandwich into her mouth.

"You hired Tommy a lawyer, didn't you." I don't need an answer. That stuff about the NO TRESPASSING sign at the 7-Eleven told me she'd been talking to somebody that gets paid to weasel.

"You didn't have to pay any bail," she says.

"You found a lawyer that works charity?"

"I had money. You needn't worry I stole it from you."

"You'd better save some for Gregory's lawyer. Gary Reed told me he was going to visit Gregory, and God knows, Gregory might just shoot him."

"You keep interfering with Gregory, maybe he'll shoot you."

"That's why I've got to stop him from getting a gun."

"If I had a gun," Tommy says, listing the people he'd shoot, starting with Gary Reed, for calling the cops after Tommy punched his nose, and ending with Squatty Body. He's the creepingest kid since Fesmire. He was into the trailer, into the kitchen, and into the conversation before I as much as heard the door close. And of course seeing it's him, Buffy didn't bark.

Oh, what a fracas we're into now. Tommy's yelling about grabbing Penny by the throat, by the ears, by both legs, what he's going to do to her you haven't seen outside a television wrestling match. Pauline, with no more to go on than Tommy's rattling anger, cheers him on like she's paid for a ringside seat.

"I've put up with it for the last time," he says.

"Oh," she says.

"What that woman won't do hasn't been written," he says.

"Oh," she says.

I'm quiet because I'm waiting to hear what she *has* done. Staying quiet gives me time to notice that Tommy ain't had a drink nor does a curse stronger than "hell" or "damn" cross his lips. So I figure he's got more hold of himself than he's letting on, more than his mother has on herself.

The upshot of it is, Penny's taken Scooter Holler to bed. When BB Eyes turned Tommy loose, with a warning that not a soul in town including his own family wanted to see him on the free side of cell bars, Tommy walked straight for his apartment. "I'd've come here if I thought I'd be welcomed."

"Course your apartment was a lot closer," I says.

"Don't you ever think you can't come home," Pauline says.

Tommy says he was lucky that he didn't actually catch them doing it. "Scooter was pulling on his pants, and she just ran into the bathroom when I got inside. Course she locked the door." By now I'm wondering how much damage Gregory and I will have to repair in the apartment to keep Frank happy, probably starting with the bathroom lock. Broken windows? Punched in walls? Staved up furniture? I'm about to tell Tommy he'd better learn to knock before entering when he lets out that there's no damage at all. When he started tiger-snarling toward the bathroom door, Penny told him if he so much as soiled the paint or split one of her nails, she'd have him in court, and assault would just be the start. "By the time I thought of taking after Scooter," Tommy says, "I heard his truck pulling away from the front."

"I'll talk to Emory," Pauline says.

Next Tommy turns the talk to where he's going to stay. I know where this is heading, so I start for Malcolm Hurd's place.

"Don't you be getting into drinking up there," Pauline warns me.

"Malcolm's getting ready for one of his veterans' bashes," I say. "He's the one does all the drinking."

It ain't but three miles to Malcolm's place, but it's a world away from my troubles. I know damn well he'll ask me to go with him to this veterans' fracas, and he knows just as well I'll say no, though I am going to charge him by the hour for any rescue missions I have to run. Least I get paid when I save him.

Malcolm Hurd is a sketch. I can't understand him, no more than I can understand anybody has money. Now Malcolm has so much money he's downright paranoid about it. His grandfather built ships, and the fortune come down to Malcolm in a trust fund that pays him five or six thousand a month. You might think Malcolm'd be happy just to sit home and watch the flies mate. But no. He ain't happy. He's sixty years old, he's owned a gas station, a construction company, and right now he's running a gravel pit. But it's funny, because the most mechanical thing he can do is spray ether in the carburetor. If his backhoe runs rough, he sprays ether in the carb. If his car won't start, he sprays ether in the carb. If it still won't start, he yells for me, and keeps spraying.

"Jim!" he'll bellow. "Jim!"

I work for Malcolm Fridays and Saturdays. Used to be just Saturdays until I quit working for the town and got on four days with Frank. I expanded to two days with Malcolm because he pays me good. With a fifteen-room house and enough land so that most anyone else in the state of New Hampshire would say he had an estate, Malcolm can usually keep me busy.

I don't get a chance to bring up my problems with Tommy before Malcolm's telling me his older daughter Pat's getting a loan for a game-room addition to her house. Her house lies just up the hill from his place. Course, I'm not supposed to know he'll give her the money for the addition, just like I'm not supposed to know he bought the house for her. (It gives him a clear conscience when he tells me to act tough with my kids.) After his daughter divorced her first husband, Malcolm let it out that he owned their house, so there'd be no splitting or sharing with the ex-son-in-law. I says, I thought it was her house. Well, he says, it will be when I pass on. "Thirty thousand dollars for a game room," he tells me.

Now they got one boy in college and the other nearly out of high school, who ain't hardly home more than to take meals like a boarder. "Pat and her husband must play a lot of games," I says.

Malcolm, he hoists up his pants and looks weasely. "She entertains a lot. She needs that room for her work."

"Okay." Only I think to myself, she's a nurse and he's a social worker, so who are they entertaining—patients? "You know somebody'd put Tommy to work? I'm afraid he's back at my place again." I ain't any more proud of this than what Malcolm is of what he has to lay out on Pat. For a moment the air fills with the heavy smell of sympathy.

"We could probably get him on down at the sawmill. Business has picked up some." He looks back at the big house of his like he expects Bernice to send him a signal through the window. "He'll have to be careful down there, or he'll find he won't be able to fill up a glove." *Careful* wa'n't the word he wanted. *Sober* was. But he don't tread too close to Tommy's drinking. And people do know Tommy for a hard worker. "Maybe Buddy Links has got something at his store and sauna."

'Bout this time Bernice comes out with a couple of coffees.

During the day we make coffee in Malcolm's garage, but by evening the pot's empty. Standing her tall, lean self next to Malcolm, Bernice looks as if she's a foot above him, though it's not more than a couple of inches. She's got a good job in the business part of the school district, so she doesn't ever let Malcolm claim she depends on him.

"Jim," she says, "he won't tell you, but I've had to send him to the Community Center for exercise. Aerobic exercises." Malcolm stares off toward the hills like he hopes it'll be a real ugly sunset. "His mind is going. Last week a man called for a load of gravel. Two days later he meets Malcolm on the street and says, 'Where's my gravel?' That was the climax. Before he always acted a day shy of forty. Lately he's two weeks past ninety. And failing fast."

Course this gripes into Malcolm, not least of all because Bernice actually is sixty-two, two years older than he is. He's told me before that some women wait until they're eligible for social security before they start picking on their husbands. But she's been pecking at him for years, and he's been deserving it. I thank him for the job recommendations for Tommy, and I say good-night. He don't answer, so I say to Bernice, "He knows it's night, don't he?"

Next morning I'm in Malcolm's garage pouring my first cup of coffee.

"Jim!" he bellows.

Out of the garage I come, still holding my coffee because it don't do to let Malcolm know I'm too willing.

"This goddamn car won't start." He's emptied the ether can and pitched that to kingdom come. It is a cool morning, but it's a cool summer morning, and ether won't do no good. He'd take diarrhea medicine for a cough if it was the only medicine he had. Now he's swearing at that Lincoln Town Car like he could scare it into starting. Now I'm talking about a sixty-year-old man that stands about five foot nine and weighs about a hundred and fifty. Maybe on a good day, he could swear the car into starting, but this ain't a good day. I can see that. Already he's cranked the juice right out of that Lincoln Town Car.

"Go get that battery charger," he says, snarling out the words like he was picking chin whiskers out of his feed.

I grab the rubber grip and wheel the machine down the driveway. I still got my coffee, and I'm smiling. Around Malcolm I'm one of the smilingest sons of bitches you ever see. As I'm clamping onto the battery terminals, Malcolm frets himself back and forth fit to furrow the driveway.

"You sure you got the right post?" he asks, flipping his hedgerow eyebrows up and down.

"Well, if I ain't, it'll blow this car all to your daughter's, and you won't have to worry about a game room addition." Then I go ahead and get the car running. Boy, don't that make him mad.

"Hop in," he says. Before I know it, we're all the way to the city, and he's kicking the tires of a three-year-old Fleetwood Cadillac. Now the Cadillac's three years old, and Malcolm's car's ten, but that Lincoln ain't got but fifty thousand miles on it and an eight-hundred-dollar paint job not a year ago, so they come down to the Lincoln Town Car and seven thousand to boot. There's a kid hanging around swishing a rag over windshields but mostly looking at his own reflection. I'm thinking maybe Tommy could get that job if the sawmill or Buddy Links won't hire him. Malcolm says, "Tell your boy there to put the plates on the Cadillac, and I'll be gone."

On the way home Malcolm asks me if I know a good restaurant to take Bernice to celebrate defeating that Lincoln Town Car. Sometimes I take Pauline to the Shore Inn over in Lathan's Landing. Get us a real nice baked haddock there.

"How much?" he asks.

"About fifteen, twenty bucks for the two of us."

"Fifteen or twenty bucks!" he hollers. "No wonder you never have any money. You can get a hamburger and a drink right at the town diner for under three dollars. Just as good too. Hamburger and a drink."

Like I said, Malcolm's plain paranoid about money.

Come afternoon we're loading up at Malcolm's gravel pit, which he owns half of along with Frank Reed. The sun carries a dusty, dry smell. "There," he says, pointing to a scooped-out place in the hill, "I told you Frank's been taking gravel out of my side."

"Malcolm, I work for Frank Reed. He don't operate like that."

"He's an outlaw. That's just what he is. He cheated you out of that tax money, didn't he?" And there wa'n't nothing to do with him but he must race right over to Frank's.

We pull into Frank's yard like we were going to rob the place. Frank, sweating a little, steps out of his office and Malcolm starts right in on him about stealing gravel.

"Must be Gary's loaded gravel out of your side," Frank tells him. Malcolm fidgets. "Take a load out of my side to even us up," Frank says. "Hell, take two loads if you want. I'd have Jim load the gravel instead of Gary, only you've sewed up all Jim's spare hours."

"Okay," Malcolm says. "We've been friends a long time."

On the way back to the gravel pit, I say, "There, are you satisfied now?" I light a cigarette and blow a little smoke out the window. My Tommy's got a cockeyed temper, but at least he's got youth and drinking as a reason. What cactus pricked Malcolm on this fine day when he's gone and bought the car he wanted right off the lot?

"I told you he was an outlaw." Malcolm's not looking at me, just dead straight ahead, as if keeping his eyes off that hollow

Gary scooped is harder than straightening bent metal. "I'm having this pit surveyed. I'll have surveyor's stakes all over this place."

The pit runs over a hundred acres, just Malcolm's part alone. "Do you know what it'll cost you to survey this?" I ask him. "Do you know how many loads of gravel Gary Reed'd have to steal—"

"Let's get this load going. How's that boy of yours? Did he go to the sawmill?"

I know why we're changing the subject, but I tell him Tommy was leaving for the sawmill about now. He couldn't get up in the morning worth a hangnail, but once he said he'd go, he'd go. He wa'n't no goddamn Fesmire.

We're delivering to a new customer. Malcolm says, "This is a very nice fella. This is a Doctor of Psychology."

We pull into this Doctor of Psychology's yard and wait for him to point where he wants us to dump the load. He points a tanned arm between his garage and driveway. As Malcolm backs up, the man tells me the gravel's for a tennis court. I hope he'll make more use of it than Malcolm's daughter will of the thirty-thousand-dollar game room, but when will he do his Doctoring of Psychology? Being around money makes you see your troubles in a simpler light. Why, if Pauline and I were to put in a game room or tennis court, deciding on the right location and finding time to play would drive us crazy, and we wouldn't need Tommy and Lisa at all for the job.

After we unload, the Doctor of Psychology's brushing dust off his white shirt. "That's a nice-looking load of gravel, Mr. Hurd," he says.

"Yes," Malcolm says, as if he's never seen a nicer-looking load of gravel himself.

"How many yards is that?" asks the Doctor of Psychology.

"Six," Malcolm says, still smiling.

"Yes, that's nice-looking gravel." I begin to sense this Doctor of Psychology mostly practices his Doctoring of Psychology outside his office. "How much is it costing me?"

"Thirty dollars," Malcolm says, only he's not smiling at the nice fella.

"You'll send me a bill, Mr. Hurd?"

Malcolm tears right into the truck, outs with his pad and pen, and writes the bill out so fast you'd think he could set the whole Bible in longhand if you gave him another ten minutes. "There," he says, handing the bill to the Doctor of Psychology, "I skipped the mailbox and sent it right from my hand to yours."

"Yes, Mr. Hurd," the Doctor of Psychology says, and tucks that bill into the pocket of those white tennis shorts. "I'll send you a check."

Although he don't often smoke, Malcolm bums a cigarette from me on the way back. "Malcolm," I says, "I guess he is a Doctor of Psychology. From the way he practiced on you, he must be one of the very best." I expect we will get his check at the end of the month, but I don't believe we'll see any more of that Doctor of Psychology's trade.

We get the dump truck parked, Malcolm sits in his pickup, turns the key, and click, click, click. Oh, mister man, wa'n't he raving! I've been around him enough to know that's what happens to a man with money, but still I'm not prepared for his next act. Down he climbs out of that truck, puts one foot in front of the other to walk over to the backhoe loader.

That backhoe bucket-loader turns and lines the truck up in Malcolm's sights. "Oh, no," I says. "I can't believe this!" With that backhoe loader moving at good speed, he hits that truck square with the bucket like to take a bite out of it and gooses it to rolling. Down out of the backhoe he runs, after the truck like a man chasing a demon. I figure he'll have a stroke and two conniption fits before he gets to the truck, but, no, I'm wrong. He reaches the truck, sets it in gear, and pops the clutch so that the motor is fairly humming by the time I get up to him. I scuff my feet in the hot gravel so I don't have to look at what I know is his shit-eating grin.

"There," he says, "I got the son of a bitch going."

I let him stay happy for a minute or two because he ain't seeing what I'm seeing—the truck bumper all stove in from them bucket teeth. I know next week I'll have to take a giant hammer-plane to pound out the damage.

7

seven

JIM

I can sleep through the night bird's screech, the cat's scrowl, and even the fisher cat's luring false cry of pain. But midsleep, the telephone's ringing drives nails into my head. I'm out of the bed before Pauline can ask what's going on—be it Frank Reed throwing Lisa out of her apartment or Tommy calling from jail or poor Gregory with some supernatural warning, as if his natural horrors aren't enough.

It's a collect call. Anybody knows me knows I ain't got any money to pay for collect calls. You'd better send me a postcard and write big because my reading ain't up to snuff. I hear shouting on the other end, sounding like Malcolm, but I think, no, it can't be Malcolm. He wouldn't call me collect, not with all his money.

But it is Malcolm. The RV park is throwing him out for the

ruckus he and Buddy Links have caused, and neither one of them is sober enough to drive that big class-C motor home. I tell him I'm going to charge him by the hour for both me and Pauline because I don't want to chance rousting Gregory at this time of night.

All the way up there Pauline's talking about drinking. It's a good hour's ride, which is going to be more than I can stand about my past, so after a while I remind her that Tommy's getting red-eyed and puffy-lipped from all the booze he's swilling, and he looks hell-bent for jail, where I never landed.

Her eyes twitch back and forth like the tail on an angry cat. "If people didn't pick on him, Tommy'd be all right. It's that damn Penny—and the cops. Talk about self-control, your friend BB Eyes can't lose weight enough to keep from having a heart attack. And suing the town. Tommy never talks about suing the town." Driving always gives Pauline a bossy edge.

Outside the RV park, Malcolm's rig sits with the running lights on and the flashers blinking. There's a city cop in his cruiser right next to the camper. "We always expect a little rowdiness from the vets when they hold their convention," he tells me. "After what they gave in the war, we figure they're entitled, but those two staged enough damage for the whole battalion. Now are you sober enough to pilot this land yacht home?"

"I hired him, didn't I?" Malcolm's leaning against the RV door and looking like a tilted mushroom. "Of course he's sober." Most of the belligerence has leaked out of him, though he's got to put on a little show.

"And get that headlight fixed," the cop tells Malcolm.

It ain't only the headlight. The whole right side of the nose looks like it tangled with a pissed-off moose.

"You related to him?" the cop asks.

"No."

"Well, see that you keep it that way."

On the drive back, with Buddy Links passed out on the sofa, Malcolm tells me about the bathroom. "We're not long in the spot I called to reserve—otherwise they'll plunk you right by the dumping station, or put you where you'll need a shoehorn." When he's drunk, Malcolm rambles like a kid coming home from school. I just let him ramble. He ain't slowing down the RV none. "I've got my trusty CC out and mixing up highballs when Buddy says he won't have any. Says whiskey causes too much trouble. Says he's going to drink beer. He's got his own six-pack in the refrigerator."

I am amazed because I never thought I'd see Buddy Links pay for so much as a fart on one of these excursions, but here was proof positive right out of Malcolm's mouth. And, oh, wa'n't Malcolm hot. He bought only the best whiskey, which Buddy damn well knew.

"Malcolm was sitting in the crapper when Buddy had to empty his bladder. "'No, sir,' I told him, 'I don't rush my movement for no man. It's the start of hemorrhoids.' Buddy storms out heading for the public toilet because with all that beer in him, he can't wait. Well, if I'd wanted to use a public toilet, I wouldn't have spent all this money on an RV with a crapper, now would I?"

"I think they all have crappers, Malcolm."

"And all that beer! Drinking beer like that will ruin the kidneys of a middle-aged man faster than cancer or hepatitis or any of them. A guy like you can drink a six-pack and hold it in all night. Buddy—"

"I don't."

"What's that?" he asks.

"I don't drink a six-pack." In fact Pauline don't like me even to drink those no-alcohol beers.

"It made me mad," Malcolm says, his voice loud and gurgly like an old-fashioned toilet. "Him going to that public bathroom. So I broke my rule and hurried my movement. And that made me madder, so I got behind the wheel and drove right over to that wash station and right into the wall on the men's room side."

Luckily, it was cinder-block construction and a good mortar job, or he'd be paying for that whole building. Lucky too that Buddy Links was the only gent in the gents. But it gave his RV a broken nose I'll be a full weekend repairing.

"Malcolm, did you take a minute to disconnect the water or the electric or the sewer?"

Oh, now he don't look so chipper. He knows he ripped pipe and plug and hose right out of their connections, another wicked repair job he'd have to hide from Bernice. "Careful on these bumps, goddamnit," he says. "I think I may have raised a hemorrhoid. I knew I shouldn't have rushed my movement."

When I get him home, he offers to ask Bernice to drive me home. "The walk will do me good," I lie. I'd just as leave Bernice took all her chewing out on him that deserves it. Buddy Links keeps snoozing in the RV. Walking up his driveway, Malcolm's got his hand down his pants looking for that hemorrhoid. I laugh loud enough to cause him to turn around and glare at me.

"It won't be funny if I have to have an operation!" he yells.

All in a single stride Bernice comes out the front door. "Jim, where's the other damned old fool of a soldier?"

I hook my thumb at the RV, but I keep my distance because Bernice can move quick. She ducks back into the house.

"Let me know if that hemorrhoid blossoms," I tell Malcolm.

It's well past dawn when I turn onto Two Captains Road with hardly a mile to go and happy as hell that I have a day off and between Pauline and me earned better than a day's pay anyway.

Blat, the horn goes before I hear either motor or tires, and I'm in the ditch because without even looking I know this is Emory. "Kind of nervous, ain't ya, Jim," he says as he steps out of that Ford pickup of his.

This tumble in the ditch ain't hurt me none, just brought me full awake. "Emory, did I ever ask you to cause trouble for me, or is this just your way of being friendly?"

He reaches a hand down like a weapon and yards me up out of the ditch. "Do you remember when we were kids back in the old neighborhood?" His eyes scan above my head as if he might be sighting that old time and place. "We all had geese and ducks, and those ducks and geese all walked to that little stream, and when they were done, they all walked home. They all knew which house to go to. On a summer evening we'd watch them."

"Yeah, and we never thought of throwing rocks at them. We never said, 'Let's see if we can kill them.' " I guess that's when I got to liking birds, though I go in for the fancier ones now, pretty ones. Pauline says you can't have too much beauty on a place.

"All the chickens too. They'd go off, and come night, they'd all find their way home."

"Emory, while we're cackling neighborly and all, let me ask you a question. Didn't Gregory give you money for that land he's built on?"

"God's own truth, Jim, he never bought it. Never did. I never put a deed in his hand." Emory explains about boundaries and subdividing, and how Gregory ought to have bought a full section. He gives one of those choking laughs. "And Gregory took back his earnest money to pay for Elizabeth's stone."

In all this detail about boundaries and acres, I smell something else, not a solid smell like Fesmire, but a weasel smell, a reek that tweaks my nose like old spoiled blood. "You afraid of Gregory?" The sun's getting higher behind him but not high enough to account for the sweat I see accumulating on his hairline.

"I'd like to do this the easy way."

"Speaking of old times," I says, "do you remember when you got that first bike of yours? You were the only kid in the neighborhood to get a brand-new bike. You wanted to show it off, so you rode it down the path to the stream where we used to play. Only you forgot there was always a pile or two of fresh cow manure in there where the cows wandered. You slid that brand-new bike into one and yourself into another. Your mother was so mad she took the stairs two at a time, yelling 'Emory' all the while. Helen and I thought she was going to murder you. 'Emory!' " I laugh thinking of his mother with a voice that could crush cans, threatening every bone in Emory's body. "She threw you right in the stream to wash the shit off you."

Emory wipes the whiskers under his nose. "Nowadays they'd call that child abuse."

"I suppose they would."

"So what's your point, Jim?"

"How come you can be all friendly with Pauline and give her money for Tommy, and you can't cut Gregory a little slack?"

"You really want Gregory living out there on his own?" He heads back to his truck. "Or is this about Pauline?"

As his truck kicks up dust, I look and see that both my forearms are locked tight with the veins swollen. But I'm glad he's gone. I'm not sure I can still win a fight, no matter who comes out on top.

The mourning doves keep busy flying from the utility wires to the ditch, occasionally cooing. Poor Gregory has so much trouble inside his head, he doesn't deserve any from outside. It ain't right.

Just a glimpse of someone's back as he creeps around my trailer sets me right off to creeping. I'm going to lay the prick out before he can do something to disturb Pauline. Right by my shed stands a shovel, but I mistrust myself to hit him too hard, so I pass it by.

I'll take care of him with my bare hands and keep the damages respectable.

From the trailer's side door comes a scratching kind of sound I can't make out, which causes me to wonder why Buffy ain't barked or growled. Usually, it doesn't take too much out of the way to wake him and set him to a racket that would start the rocks in the wall to complaining. There's that scratching noise again, worrying me because I don't know what in the hell he's doing. Deep down in my throat, I work up as big a roar as I can conjure, then I let it out as I run around the corner and lunge for his neck.

"Father, what the fuck ails you?" Tommy's standing on the step with a ring of keys, one stuck halfway in the door. "Are you practicing for a stroke?" He reaches for a cigarette. "When did you take to locking the trailer at night?"

I thank the stars I didn't grab that shovel because I'd've brained him sure. He's using the wrong key, though he swears uphill and down we must have changed the locks on him. Then he says he wonders if I'd let him stay in jail those extra hours just to let Scooter have a shot at Penny to break him up with her. By the time we're sitting in the kitchen with our coffees and Pauline's opened up a package of Danish for Tommy to eat in his misery, both of them have blamed me as if I'd pulled back the bedcovers for Scooter and Penny.

Tommy says, "You don't like her, you argue with her about something every time you come over, and she says you won't even lay claim to Aaron, who is your own grandson."

What can I answer to that? It's mostly true. I wait for Pauline to speak up because though I mistrust Penny, Pauline hates her. She takes Tommy by the wrist. I see she's going to explain, and Tommy is going to understand.

"Your father ain't been doing the best he can by you kids," she says, "but I'm helping him to change. He's got to thinking he's a sly old dog when he's just a stubborn one."

Don't that beat the hell out of the devil! I'm not about to argue because I could as easy talk fall geese into flying north as turn Pauline to seeing that her children make mistakes. "And if you're staying down to Lisa's, you stay two feet to the good side of steady," I tell him. "Your sister doesn't need to lose her lease over your ramming."

"There you go, blaming Tommy," Pauline says. "Course it's the Reeds pushing the lease business, but you won't go against them."

"Where else am I going to stay?" Tommy says. "You don't want me back here, though I bet Gregory's welcome any night."

"You won't have Lisa's place if she loses her lease," I say.

"I need some clean clothes to work for Mr. Links," Tommy says. "I was hoping I'd left some here."

He hasn't left anything here but a hole in my pocket, and he knows it. Most people would find clean clothes when they took them out of the Laundromat, not where they used to live. And I'm having a hard time believing that Buddy Links told him he'd need clean clothes to stack wood and put away stock in the back room. "Buddy giving you a promotion, is he?"

"He says it's not good for business if the customers see one of his employees looking all raggedy."

The long and short of it is Pauline says she'll drive him up to the mall to buy some new clothes. I suppose it's only right for her to yank some money out of one of her brown envelopes to buy him some new clothes and make him feel better over his girlie playing snuggle bunnies with his cousin. If you got a girlie like Penny and a friend like Scooter, you're guaranteed to be the radish. Course nobody wants to be the radish. I remember when Emory and I were friends back before I was the radish.

So I'm lying in bed trying to sleep but thinking back when I used to lie here waiting to hear Fesmire trying to creep into Lisa's room.

The winter after he got shot, Fesmire started talking in initials. He learned a whole new alphabet and could rattle off WIC and AFDC until I had to ask Lisa to translate just to hold a conversation with him. I swear that boy could make water run uphill the way he reverses the natural order of things. Why, he managed to have his baby girl support him instead of the other way to. He was getting food under one set of initials, food stamps under another, and checks to fill in the chinks from a third. I wished I could learn that language.

Back then, Gregory was making a little money on the side cutting cordwood out of four-footers he stacked the summer before. I told him to saw a couple of cords into stove lengths, and we'd drive it up to Fesmire to help them go easy on the fuel bills. If Lisa was going to live on assistance, I guessed I could assist too.

Rain and cold chose to settle the morning we piled those stove lengths into Malcolm Hurd's dump truck. Gregory ribbed me about slowing down with the burdens and cares of old age. Out of the truck in Fesmire's yard, I lighted a cigarette and took a slide into a big maple. I coughed out a good, loud, mouth-filling curse.

"That's it. That's the one shot me." Up on the porch, Fesmire, sweater, vest, wool coat, and hat, stood with a cup of coffee in one hand and his pipe in the other. Turning over his pipe against the rain, he stepped off the porch to look at our load. "Better than three cords," he guessed.

"Where do you want it?" Gregory asked him.

"They'll stack right between that fiendish maple and the shed."

"Where are you headed?" I asked him as I started to stack the cordwood.

"Go ahead. I'll be out in a minute."

As Gregory and I worked along, I threw an occasional glance

at the house for Fesmire. I was beginning to worry maybe the boy hurt himself in there, broke a nose hair on that coffee cup. The truck bed was empty, the wood nearly stacked, when I smelled Fesmire.

Out he came, pipe flipped upside down again, coffee cup in one hand, and sign in the other—WOOD 4 SALE. He balanced that coffee cup on the row of wood, grabbed the last stick of stove length off the ground, and plunked it on top of the bent edge of the sign. WOOD 4 SALE.

"You might've left a little more air in it when you stacked it," Fesmire said, "then I could easy claim four cords when I come to sell it." He snagged his coffee off the woodpile and took a sip. "I can't burn more than five cords without setting the place ablaze, and I got that and more too out back."

"You put that chain saw to use?" Gregory asked, because a month ago he'd fixed the McCulloch that spit out that bullet and he'd brought it back up to Fesmire.

"Didn't have to. CAP sent up five cords of cut-and-split as part of the fuel assistance program. Come in and get a coffee. Lisa's made some fresh."

"While we were unloading and stacking," I asked, "just what the hell were you doing?"

Fesmire kept moving, giving me barely a chance to catch his scent as he explained. First, he got caught short and couldn't very well work with a turd halfway down his trousers; second, he had to paint the sign because he didn't want the neighbors thinking he'd received more than his fair share of the CAP wood; and third, he had to help Lisa fix the coffee since, like her mother, she still held back on the makings, so her coffee poured thin and weakened his kidneys. Fesmire favored logic in his explanation, giving me the old one, two, three.

We sat at the dining room table where Lisa brought Gregory

and me coffees, fresh and, as Fesmire claimed, strong. "Rebecca's sleeping right now," Lisa says, "but you can tiptoe in to see her."

To save heat, Fesmire'd closed up the second floor so the crib and his and Lisa's bed too, took up most of the living room. With any luck he'd be able to sell half that CAP wood come spring. I saw a new television set sitting on top of an old one, more or less in line with the bed.

"Come into a little money?" Gregory asked his sister.

"I got a deal," Fesmire said. "Traded that McCulloch chain saw for it. Lisa didn't like watching that old black-and-white set Pa left."

"It does make a good pedestal, though," I said, burying my face in my coffee to escape the stench of Fesmire.

Rebecca, lying in her crib with a pink panda Gregory'd bought her, looked all Hutchins. She sported blond curls and a sweet mouth, just like Helen when she was a baby. At least God didn't curse the child with that long nose of Fesmire's, but if I was to break his nose, oh, there'd be no end to the names I'd be called at home. Look what happened when the tree shot him, and I wa'n't even there.

Pauline would want to know how much the baby's grown and if she coo-coo'ed. There ain't a thing about babies Pauline doesn't like. That's why I take care of the birth control. I wanted to talk to Fesmire about birth control, but private because it's a little more delicate than trying to choose between diesel or gas engines.

Telling him I wanted to see his CAP wood, I edged Fesmire out to the back porch. Scattered around the backyard lay at least five cords of prime-looking, split stove lengths, which Fesmire didn't have to touch with ax or saw.

"Fesmire," I said, "you and Lisa are just about making it right now, with Rebecca and all, am I right?"

"We do okay."

"Now, I ain't trying to insult you, just give you a little advice from experience. You haven't finished paying Rebecca's hospital bills, have you?"

"They ain't going to repossess her if I don't."

"Here's the point," I says, sidestepping the swamp of Fesmire logic. "If you don't take some precautions, Lisa'll wind up pregnant again. Do you follow me?"

"As long as Lisa stays sober, she'll stay unpregnant."

A fist has formed at the end of my arm. "I'm talking about birth control, here, mister man. Now if you need me to read off specifications, I will."

"No need to get hostile. No need for hostilities at all," Fesmire says, sucking noisily on that upside-down pipe, "because I don't believe in birth control. I'm death against it. It ain't natural. It don't feel natural. You got to admit that. No, sir, it's straight-out poison to me. Words ain't going to change it. You can't make it natural, and I'm foot on the ground opposed to anything about it that would run contrary to nature."

There it was. I strolled into the house to see if I could talk some sense to Lisa.

"I married Leo, Daddy," she said, pouring more coffee into my cup. "I can't cross him on something like that. It would break his heart."

I sipped the coffee. Funny, I had forgot his first name, forgot he even had one. It was touching to hear her call him Leo, but it wa'n't good enough to keep me from speaking. "You birth him about two, three more kids, it'll about break the bank."

"I thank you and Gregory for the wood, Daddy, I really do, but I don't see why every time you come up here, you have to turn hard on Leo. He's my husband and that baby girl in there is his daughter as much as mine." She turned her back on me and set herself to fooling with some dishes, which I figured she was doing so I wouldn't see her cry.

"I remember the time," I tell her, "when you'd sit in my lap if a cry set you back."

"I'm not a child anymore. I'm a mother."

Then I saw she wa'n't washing dishes at all. She was fixing up a bottle for Rebecca's feeding. I wondered Fesmire hadn't fussed over her not breast-feeding the baby all the time, but I tucked that question into my back pocket. I'd stirred up enough trouble for one day. I took the bottle from her and went into the living room to feed Rebecca. I had to sit on their bed because there was no room for an extra chair in the place. Still, I sat comfortable with my granddaughter in my arms, her blue eyes watching mine as she suckled that bottle. She'd drunk about four ounces when her father stepped inside.

"You know, I been thinking," he says. "Maybe before you go, you and Gregory could stack that CAP wood for us. My back's been bothering me to beat the band lately, and my foot ain't completely healed from where that chain saw of yours shot me."

The only thing I was holding with heft enough to throw was Rebecca. Curse those plastic baby bottles without weight enough to conk his head. He stood there, lean and lanky, sucking in a good stream of smoke, and stared at this fool of a forty-five-year-old father-in-law that he'd foozled again. In my arms Rebecca was blowing bubbles and cooing like a dove, which was a good thing because it took most of the throwing desire out of my arm.

"All right," I said, "we'll do it. But after we leave, don't you look to see my truck making tracks in your yard again."

"Well," Pauline said when I got home and told her about the mother lode of wood Fesmire's developing up to his place, "you can stay to home if you want, but I'm not going to miss seeing Lisa or Rebecca either."

The eye-stinging smell of liniment came off my back where Pauline was rubbing it in. "Maybe Fesmire'll rent Lisa and the baby out to us."

Two and a half children later there was trouble at Fesmire's. Not that we hadn't had troubles enough of our own. None of that could I lay to Fesmire, but what was going on at his place he couldn't lay to me either.

Pauline came back from there and warned me not to let Gregory visit lest he see his sister's face all bruised. "Pregnant as she is, he dared hit her?" I asked. Never mind what Gregory might do, I was ready to mount Fesmire right onto my truck and use him for a bumper guard.

"Oh, she's so skinny, Jim, worse than when she carried Rebecca. She was sitting on the couch with a stuffed, white unicorn, and I believe that unicorn outweighed her. I believe he's starving her."

"Did she say he hit her?"

"Yes."

I was thinking, I'm the one who'll have to go up there and bring her home. Pauline would cry herself into a puddle; Gregory would thrash Fesmire into mash. That left me to amputate Fesmire from the Hutchinses.

Then Sunday came a phone call from one of Fesmire's neighbors, a woman who wouldn't leave her name because she said she'd dealt with Fesmire before. She told me Fesmire had dragged Lisa and the children outside and was yelling and screaming and waving his gun around. She called the police last week, but by the time they reached the place, everything was calm and quiet. "If it was my child, Mr. Hutchins, I'd have her out of there."

All the way up there I seethed until my stench matched Fesmire's. The sunlight filtered through the new leaves in Fesmire's trees as if it didn't know the dangers of the yard it entered. The woodpile was gone, the johnboat was in the water, and Fesmire was standing with Lisa and Rebecca and Seth on the porch. The gun he held was not his old .22 squirrel gun but a pump shotgun.

I pushed the shift up into park and just let the old diesel tick away while I watched Fesmire. He shifted his pipe to the left side of his mouth and flipped up the brim of his wool cap before raising the shotgun to his shoulder. With a pull on the shift lever, I was in reverse and ready to floor it when I saw Fesmire wasn't aiming at me but at something off to the side and nearer the porch. I slid back into park and counted one, two, three: Lisa, Rebecca, Seth. As I stepped out of the truck—*boom!*—Fesmire squeezed off a shot. Skin and stuffing flew in the air, crowded with children's cries. I wondered if he'd shot the dog, Fesmire's ferocious German shepherd? No, the dog started yowling at the end of a chain wrapped around the porch railing.

Fesmire pumped a fresh shell, shifted the muzzle to the left—*boom!*—screams and fur rushed to fill the air again. Lisa tugged at Fesmire's arm. He pushed her away like a lazy fly in August and pumped the shotgun again.

"Fesmire!" I yelled. "Fesmire!"

"One more," he said. As I ducked behind the truck door, he let fly another round. The air turned powdery white. I couldn't see what he shot, though I knew it wasn't anything anybody would get to eat, not after those shotgun blasts demolished it.

"Fesmire!" I yelled, but I didn't move until I saw what he was going to do with the shotgun.

"Get off my land!" he said.

"Fesmire!"

Without raising the shotgun, he walked to the end of the porch and slipped the German shepherd's collar. The dog, all teeth and tongue, rushed at me with a growl. Hiding behind the truck door, I yanked the tire iron from under the seat. Just as the dog reached me, I swung the door open, but he lunged to my left. Teeth dripping with drool snapped at me while I poked the tire iron at him. Lisa's whistle from the porch turned his head, then I cracked his skull with the tire iron. A second whang finished him off. I started across the yard to get Lisa and my grandchildren.

Ten feet from the vehicle with no place to duck for cover, I scanned the shooting gallery. Dust and fur had settled on the site. The large pink panda I've seen Rebecca so often hug still sat on a stump, headless. Next to it stood the white unicorn. Lisa always favored stuffed animals. Fesmire would never buy any. He said the kids had a mother and a father to hold them, they didn't need stuffed hugs.

"Fesmire!" I yelled.

"She's a drunk, you know," he yelled back. He held Lisa by the back of the neck, though the shotgun pointed safely to the ground. "Every minute I'm gone she's gobbling booze. That's where all the extra money goes."

Lisa slipped his grip. "He's lying," she said. I saw more clearly now that skinny though she was, she was pregnant. I walked toward the porch again to draw his attention from her. I was moving in low-low, but I was moving.

"I didn't even know about the money your wife was sending up here," Fesmire said. "I found one of the letters. You better look on the back of those checks, see where Lisa cashed them. It wasn't at the bank. Drunk!" he shouted at her. She didn't budge an inch.

Tire iron on my shoulder, I pushed my boots across the yard. "At least she'll be a drunk among her own." I walked right into his face where he couldn't raise his shotgun as fast as I could whap him with my tire iron.

"That baby's not mine," he said. "She got it putting out for booze. That's what she does when she can't find liquor money. Whore! Slut!"

Down flew the tire iron, whamming him on his arm. The shotgun hit the floor and let loose. I looked for bloody children. Bloody daughter. Then I saw the blast had only taken out a section of railing. I told Lisa to pack things for her and the children and get into the truck.

"You see that fucking unicorn there," Fesmire said. "He gave it to her, the blond asshole she's been fucking, that nephew of yours, Scooter Holler. You wait. That baby'll be near as white as that unicorn. You wait."

I kept him backed to what was left of the railing. Even when Lisa and the children came out, I wanted to punch his face. What kept me from it was the new smell coming off him. A stink I'd never scented before from him, the stink of fear.

All the time we were walking to the truck, I kept my hands full of suitcase. *Boom!* He blew that white unicorn all to pieces, and I wished I had taken the shotgun from him.

Lisa's baby came out light skinned, nearly white enough to spoil my joy and put that goddamn unicorn in my dreams, but Lisa got her tubes tied, so there won't be more, Fesmire's or anyone else's. She does drink—drinks too much. And she does turn to men for liquor when she can't wrangle the money out of her mother. I don't know if that baby belongs to Scooter, but I guess it ain't Fesmire's. No, hard as it is to believe, Leo Fesmire too has his problems. I regret pounding him.

Much as I'd like to blame all Lisa's troubles on Fesmire, I see she's brought on more than a few of her own. The meanness in me makes me smile. I guess he honestly believes that youngest child's not his, else why would he persist in not allowing Alison to visit him when Rebecca and Seth seem welcome anytime? At least that's what I get from his mother. Fesmire don't talk to me at all. I don't think it's because he's mad. I think it's because he's embarrassed. I figured after Lisa left him, the first thing he'd do would be to find another meal ticket, but he didn't. He still lives up there in his parents' house and moves the johnboat off and on the porch with the seasons, but he don't live with no woman. Lisa says she don't care what he does if he'll just send the support money, which he usually does but only to the tune of about twenty-five dollars a week. He says neither she nor the littlest one deserve any of his money, and as for the other two, twenty-five dollars is more than he allots himself. "Course," he tells her, "I don't drink all mine up."

8
eight

JIM

It's late morning by the time I get back up to Malcolm's, and already Bernice has got him talking to himself because she called Donner's Electric to come fix the clothes dryer. "Twenty-five dollars just to look at it," Malcolm says.

Malcolm says we'll fix the dryer. He figures to control the money in his household. He's paying me eight an hour, so he decides I can fix the dryer cheaper than Donner's Electric. We drag the machine over into the garage. Bernice, she's into her car and down the road. That woman may be a lot of things, but fool ain't one of them.

We dig right in, and it ain't long before we got white metal sitting on the floor and colored wires hanging in the air. I tell Malcolm maybe we ought to get someone else to take a look since we wa'n't seeing the source of the problem. About this time along comes Buddy Links. For far less than twenty-five dollars Buddy decides the problem must be the house wiring. So we all tramp to the cellar and trace the line back to the circuit box. Buddy stares at it.

"It ain't getting enough juice," Buddy says. "You got these one-ten lines running to her."

I'm thinking the dryer has worked fine on that same wiring, and nobody sneaked in at night and changed the lines.

"Jim," Malcolm says, "go upstairs and call Donner's Electric."

When I get back to the garage, Malcolm and Buddy are talking Granny Smith apples. Now, Malcolm's father was a playboy, and his mother was a playgirl. She never came closer to making an apple pie than a goat did to building a barn. And Buddy's family was so poor, any apples they might've ate, they swiped from the back of a neighbor's tree, which wouldn't have been of the Granny Smith variety. I don't say a word.

They've about played out the apples when the electrician shows up. "What's that?" he says.

"It's a dryer," Malcolm says, like he thinks the guy needs an answer.

"It might have been once," says the electrician. He's already considerable smarter than Malcolm's bargained for, to say nothing of expensive.

"We think it's the house wiring," Buddy pipes up.

"Why did you tear the machine apart, just to give me some overtime?"

Of course there ain't nothing wrong with the house wiring. There ain't nothing much wrong with the dryer either, except the switch that cuts the juice when the door's opened. That's shot. That was the whole problem, a two-dollar switch. The electrician has that installed in five minutes, but he's another hour rewiring all the panels. Oh, Malcolm looks sick. And isn't he sick when he sees the bill. Bernice pulls in the yard, Malcolm just says he doesn't want to talk about it.

Next thing I know Dorcey's got Malcolm in a dither. Dorcey was housekeeper to Malcolm, practically raised his kids, but she got up in her seventies and decided she didn't want to keep house anymore. Yesterday a young man had talked her into sealing her roof. He charged her six hundred dollars, just the amount she'd been fool enough to tell him she had, but she couldn't find it, so he took her to the bank to cash her social security check for four hundred dollars and said he'd be back for the other two hundred.

"Who was it?" I ask.

"It was a White from out on the White Road."

"There aren't any Whites on the White Road."

"This is some guy putting the swindle to old people," Malcolm says. "Get a ladder."

We buzz downtown, and I climb the ladder. Dorcey's ain't much of a house, four rooms down and a half attic up. What the guy had done, he'd bought a couple gallons of that silver stuff they use to seal trailer roofs and just sprayed it. It was all over everything, moss, pinecones, leaves, branches. Lisa's kids do a better job with spatter paint in grade school.

"Dorcey got ripped off," I tell Malcolm.

"Well, he ripped off the wrong person." Malcolm turned to Dorcey. "You get a receipt?"

"I had one, but he took it back when I couldn't pay the whole bill." She went right to pieces. Malcolm, he's got an arm right around her.

"Now, Dorcey, that money ain't gone and slid through the cracks. It's in your house. If this character comes back for his two hundred dollars, you call me."

Malcolm and me stop at the police station to see BB Eyes.

BB Eyes says the guy ain't likely to show up for his two hundred because these operations are strictly fly-by-night deals.

Malcolm drops me off at Dorcey's to help her look for her six hundred dollars. "I'd help too," he says, "but I've been known to mislay a freckle." The truth is, the sight of a wet face is a horror show to him. He tells Dorcey he'll make good the four hundred she give the roof sealer.

I turn the place upside down—couch cushions, mattress, cookie jar—before Dorcey remembers that the last time she saw the money, she'd been sorting through some old magazines. Right in the middle of one of the old *National Geographics* was the envelope with her six hundred dollars.

"Did you save all these?" I ask her. There must be a couple of hundred years' worth of moldy old magazines, enough to set off asthma and two cases of double pneumonia.

When I call Malcolm with the news, he says, "Tell her to keep her money in the bank and throw out them goddamn magazines!"

It turns out Dorcey's happy for me to bundle the magazines because I tell her I'll truck the lot down to the collectibles store. Course I'm just going to take them to the recycle center at the dump. Good-natured as can be, she tells me to give the profit to Malcolm for all his help. Outside, loading the *National Geographics*, I see Scooter Holler stride right up to Dorcey's door and put knuckles to wood as if he were a minister paying a social call.

"I'm here for my two hundred," he says to her.

"You're here to return her four hundred," I say. A head taller than me, he curls a grin like he don't know whether to run or hit. "Or would you like to talk to BB Eyes about this deal?"

"I need extra now that I'm supporting that grandson of yours," he says. "I've been trying to scrounge up some small jobs, oiling driveways, sealing roofs."

"Come on, Scooter," I say. "Give her the money back."

He yanks out his wallet on a chain. "I'm out two buckets of sealer. Cost me fifty bucks."

"Cost you more to talk with BB Eyes," I tell him, then he quits the weaseling and yanks Dorcey's four hundred dollars from his wallet.

By late afternoon Malcolm's drinking a sorrowful cup of coffee, and I tell him it's quitting time. He slips me a double sawbuck along with my pay and says to take Pauline for a baked-haddock dinner. But he warns me not to let Bernice know. Malcolm is a sketch. I don't know a man I understand less or like better, not that I'd let on to either one to his face.

The next day Pauline grabs the money Malcolm paid her and some of what he paid me for the RV park rescue and drives Tommy up to the mall for more clothes. Seems as though he dirtied the other ones she bought him chopping wood for Buddy Links' sauna. I guess that's a good sign, even if Tommy ain't figured out how to use the Laundromat. "Well, what's he going to wear while he's washing his clothes?" she asked me. "Stand there naked until BB Eyes arrests him for indecent exposure?" Course I know he had some clothes before he decided to become a fashion model, and they weren't all pink ladies' underwear.

It's my day off, but I ain't sleeping. There's a quiet outside that ain't right. You'll notice that stillness just before storms, sort of like no one's breathing it. Right now I hear that quiet, only I can still see sunlight, so I know no storm's coming. Sliding into my shoes, I'm down the hall and out the door, thinking it can't be anybody or I'd've heard a car or Buffy would've barked, one of those warning signs.

Standing in the yard is bristle-brushed Scooter Holler. "Uncle Jim, I want to thank you. You did me a good turn over that roofing deal, letting me go. At first I was pissed, I'll tell you, because I been trying to get money ahead since I moved out of my house.

Living with Emory is like running second best to a dog with the shits."

"Penny charging you rent?"

"I wanted to ask your advice about that. I can't talk to Tommy, and I don't trust any advice my old man would give me."

Sitting out in the lawn chairs having a smoke, he talks and I listen. I ain't feeling good enough about him to invite him in for tea, but fighting and feuding ain't anything I want a steady diet of either. He winds words around about not wanting to hurt his friend, meaning Tommy, and Penny not wanting to hurt Tommy, and he's sure Tommy doesn't want to hurt anyone.

"Here's the thing, Scooter. Nobody wants to be the radish. No matter which of you ends up with Penny and which doesn't, either one of you could feel like you're the radish."

"Or both of us," he says, which may be the smartest thing Scooter Holler has ever said. Only if he's smart enough to see that, why can't he see how worthless Squatty Body is from the start? Could be he sees her as an easier way to make a living than roofing or living with Emory. Myself, I'd rather suck shit from a dead hen's ass.

"You'd do Emory a favor if you told him to steer clear of Gregory for a while," I says. "Gregory might have a gun."

"And would you tell Tommy he ought to stop over? If he don't want to talk in front of Penny, we can meet somewhere."

"He's staying with his sister. Why don't you call him there?"

"I'd feel better if you spoke to him."

"You see the way it is, Scooter. Nobody wants to be the radish."

After he drives off, I circle to the other side of the trailer to see what's up with Buffy that he didn't bark. There he is sprawled on his doghouse. Up close I see he's got some cloth between his paws, which I identify as one of Tommy's shirts, which naturally ain't clean. It must have been that kept Buffy from barking at Scooter.

I go back inside to lie down. Right now I envy Fesmire. I really do. That guy could fall asleep in the middle of a trial for his life. He was probably born sleeping. I look at the clock. The second hand's not moving. So that's something else to buy that I can't afford, but on a hunch I try the light switch, and that doesn't work. Bending in the dark closet with my cigarette lighter, trying not to torch a dress of Pauline's, I see not a one of the switches on the circuit-breaker board has moved. I shift my head back to try to read the fiendish lettering, to see raised OFF's and ON's painted the same gray as the box. They sure don't manufacture these things for the convenience of some farsighted, middle-aged fool like me without a flashlight or glasses.

A telephone call over to the Glebes' tells me they've got electricity. I wonder if Pauline skipped paying the bill again. Once before she did that when she needed money to pay Tommy's lawyer, but I intercepted the power company's shutoff notice and hustled the money right off to them. I suppose the utility money could have gone for Tommy's bail or maybe Pauline's spreading it around at the mall so that Tommy will own enough new clothes he'll never have to wash them. Here in the dark trailer I take summer for a blessing because at least I ain't cold.

Out in the kitchen I've poured water up to the coffeemaker's four-cup mark before I realize that won't work either. It don't take much of a change in your life to make you feel foolish. Sometimes I feel like old Buffy has simplified life just about right. Why, after a while even Fesmire, young as he is, got outfoxed.

Then, I think, I didn't hear a truck. Buffy didn't bark. Outside, one look tells the story. Like a limp dick, the cable hangs loose below the meter. Bastard knew enough to pry it off on my side of the meter so I'll have to fix it instead of the power company.

Nothing fancy, probably the shovel I see lying on the ground, pried that cable right out of the bottom of the meter box. Quiet too. He must have dropped it when he heard me coming to the door. Took one of Tommy's shirts from Squatty Body and tossed it to Buffy to give him Tommy's scent. That's why Buffy didn't bark. And that son of a bitch sat here listening to me passing advice about no one wanting to be the radish. And thanking me for it just as if I were loaning him tools. I'll say Emory's raised him well.

When I was younger, I never admitted to being tired. But right this minute I'd skip food and a cuddle and a view of the sunset just to doze away until tomorrow morning. I'd like to splice Scooter between cable and meter and watch him fry. And I think here's another occasion where having a gun would put me in more trouble than a tomcat with two cocks.

My first thought sends me to my truck for my jumper cables with the idea of patching into the line and connecting to the wire that runs into my trailer. I'm holding the shiny black and red jumper cables like a pair of tropical snakes and thinking all I need is for someone to see this rig and report me to the power company and I'll be right alongside Tommy in the jail.

The fused seal doesn't say DO NOT BREAK UNDER PENALTY OF LAW. It's just got numbers on it. As careful as I can, I snip the wire, slide it out of the metal band, and peel the band from around the meter. With a quick tug, I unplug that meter and set it on the ground before somebody driving by with shares in the power company reports me. Now if you imagine I'm thinking about sex while I'm sticking the cable back in, which I also have to strip and straighten, you're dead wrong. I'm hoping the two-hundred-forty volts coming into this box don't fry me. Just the sweat on my hands has humidified the air sufficient to jump a jolt right across those tongs. I'm one happy guy to plug that meter back and fit the band around it and even slip the metal seal back. The meter's wheel is turning, the juice is flowing, and I'm thinking I could have set the dials back a little while I had the damn meter on the grass. That thought starts the sweat at the back of my neck.

Time I've restored electricity to the trailer, Pauline comes back. Tommy, wearing his new duds, stopped at Squatty Body's, which makes me think we weren't needing those clothes so much for work as we wanted to model them for Squatty Body. At least he'll be a well-dressed radish.

As Pauline walks into the house, the goddamn phone rings. It's like there's some maternal magnetism that attracts rings from the telephone.

"Don't, for God's sake, answer that phone."

As usual, she picks up the telephone, and I hear those dread words: "What's wrong, honey?"

It's Lisa's Rebecca. Little Alison has fallen on the table corner and cut her forehead, which won't stop bleeding. Rebecca says she's tried and tried, but she can't wake her mother up.

"Christ," I says, "it's past noontime."

"Lisa always was a heavy sleeper."

I know better than to say anything as we head to Lisa's apartment, where Pauline'll find out for herself.

What she sees makes an impression all right. Lisa's stretched out on the couch not even hungover because she's still drunk. With her on the couch is a lowlife with nothing on but the grayest kind of underpants. "You might have thought they was spun out of dust bunnies," Pauline says. "I've swept cleaner things from under the motel beds."

Pauline closes Alison's cut forehead with one of those butterfly bandages. I shake Mr. Underwear awake and tell him to head out the door. He fumbles into his jeans, then falls back on the couch. I hurry him along by telling him Pauline will bandage his asshole shut if he don't meet daylight in the next two minutes.

"She's nothing but a whore!" Pauline says, laying Lisa right next door to her sister in the cemetery, only without any stone Cabbage Patch doll sitting at her head. Coming to, Lisa moans, only it ain't real clear what she's moaning about because she throws her arm around her mother. "Who was that?" Pauline asks her. Pauline shakes Lisa and asks again, but all she gets is another moan. "I don't believe she even knows that louse's name."

Mr. Underwear probably wa'n't the only louse in and out of the apartment last night, but I'm not going to tell Pauline. I don't know whether it's booze or drugs or what, but Lisa's turned careless. She's going to lose that apartment, she could lose those children, Christ, she could end up in jail.

I didn't worry about my kids when they were little. Maybe I should have. Years ago I raged when Tommy was expelled. Then when Gregory wanted to quit school, I could have chewed through a porcupine's butt. I was mad that he'd turn out like me and have to scramble for the short-end jobs all his life. Elizabeth, who did so well in school, who liked baton and Girl Scouts and all that, I never worried about, until the pond had already swallowed her up. Then, I worried about her through Pauline.

Now, I worry about Lisa's kids. Not just about her losing them, but about some drug-drenched turd ball bothering them. Not every guy goes to the apartment is going to satisfy himself with Lisa. Who's to say the panty thief won't end up at Lisa's place with something more perverted than stealing panties on his mind? God knows she ain't checking references.

With Alison bandaged and Mr. Underwear stumbling off down the street, Pauline has got Lisa up, and Lisa's sick. "She's got awful pains in her side," Pauline says.

We drive her and the children to the hospital, Lisa moaning like a cow about to freshen and those three kids as quiet as frozen ground. Pauline's crying. She says she can't bear to lose another child. I buy a coffee in the hospital cafeteria, and I get the kids some ice cream, but they don't more than move it around like it's a little animal they're trying to wake up.

"Don't worry," I tell them. "Your mother will be okay."

"No, she won't, Grandpa," Rebecca says. Sometimes I think she ain't only Lisa's oldest, she's the oldest child on earth.

As it turns out, Rebecca is right. They keep Lisa at the hospital because she's underweight, run-down, anemic, and suffering from some kind of infection. That means the three kids come home with us, and Tommy gets Lisa's apartment to himself and whatever colony of under-the-rocks friends he'll invite over. Naturally, it don't seem right, particularly when I'm cramped up on that couch Pauline made Fesmire sleep on. Too many nights on this and I could feel some sympathy for that character, stench and all.

It's three nights before Lisa comes home with some pills and the doctor's warning to stop drinking or it'll kill her. By the time I show up at Malcolm's on Friday, he's giving me hell about my taxes: "If you didn't spend so much on those foolish kids of yours, you could pay your tax bill and not have liens going back two years."

"That far back? I didn't know it'd gone that far."

"It'd've gone further, only I paid a year of it." He looks away a minute like he's embarrassed for both of us. "Jesus, Jim, you got to tend to your own business and let those kids tend to theirs."

Like you do with your daughter? I think, but I just thank him for the tax money. He knows I can't keep a mourning Pauline from squandering what we do have on the kids. Course his advice ain't shit because without a cough or a twitch he tells me we'll be working at his daughter's place today.

We're going to seed a patch of ground down by his daughter's thirteen-thousand-dollar swimming pool, a pool that Malcolm bought. Now it's taken some little while for us to go over there to do this job because we haven't been speaking much to the son-in-law since late winter when Malcolm took him and Buddy Links snowmobiling.

Before we'd left, Malcolm gave Buddy Links a hundred-dollar bill to spread around the state liquor store, and on the way, he bought the son-in-law a brand-new snowmobile outfit, from boots to helmet. Bernice, she baked Malcolm three of the nicest casseroles you ever saw to take for that long weekend of machining. He loaded them in the back of the truck along with the snowmobiles. The only thing that got used was the Canadian Club. After Malcolm got drunk, punched the son-in-law, and threw the TV out the motel window, they didn't even get to stay one of Malcolm's three nights', paid-in-advance reservation. The son-in-law kept the purple and black snowmobile suit, and as for the casseroles, Malcolm's dogs got them.

But bygones have gone by, so now we're up to the son-in-law's to spread grass seed. Malcolm's got three, four hundred pounds of lime and a bag of grass seed sitting in his truck bed. Then he spies a bag of seed in their garage. "Jim," he says, his eyes lighting up, "that's grass seed."

"It's oats."

"No, that's grass seed." He dumps that lime in the spreader and tells me to go to it.

"Don't you think we ought to cover the swimming pool first?" I asks.

"No, I don't."

The wind blows, and we drag that spreader of lime and oats right along. We're a couple of hours on that job, and then, oh, boy, does he think of that pool. The water's turned milky with lime and seeds floating over the surface. We have to change the pump filters five or six times to clear that pool.

9
nine

JIM

"You know that underwear thief has stolen again," says Gregory, sliding his hands around his Big One coffee as if he needs to keep them warm. "And he's planning worse."

I'm looking around for his gun. "How do you know?" I won't contradict him.

"I hear it." The last time Lisa come up here, she washed his pots and dishes. The pots make a jumbled pile where she left them. He keeps a jerry can of water for his coffee. I don't know what he can be eating. He used to buy ice off Buddy Links for his cooler, but Buddy told me he ain't bought any for a couple of weeks. "I always hear about bad stuff with Tommy. Now they're talking about how bad Lisa is."

He ain't the only one hearing talk about Lisa. They aren't even careful around me anymore. Gregory ain't much weirder than the rest of the galloping gossips.

"Tell Lisa not to come here anymore," he says. "She shouldn't have those little children either. You let bad people around you, they infect you. Pretty soon you get so you're just as bad as they are. And don't tell me about being careful. It won't work."

"Didn't Lisa come up here with a nice cooked dinner for you?" I remind him. She roasted a small turkey and stuffing, mashed potatoes, steamed broccoli, and baked an apple pie. She even bought cranberry sauce, though with nearly four hundred bucks a month in food stamps I don't guess that much dented her meal planning. She and the kids brought this feast up to him. Course Pauline drove them because Lisa don't have a car to drive, and they all sat around like the royal kings of England with napkins and everything.

"She's my sworn enemy." He purses his lips and strains his neck. "She ain't lurking out there, is she?" Right on my collarbone he locks a claw as he stands to stare out his window. Quick like, his eyes shift to the ratty trunk he keeps by his bed, then he goes to staring out the window again. "If she's there, I'll shoot her."

"That don't make sense, Gregory."

"Sense ain't sense." I pull away from his painful grip, and he gives me a nasty little smile. "When I leave your trailer, I tune you in on my radio so I can hear everything you say. From what I been hearing, I don't want Momma coming up here either."

"Is she your sworn enemy too?" I watch him close to see if he's going to stare at that old trunk.

"Just make sure she don't step foot on my land, unless you're with her."

"Gregory," I say, trying to change the subject. "Are you eating? The only thing I ever see you put in your mouth is a coffee. You'll make yourself sick if you don't eat."

"You don't see a skinny dog here, do you?" He goes to his cot where the hound he calls Dog lies. "Can't count his ribs by eye. No sick, old dogs at my place."

"Buffy's not sick. He's just old."

"What's the difference?"

It feels a long way down his road. All the while he sits next to me in the truck filling the air right up to the sunroof with silent hatred. I wonder can he be swiping women's panties. Mad as he is, I can't feature him slipping far enough off from angry even to get a hard-on, much less use it.

At the end of the road I tell him, "Get yourself something to eat," and put a ten in his hand. He hops out of the truck, unlocks the bar, and holds it up while waving me through. Lumbering back toward his place, he walks like it was no more jaunt than moving to the next room. He can carry an awful heavy sack of mad without stumbling.

I'm about halfway to Malcolm's when I spot that ten-dollar bill just lying on my floorboards. First thing I says to Malcolm, "Gregory ain't taking care of himself." And it is a hard thing to say. I'm swallowing more than pride, I can tell you. If Gregory's crazy, where does it come from and whose fault is it? Either way you figure it—upbringing or birth—it comes right back to the parents. Which is me. Pauline too, naturally, but me, my feeling at fault and to blame like I'd taken a stick of kindling and beat a soft-haired pup with it.

Nursing a coffee and wishing it were a beer, I sit outside while Malcolm's on the phone with a lawyer. When Malcolm comes out, he says we have to get into the legal psychology of the case. I ask him if he called that Doctor of Psychology he delivered the gravel to.

"He did pay me, you know, Jim," he says, which may or may not be so, and the check may or may not have cleared, but Malcolm wants me to know he's right on top of things, particularly that Doctor of Psychology, lest I think he made some error of judgment.

Judgment is what this deal with Gregory is all about. Judgment's the ticket because Gregory's of age and can't just be locked up, you see, but only if he's a danger to himself or others. Well, I thinks, if that's the qualification for installing someone in a room with the lock on the outside, I could name a long list of qualifiers without even searching beyond the town line. But Malcolm says this is technical stuff, not just whether Gregory might be sick, but what he might do, which has got to be predicted by one of these doctor-of-psychology fellas or a judge.

"He ain't doing well up there, Malcolm," I says. Cripe's sakes alive, he's living like an animal in a cave, awful as it is to say it. It don't make a lot of sense that Tommy may end up in jail where they'll house and feed him, while they'll leave Gregory, sick with craziness, out at his place like an ugly three-legged dog no one wants. Malcolm just says that it's the law. If it's the law, I'll have to work with it. I ask him could we send his Doctor of Psychology, and Malcolm says no, he's too busy with his tennis court.

Malcolm says he'll take a social worker out to visit Gregory. It seems like dumping all your laundry right in the middle of the street, but the way Pauline and Lisa take it, I'm the one to blame, picking on Gregory for being different, and trying to run his life. *Crazy* they won't have no part of. They say whatever's wrong with Gregory will work itself out without any interference from me. What did I want to do anyway? Get somebody to call him crazy and lock him up? Then what? Who'd pay for it? And when Gregory got out, why, he'd hate me. Hate me forever. And who could blame him?

"I lost one child," Pauline says to me. "I don't mean to lose another." And she goes right into a crying jag every time she says it.

I ask Malcolm why the state has to send a social worker. God knows they poured help on Fesmire with both hands. Malcolm says he called that lawyer Gregory built the chimney for, and he explained the best thing would be to persuade Gregory to commit himself to the mental hospital. Good God, I think, if the social worker goes up there and tries to talk him into signing up at the nuthouse, why Gregory'll spatter-paint the wall with him, then come looking for the rest of his sworn enemies. Malcolm says he'll accompany her. I figure that's like carrying a can of gasoline to a fire.

GREGORY

Right away I know trouble traveled here. And I know I have to use caution and care because stepping out of Malcolm Hurd's truck is this strange woman carrying a lean leather case. Malcolm introduces her, but I jump the juice in my mind so as not to know her name because if I let her name live in my brain, it will linger there to ambush me. It's a wonder not a word about them came from my radio. I don't let on to a thing, so they don't know how far they aren't fooling me. She asks me if I mind if she comes inside to ask me a few questions.

"Inside or outside, it don't make no never mind to me."

Once we're inside, Malcolm says, blunt's a barrel, "What you got in that old trunk, Gregory?"

"I thought the social worker woman was going to ask me the questions," I says. "Did you ram my gate," I ask Malcolm, "or did you get good at picking locks?"

"I had to prise it off," Malcolm says. "What you need to be locked up here for anyway?"

"You lock your doors at night," I say. "Father told me. Said you swore to shotgun any son of bitch who'd try to break in. Guess you and she are lucky, huh?" I smile at the woman, 'cause I don't want to scare her. I catch her shift her sharp eyes from Malcolm to me to the trunk. "That's my bureau." I see the woman and Malcolm Hurd still staring at the trunk. I walk right over, grab ahold of the hasp, and lift the lid. "See, just my belongings." I moved the gun after Father's last visit. I knew. I ain't letting on where it is.

"Mr. Hurd," the social worker says, "I think Gregory and I will be quite comfortable talking together here."

You could beat me breathless if Malcolm Hurd doesn't stand himself straight up, says he'll go buy me a new lock, and strides right out my door. I watch him twist his truck around and rattle off down my road.

"Mr. Hurd tells me you built this place by yourself," the social worker woman says. She can't take away my property. They have to send a sheriff for that. I offer her a coffee because the snake's slipping up my neck again to nibble my brain. I fire up the Coleman.

"She ain't finished yet," I tell the woman. "I haven't wired but that unit out there on the utility pole. You know they want over a hundred dollars for a two-hundred-amp service unit?" She's watching me pour water into the coffee cups like she needs to know if I'm going to poison her, just like Mary Beth at the 7-Eleven kept watching me instead of scoping Scooter Holler. This

social worker woman harbors no harm, or I'd've heard. She and
Malcolm Hurd hope to find my gun. "I ain't got milk today
because my cooler run out of ice." She smiles and takes the coffee
and sugar and spoon, like a little girl playing teatime. Elizabeth
used to line up her dolls and play teatime. If that bastard stole her
underwear, I'd kill him, whether it was Scooter Holler or not.

"Gregory, do you ever think of hurting yourself?"

"How?"

"Any way."

"No." Do they think I bought the gun to shoot myself? I
would've purchased a pistol. "That don't make sense."

"Do you want to hurt someone?"

How serious is she? She sips her tea dainty. Ladylike. "I don't
hurt anyone unless they want to hurt me."

"Do you think someone is trying to hurt you, Gregory?"

"There's always someone trying to hurt you. You don't know
but right now that pervert might be stealing the underwear out of
your bureau."

"Gregory, do you want to hurt me?"

"No. You're not trying to hurt me."

She asks me what my plans are for the place. I want to finish
the upstairs, which is just beams and boards with a ladder to
climb up there. By God she hikes right up that ladder.

"You do good work, Gregory."

"Can't paint for shit."

"Maybe you could hire that done, what painting you'll have."

"I don't hire nothing. There's where you let people hurt you
and cheat you and tell you what to do. I'll build it all myself. I
ain't no lawyer to hire things out."

"You don't need to shout."

I wasn't shouting. Sometimes I got to speak loud to carry over the crunching the snake makes in my braincase. It's a cracking kind of noise, nasty, nipping off bone bits while I'm trying to talk. "It's noisy. Can't you hear it?"

"No." She sets her cup down tenderly, the way Elizabeth always set hers in the saucer.

"Can't you hear the snake?" I ask the social worker woman.

"Is there a snake in here, Gregory?" She pushes her chair back from the table, and I hope the leg I wired won't wobble. If she were to fall with that hot coffee leaping into her lap, she'd burn herself bad.

"Careful. Caution."

"Do you keep a snake in here, Gregory?" She's looking under the table. "They only told me about the dog. They never said anything about a snake."

"He only bites me. He's a very shy snake. Many of them are, you know." I wish she could hear the snake or maybe even see it. At home I looked in the mirror when the snake mashed into my mind, but I couldn't make out the snake itself. Only my face twisted and turned like those pictures of people slowing down real fast in rockets and stuff. The snake can do that, slow me down suddenly, slur my face and slice my words into parts I can't pronounce. If it starts happening now, I'll run out into the rambling woods and whistle this woman away.

"Do you keep the snake in a cage, Gregory?"

"I can't control him like I can Dog."

She's out the door. Dancing in the dirt like she has to pee, she says, "Where's Mr. Hurd? Why isn't he back?"

"You want me to drive you somewhere?"

She shakes her head like she's saving a snake in there for herself. It's a wonder she don't addle her brains. Backing away from me, she shakes her head and searches for Malcolm Hurd. Here he comes, handing me a new key to the new lock he's set on my gate.

"I'll lock it on my way out, Gregory," he says.

No harm done. She, nor Malcolm Hurd, meant me no harm. That's why I didn't hear helpful hints on my radio that a raid would rush up my road. I hear Momma and Father on the radio after I leave their trailer. They talk about me, Momma always trailing tales of torment. She's my enemy, no matter how many times Father tells me she isn't. If she wasn't, he wouldn't have to say it all the time.

JIM

"Jim," Malcolm says, "here's the story."

He ain't happy. He fidgets like a caged rooster. The state woman can't order Gregory locked up. Old Gregory, cagey with craziness, didn't threaten or yell or carry on, but at his worse only made talk about a pet snake. She told Malcolm that wouldn't count against him in her assessment of his mental status.

"Mental status!" I says to Malcolm. "He ain't got any mental status. And he ain't got any pet snake. If he were any crazier, they could declare him a national wildlife refuge from the shoulders up."

About all I can understand is that they know Gregory is crazy, but he ain't crazy enough for them to lock him up. As far as they care, he can just spend the winter out in the woods. I'm afraid for him.

"I hate to put it this way," Malcolm tells me, "but he's got to talk about killing himself or threaten someone. That's how the woman explained it to me. I know this is hard—"

"It's hard just thinking he's crazy. Is there anything they can do for him if we can get him to the hospital?"

"I don't know."

"He don't keep no snake," I say, "but he does keep a gun."

Maybe if Gregory starts an open fire in the middle of his house and roasts up children and puts a noose around his neck, maybe then they'll see if they can help him. If they don't just shoot him. By then the whole world but me will own a gun.

I'm just too disgusted to sit around talking to Malcolm, so I thank him and head off. I'm in one of those moods that could carry me clear across country. Ten, fifteen years ago, these moods would attack me. I'd grab a six-pack with all intentions that it would ticket me clear across the United States, leaving troubles, regrets, and sorrows behind me in the great state of New Hampshire. Of course by the time I'd drunk those beers, they'd slowed me down enough so that I couldn't even cross the county line much less state borders. I'd come home to hear Pauline tell me I was useless as a toadstool. She always blamed the beer and not the man-itch to move. I never tried to explain it to her.

There right at the dirt turn off of Two Captains Road sits the squad car. I pull up behind it, but even out of my truck I don't see BB Eyes. Peering off into the woods, I give him a holler.

"Don't you move an inch." Solid metal prods my spine. "What the hell are you doing here?"

"BB Eyes, get that fucking gun out of my back." I'm as mad as I am scared and unwilling to unhand either one. "Is that thing loaded?"

"Safety's on. Now you best not stick so close to me, or I'll have to charge you with interfering with an official investigation."

I turn, and he holsters the gun. "What brings you and your against-regulations stomach way out here? Which one of my kids are you hunting now?"

"The underwear thief. The state cops tell me he's not danger-ous. The psychological profiles for these guys show no violence, which is why the SP aren't hogging this case for themselves. But people in this town are worried, and it's people in this town who pay my salary."

"Seems like you're peeing down your pant leg just to keep your feet warm."

"People in town don't pay much attention to some PP from a shrink up at the capital. They're worried we got a raping murderer running loose."

"What's PP?"

"Psychological profile. Like I told you."

I tell him about Gregory and the social worker woman. "Seems like nobody knows what crazy is anymore. I think of my son-in-law, Fesmire, and I think I must be crazy for working all the time. I wonder if poor Gregory ain't worked himself crazy."

"Your boy Tommy don't put in too many days working. Not to throw it in your face, but if I catch him stealing, he will go to jail."

"He ain't stealing no women's underwear."

"No, he don't fit the PP. He's as assaultive to cops as if we'd shoved a blackberry cane between his cheeks."

He laughs, but there ain't no more hilarity in it than there is to old cold bacon. I'm thinking it's a hell of a fix when a man gets to wishing the son they won't put away gets arrested and the son they will escapes. Not that Tommy will escape much longer. This next trial of his will likely land him in jail if not into prison. Then he better keep his yap tamed, or they'll tame it for him. And poor Gregory. I guess it's too much to hope that those voices will tell him something good.

And why is BB Eyes here? Just what underwear thief is he laying for here at the dirt beginning of Two Captains Road? Who does fit this scientific PP the State Police provided so he could stand on tiptoes and see over the heads of the rest of us? It's my poor Gregory is who it is. Does BB Eyes think he'll be doing me a favor arresting Gregory as the underwear thief and putting him into a warm jail cell with three squares a day? Poor Gregory, it'll be all he needs to have someone really following him. What a horror, to wake up and find out what you've been dreaming is real.

And why is Emory Holler sitting in his truck with the motor running? Not so far from my place but what Pauline could smell his farts. Before I can reach down for my tire iron riding easy between the seat and the door, Emory's out of his truck and reaching behind him. The bastard must have taken to tucking a gun behind his back, but I'm too tired and stubborn even to duck. Out it comes. Only it ain't a gun, it's a wallet on a chain. He plucks out two twenties.

"That's for the damage my boy done to your trailer," he says. "I don't ask you to excuse him. If you want to prosecute, you go right ahead. That's your right, which is exactly what I told Scooter."

These double sawbucks I'm holding don't look counterfeit, but something about this deal sure as hell does. "I figure most of Scooter's problems are going to be with Tommy," I says, "unless he's going to make a career out of fleecing old ladies like Dorcey." Actually I doubt he and Tommy will fight over Squatty Body, but if Malcolm Hurd gets wind of Scooter's pulling shit, the boy will end up in prison. I suppose a proud man would throw Emory's money on the ground and spit on it. Me, I tuck the money right in my pocket and remind myself not to tell Pauline I got an extra forty bucks.

"Jim," Emory says, "do you suppose we could get back to being friends?"

"You know Scooter had that same honey-flavored tone when he come here asking me advice about his love life. Then, the next thing I know, I'm juiceless in my trailer. Now, I don't mean to insult you nor nothing, Emory, but I might want to drive in crawler gear while I approach calling you friend or family again."

"Look, Jim, I've got six in the truck I'd be pleased to share with you if you invite me into your place."

"I don't believe Pauline would be happy to see me drinking."

"A fine woman," he says. "Tell me, Jim, what's it like to be married to a babe?" He snaps a Bud out of its plastic collar, then tongues the foam off the top.

"To tell you the truth, Emory, it's goddamn expensive."

Tossing back a quick third of his Bud, he asks "Why?" like he really was concerned and might dig into his wallet for another twenty.

"I might have to buy a gun to shoot your ass the next time you come calling."

LISA

If I haven't got troubles enough with all this pain, and Frank Reed going to throw me out, now Leo's threatening to come down and take Rebecca and Seth away from me. Like a fool I got drunk and called him about having to find a new place, and he figured out I was partying here. What you and Scooter do with that one kid of his is up to you, he said, but I'll snatch mine out from any dopers' den.

Scooter said he and Tommy could put such a scare into Frank that Frank would beg me to stay. But Tommy's not out of walking distance to jail. And I'm not asking either one of them or both together to tackle Leo Fesmire. Not with what I know about him, which I've never told anybody, not even Momma. Not even Gregory.

These kids are driving me crazy. Daddy doesn't remember when we were kids he could just let us go, run in and out of the old place. If we got hungry, we grabbed a slice of white bread, and if we got hurt, we pasted on a Band-Aid. Anything we did, we did ourselves, whether it was yelling or running or sitting quiet and watching the peacock fan his tail. If I let my kids outside, they'll be hit by cars or arrested for loitering. Then Leo will be onto me saying I can't take care of them. If I go outside with them during the day, there's always some old hen calling me a lazy welfare bitch. Daddy doesn't remember that he didn't raise us. We just grew up.

When I lived with Leo, he told me I worried too much about the children. Children are the last things I worry about, he used to say, because children are naturally happy or naturally sad. That was Leo's philosophy. He was full of philosophy. He imagined one day they'd be teaching about him at the university. I believed it too. Leo convinced me of that along with a whole lot of other things. He said if a man was right, all he needed do was stay home and sooner or later the world would discover it and find him out and celebrate him for the philosopher he was. Look at Einstein, he'd say, and I'd nod my head, though I never did know exactly what he meant. Then one day I said, Leo, I wasn't raised. I just grew. And I've got to say it's held me back.

He didn't like it, and right then he began pulling away from me. He'd just suck on his pipe and tell me, Look at Einstein. I think he took to smoking that pipe and wearing his hair long because he thought it made him look like Einstein. It did, a little. Leo never wanted to look like a rock star or a movie actor, never strutted the way most of the boys did, the way Tommy still does. Father was right when he said there wa'n't no peacock to Leo. "Fesmire," he calls Leo, claiming never to remember that first name. Father never thinks that the dislike he took to Leo poisoned my marriage from before it even began. Sometimes I wonder Father even thinks at all.

Leo thought all the time, philosophizing or scheming, but often so lost in thought he lost touch with reality, at least the part I lived in. By the time he came to accuse me of deserting him for Scooter, I'd felt deserted, starved, and abused. And I never had to give pussy away to have friends, no matter how mean he likes to talk.

The house stinks of pussy! he yelled. Next thing I know you'll be bringing them in to fuck Rebecca. Then he slapped me. Kept his hand open in a weak moment. He expected me to keep having kids just to satisfy his ego.

His long nose twitching, he walked around the living room, picking up Rebecca, picking up Seth, going into the kitchen to check out the refrigerator, then to the bathroom where he opened the medicine cabinet and popped the top off the toothpaste. He didn't want me to buy deodorant or perfume or hairspray, so the toothpaste was the cabinet's only occupant. Even toothpaste, he said, wasted his money, but he allowed me to have it because I'd grown up with it and would go hyper if he made me follow his way of brushing with baking soda. You don't know what all those chemicals do to your mind. Tell me that ain't from years of sucking up false pharmaceuticals from all these fancy toothpastes and deodorants. Then he stopped his philosophical speech and got right in my face and yelled, This house stinks of pussy!

Leo was the smartest guy I ever knew, and that includes all the doctors and lawyers Father knows through Malcolm Hurd. All those smart men trying to lock Gregory up in a loony bin. There's a treasure trove of smartness around here, none of it making my life any easier, none of it any better than what Scooter gave me when I was half-high with vodka and he was kissing my mouth like I was the sweetest thing.

Course there ain't nothing sweeter than children, but they do drive me crazy, especially Alison, 'cause I'm so nervous. The kids are watching TV in the living room and their cereal bowls are in the sink. Momma says, "You've got it easy. Your children pick up after themselves." She doesn't know how hard it was to train them with Leo not giving a shit and me not having any training myself. Nor does she ever think I've still got to wash the cereal bowls and put away the boxes and sweep the kitchen floor and wipe the counter—and a lot of stuff she never did. Or did so seldom the place never looked clean. I hate to throw it up in her face, but if she pushes me, one day I will. I'll just tell her what growing up was like. How Father can wonder that Gregory acts odd is beyond me. Looks to me like Gregory's just trying to live the way he grew up. It's a wonder we're not all nuts because we sucked up four ounces of crazy with every bottle of formula when we were little.

By the time I get the kitchen cleaned up, my head's starting to clear. I brew myself a nice cup of Red Zinger. The herbs remind me of grass, the sweet, high smell of grass. But right now I just want to stay quiet and still while the kids watch their shows. They like that Discovery Channel with all the animals and nature. Father encourages them to watch those shows, like they're going to get the education he missed. He says it calms them. I wonder how calm he'd be if I told him about Leo.

After yelling about pussy stink, Leo shoved me into the bedroom and got the toilet plunger and said, All right now, I'm going to pump out that foreign come.

You touch me with that filthy thing, I'll claw your eyes out while you sleep, I told him.

He set the plunger on the floor like he used to lean his rifle against the porch railing, then he slid the bureau in front of the door. Skinny though he is, Leo's strong. That door didn't lock, so

I knew what he was doing. His dark eyes lit up, meaning to scare me and taking delight in frightening me all at the same time. When he walked to the bed, he moved stiff-legged, like a scarecrow on the prowl. And he left that red rubber plunger just where he'd set it.

I'm going to clean you out, he said, because you ain't fit to sleep in my bed.

Leo knew all kinds of tricks to hurt me. Once he yanked me upside down and stood on my fingers and bent back my big toe until I thought I'd pass out from pain running into my blood-pounding head. It barely left a faint blue bruise at the joint, like I might've stubbed it. Another time he got behind me and twisted my head like he was unscrewing a stubborn lid. Don't make me slip, he told me, or I'll snap it. I'd seen him kill things that way, rabbits, chickens. I was scared he would snap my neck just enough to paralyze me without killing me, so I'd spend the rest of my life as just a head. Just a helpless head. He told me he could do that. Right here, I know the right pressure, he said.

Pressure is what he used that time after Scooter. Quick as a thought, he pressed his hand against the side of my throat and closed off the artery until I went black. When I came to, he already had my pants off and my arms and legs tied to the four corners of the bed.

Maybe you can't help it, he said. Drinking and whoring. Maybe they come as natural to you as scratching an itch. Then he talked about Father's drinking, which I'd told him of, what I'd remembered of it, and he said it must have shamed me, and it was a shame. And the whoring, he said, maybe that came from sleeping with Gregory in the cramped quarters of that little house.

Roughly, he spread my knees and stared at my crotch. I don't see it leaking out of your hole yet. I'm going to help it. He grabbed the plunger from the floor and brought it up close to his face to inspect the thick red rubber of its suction cup. It's clean enough for your filth, he said.

I couldn't speak. I was too scared to threaten him or promise him or beg him. He was going to work that thing to suck my insides out. Philosopher that he featured himself, he could turn mean quick. I went to screaming. Somewhere screams answered me. The kids? The kids screaming from outside the door?

When I opened my eyes, I saw the screams weren't sympathy. They were rage. It wasn't the children, but Leo, bellowing and raging enough to show me I'd have to leave him forever. And I'd have to live after he'd sucked my insides.

The hard red cap touched me, prodded me, like poking at an animal. He pushed the filthy rubber between my legs, rubbing the nasty thing against my flesh, this toilet tool in my open self. He stopped shrieking and started telling me not to get excited, just because it was bigger and harder than Scooter's cock. It's just as dirty too, he said, full of dirt, like you like it. Try not to get all juiced up and stink the house up even more with your goddamn stinking pussy juice.

And he kept touching me down there with that shit-sucker, which is why I hurt down there now. The bastard, he infected me. I called Momma to ask her to get me some Tylenol. All I have in the house is food stamps, which I can't buy medicine with, I tell her. I tell her to bring money, and I'll give her my food stamps. I've got a hundred dollars' worth left from the three seventy-five they give me this month. I don't even care if she just brings me fifty dollars, fifty dollars and Tylenol for this killer pain down there.

That's why the kids drive me crazy. If this killer pain didn't rage in my insides, like being pregnant with a case of broken bottles, I could concentrate. Instead, every sound one of the kids makes pushes and shoves me, yanks me, tugs me, "Momma,

Momma, Momma," always asking, even if Momma thinks I've got them all trained to do for themselves. And I don't know when Leo may show up.

GREGORY

They say Emory killed Aunt Helen. I'm going to gawk at his place for a piece of evidence. Or the pink panties. If he or Scooter are stealing panties, I'll put them in the paws of the police. Then Emory won't try to launch me off my land, and I can leave my shotgun alone. A man who'll murder his wife ain't above stealing pink panties.

You'd think with this sizable spread of his, Emory wouldn't need to steal my land. He's like those old pharaohs of Egypt with their pyramids and kingdoms and miles of desert to deliver them to the far end of forever. Fear is what it is. But all I need is my little five-acre plot and my place. That will keep me fine. And set the snake outside my brain. It's all Father has, five acres and the trailer. And I don't even need a trailer because I've constructed my camp right on my land. And Emory'd better leave me have it.

He leaves his wide windows uncovered. He must think with all his land of plenty no one can peer at him, but he's got a penetrable perimeter. Woods are no walls to someone like me who walks. I slip past fruit trees and pool right up to his patio, sliding on my stomach. I slide my way to his windows.

He wouldn't want anyone to find evidence of his evil, so I figure he covered it up in a closet. He'll be buried with it like those pharaohs when he passes, piled up with all his belongings, safe and secure. But if I find the foul evidence of his crime or the pink panties, he'll be buried in prison. No pharaoh he.

He's dumb not to own a dog. At my place Dog would already

be barking at anyone attempting to barge in. I see Emory sitting on his big settee. Scooter's gone, which is good because Emory won't display his stuff with his son there. Scooter's at Penny's, or he's off stealing pink panties. I need to catch Emory at a crime.

Father said he'd have to take my sales agreement to an attorney. He said a lawyer'd look at the deed to see if Emory could evict me off my land. But Emory didn't send me a signed sales agreement. We agreed. We shook hands. I gave him money. I can't help it if he changed his mind later, but Father said the lawyer said it wasn't likely we could win in court without the sales agreement. Father talks to lawyers a lot.

The snake's seeping out of his burrow to bite me. I can't get any coffee here. It hurts.

Emory's watching television. A man and two women sit by a hot tub, taking off their clothes.

The two women look pretty. They are completely naked nude. One's blond, the other's dark. I can't hear what they're saying, but when they take off the man's trunks, he smiles. There's a gold chain around his neck, and nothing else on any of them. All naked. I know this isn't regular TV or even cable. I think this is one of what Tommy calls fuck flicks. I've never watched one.

Emory stands. He's wearing sweatpants. When he pulls them off, I see he's wearing nothing underneath. His penis swings soft just like the penis of the man in the movie. Sitting on the settee with his sweats at his feet, Emory lets his hands lie on his legs.

The women in the movie move on the man. They fight for his penis, putting it in their mouths until it is stiff. It grows very big. Emory stands. His penis is small. It is not even stiff. The man in the movie is pushing his penis into one of the women. Emory holds his wrinkled penis. He lets go and sits. My penis hardens.

It's a very confusing movie. Maybe if I could hear them talk, I could understand it. The snake chews my brain like chocolate taffy candy.

Now they're all sitting beside the bubbling pool. The women push the man down and play with his penis. Emory is playing with his penis, which is still soft. I figure this is a tempting time to penetrate the place. I watch for wires as I check the windows, but the house isn't alarmed. The second sash is closed but not locked, so I slide it open, and I'm in slick as shit.

Now I can hear the movie. It's music and bubbling water. From the doorway to the hall I can hear the women panting. Quietly, I click open the closet door. Nothing. Not even clothes. There's a bed here, made up, with a spread and all. It must be a spare room. Looking from the hall, I see Emory as he mangles his meat. The women in the movie wear smiles and sweat as they pound the guy's penis.

The doorbell rings. Emory turns off the VCR. When he twists around to tie his bathrobe shut, I see his penis, still soft and small. As he answers the door, I scoot down the hall and into the next room. His bedroom. A big canopy bed for the pharaoh, missing only a crown, a crest, a coat of arms. No wires at this window, so I flip the lock and open the glass in case I have to leave in a hurry. I hear him talking to a woman, a real woman, not one of the women in the movie. That's good. I'll know where he is. I start my search in the closet.

Shoes and boots, fancy boots with buckles and even a god-damn snakeskin pair. I don't touch those. In the back, beyond the boots, hides a box and a videotape. I slide them out. On the top of the box is a garden scene with women holding umbrellas, though it isn't raining. This part is porcelain. All along the edges filigree decorates the wood. There's a little hasp but no lock. I open it.

The snake fangs into my mind, frantic to puncture me with pain. I cock my head to the hallway. I can still hear the talking but not the words. Inside the box are photographs, a whole batch of pictures, a lot taken with an old Polaroid.

Some of the Polaroids show a naked woman. She's dancing, holding up her arms, swinging and swaying. She's short with big breasts. It's only when I look at the other pictures, where the woman wears clothes, that I see the woman is Aunt Helen. This could be evidence. I remember her funeral, some years before Elizabeth died. A lot of talk in town, but not in our house, not like when Elizabeth died. Your uncle pushed your aunt down the cellar stairs. Now he's got all her insurance money, they said, and he's going to get away with it because he made it look like an accident.

I hear talk in the big room. I shove the pictures in the box and close the porcelain portrait cover. From the doorway I can hear the woman's voice, familiar, friendly, family. It's Momma. She's unbuttoning her blouse. Swishing and swaying in front of pharaoh at his settee, she takes off her bra and slides out of her skirt and slip. She's doing this dance, only there's no music. I can't see if Emory's robe is open. His hands stay still. Momma has big breasts, like Aunt Helen's. She has a slender stomach with a little roll of fat that shows around her hips as she pushes her panties off.

The snake gnaws at me, but I see Momma dancing. I close my eyes to make her go away, but when I open them, there she is, dancing.

She's my enemy. She snakes her bold body before Emory. Emory stays seated in his settee. I bet he's got a great big smile now. I bet his penis pulses purple and is big and hard. I hate them both. Inside my brain the snake slithers. The snake tunnels.

Momma turns. All herself is bare body, completely naked

nude. A mole on her butt shows. Everything shows. She doesn't hide anything. She dances her sexy self for Emory, showing him everything. I can't stand it. All his guns are in that room, else I'd run and ram through the cases and grab a gun and blast that naked body and punish pharaoh until his horse cock hung as flat and useless as a hound's ear.

Oh, it hurts. And she's still doing her dance. Emory stands. I'll get my gun, that's what I'll get. They'll be sorry for making me hurt. I won't wait for Emory to turn around, to see his big hung, horse cock. He turns, but he's pulled his robe over his penis. I know what they want. They want to come to that other room and fuck and suck. That's what he uses that room for. I'll find them in the fuck and suck room.

Here he comes. I return the lovely ladies box, take the video-tape, and bear it out the window. My fingers are strong. I slide the window so closed, he'll never know I invaded his pharaoh's palace. He thinks all his putrid pollution stays safely secret. Wait until I put my gun to his head. Then we'll see about this hard horse cock. And Momma too.

I hate this hurt. All the way down, I hurt.

10
ten

TOMMY

If Penny thinks she's just going to kick me out and keep Aaron so she can live on the support money, she'll be weeping worse than Momma.

"Hello, Penny," I say.

"Scooter ain't here." She's all cleaned up, her hair brushed back, her lipstick on like she's looking for work. "He said he'd be right back, only he ain't. There ain't a one of you guys can tell time."

"I got a job. I'm getting a regular paycheck working for Buddy Links."

"Splitting firewood for the sauna, washing towels—why, Tommy, I bet you're even setting money aside for a Camaro."

"I am."

"Let's see it." Now she's the angry Penny, the smart, conniving Penny, the hot Penny, who turns all her sex and passion whichever way she wants, and I never know which way it'll flow until she spins open the big valves and lets her rip. I know once she shoots it out, she can't stop it or even control it until she's run bone-dry.

I flash five twenties by her like I'm showing a poker hand. I like twenties. They're impressive enough and everybody takes them.

"So, how much of that am I going to get?" She doesn't put her hand out. She knows if she were to stick her hand out, I'd knock it away, just as I know if I were to put my hand on her body, she'd knock it away.

"How much of it you want?" I'm weaseling on this because it's all the money I got.

"It ain't how much I want. It's how much I need—which is all of it. For me and Aaron. Scooter hasn't paid a lot of bills around here."

I give her four twenties. "Maybe he's waiting for Emory to pay them."

"Emory offered, but Emory Holler always expects sugar for his money."

So Emory's after Penny. I guess he ain't scored here or Penny would've said. She don't hold nothing back no matter what.

"I keep the door locked." She pulls two Buds from the fridge. "Just as long as he doesn't take to stealing my underwear. I don't have money to be replacing panties like they were Pampers."

We're both laughing as we pop our Buds. "I wonder who is stealing that underwear."

Penny pulls a long face. "Why, Tommy, it's your brother. Didn't you know?"

"Sure it is," I say, laughing. "I can just see poor Gregory decorating his camp with silky undies. One touch of his calloused hands, those panties would shred to dust."

She nods her head up and down. "He's doing it, you know. And BB Eyes is going to catch him."

"That makes as much sense as feeding meat loaf to a cow." Aaron's up from his nap, crawling on my belly like he's exploring the moon. "First of all, Gregory's about as interested in women as Aaron is, for Christ's sake. Second, he's more down on stealing than all the gods back to Moses."

"Your brother ain't stealing women," she says, taking Aaron's little dragon rattle and shaking it at me. "He's stealing their underwear."

"Who told you all this bullshit?"

"BB Eyes."

From the closet I get Aaron's backpack and tell Penny I'll take him for a walk. It's a cinch he hasn't breathed fresh air all day.

"You be sure you bring him back," she says, "or I'll have law on you that'll make BB Eyes and the DMV look like Girl Scouts."

Down at Reed's, I take Aaron through the storefront, where he's grabbing at red jugs of STP and black jugs of oil until I slip a bright blue mini–ice scraper into his hand.

Out back, Father doesn't even stop work to pick up Aaron, just grunts at him.

"Got your boy out for a stroll," he says with his gift for remarking on the obvious.

"I figure it'll dress up my image so that when I step up to trial, the judge'll know me for a family man." I see Frank has gone out front, so I barge right ahead and ask Father about Gregory stealing women's underwear, even though it makes me look as foolish as an old man's hard-on.

"BB Eyes thinks so," Father says. He backs away from under

the car and fits a welder's helmet over his head. "He's even taken to spying on your brother."

"That's bullshit!"

"There's considerable trouble with Gregory," Father says. "Watch his eyes." He waits a minute for me to cover Aaron's eyes before he sparks up the garage.

"He ain't troubled women before."

"He ain't done a lot of things before. Neither have you."

Aaron's crying before I even see Frank holding the ice scraper he's snatched from the kid's hand. "Teaching him to steal before he's even out of diapers," Frank says to me. "You are a disgrace."

"What are you—"

"Now I want you out of my place," Frank says, pointing the ice scraper at me like he might shoot me with it. "You don't come in here again. If you need to talk to your father, you come around to these bay doors. And you still stay outside."

"Hey," I says, "you don't have to go all hyper."

"You've assaulted Gary, ruined your sister's apartment, and made your family's lives as miserable as you can. You're going to end up in prison. You may think you're as hard to catch as a winged eel, but they'll get you, boy. You better believe that."

I've listened to more than I need to and with Father not saying a word to stick up for me either. "No wonder your wife don't like you," I say to Frank. "You don't know how to be anything but disagreeable."

I take Aaron out the back door while Frank sputters, "What d'you say about my wife?"

I'm lucky I'm traveling with Aaron this minute, otherwise I'd probably be into a fight with Frank. I wander down past the torn yellow crime-scene tape toward the brook.

Away upstream from Frank's place lies a small sandy stretch like a beach. A poor beach, Lisa calls it, for poor people like us to bring our kids, let them dig their toes into the sand and drink Kool-Aid and eat egg-salad sandwiches. I set a cigarette floating for Aaron to watch. He waves his little hands bye-bye as it spins and jounces in the stream.

I don't live like wasting one cigarette is going to ruin the national economy and sell the whole state of New Hampshire to Japan. That's Father's line. All the time worrying some act of his will set the whole world spinning right out of orbit so we'll all fall into the sun and fry. And as we're going down, he thinks we'll be chanting, "It's Jim Hutchins's fault," over and over again. Jesus Christ, I'm glad I ain't got a worried mind.

It's the last time I'm going your bail, Tommy, he always says. Of course he gives me the money and Momma comes up with the lawyer's fees, else I will go to jail again, and there ain't anybody in the family wants to see that. Especially me. I'd like to have a chance for life to stop buzzing at me so I could get back to my art, and not just airbrushing goofy shit on four-by-fours either, though I could go that way awhile. I just can't stand routine. Gregory could lay bricks one right after another like there was no deeper pleasure. No wonder he's going nuts. Poor bastard. I may lightning-rod trouble, but I ain't crazy. And I ain't going crazy. So Gregory stuck out school and graduated. So what? What's it got him? He's going nuts.

Who the hell would be stupid enough to bring stolen women's panties here, jerk off in them, and bury them in sawdust? I don't really care except I don't want to see the crime fobbed off on Gregory—or myself, because once they label you nuts, life turns rougher than a nor'easter. There ain't nothing this town won't blame on a Hutchins.

When we get back on the street, Gregory pulls his truck to the sidewalk, slams on the binders, and whips out the door.

"Good thing you got your boy with you," Gregory says.

"What's up?"

"You stole my gun." His thumb stabs into my shoulder sending paralytic pain up my neck. "Momma is out there nasty naked dancing for Emory. I've got to get my gun." He shoves me back.

"What would I want with your gun?" I pick up Aaron.

"You sell what you steal." His hands open and close on empty air. "I need my shotgun to shoot them."

If I weren't holding Aaron, he'd be whaling on me until I told him where his shotgun was. "Maybe you hid it so well, you can't find it."

Oh, Jesus Christ, that sets him into a wicked rage. He's cursing Emory and Momma and me, we're all his sworn enemies, and he'll kill us all, and he ends up right in my face. "How'd you know it was hid if you didn't steal it?"

"Father told me." I figure as the only adult who isn't Gregory's sworn enemy, he'll be spared killing. "He's got your gun."

JIM

"Give me my gun," Gregory says.

I'm standing here with a two-gallon plastic container of grain in one hand and a bucket of water in the other. "Do you want to help me with the birds?"

"You set out to feed 'em alone, you can finish feeding 'em alone." He's as tousled and filthy as if he'd slept under a porch. "I know Momma ain't here. I'll bet you don't even know where she is."

Since she's become his sworn enemy, he won't come here unless she's gone. I know it's the illness driving him to act this way, but it measures the same as most any meanness you'd set a rule to. "Let me finish here, we can go get us a cup of coffee."

"She's your enemy too. That's why you don't know where she is. Get my gun, and I'll tell you where my wandering Momma is."

How he knows I've got his gun is beyond me. I didn't want Malcolm to leave it here, but Malcolm didn't give me much choice. He laid it on the couch along with a box of shells and said, There. If Gregory calls the cops, I won't have the gun, and they won't bother you because you're his father. I told him Gregory wouldn't call the cops because he's petrified of them. I go ahead and finish feeding up. I'm hoping the peacock will fan so I can make Gregory look at something pretty. Naturally, the bird just drags his tail through the dirt to get at the grain.

"You showed yourself real smart stealing my gun," Gregory says. "I figured Tommy took it, but he don't have it. You were smart to find it, but how'd you get past my gate?" He stares down both directions of the road. "That's gnawing at my knower. How'd you get past my gate?"

He never thought when Malcolm bought that new lock for him, it came with two keys. Malcolm just kept the extra one. "Gregory, I ain't been to your place except when you were there. If I could pick locks, I'd be opening bank vaults, not fooling around out to your place."

"Don't you call me no fool!" Gregory yells. "You footed it, that's what you did. See, I ain't a fool. I can figure out my own father. You can't fox me."

"I ain't trying to fool you."

"I ain't a fool!" He's yelling so I wonder the Glebes ain't called the cops. "You're the fool. You don't know where Momma is, and she's making a fool of you right now."

I don't know why he's got it in for Pauline, especially when she's all the time telling me to leave him alone. Out in the barn I set down the feed dish and take notice of the grain bag. "Old Mr.

Rat's made himself busy here," I tell Gregory. "Charley ain't doing his job out here."

"You feed him too much," says Gregory, running a boot toe to the hole. "Charley won't chase no rat to chew on if he's got Momma opening cans of cat food in the house. Momma's always opening something. Only you're deep in the dark."

Meanness rots inside him. "You could brick me up a box to keep the grain away from Mr. Rat." I'll say what I have to, to wall Gregory away from meanness and guns.

"Be cheaper to put it in a plastic barrel. Or galvanized," he says. "Or have you moved to modern like Tommy so you don't mind spending scads of money?"

"Gregory, if everybody I owed money to would vote for me, I could be elected president."

"No elections. Momma collects cash. She doesn't push for president."

"Let's go get that cup of coffee. Your truck or mine?"

He won't ride to town because he knows I've got a good, economical (he says) coffeemaker right inside the trailer. I wonder if he knows I've got a good, economical shotgun lying on the couch. The way he's pushing, I'm beginning to believe he may have heard something right from those voices on his radio.

"You get my gun, I'll cook the coffee," he says. "And while we're drinking it, I'll drop the big bomb on Momma."

"Gregory, what are you talking about?" I know asking him is close to asking the cat what he's dreaming, but I got to say something.

"Oh, you'll want to kill her after I tell you what I know, what I saw her do with Emory."

"Emory Holler?"

"Get my gun."

"I ain't got your gun." I always figure if you're going to lie, just keep at it.

I put myself and sunlight between him and the trailer because if he gets in ahead of me, it'll be all over. I don't know if that goddamn gun was loaded when Malcolm laid it on the couch.

That claw of his pinches hard on my neck cords. "Get my gun, goddamn you," he growls.

"Cursing me ain't going to make me do what I can't do, Gregory." I shrug out of his grip, but he steps up and clutches me again. I'm not going to be able to shake him many more times. "Quit grabbing me, Gregory. I ain't got your goddamn gun."

"Don't you turn into my enemy." He shoves me. "Momma's my sworn enemy, and she should be yours. So I'll yell it to you, then you'll go and get my gun." He bear-hugs me and shouts so my ears hurt. *"Momma's over there completely nude naked. Right in front of Emory. A feast for his eyes. Stripped herself."* He pushes me toward the trailer. My chest aches from his grip. *"Nasty naked dancing."*

"My gun," he says.

"No."

"Fucking, fucking Emory!"

"No." I'm backing around the corner.

"I'm no fool." He grabs my throat. "I'm no fucking fool."

I punch his stomach, just muscle, no fat, no air. Out of surprise he lets go of my throat. Then he just flings me to the ground and makes for the trailer. He won't have any trouble finding the shotgun. I'm after him, but he's through the door before I make it to the steps. Out he comes with the barrel pointing and his fingers inside the trigger guard.

Backing up, I turn the corner by the shed. As he comes around, face set and white as mortar, I grab the shovel. Gregory don't deserve this. Both hands, swing hard. One swing. I ain't got no three strikes. He comes around the corner, gun first. I kneecap him.

Crack. God, what a sound. He's down on the ground. I snatch the gun from him. He's whimpering, but I don't dare listen to him. Inside the shed is a coil of rope. I've hog-tied him before I realize he's quit whimpering. He ain't making a sound. Then I break open the shotgun and dump out the green shell.

"I just hope to God I ain't injured him permanently," I tell Malcolm on the phone.

"You say he attacked you?"

"Liked to kill me." I try to keep the snuffle out of my voice. I'm standing where I can see Gregory out the window, through he's not clear because my eyes are so wet. "Jesus Christ, Malcolm, I knew I wa'n't going to get more than one swing."

"That's right, but now we got to figure this thing out."

"I need to get off the phone and call the ambulance. Hell, he ain't even squirming out there. I may have just made him even crazier."

"Hold on. You let me do the calling."

Calling he does. The next thing I know, I got lawyer and ambulance and cops so on my property there isn't room for BB Eyes to step foot on Hutchins land. We have to stand out on the public road to talk.

"What you're going to have to do," says BB Eyes, taking out his official, bought-and-paid-for-by-the-town citation pad, "you're going to swear a complaint of assault against Gregory."

TOMMY

"If you're here about Scooter," Emory starts, "that has nothing to do with me."

"Scooter and me are friends," I tell him. He's blocking the door like he's talking to some goddamn Jehovah's Witness. "When you step out of my way, you can get me a beer."

"Why would I want to do that?"

"Because we're going to talk about my mother."

His "den," as he calls it, looks like an arsenal: gun racks, gun cases, rifles, shotguns, pistols. Maybe somewhere is a display of stolen pink panties. If he's perverted like Gregory says, he might be perverted enough to lust after pink panties. I ain't having that fobbed off on my brother.

"Here's your beer." Emory hands me a can of Bud.

"A glass. When I'm drinking in such swanky surroundings, I expect a glass. Just like in a fancy city bar."

"They're in that cabinet."

The leather of his couch squeaks a little when I slide over to get a glass out of the oak cabinet. On the top sits a picture of Aunt Helen. What a fucking hypocrite. The door shuts as quiet as a lie in the dark. "So you like my mother naked?"

"Your father heard that shit coming out of your mouth, he'd make you eat toilet paper."

"My father will hear about it unless you turn loose of trying to evict Gregory off his land."

Reaching behind him, Emory gets his smokes, lights one, then tosses pack and lighter to me. I bend to light mine and hear a click. "That was a shell going into the chamber," he says. He's holding this little automatic and keeping it pointed at me. "Now let's talk about threats before you finish that beer and get too drunk to follow common sense."

I tell him I know Momma comes over here to fuck him. I tell him she strips, dances around, and then they do the horizontal bop. I tell him I've seen them, and I'm not the only one. Then I tell him he can stick his cap gun up his ass.

Bam!

My cigarette and my beer are in my lap. My crotch is burning, wet, and I'm looking for where I've been shot. I get my cigarette to my mouth and suck in a big drag. The leather next to me shows the torn hole where the bullet went through, maybe a foot from me.

"This goddamn thing always did shoot wide. I don't know how much you been peeping, but I do know you for a failure at most everything you do. I'm sure your mother would gladly tell you why she comes over here, but I'll spare her that. She comes here because she needs money, money for your bail, your lawyers, money you ain't got. And as far as I can see, your father ain't either."

I tell him my mother's still alive, which is why Father's not rich like he is. I listen for the click of another shell going into the chamber. Maybe it's already in there. I don't know shit about guns.

"Kind of perverted, aren't you?" Emory asks. "Watching your mother dance naked. You into swiping underwear too?"

"I don't swipe a thing. I got a regular job with Buddy Links, and I got a kid to support."

"A regular upright citizen. Looks like you pissed your pants there. Maybe you didn't drink enough to hold your courage." Sliding right over at me, he sets his hairy face breathing distance from mine. I see he left that goddamn gun on the chair arm. "I don't know what you saw, only you didn't see me screwing your mother because that never happened. You know it, and I know it."

I got nowhere to squirm pinned here on this leather couch. I couldn't even get a knee into his nuts. I don't know how much Gregory saw. I know he was mad enough to shoot Momma and Emory both. He sure didn't doubt Momma was naked. He said that word so many times, it began to sound funny. He ain't so wacko he can't tell naked when he sees it.

I reach over to grab Aunt Helen's picture, the only thing within arm's reach to hit him with. I make it about halfway when he locks onto my wrist. "How come you're hounding Gregory off that land? For Christ sake, we're family."

He pushes up and retrieves his cigarette from the ashtray. "Your brother's nuts. Don't you know that? Your father's got him locked up in the New Hampshire State Hospital. Pretty soon, it'll be two of you Hutchinses being clothed and fed at taxpayers' expense."

"I'm not going to any goddamn jail."

"Maybe they'll get your father or your sister next. I'm sure they don't lack reasons to go after either one."

"For someone who got away with killing his wife, that's a ballsy thing to say."

"You little peckerhead."

I can beat him to that gun if he goes for it.

"When Helen died, people couldn't get in line fast enough to accuse me of harming her. I couldn't get through burying her before BB Eyes paid me a visit—and no condolences either. And that's saying nothing of when the State Police sergeant came through my house with a tape measure and a Polaroid camera. And you wonder why I stick to the law with Gregory? After what I been through? Why, if he were to get hurt out there, he could sue me. I could lose everything." He stops to scratch at the beard again, so I'm about to ask him about fleas, but he has more to say. "Look, it's a good thing you're your mother's son, or I would have shot you—for a burglar. And there ain't a soul in town would've questioned it."

He turns his back, and I've got his gun. Just as quick as that. And I step right out of arm's reach. I like the feel of the gun in my hand. I'm going to like this. Emory takes a drag, then sets his cigarette in the ashtray, as if he's going to take care of me. Well, he ain't stupid. He knows I can shoot him. I don't say anything. I don't have to say a word. I like this.

"Tommy," he says, "the way things are done now is according to law. Look at how your father handled Gregory."

He explains out how easy Father and Malcolm Hurd railroaded Gregory right to the nuthouse by charging him with assault, having the police take him to the shrinks instead of jail, and getting him locked up as an emergency admittance. Before anyone knows it, Gregory is swallowing pills and walking around with a glazed look in his eyes. In fact hardly anyone does know about it, including Momma and up until now—me. I don't go out to Gregory's place uninvited. The last time he saw me was when he came looking for his gun. That's when he told me about Momma dancing naked. So maybe he is nuts. Maybe he didn't see Momma naked at all.

"I'll have your brother off my land by law. You know, with an involuntary commitment, you can be walking around the state hospital for five years with so many drugs in you, you'll be pissing down both pant legs and think you're standing in the shower."

Gregory don't lie. He never did. And I can't believe he hallucinated Momma and Emory because the strongest drug he ever took was a cherry Coke. Something ain't right here, and I figure maybe Emory's got the biggest bluff going.

"If you're going to shoot, you'd better kill me, because otherwise I'll have you up there with Gregory. And your mother would believe I was doing her a favor by not sending you to the jailhouse."

He stands. He better not think I'll let him just walk over here and take this gun away from me like I'm some doofus. Bad enough

Penny's wringing my dick with both hands, but it ain't going to be any man putting me in pain, uncle or no uncle. He steps forward, and I step back. He steps forward, I level the gun at him.

"I'll gut-shoot you, Emory. Think of it as payback for killing Aunt Helen."

He shrugs and spreads his arms, then, *wham*. It's like he's clapping a fly between his hands, only his hands don't meet. *Smack*, his hand whaps my face, jars me, pushes my head around. I barely feel his other hand steal the gun from me, just a quick pain as the trigger guard rips past my finger.

"Now, you little shitheels, I'm going to shoot you."

I blink the tears out of my eyes. "Fuck you," I say. I watch the tendons and muscles of his wrist, but there's no movement.

PAULINE

I want to tell Jim right away, the minute he opens the door and whistles to Petey and picks up Charley and rubs him between the ears. The way he thinks he knows how to please everything and everybody, it just puts stones in my shoes today. But I don't tell him. Instead I make the pot of coffee I know he wants and listen while he rambles on about what kind of salad he'll fix to go with the spaghetti and meatballs he's going to make. Since he's started cooking, you'd think everybody ate their food raw before he arrived on the scene.

"Jim, I want you out of here."

"You want to go to a restaurant?" he asks, as if we have spare dollars growing out of his thinning hair. I stare at him. He didn't shave today. I've noticed lately he'll go two or three days without shaving as if he can save enough on razor blades to pay off our debts.

"I want you to leave, get out of here. I don't want you living here anymore."

"Oh," he says. Just that. "Oh," as if he didn't hear me right the first time. He sloshes coffee into his mouth, sets his cup by the pot, and says, "I got to feed up."

"I did that." I was so mad when I got home, I fed and watered the birds, else I'd've been in the trailer thrashing. "Put your clothes in a bag and leave. Unless you got a suitcase you can call your own. God knows you've got little enough else."

"All right," he says, refilling his cup like he was pumping gas for some cranky customer, "all right. What's up now?" He sits and shakes a cigarette out of his pack.

"It ain't bad enough what you did to Gregory, then you just kept a lying silence to yourself and Malcolm Hurd and BB Eyes." I throw my cup right on the floor. "I suppose everybody from here to Boston knows about it! Everybody but me!"

"Gregory was going to hurt himself."

"Now look what you've made me do," I tell him. There's sticky tea on the floor, and naturally my cup is all smashed. If he so much as reaches for the Super Glue, I'll seal his eyelids with it while he sleeps.

"Do you want to hear about Gregory or not?"

"Just don't you lie to me, mister, because I've had more than I can stand of lying."

So he starts in about Gregory. It's nothing I haven't heard before, insulting Gregory about his eating and washing. He says Gregory couldn't take of himself.

"You couldn't either when I met you," I say.

"No, but I was smart enough to get someone to help me."

"Then all Gregory needed was some help. Like when Lisa went up there and cooked him that turkey dinner. He didn't need someone to get him locked up in an insane asylum!"

He says Gregory was getting ready to hurt people, to hurt us—Lisa and me, he means. He says Gregory really was crazy, hearing voices and hating people he had no reason to hate. He'd said I was his sworn enemy. He'd bought a shotgun and was mad enough to use it. I let Jim tell his whole story so I can see if he's lying or leaving out the details or pulling any other tricks I've known him to use.

"And you don't think Gregory'll be mad when he gets out? You don't think he'll hate you for what you did to him? Then he might try to hurt you."

"Gregory'll be okay."

"And what about his knee?"

"The doctor said he'd be okay."

"The same doctor who claims he's crazy? Why would I believe him?"

Without drinking coffee or puffing on a cigarette, Jim starts on new stuff, stuff I haven't heard, stuff I listen to real carefully. Of course, it's all full of more insults to Gregory, the doctor saying the boy's schizophrenic because his brain is all messed up. They've started him on drugs, and they're going to keep giving him drugs, and they're going to make him take drugs for the rest of his life. And they're calling that helping him.

"If they know what he's got, why don't they cure him?" I ask.

"Because it ain't something you get cured of."

"I'll tell you what I think. Gregory was heartbroken over Elizabeth, and he's still grieving. It's grief has him in its dark arms. Now, I ain't a doctor, but I know my son, and unlike some other people I could name, I know common sense."

Oh, no, Jim can't believe that because he'd rather believe the fancy phrases of some doctor who's adding chemicals to Gregory's brain. He'd rather believe our own son was going to hurt us rather than understand the boy is frightened and grieving. I tell Jim I'm going up there to visit Gregory and see how soon I can get him out of the place. I don't even like to name what it is.

"I wouldn't do that. He's not ready to see you. The doctor says it might set him back."

"I'm his mother." Jim doesn't say anything so I tell him, "Jim, you put Gregory in there, you get him out."

"I can't do that. He's in there all legal now because he came at me with a gun."

"I thought you said it was me he wanted to hurt! Now I see the truth is different. Well, you just go up there and get him out of that place."

"We got him to sign himself in and commit himself, and I'm not going to talk him into uncommitting himself."

"That's why you hid this whole rotten business from me. That's why I want you out of here. I'm not going to live with this sneaking and lying."

Wham! Jim's fist hits the table like he was trying to drive nails through it. "What I want to know is, who told you all this?"

I'm not going to tell him. I say he's the one that hid and lied and he has no business asking me anything. I say I'll tell him just what I want from now on and no more. The same as he treats me.

"It was Emory Holler, wa'n't it?" he says, chewing the words. "My fucking killer brother-in-law."

"At least he had the decency—"

"Decency!"

"Yes, decency. He told me so I wouldn't be wondering and worrying about what's happened to Gregory and why I wasn't seeing him anymore."

"You weren't seeing Gregory because you were his sworn enemy." Jim sticks his face across the table at me and grinds his teeth like he was chewing bone. "You're just lucky you weren't looking at him from the wrong end of a shotgun."

"That was you. That wasn't me. I don't believe Gregory hated me."

"Emory wouldn't tell you that, and he didn't tell you Gregory'd watched you over there."

"What's that supposed to mean?"

"You know what you did over there." He's out of his chair and over to the wall. "Maybe I should get out of here."

When he turns, I know I have to say something. I don't know how to explain it the way it happened, the natural way I felt. "It didn't have anything to do with money. Nothing happened, you know, because Emory's impotent."

"At least that's what Emory tells everybody."

The telephone rings, and he points to it. When I tell him it's someone asking for Mr. Hutchins, he whispers to say he's not here. "What's that about?" I ask him after I hang up. "More of your lies about Gregory?"

"I ain't got any friends who call me Mr. Hutchins. And right now I don't want to talk to anyone who isn't a friend."

JIM

At least at work I got answers when Frank starts harping at me. He says, "BB Eyes claims last time we changed his oil, it dripped on his driveway because we didn't tighten the drain plug."

"The problem is his pan's deformed." I don't tell him the pan's deformed because his boy, Gary, yarded that drain plug with an air wrench a couple of changes back instead of just installing a new plug. Ever since Tommy notched his nose, that boy's been madder than a bee in a bag. "I don't guess he'll want to pay for a new oil pan."

Up on the pole lift goes BB Eyes' car. I install a brand-new drain plug with a brand-new washer. I lower the car and pour in four quarts of premium oil. I raise the car. Frank steps underneath, wipes the pan with a rag, and waves the oil stain under my nose. You'd think he was a cop finding blood on the carpet. "I want everything as clean as a new toothbrush," Frank tells me.

When you've got something deformed, you've got to twist the torch on your creative flame. Teflon, that thin tape plumbers wrap on threads, forms a good seal. I stretch a couple of turns of the tape around those drain-plug threads, like a custom-fit condom, and don't it seal just as nice as pie.

"You get yourself in here, Frank Reed, and you run that crimestoppers cloth under this oil pan and tell me if you find even the idea of a leak."

He wipes. He wipes it twice, though he ain't waving that cloth around like a yellow flag. He tells me to clean out that oil container I drained the crankcase into so he can still sell it out front. I tell him it's a good thing he don't run a whorehouse.

"Why's that?" he asks.

" 'Cause you'd claim every one of them for a virgin, every time."

"When you make out that bill, put down three dollars and a half to install that Teflon tape."

"For what? You can rewrap that tape and sell it for new, even if it is short a couple of inches. It isn't the only thing around here that's—"

"For your time."

"Three dollars and fifty cents to wrap a piece of tape around a drain plug? That's crazy."

"That's what's wrong with you, Jim. You forget we're here to make money. At least I am."

"I could make this into a profession. At three-fifty a pop, I can wrap Teflon tape all day. I'll be a professional Teflon taper. Hell, for four dollars, I'll give them the color of their choice."

"Pass me that new roll of tape, before you get it all greasy."

I can't wait to see BB Eyes after he lays eyes on the bill for his oil change. He'll lose pounds just in sputtering.

Gregory's in the hospital three days, and I've just now thought to check out his place. Or what he claims for a place, because without that piece of paper he might just as well poke holes in his pockets. Using the key Malcolm kept, I unlock his gate and drive down the road. I'm happy that at least Gregory's out of the rain and getting a table set for him because I believe otherwise the boy would have starved to death, if he hadn't killed somebody first.

He never locks his door. Never put a lock on it, I guess, figuring the only people he worried about bothering him would be kept out by that locked gate. It's only when I open the door that I remember Dog. The animal is halfway to my throat when I see him. Before I can raise a foot to kick him, he's on my chest, and I'm flat on my back. Slobber and smell come off him like a bad rain. I fold my hands over my neck to protect myself. Dog drags his wet, coarse tongue across my face.

"Goddamn you," I say, getting up. Wagging his tail and scootching down his forequarters, he lolls his tongue like one of those poor retarded kids. "I guess you must be hungry."

I locate Gregory's cache of dog food cans and spin one open for Dog. He eats that in about two bites and whines for more, but I tell him to wait. He'll choke it down so fast, it'll just be puke on the floor a minute later. Of course I'll have to take him somewhere, either home or up to Malcolm's. Malcolm's always taking in strays of some kind. Besides, if I were to take Dog to my place, either Charley would scratch his eyes out or Buffy would chew his leg off. And that ain't saying a word about what Pauline would do to me.

I open Gregory's cooler and stench comes up like a hard right. A half-gallon carton of milk sitting in melted ice. By the way it smelled, that milk might have come from the cow that stepped off Noah's ark. I dump milk and water and moldy carton out back, leaving the top open on the cooler, and making sure Dog doesn't run out there and lick up that slop. Nature's most perfect food. Well, doesn't that just go to show you. There ain't a thing you can't spoil if you wait long enough. Thinking about that comes too close to home, so I head back inside.

There ain't much stuff to dig through. His tools won't go bad unless the roof leaks on them, which it won't. He's shingled that tight. I don't know what he's done with his clothes. Excepting a winter jacket and an old flannel shirt, which Dog made into a bed some time ago, there ain't a stitch around. I hope he don't need much to wear at the hospital. Right under his alarm clock, which naturally has run down, is his money, the bills all jumbled with ones next to a twenty, then a ten and a five and another twenty. If he was eating regular, he might have used the money for napkins. I'll get them into his bank account for him. Then I lay eyes on the damnedest thing. A videotape. Now what the hell would he be doing with a videotape? He don't own a VCR. He don't even have electricity.

Why they needed more than one look to call the boy crazy is beyond me. They tell me his knee will be all right. Just swollen and bruised is all. He may take that medication the rest of his life, but at least he'll have a life. He don't remember much, including me whacking him with that shovel, though it still ain't a good idea for Pauline to visit him. Nothing to upset him, the doctor says, until we get the medicine to working. I guess she must still be his sworn enemy. If he believes what he told me about her and Emory, I can see why that just made him crazier.

Pauline says it's grieving over poor little Elizabeth that drove him around the bend. And Lisa blames it on the hard way they were brought up. The doctor, he says it's just something screwed up in Gregory's brain. They can't fix it, but the medicine will allow it to work, like you keep adding oil to a worn motor and you don't run it too hard, and it'll last a good while. Even if you have to wrap the drain plug in Teflon tape.

I get out my glasses so I can read what's written on the videotape. It ain't a regular movie because the label bears handwriting. It ain't Gregory's writing, unless he changed that too. It says "Dancing," and right out loud I says, "Ain't that the damnedest thing. I never knew Gregory to take any interest in dancing."

I whistle Dog into the truck and run him up to Malcolm's. If Malcolm keeps him long enough, Dog'll be living in a house with combination windows and a sign over the doorway saying DOG. Not because Malcolm has to label every creature he owns but because every pet has his name on his house, like Guitar, the donkey, has GUITAR over his doorway. I call them pets, even if Malcolm's always correcting me and saying they're "farm animals." These "farm animals" lodge in better houses than a good many people I know. We just settle on calling them by their names, Guitar or SloMo; that seems to suit best all around anyway.

"We were looking for you," says Sergeant Dumont when he gets me in the cruiser. He ain't half so fat nor a quarter as friendly as BB Eyes. And since they made him sergeant instead of giving him a raise, he figures he's got to take the trim out of the sails of anybody who lives in town. "You're driving a vehicle with an expired inspection sticker."

You'd think since I inspect at least three vehicles a week, I could remember to slap a sticker onto my own truck. "I'm still within the grace period."

"No, you're not within any grace period." He gives that narrow mustache of his a stroke. "You're in my graces. For now. Let's see your driver's license, if you're carrying it."

Of course I'm carrying it. It's about the only thing I got to weigh my wallet down. Naturally, it's expired. Dumont doesn't need to look at it for more than a minute before he goes to buffing that lip caterpillar of his. He's on the mike calling it in, and I'm hearing talk coming back about bench warrants for my arrest. I'm afraid the sun is going to glare right off that mustache of his before we're through here, blinding motorists and causing accidents up and down this road. He says if those warrants are for me, he's going to have to cuff me and take me in to the station.

"That's good, because in about five more minutes I'm going to need a bathroom, which I know you got real handy down at the jail."

"This your right DOB?" He's pointing to something on my license I can't make out without my reading glasses. I tell him I can't see it. "Driving without corrective lenses," he says. He may wear those whiskers off his face before we're through here.

"What's DOB?"

"When were you born? You do know that, don't you?"

When I tell him, he calls it in over the mike. It turns out the bench warrants are for another James Hutchins. I didn't know there were two of us hard-luck guys in the state of New Hampshire. Maybe the other Jim's worse off than I am. God pity him. I notice Dumont ain't written anything down yet, so I wonder how long a chat we're going to have.

"Look, I got a wife to home crying about the kids twice a day. It's about all I can think about."

"Tend to this," he says, giving me back my license. "And get a sticker on that truck. You know I can make you leave it right here. That's what I should do, by law. It will pass inspection, won't it?"

"What were you looking for me for?"

"BB Eyes found something out to your place. You'd better get on home and see him."

I no more than slide behind the wheel of my truck, then Dumont's blue lights jab into my mirror. He pulls up beside me and yells out the window, "Let's be wearing those corrective lenses. At least do one thing right."

I don't need only reading glasses, and I don't need those to drive, but I'm not going to show Dumont my license again, so I slip on a pair of sunglasses Pauline left in the truck. The frames are blue and decorated with rhinestones. Dumont's smiling as I drive off.

BB Eyes is not smiling when I pull in my yard. "You selling your story to TV? Or have you just plain lost your mind?"

I yank Pauline's glasses off my face and fling them onto the seat. Sometimes that woman's need for beauty is worrisome. BB Eyes gives no chance to ask questions.

"We found another pair of pink panties, right here on your property."

"Maybe they belong to the other Jim Hutchins."

"You are nuts."

"Just a suggestion."

He's got to show them to me, the dirt- and scum-covered panties, like they were a prize rainbow trout he'd just landed. There ain't nothing pretty about them. There ain't nothing to excite the eyes or the heart. Sitting in the plastic bag, they look like something you might've washed a car with. I tell BB Eyes he might want to keep them to use as a rag for checking oil leaks.

"You don't seriously think I'm the panty pervert?" I look at those little dark eyes of his, but there ain't a hint of humor in them. Not a hint.

"Jim," says BB Eyes, holding the panties up like he expects me to grow a guilt-proving erection just from gazing at them, "when guys get hard up, they can turn to most anything. We had to take a citizen to emergency last month who got his dick stuck in a garden hose. It wasn't a new hose either. Ain't no law against it, but I'll tell you what. Cutting off that length of hose so's to fit him into the cruiser turned my stomach. I would've called the EMTs, only they won't handle drunks. Now I happen to know you got good reason to be hard up."

"How did you come to look on my land?"

"Telephone tip."

When I ask him, he tells me he doesn't know who made the call. Course BB Eyes ain't never been above lying. He says even though they got this fancy device that displays the number of the telephone the guy called from, it was a pay phone. They ain't running tests on the jism in the panties because the state lab doesn't run DNA tests. Nor the FBI either. Those labs wouldn't charge the town to do the tests, but for a case of this nature, BB Eyes would have to send "the sample," as he calls it, off to a private lab. Somewhere in Texas, he thinks.

"And they'd charge the town?"

"A thousand dollars, for starters. It wouldn't come up with no name on it. We'd have to pay for each sample, each time we tried to match a suspect. And we'd have to have reasonable cause or persuade the suspect to donate a sample voluntarily."

"Expensive," I say. "And messy to boot."

"Basically, the state considers this a case of petty burglary. That's why they're not trying to horn in. There ain't any glory in this case."

"It's about like catching a Peeping Tom."

"But it's progressive. People used to think that these guys are harmless, but for the past five years or so criminologists have been saying these crimes are progressive." He says not all people who smoke pot go on to use cocaine and heroine, but all cocaine and heroine users started drugs by smoking pot. "It's the same with these sex offenders. If we can find the guy, get him to confess, we can help him."

"And I thought you were just trying to keep the selectmen at bay." He says nothing back, which tells me I'm at least partly right. "If you're waiting for me to confess, you'll have them guinea hens roosting on your shoulders before you leave."

"Then you ought to think about who would set you up."

Inside the trailer I slide that videotape into the VCR and sit back to watch whatever's got Gregory's interest. I can tell you the thought of pink panties has worried my mind more than once, so I'll be relieved to see no stolen women's underwear. Relief ain't in it though. There's my Pauline shedding her clothes as she wriggles her fine woman flesh around Emory's den. I know I didn't take this video, nor can I imagine Gregory did, so I guess that leaves my brother-in-law. The son of a bitch who told me he was impotent. I wondered at the time why a man would tell such a thing on himself, but I ain't got to think about it anymore. I understand it completely now.

She's moving her naked self around on the television as sexy as can be. The tears are starting. I don't leave it on to watch the real dirty parts.

11

eleven

PAULINE

Jim wants to think I'm a whore, believing I have sex with Emory, and Emory gives me money for it. I don't know why but men will choose to believe anything that'll make them unhappy. And now here's poor Gregory doing the same thing, while inwardly dwelling on poor Elizabeth's death, just dwelling on it, as if he could have saved her. I swear that's what eats the poor boy and makes him hate so. No matter how many times I told him, Jim told him, even Lisa and Tommy told him, that he'd done all anybody could to save her, he still blames himself for failing to bring her back to life. Just like Jim is blaming himself for failing and for the kids' failures, which is why he's so mad, and why he wants to believe the worst about me and Emory.

Gregory couldn't have seen anything except my car parked at

Emory's, so he must have exaggerated. Now Jim exaggerates, just like all men when it comes to sex because they always have to exaggerate, making it better or worse. Besides, I never ask Emory for money. I just tell him what's needing, and he gives whether I dance for him or not. Usually I do dance for him, but that's because I like to dance for him. The only time Jim would sit still long enough to watch something would be something on TV. If I was naked, he wouldn't want to watch me dance; he'd just want to go right to loving. Course Emory can't, which is another reason I like to dance for him.

"Do you?" he asks.

"Of course," I say, looking at him sitting in his chair and wearing his bathrobe as if he's getting over some illness, "why else would I do it?"

Sometimes I put on a tape, like his old Herb Alpert tape, maybe play "A Taste of Honey," but often, like today, I want to move to my own rhythms, so I don't use any music. Emory watches everything I do, his eyes as full of excitement as the rest of him is empty of it. I asked him why he didn't go to a doctor about it, and he said he did. One gave him tranquilizers to stop him thinking about sex, and the other told him to talk about Helen's death. As if that would help me, he said, the very thing I'm trying to forget. So I dance for him bringing him happiness he says he can't find anywhere else. And we never talk about the lie I told BB Eyes and the insurance investigator about Helen's death.

As I move my body, I check his eyes, noticing which moves please him, which keep me in charge here. I know a tilt of my hips and a half spin makes him breathe faster. I can almost feel his breath. My blouse I take off in front of him, but I turn to undo my bra so I can surprise him when I bring my bare breasts to his eyes.

When I started dancing for him, I didn't take off my clothes, none of them, but after a couple of times I knew he'd never try to touch me. I knew I was safe. At first I just bared my chest, but when I saw how that pleased him, I went the whole way naked. In a funny way it's easier to dance that way, nothing holding you, hiding you, just you, free to turn, bend, twist, move in any way you want to. His eyes are applauding me. He is my captive audience.

I know it's selfish, but I dread the day he gets back his potency because after that I won't be able to dance for him. It wouldn't be fair to get him all aroused and not let him touch me.

I slide out of my panties, knowing it won't be long before he reaches the emotional climax he says substitutes for the other. I know I am in charge here as I see him shift in his chair, so I turn slowly, letting my hands graze over my skin, not quite touching myself, gently stroking, the way a perfect lover would caress me. My rhythms beating on their own, I am in charge of this whole room. Emory's eyes are full of me. My body enters his brain. His eyelids fall, fall, fall, and close. I am done.

As I dress, he offers me a beer, as he usually does, his little joke, knowing I'll refuse. Of course, he brings me the iced tea without my even asking for it. Could this thoughtful man have murdered Helen? Right after her death, people called me a liar and him a killer, which preys on his mind as much as grief for her death. Grief for Elizabeth still lives in me and darkens my days, but not guilt like Gregory feels, not horror over the gossip like Emory suffers. Helen fell down the stairs and broke her neck because her knees weren't good, and anyone who really knew her knew that. Course Emory came into that money, but it's not like he was planning to run off to California or someplace. It comes back to the same thing, people want to think the worst all the time.

Emory too is dressed, wearing his clothes from the Town Laundry because he says he never could get the hang of washing clothes.

"I hear BB Eyes found panties on your property," he says.

"They weren't mine, but maybe they'll take Jim's mind off me for a while."

"Is he threatening you?"

"He doubts you're impotent."

"Wish I could doubt it." The air goes pink with sadness. "I told him about it long before you started coming here."

"He thinks you lied. He lied to me about sending Gregory to the hospital, now he accuses us of lying." I feel funny saying "us," but Emory doesn't notice it.

He tips his beer up like he's a teenager showing off. "Next time would you mind if I videotaped your dancing?"

I didn't like it when he made the tape before because I imagined him sitting with his remote, going over certain parts, like he does with those X-rated movies of his, and he'd be the one in charge. "Are you tired of the one you made before?"

He lights a cigarette. "I know it's got to be in the house somewhere, but I just can't lay my hands on it."

"I hope you haven't left it out somewhere. If I thought Scooter—or anyone besides you—was watching the tape—" I gulp my iced tea. "You don't think Jim—"

"He hasn't been here in over a month. No one's broke in. Besides, I keep the tape in my bedroom closet. What would he be doing there? I must have just set it down somewhere. I shouldn't have told you. I've just upset you."

"Don't say that. Don't ever keep things from me. That's just what Jim did with Gregory, and I hate him for it."

He finishes his beer, crunches the can, and goes to look for the tape. It's beautiful in this den with everything clean, and everything working, everything clean because Emory has it cleaned. The cleaning woman!

"She never comes in here," says Emory, showing me this closet with Helen's jewel box.

The bedroom with its canopy bed and gleaming bureaus is so beautiful I just have to lie back on the bed, which is the most comfortable bed I've ever lain on. Emory has this all to himself. He lies down beside me, our faces so close I can feel his whiskers, though they aren't actually touching me.

If Jim took the tape, he wouldn't just be suspicious, he'd know, but he'd know I was only dancing. I tell Emory I've got to get home because we're going to move Lisa to her new apartment.

"That goddamn Frank Reed threw her out!" Emory's leaning on his elbow and looking at my face the same way he watches my body when I dance. "Christ, Jim works for him."

"He's letting her move into his other building, farther off Main Street." I run my fingers up the flesh of his forearm, heavier than Jim's, not so veiny. He offers me money for her rent, and I take it because I had to scrimp to come up with the security deposit. The rent itself ain't much because the housing authority takes care of most of it.

As we're packing, I'm trying to cheer Jim because he looks like somebody stepped on his tail. "Lisa's going to keep this new apartment just as nice as if she owned it," I say.

"Lisa's trouble ain't keeping an apartment nice. The trouble with Lisa is keeping an apartment at all."

We've just loaded Lisa's couch onto the truck when Penny shows up, Aaron in one hand and a cigarette in the other. I bought them a perfectly good little stroller, but she'd rather walk over here looking like the slut she is.

"I haven't seen Tommy lately," she says.

"I ain't seen him either," says Jim, "but that's because there's work to be done."

"Tommy never shirked any work," I say, because I won't have him bad-mouth one of my children to this slut. Bad enough he's put poor Gregory in the State Hospital.

"Well, he's shirking on his payments." Penny says she hasn't received so much as diaper money from Tommy in over a week. He hasn't even shown up.

Of course I know that because I sent Tommy down to my grandfather's in the city to keep him out of town. If he gets somewhere he doesn't have the ugly reputation, and the police aren't constantly watching him, and bad companions don't lie around like rabbit snares, then the boy might have a chance in life. I don't want him going into court with more charges hanging off like tags at a yard sale.

"He'd better show up soon," says Penny, and she shifts little Aaron on her hip like he was a bag of groceries she'd like to set down. After a drag on her cigarette, she uses it as a pointer at Jim. "One way or another, I've got to have some money."

"Get it out of the Hollers," Jim says, slamming up the tailgate, "whichever one you're fucking this week."

"That's crude," Penny says. "I don't need to talk crude. Maybe I just need to drop Aaron off at your place and let you take care of him and pay for him. And Tommy ain't the only one who can talk to lawyers."

I'd like to sue her, sue her for all the pain eating away at Tommy's heart. All his drinking, and the ramming that comes with it, I lay right at her door. Jim don't go along with me because he can't blame her for all Tommy's wrong, but I say she's caused more than half, so she can claim it all. Without her, Tommy'd never have to slink. It's that slinking turns him bad.

"You want a ride?" Jim asks Penny. But she turns it down, probably because she's on the prowl. That's what I tell Jim as we leave for Lisa's new apartment.

"You know," he says, "if Tommy stays disappeared, maybe Lisa'll have a chance of keeping this apartment."

Just because Tommy's gone doesn't mean the boy's slipped all the trouble in the world. He may still need help. "You don't know where Tommy is or what hurts he may have, so that sets your mind to rest."

He tells me he's worrying about losing the load. "Right now that outboard chair disappeared from my mirror." But of course he keeps on driving as if he won't be satisfied until Lisa's furniture bounces right out onto the public road.

"Stop the truck and give me that tie-down." By the time I've set the hooks in the truck's side panel, I feel like walking home, getting in my car, and driving down to the city to see Tommy. For once Jim senses something wrong because he's out of the truck.

"I been thinking that with Tommy gone, life for us might settle down to an off-and-on rain instead of a constant hurricane," he says. "That's all."

"That's just the trouble with you. You want to blame Tommy for all your troubles. You want the children's lives to be no more bother to you than a mirror. Well, mister, your life wasn't like that, and you've no right expecting theirs to be. You think you stopped being their father when they turned twenty-one?" I step away from the truck. I don't know where I'm going right now, just away. His hand isn't hard, but it stops me.

"The trouble with me is I'm about scraped to sore and oozing with being told what the trouble with me is." I'm watching his eyes watch mine. "You know where Tommy is, don't you."

As I'm telling him, blue lights flash the arrival of BB Eyes and the patrol car. He pulls up tight behind the truck and leaves those staring lights on. "Least he doesn't have his gun drawn," I tell Jim as BB Eyes tugs himself out from behind the wheel.

"You find more scummy underwear?" Jim asks.

"Doing my duty protecting a broken-down motorist from traffic. Regulations," says BB Eyes. He rubs his hands across his belly. "Heard a word I like today. *Portly*. Ever heard it? I prefer it to *fat*. Asking all my friends to become familiar with it, drop it into their regular conversation. 'A portly gentleman.' That's what my lawyer calls me. Now Tommy ain't the only one in town with a lawyer. Speaking of Tommy, I heard he's gone."

"Everyone's talking to lawyers," I say.

"Being out on bail," says BB Eyes, "Tommy has responsibilities."

"You know he don't live with me," Jim says. I wait for him to say more, to name city and street where Tommy can be found. "I'd think you'd be happy he's not in town."

"If he's left the state, we'll have to prosecute him as a fugitive."

If Jim tells BB Eyes where Tommy is, I'll walk right now. "You're saying you'd spend taxpayer money to bring him back to the state of New Hampshire," Jim says, "then you'd put him up in prison at state expense?"

BB Eyes sets his hands on his hips, one right above his gun. "About the same time I'll believe you don't know where he is."

"I ain't broke down here, BB Eyes," Jim says, "just had to fix a bungee."

"Maybe I should follow you, to see you get this stuff moved safely."

"Maybe you should," I say, and move toward the cab, "and help unload too."

"That might be too much kindness," BB Eyes says. "Don't forget 'a portly gentleman.' "

He follows us a block, with the blue lights off, then turns

around. It's a good thing he does, because when we get to Lisa's, there's Tommy himself.

JIM

I've got to make some money today, so I head off to Malcolm's to put in some hours for the IRS. On the way I stop at my shed where I've tucked that videotape in the grain sack. Maybe the rat'll eat it. I'm feeling miserable.

I'm sitting here, hoping my legs will stay attached. Something bites its way into every sore spot in my stomach. I ain't prayed since I was a kid, but I get down on my knees. I don't know what to ask for. Bring Pauline back to me? Give me money? Straighten my kids out? "Jesus Christ, damn it all to hell. Just take some of this fucking pain away."

Out the window I see the peacock striding across the yard, and even he doesn't feel like fanning his tail. I smell sorrow, like I remember from Pauline after Elizabeth died. On the first day she woke up and knew Elizabeth was never going to be in the house again, the red left her heart. I tried to keep things going, but I didn't know what to do. Now she's perking up, but she's like a different person. And it's a person that ain't got much use for me. Shuddering and leaking, I think about Gregory's gun. I could lie down on the bed, stretch the gun out the length of my body, and use my toes. I don't like thinking of beds right now. It's like rubbing my own nose right in it. It's time to get to Malcolm's.

"Do you pray, Malcolm?" I ask him.

I don't know how Malcolm does with sadness, but I do know he don't have any trouble letting mad out. Mad comes out of Malcolm on its own accord. "Not often," he says.

I'm a little later than usual, so he's made the coffee, which is outrageously foul. It's finishing up whatever's left of my stomach. "What do you ask for?" I say.

"It ain't exactly prayer."

"You pray to God?"

"Once in a while I get brave enough to ask for help. I guess that's about what God is."

But it ain't God that's replacing the headlight on the 'dozer. "What d'you run into?" I ask him.

"I took a wrench to it. Son of a bitch wouldn't start." He punched them both out, after the ether spraying didn't work. Malcolm's mad leaks out fine.

Malcolm's got me replacing a couple of clapboards the Great Dane has destructed off the house, and that damned donkey Guitar bites at my shoulder. Gnaw, gnaw, and I give him a push. Gnaw, gnaw, and another push. Now these ain't love bites either. Babies is what these donkeys of his are, damn nasty babies.

Malcolm goes in the house to call this high-priced carpenter who's going to help us install a cupola up on the garage. For what I can't imagine.

Back comes Guitar for another chaw on my carrot-shoulder, so I turn right around and smack him in the snoot. That backs him off until Malcolm returns to ping a final row of nails into a clapboard. Nails are flying through the air. Oh, boy, don't that make that donkey mad. He bites right into Malcolm's pants and drags him out into the yard until he tears the seat right out of them pants.

"Now, what d'you suppose ails him today?"

I shrug my shoulders by way of a lie. It feels good, this little lie, I've been surrounded by such big ones.

"Put him in his house, Jim," says Malcolm, heading for his house and a fresh set of trousers. "He ain't fit company today."

So I lead that big donkey (he must go better than a quarter

ton) over to his house, with his name over the door, and I ask him would he like one of his combination windows opened. His big brown eyes ask me if I'd like a kick in the ass. I leave him and help Malcolm set up the ladder between Guitar's house and the garage.

The high-priced carpenter and I get the cupola on the roof. "What I'd like to know is what kind of operation is this?" the carpenter asks me. "What is your position here? Just what is it you do?"

I figure he'd like to edge me out of my job, so I answer him right up. "Look, Malcolm pays for things, that's what he does, and when I notice any of you fellas slack of work, I find something for you to do. I keep you guys in work. You notice you've had a lot of work since I took up with Malcolm?"

"Yes, I have."

"I do that, and I follow Malcolm around and make him ugly. That's the drastic part of the job."

Malcolm's happy enough with the position of the cupola to come up and see can he jam a few nails in it. Time he reaches us, he figures out he's left the box of galvanized nails behind, so he sends me to get them. When I near the edge of the roof, I see that's all that's there, just the edge of the roof. Down on the ground lies the ladder like some kind of victim. And standing by it is Guitar, looking sassy and generally pleased with himself.

"Malcolm," I call up to the peak, "did you want to test my jumping abilities today?"

By the time he rouses himself over to see the fix we're in, Guitar has taken to kicking the fallen ladder. "He don't like anything foreign in his yard," Malcolm says, kind of philosophical.

"I know just how he feels," I say, and head for the top of the roof.

"Where are you going?"

"I want a good look at Bernice when she sees us up here."

I get a good look too. She's still laughing when she comes out of the house.

Bernice, she points up at us with one hand and covers her laughing mouth with the other. For the first time in my life I wonder if Pauline would help me if she found me in a fix like this. I guess she would. I've never known her to be mean. Course, I never knew her to dance naked neither. And I think she's got years and years to surprise me yet. Her mother's still alive, despite smoking and drinking and weighing about the heft of a year-old workhorse. And her mother's father is still alive, registering a level ninety. He lives in the city.

I don't remember a lot of surprises in our early days, except when Pauline turned up pregnant. Life was hard and sweet, and I figured that was what it was supposed to be, if there was any supposed to in it. I had to sit down with pencil and paper to figure if I could afford to move out of my room and into an apartment with Pauline. Pumping gas, replacing mufflers, tune-ups (which in those days meant points, rotor, and condenser on top of plugs and timing), all brought me a buck and a half an hour. So I started putting in an extra half day Saturdays, strictly mechanic work, no gas, for time and a half. Then I could afford the apartment.

First we had to get married. The landlady wouldn't let us move in unless we were married. I know you, Jim Hutchins, she said, and I know you ain't married. Matter of fact I don't know but one reason why anyone would marry you, she said. Course, she was right there. Pauline had started to show. She wouldn't be able to keep her job at the laundry much longer, so money would get tight before it'd get better. And I was trying to set aside money for Gregory's birth because naturally we didn't have any health insurance in those days. My sister helped us. And Pauline's pa would always lend a hand getting furniture, even if it was stole.

You didn't want to ask his help building or painting or anything, but he could come into possession of more stuff than two honest men could work for. Practically steal to color, though size befuddled him. Once he brought us down a yellow refrigerator that wouldn't fit under the cabinets. It didn't really surprise me. What surprised me was that he was sober enough to drive it to us.

I didn't drink much in those days. Later, when we spent a spell living amongst Pauline's family, I started matching Pa bottle for bottle. That was a disaster. We both lay in the same trough for a while. Now he's dead. Been dead. When you're young like Pauline and me were, you never think you're going to have to go through deaths. Going through births was hard enough.

Malcolm says he's getting rid of Guitar. He's put an ad in the *Buy or Sell* for him at two hundred dollars and listed my phone number. "I don't want a lot of lunkheads pestering me with foolish questions and trying to arrange for free donkey rides for their brats. I been down that road before."

"You don't mind if I charge them for the rides?" I ask him. "All the lunkheads that call my house?"

When I get home, there's not much talk between Pauline and me. I make coffee for myself, but I ain't got any appetite. I sure don't have any appetite to talk about that videotape. I don't even turn on the TV. I'm sitting here watching the fish make slow turns in the tank, thinking of Gregory reaching in and popping one in his mouth. After a while I begin to understand how he could do that. Then the telephone rings. I think it's somebody calling after that damn donkey Malcolm's selling, but it ain't.

"Is the Criminal there?" says this woman's voice.

"Criminal?"

"Criminal. Thomas Hutchins," she says like she's explaining addition to a grown person. "You got any other criminals there?"

That ain't anything I want to talk about over the telephone, so

I just say, "To tell the truth, ma'am, Tommy don't live here. Hasn't for some time now."

"The Criminal isn't there, then?"

Now I don't know who I'm talking to, bail officer, welfare, or what. "I don't even care to know where Tommy is." Pauline looks at me like she'd gladly put a little rat poison in my coffee.

"I suppose you'll claim not to know what he's doing either."

"To tell you to the truth, ma'am, I really don't."

"You're a fine father, do you know that?" Her voice ain't getting louder, but if it were next to lumber, it'd make short work of a two-by-four. "Do you think you're a fine father? Or any kind of a father at all?"

"You understand he don't live with me. Now if you'll pardon me, who am I talking to and what is this all about?" I'm hoping she's got the wrong Hutchins family or the wrong Tommy, only she don't.

It's Alice Jewell, and the mad in her voice disguised it. Tommy's been feeding liquor to underage kids. Her daughter, Mary Beth, threw up last night from all the booze—*and whatever else*—the Criminal gave her, and Alice Jewell is sure Tommy isn't giving away anything out of the goodness of his heart. And she knows Mary Beth doesn't have any money to pay the Criminal with, but she is also sure there are other kinds of payment.

"You're his father," she says like she's a judge handing down a sentence.

Of course I can sympathize with the woman. You don't have to tell me twice it's hard raising kids, but Tommy's seen eighteen come and go. And twenty-one too. "I'm sorry, but I didn't know nothing about it."

"If you're not going to do anything about it, the police will," she says, her voice sharp and pointy again. She slams down the phone.

"Alice Jewell has peddled her ass more than once," says Pauline after I tell her about the conversation. "She needn't stick her nose up in the air at our Tommy."

I say I thought she and Alice were friends, good friends. Now I know she's got a better friend in Emory. Course I don't say that. I say, "I don't guess anyone Alice Jewell slept with was under-age."

"You know why she's threatening with the police?" Pauline says. "She's been carrying on with Sergeant Dumont, who happens to be her landlord, and whose wife doesn't know that Alice is paying her rent on her back. She even bragged to me about it."

I say I'll warn Tommy about it. Pauline says the police will have another cause to hound Tommy. Course I don't think they were looking for any extra, but I keep still. I let her rant. Again I say I'll speak to Tommy.

"You warn him," says Pauline. "That's just what you do. You warn him." She's throwing a can of tomato soup into a pot along with a can of chicken soup. It just about turns my stomach to watch her. It's a recipe she got from Lisa, who learned it from Fesmire. I'm about to tell her to take my portion over to Emory Holler when I get the chance to have that talk with Tommy after all. Lisa calls her mother and says Tommy and Scooter Holler are down to her new apartment drunk with a couple of underage girls. One of the girls is out of her head on drugs.

"That wouldn't be Mary Beth Jewell?" I ask Pauline.

"No, that's the other one."

Tommy must know the sound of my truck because I haven't switched off the motor before I see him dive through the open window on the side porch and take a header over the railing.

"Tommy," I yell, "pull your pants up." And that's all there is of my warning. At least I did warn him. Yanking on his pants and running across the yard, Tommy looks like he might make Massachusetts before morning. I ain't chasing Tommy. What would I do if I caught him?

In the apartment sits Scooter Holler so drunk he can't yell above a normal voice. There's a tall queen with dark ringlets talking to Lisa so fast I figure she's got to be repeating herself about every five minutes. So that leaves Mary Beth Jewell, who's looking out the window Tommy left by as if she expects to see a comet or something. When I tell them to leave, she turns her lumpy, rumpy self around and tells me to fuck myself.

I figure she's feeling out of sorts because her honey just took off. I tell them again to clear out of the place. I'm thinking I got up early this morning to move Lisa over here because she lost her last place over just this kind of raccoon wildness, and there doesn't want to be anybody thinking I'm looking forward to getting up early tomorrow morning to move her to another apartment. I'm losing money on this deal all the way around. Besides, Frank Reed don't own enough buildings to keep this game running indefinitely.

"I'll leave when I'm good and ready," says Scooter Holler, more to the two girls than to me, "and I ain't either." He lolls back against the couch and slides a hand up the dark-haired beauty's leg. So much for his love and devotion for Squatty Body. Maybe there's good to come out of this yet. Scooter sees I'm still standing here. He rolls himself up to a sitting position so he can puff out his chest and jostle his shoulders to remind me he's bigger and stronger and younger than I am.

"Why don't you just leave us alone," says Scooter.

"You're all drunk, and I'm sober. If I go out to my truck for my tire iron, there'll be some bloody heads in here, and none of them will be mine."

Scooter stands and tries to make a fist, which is like trying to pick up a rotted tomato. I head right out to the yard, pretty sure they'll follow. I grip the tire iron before I turn around. Any fracas I want out here. The tire iron calls my arm to swing it. Out comes Scooter to give me a hassle with the two girls for audience. Lisa slams and locks the door behind them. She can be smart when she wants to.

I wish they had run like Tommy, all the way to Massachusetts or down to the city, out of my sight. I wish they'd run now. I'm tired like I used to get tired plowing roads for the town twenty-four hours straight after a big storm.

"Look, I'll drive you down to the end of the Dingley Road, past where Two Captains Road turns to dirt. You can hoot and holler there all night."

"No, dude," says Scooter, "we ain't decided where we're going next, but it ain't going to be no barren puckerbrush."

He just sits on the ground. Somewhere in his brain lies the knowledge that they've left their booze and dope in Lisa's apartment. If I leave them here, they'll be back inside if they have to break windows. Sliding through broken glass won't even slow them down.

It's late. Even my toes are tired. I'm tired of Scooter and these girls. I'd just as soon kill the lot of them. "Okay, I was young, and I've been hassled by the police, but I will call them if you won't leave. I'm telling you a ride to the Dingley Road is a better deal than a ride to the cop station." I'm looking at Scooter with those two drunk underage girls and thinking I ought to just call the cops and stop giving them chances.

"You can't tell us what to do," he says. "You can't even tell your own wife what to do."

I hit him. The tire iron mashes right into his back, then upper arm. He's rolling, and I know the next swing will take his god-damn head off. The tire iron sings to me. At the end of my arm it flows in a sweet and right arc, back, back, then forward to smack into his pumpkin head. I expect to see cracked orange flesh. He ducks. The dark-haired queen helps him up over the tailgate. He's holding his arm like it might fall off if he let go. I use the tire iron to point Mary Beth to the cab.

The minute I get in next to her, Mary Beth says, "If you start that motor, I'll scream rape."

Now, I'm hard-core. "Go ahead and scream, but you'll find out you ain't dealing with a dud here. You scream rape, and I'll mash your head in. When the cops come, you won't even know what rape is." She sits next to me with her arms folded over her chest and taking big, slow breaths.

It's dark and wet at the end of the Dingley Road, but it ain't near any water. I guess they'll be safe enough. Through the open window I can hear them hooting and hollering nearly a half mile down the road. I'm going to call Alice Jewell when I get home to tell her where her precious child is tonight, but first I stop back at Lisa's just on a hunch. And sure enough, there's Tommy.

12

twelve

TOMMY

I don't want to talk to cops right now," I tell Father. Lisa's gone to bed, which is what I want to do because I've been up since three o'clock this morning when the city cops knocked and entered. Luckily the stash and me slept in the back bedroom, for safekeeping, as Grampy said, so I slid out the window and down over the shed roof. I'd've taken Uncle's car, only I didn't need to be picked up with a paper bag full of pot.

"I don't get the attraction to Mary Beth," Father says. "Alice says she'll go to the cops."

"The bitch has probably told her boyfriend Dumont already." I bum a cigarette from him because if we're going to sit up half the night, we might as well smoke. "Don't worry, Mary Beth'll never testify against me, and they ain't going to catch me with my dick out."

Father's spraddled in the stuffed chair, barely smoking his cigarette, like he only lit it up for politeness. Father's getting old. "To tell you the truth I was more worried about what you were doing with Mary Beth Jewell when I thought you had the heartache for Penny." Now he takes a quick drag and spits out smoke like he didn't want it to linger. "What, are you and Scooter Holler pals again? I'd think that was like kissing the rattlesnake that bit you."

"Scooter and I been friends a long time." And family too, though I don't bring that up. "Penny wasn't worth fighting over." I wonder he don't raise Emory. I wonder how much he knows about Momma.

"Don't forget you got a little boy lives with Penny."

"Penny'll take care of Aaron. Aaron's her meal ticket."

"She thinks you're her meal ticket, and she won't go to the cops like Alice Jewell did. She'll go to welfare."

"Lisa never got very far hauling money out of Fesmire. I guess I'm at least as smart as him."

"Ain't nobody got money out of Fesmire." Father stubs out his Camel. Damn short smoke if you ask me, hardly worth the puffing, but that's the way Father likes them. He grinds his butt in Lisa's ashtray, then he asks me about Emory Holler. He asks me if Scooter ever says anything about Momma going over there. He asks me if Emory's gone down to Boston to take a cure for his impotence.

"Scooter don't talk much about his father," I say.

"Yeah, well, the little asshole had something to say about your mother. If it was my mother he talked that way about, I'd take a couple of years out of his life and make him wish I'd taken them all."

"Father, don't tell BB Eyes you saw me."

"I ain't the one who fucks up this family," he says, and out the door he goes.

I wish I could rely on him, but after Penny I don't rely on anybody. Besides, Father's so roaring pissed-off over Emory and Scooter, he might trade me in to BB Eyes if he figured the cops could do something to the Hollers. Not that that's very fucking likely. Anyways, it probably ain't safe for me to spend the night here, and it for sure ain't safe for my stash to spend the night here. Good stuff, Uncle said, no stems, no shit. So, paper bag with two big Ziplocs under my coat, I walk along as innocent as if I were going to grade school.

Back in fourth grade I had this teacher, Miss Hamblett, who liked my art. Up until then I hadn't gotten into trouble much, but I hadn't seen many smiles from teachers either. Miss Hamblett taught us all about hawks, their migrations and hunting and even the different types, like buteos, and took us out for a "hawk watch," where we got to sit in this open field instead of being all shut up in school all day. She was real taken with this hawk I drew. I chose a peregrine falcon because it has the most interesting face of all the hawks, like a mask, and it's the fastest. I drew speed lines as it dove on a goldfinch. Miss Hamblett asked me why I drew a goldfinch as prey, and I told her I read that the peregrine falcon fed on other birds. That's why it's useless and mean, Kari Reed said. Miss Hamblett shushed her and told the class how beautiful my drawing was.

Miss Hamblett was a short, roundish, young teacher, and even the next year in fifth grade when I didn't have her for a teacher anymore, she'd tell me to stop in her classroom and show her my drawings. I would sometimes. I told her that drawing the falcon was easy because I copied it from a book in the library, but she said just doing the drawing proved I had artistic talent. I liked her. I also got the hots for her. I used to beat my meat thinking of her. That's the most school ever meant to me. I should look her up someday if she's still around. She was still teaching at the elementary school when Elizabeth was in fourth grade because Elizabeth said Miss Hamblett told her about my peregrine falcon drawing. Course Elizabeth always did well in school. Girls got it a lot easier with teachers. Except Miss Hamblett. She was fair.

It's a long walk out here, and I'm out of cigarettes. I hope there'll be some when I get there, or I'll have to smoke some of this weed.

Who am I to be seeing a nice person like Miss Hamblett? A dope-dealing hard case, a brawler with cops, living by my wits. It's a different world from what she lives in. I still like art. If I had my airbrush, I could make designs. I could probably make a good living doing vans and pickups. Then Miss Hamblett could be proud of me. I could go to her house and tell her I'll put anything she wants on her car. Free. And I know she won't pick out some cartoon foolishness or some tired old cliché scene so wornout they won't even use it in advertisements: The Lighthouse, The Mountain, The Red Barn, The Sunset. Miss Hamblett's not sappy. No teddy bears with pink ribbons like the geezer bikers stick on their reconditioned Harleys. Maybe she'd like that peregrine falcon.

Too bad we're in different worlds. As it is, she probably wouldn't even speak to me. I come up to her door with a six-pack and some weed, she'd be on the phone to the cops. As soon as she locked the door. I'll bet she doesn't even know who I am anymore.

Gregory ain't got a lot of hiding places here, but at least there's a pack of cigarettes. And they're filtered. You go to jail now, you can't smoke. On top of your sentence, you get a nicotine fit. I suck down a good drag and look for a place to hide my stash. Under the bed's too obvious. There ain't a bureau or a cabinet in here. You'd think Gregory was a hermit the way he's laid this place out. Used to be cartons of dog food, but I guess Father took them when he took Dog up to Malcolm Hurd's. Good old practical Father. Down to Lisa's busting up a party while Momma, his own wife, puts in her party time with Emory Holler. Everybody suffers.

There's no paneling or wallboard to slip my stash behind. Naturally Gregory ain't insulated this place because cold weather won't set in for another couple of months. No, Gregory won't insulate until November, if he's out of the hospital by then, and if Emory ain't claimed back this property, but Gregory will insulate, and he'll caulk the windows because he's a frugal guy, a tree-hugging woodsman, if you can have such a thing. Trees growing practically out of his plate, but he won't cut one down unless he needs it—for fuel or to sell.

Except that shade tree he cut down by the hospital when Elizabeth died. That had been me, I'd've done jail time for that. Disturbing the peace, malicious mischief, destruction of property, causing a riot, interference with interstate communications. They'd've thrown that in because one of the branches took out the television cable. Think of that, rich people in that neighborhood deprived of *Masterpiece* fucking *Theater* half the night because a regular guy went off his nut with grief. BB Eyes must've fixed it up with the cable company. I know if it'd been me, I'd've had to pay some guy forty dollars an hour to relink the broken cable. But that's all right. Gregory had enough trouble. Still does. For all his honesty, about all he's got is this place, which Emory may very well steal out from under him, and a collection of sorry-looking chain saws. I know for a fact that pitiful-looking red Homelite sitting by the woodbox ain't run in years. They likely don't even manufacture parts for it anymore.

But good old Gregory drained the fuel tank. Of course he did, the frugal, thorough son of a bitch, so the gas wouldn't varnish up and clog fuel line and carb. Father taught us that years ago, and whatever Gregory learns, he does. Gregory has even left the cap loose so as not to trap any gasoline vapors in the tank. No wonder I wind up in jail and he winds up in the home for the sanity-challenged.

I can't smell gasoline from the tank. I fold the bag carefully, watching that the Ziploc doesn't unseal, and slide it into the Homelite's tank. I screw the cap back on and, just like Gregory, leave it a little loose. That's the way I like things, a little loose. There's still the other bag to hide. It won't be a big deal if I get picked up with a baggie, but with my stash on me, they'll charge me for dealing. They'd just love that.

It's a cinch I'm not going to put it under his mattress or someplace dumb like that. After all, it ain't only cops I'm hiding it from. Who knows who else will come in here. Gregory ain't even put a lock on his door. He did polyurethane the door so it wouldn't weather. Over in the corner sit a couple of cans of poly and a can of enamel. One of the poly cans is practically empty, the stuff at the bottom having plasticized. Just as Father taught him, Gregory punched nail holes along the rim of the can to let the poly from brush wipes drip back into the can. I'll bet Gregory's never gotten laid because Father didn't teach him how to do it.

A couple of smacks with the heel of my hand seals the lid down tight. I wish I had something to eat. I'll have to go buy something after I take a nap. I'm tireder than I am hungry. This mattress of Gregory's wouldn't win any prizes at the Inn Keepers convention, but it's a hell of a lot more comfortable than the metal bunk and blanket at the jail cell.

I wish Mary Beth were lying here with me. She is so soft. The skin on her face feels as smooth as the lovely skin on the bottom of her breasts. I know their nipples carry the most sensitivity, but the underpart of women's breasts always seems the most delicate to me. Her whole body just heats up when I kiss her. And her telling me that excites me.

Not like Penny. She couldn't ever tell me anything. Oh, she'd always do it, but, hell, she'd do it with someone else if I weren't around. She wouldn't talk about how she felt. She sure didn't go out of her way to make me feel good. Her tits don't have that special softness like Mary Beth's. Course I'd never tell Penny that. Scooter, he told her that, even if it weren't true, just for laughs. He said he'd tell her her tits were covered with green moss, only she could see he was lying. He said he told her that her asshole was crooked. Asked her if she was part Japanese. I told him that was bullshit about Japanese women having slanted twats. He said he didn't care. He figured it made his lie about Penny's asshole more believable.

Course I got to deal with Penny still because of Aaron. I told Mary Beth I couldn't respect a man who abandons his children. That's what Fesmire's done, as far as I can see. Whether or not he believes Alison is his, he knows Rebecca and Seth are. And he married Lisa. He's their legal father. I could never abandon Aaron. I know I'll have to deal with that cheating slut until he's eighteen unless she gives him up. Then she can come visit him at my convenience. Naturally she won't do that because she won't want to lose that AFDC check.

Cold. Hard. Pressure, pinch, pain on my ear. I swing on it, and it goes away. Ear burns. Funny dream. Pain again. "Fucking Christ," I say. I try to throw a quick hand to grab, but it slips away.

"The Criminal. Wake up, Criminal."

Mary Beth's mother, I know the voice before I open my eyes, know the bitch as well as I know I ain't dreaming. "Alice Jewell, you taking up housebreaking?"

"Citizen's arrest, Criminal." She's holding a pistol on me. It's an automatic, a small automatic, but it would do the job. She ain't got Emory's sense of humor, so I'm not going to try to take it away from her right now. I wish I had Gregory's shotgun. I'd blow this woman's head off her shoulders, then she could make a headless citizen's arrest.

"I got to take a piss. Can't arrest that first thing in the morning."

"If you didn't drink all night, you wouldn't have that trouble either. Criminal." She's as tall as me and might go a hundred and sixty, heavy in the butt and shoulders. She worked at an Agway, so I know she can heft a grain bag if she has to. She speaks in a voice like she might've swallowed a grain bag or two.

"You like doing that, don't you, calling me Criminal like you were a cop. You going to get your kicks watching me take a piss too?"

"I'm going to shoot it off," she says. "Right while you're taking your morning pee."

JIM

Malcolm's hot this morning. That damned basset hound of his son-in-law's wandered down here, and Malcolm's Great Dane chased that short-legged hound all the way home, yelping whenever it could get breath enough to yelp. The son-in-law come out in a rage, threatening the Great Dane. Things got worse in a hurry because Malcolm heard the son-in-law, jumped on his doodlebug, and tooled right up to his property.

The Great Dane didn't hurt the hound but just scared him. Those basset hounds bark and cry like they're hurt all the time. Course I don't guess I'd want that Great Dane chasing me.

I did tell Malcolm he could wait for his daughter to get home before telling her what a stinker and a nincompoop she's married to. Or he could take a nap, and I could do it for him. I've heard the sermon on the son-in-law often enough I know the words and the tune both. What I don't like is being left alone here with this god-damn farm stand and its big sign OPEN. It's all decorated with ears of corn and apples with stems and leaves. But I hate waiting on people, specially tourists, specially tourists from Massachusetts.

I set the corn and tomatoes on the stand, arranging them as best I can beside the half-peck bags of early apples. In past years Malcolm's been too busy at harvesttime to harvest, so we've just rototilled the tomatoes under to give the soil some tilth for next year's tomatoes. The corn stands in the field way into November, all dry and raspy in the wind like a bunch of old men jawing. Time we try to plow that under, the ground's knotted and miserable, and Malcolm, he's about the same. But this year I'm working extra, so we've erected this damn farm stand.

I go to putting the hay away in the barn. It's a job I enjoy. Takes no figuring, no artistic ability, and when you're done, you know you're done. And you don't wait on anybody. I've stacked just about five bales when this Massachusetts car stops at the stand. I stack another bale, but I know I ain't done. I know I'm a long ways from done because the guy calls me "sir."

"Sir, is the price on that corn right?"

"Whatever it says on the sign."

Now the sign sits square on the stand, so the guy didn't need me to tell him that. It ain't like it's an antique sign, only Malcolm's charging a buck and a half a dozen, which is about half market price. The guy carries a couple of ears over to his car, where an electric window slides down so his wife can examine the corn. She peels it back and goes through that ear of corn like she's going to perform surgery with it. I get just two more bales stacked before I hear "sir" again. Now I'm wearing jeans with stains that go back to the invention of dirt and my body ain't seen soap for two days, so what kind of fool is this guy, calling me "sir"?

"That's a good price," he says, low so his wife can't hear through the still-lowered window. Then he speaks up loud and clear, "But some of these ears have corn borers."

"If it's such a good price," I say, giving him a little religious advice, "just buy the corn and cut out the borers. Or cook it with them. They won't eat too much more anyway."

"I'd like to buy some tomatoes, but they're probably wormy."

I wait for that window to slide up, but it stays down. I go right into my sermon. "I don't know nothing about it. I take care of the hay. I ain't the stand man. We had to fire the stand man because he was thieving all the uninfected corn and tomatoes. He went back to Boston. I'm the hay man. If you want to come back, Mr. Hurd will be here in an hour or so."

Back home for lunch I answer the telephone. Pauline ain't here, so I figure she's either gone to Emory's or is bailing Tommy somewhere between here and the city. For a wonder the person calling is a woman who wants to buy Guitar for her daughter. She'd like a nice pet, she says. She's seen pictures of donkeys and shown them to her daughter, and they saw Malcolm's ad as an answer to their prayers.

"This donkey ain't a picture of a donkey." I tell her I don't think Guitar would be right for her daughter.

"Why not?"

"This donkey we're selling don't ride. And he don't pull either."

"Well, what does he do?"

"He's a male donkey. Mostly he populates the place with other donkeys."

I don't even get a "good-bye."

It makes me think about Pauline. Maybe that's the way it'll turn out between us. Not even a good-bye. I don't like sitting in this trailer by myself because I keep thinking one night I'll end up here alone, swallowing fish out of the tank like poor Gregory. They'll give us adjoining beds up there at the hospital and call it the Hutchins Memorial Room. Or could be I'll turn the other way, go roaring over to Emory's with a mind to tear out his heart, and he'll kneecap me. Only he won't hit careful, so I'll wind up with a gimpy leg, jail time, and no wife.

Where am I going to stay? I've lived with Pauline so long it's turned into what living is. But I just may need to get away from her. Maybe she'll realize something. I don't know. I do know I can't give up my mind or my knees over this deal. I feel as out of place as a mole on a sunlit superhighway.

I sure as hell can't rent no apartment. I ain't like Fesmire and Lisa and Penny, I got to pay to live, and there ain't much pay left. Malcolm'd put me up. If I was willing to tell him about everything and listen to his advice, which I pretty much know already. These things happen, Jim, he'll say, the sooner you accept it's over and get on with your life, the better off you'll be. As if he'd ever accept Bernice running around with another man. There wouldn't be a piece of machinery running on his place when he got done tearing. Nor a donkey house standing. There's a thought. If he sells Guitar, I can move into the donkey house.

I'll check out Gregory's place. He ain't got squat there, but it's free. And I don't have to tell anyone. Malcolm gave me the key to the gate. I'll just have to watch myself. If I end up eating cold dog food out of the can, I'll know I'm in trouble.

TOMMY

"Okay, Criminal, you've peed," Alice says," now take off your pants and underpants, if you're wearing any."

Alice has marched me out back of Gregory's place, threatening my cock and balls with every breath. She's on the line between crazy and furious. She tells me if I end up in court, she's heard a smart lawyer can get me a reduced sentence or probation, but if she shoots me, she'll get a jury trial, and no jury will convict her for shooting a worthless molesting rapist like me.

"I didn't rape anybody."

"Mary Beth's underage," she says, planting her foot on my underpants and sliding them across the dirt. "That makes it rape. I've got more sympathy for that panty sniffer than I have for you."

"You going to sniff my underpants?"

She loses it. I'm watching my chance because, pantless or not, I'm going to clock this bitch and take that fucking gun away from her. I'll give her a little taste of damnation as soon as I'm holding the gun. I jump.

She rears back. She must've been moving already because I don't give away my attacks even when I'm drunk.

"Lie down, Criminal. On your belly like a snake. Now crawl along here."

Every stick and protruding root tears my skin. I raise my crotch as I crawl until she stomps my back. "Crawl, Criminal! Keep that belly to the ground, or I'll shoot you right now." Dirt and all kinds of mung gets into the scrapes and cuts, burning. There's probably poison ivy here too. She's sounding calmer when we get to her truck, a beat-up Toyota. I'll have to piss her off again to get an advantage.

"My cock will be all dirty when you go to suck it."

"If I ever stick that thing in my mouth, it won't be attached to you."

I wonder where she thinks she's going to drive me. To the cops?

Off the tailgate comes this bag heavy with stuff from the hardware store, so heavy it's straining the label. Gun in one hand, bag in the other, old Alice makes me crawl to the side of the house where Gregory let this big oak stand. South side of the house, shade in the summer, sun in the winter, he said, plan a big deck or even a solarium right here.

"Back up to this tree, Tom," she orders.

Even before she runs the nylon straps of the motorcycle tie-down across my chest, I know she's serious because she's calling me by name, not "Criminal." By the way she's cranked the tension on the buckle, I know she's damn serious. There's no chance I can jump her because I can't move from the waist up. I ain't going to wring her tits anymore.

"How'd you know where to find me?"

"Mary Beth."

I can't ask her any more questions because she duct-tapes my face with my underpants. The cloth sticks between my lips and comes over my nose. I can't believe I'm going to die like this, suffocate and choke on my own underpants. I'm trying to remember when I put them on. I know I changed since I pissed myself at Emory Holler's. A couple of days ago maybe. It ain't only my sweat but some of Mary Beth's juices too I'm chomping. I'd tell Alice that if I could speak. She walks back to the truck for something, and I wonder why Mary Beth told her mother I'd be here. I didn't even know myself. I was just hiding my stash from BB Eyes. Right now I'd hug BB Eyes like a brother, even if he would be goony laughing at me.

Both hands on the bail, Alice lugs back a five-gallon black bucket. "Too bad it's not hot tar, but I don't have the time to heat it up. I don't have any feathers either." It's driveway sealant. Alice works a pair of pliers around the lid like she's opening a can of meat for herself. I squirm to slide out of the straps, but I can't budge an inch. I press my bare legs together as she starts to pour, but that just helps the black stuff to pool on my skin. I try to cover my crotch with my hands. They go only as far as the hair, which is already swimming in the sticky sealant. My cock burns with it. If I could get a hard-on, I could raise the head up out of the tar, but a hard-on is the last thing I can get, even if I were to pray.

"Here, this will help you breathe." She pulls my underpants up past my nose. Now I can only see a little. "I could've bought latex sealant, but this stuff is cheaper. Best nine ninety-nine I've spent in a long time."

PAULINE

I ask Emory to take me out to Gregory's place. I want to see it for myself. I guess I have to know just how bad it was where he was living. Bad enough so he didn't want me to see it. Sitting in Emory's big truck with the tape player and CD player and the six speakers, I think about all the things Jim and I have passed up, gone without, never had. In all our life we've never had a new car. If we did, it wouldn't come with the gadgets like this.

We have to drive clear around to Gregory's road because there's no way through from Emory's house. Emory explains to me again about selling off this whole plot of land to Wal-Mart, that he can't subdivide the acreage for Gregory, that he can't just let Gregory squat here because after so many years—

"After so many times hearing this, I want to scream," I say. "Jim says you took money from Gregory for that land."

"He asked for it back. Honestly, Pauline, do you think I need to steal money from your boy?" I know he's not lying because he hasn't lied to me. I know he's caught in a bind on this land that

Gregory can't understand and Jim won't. Jim don't like to understand about money, neither making it nor spending it.

When we get to Gregory's gate, the bar is up and the chain's dangling from it. After examining the lock, Emory says someone cut it with bolt cutters.

"Not you?" I ask.

"I figured we'd have to walk in from here."

It would have been a pretty walk, through leafy trees and low shrubs, even a patch of blackberry bushes at one place, all under blue sky. I ask Emory to stop, and we cram blackberries in our mouths like we were kids. Naturally, thorns prick our arms and legs, juice stains our hands, and Emory tries to suck the stain off my fingers but can't.

I think, what if Jim is out here? What would he do seeing Emory and me together? Have I turned wild and reckless or only foolish? Maybe Lisa and Tommy come by their own wildness out of my body from Pa, and now the wild is flowering in me. I know I don't want any fights with Jim. I don't want to hit or be hit or even see hitting.

As we come into the clearing, I see the blue of Jim's truck, only it's not his truck, it's not any truck. It's only sight of sky and my worrying imagination. I look at my scratched wrists and stained fingers, which are shaking and quivering, and I tell myself to stop being silly.

"He did a good job here," Emory says. "This is no rattletrap shack but solid-built."

From around the side comes a funny noise like a bird or small animal. Emory and I go inside to look around. The place could use a picking-up and a good scrubbing. Lisa and I could have it looking tip-top in a couple of hours. I tell Emory how I might come out tomorrow with Lisa and clean this place up proper.

"You'll be wasting your energy." He sorts through some of Gregory's machines in the corner, a chain saw, a drill, a circular saw. "I can't leave this building standing. By law I can force Gregory to take it down, but I won't do that. I'll take care of it myself."

I can see he feels bad about Gregory's place, and at least he's honest with me. I take his hand and pull him out on the porch. I wonder if Lisa and I came up here and worked our magic on the place, maybe Emory'd change his mind about tearing it down. I feel sad standing in the middle of all Gregory's wasted work. I hear that funny little noise again. When Emory turns to look for it, I reach up and kiss him. It's an awkward, sideways kiss, more whiskers than lips, just a brush of flesh, but I know I shouldn't have done it.

"When Jim and I were kids," Emory says, holding my hand and moving away from Gregory's house, "we used to make fun of this old dog Buddy Links' family owned. He had a set of ribs looked like a xylophone. We never hurt the dog or anything. In fact we didn't go too close because we figured it carried about a hundred diseases. One day when I was by myself, the dog comes out of the Linkses' yard, hobbles over to this big elm, and leans over to pee on the tree. Only the dog keeps leaning. Just leaned until he fell over. Then he was dead. His pecker just leaking out a bladderful of urine. Sometimes I think back on that dog, and I think, Jesus Christ, that's what's going to happen to me. That's just how I'm going to go."

I know what he wants me to say, but I can't say it because I already feel bad about the kiss. I swing out in front of him and start dancing, my easy way to please us both, swaying in front on him like a slender tree in a slight breeze. Under this warm sun I feel a little sweat at the top of my spine, but I know as sure as I'm a woman that I won't tip over and leak urine out of my bladder.

Emory's gentle, moving eyes turn me daring. The buttons slip out of their holes so my blouse hangs open. Unhooking my bra frees my breasts to sway in the slow rhythm of my dance as my body fills his eyes. I feel hot now. Pushing back my shoulders exposes more of my chest to the air, the caressing air. No, that's too much, "caressing" as if his eyes were feeling me, his breath on my breasts, his lips on my nipples.

"Aaoooghh!"

All to once the animal noise turn human. It's a roar.

"Aaoooghh!"

I think we're being attacked. Then I see him there fixed to the tree by the side of the house. I turn my back to cover myself back up while Emory runs to him.

"Jesus Christ, it's your Tommy. Oh, my God!"

I find his pants and cover him so he can have a little modesty, if not any more comfort. He's cursing awful, cursing his pain, cursing Alice Jewell, cursing himself, which I never heard him do before.

"How could I've been so goddamn stupid? And you are goddamn disgusting."

"At least we're not tied to a tree with a lap full of tar," Emory says as he releases the buckle on the red nylon strap that's held Tommy upright. "That is tar, isn't it? How long you been wearing it?"

"Hours. Just goddamn—what the hell were you doing?" He's talking to me now. "You're no better than Penny." He's cursing women now while Emory goes into Gregory's house looking for paint thinner to remove the tar. Tommy's worked himself up to shooting the whole race of females when Emory brings out an old red chain saw, unscrewing the gas-tank cover as he walks.

"Not that one, you fucking idiot!" Tommy yells.

Jim has always claimed Tommy swore something awful when he was drunk, but he's going the whole hog now, and he's sober.

Out of the chain saw comes not gasoline but a plastic bag.

Tommy reaches for it and screams. The tar must have set up enough to tear his skin when he moves.

"Jesus, Tommy," Emory tells him, "you'd better smoke all of this because I'd say they'll have to cut the tar off you."

"Aren't we going to call the police?" I ask.

"No," they both say at once.

I want to explain to Tommy about dancing for Emory because I see that caused him more pain than the tar Alice Jewell poured in his lap. He says Mary Beth begged for everything she got, so he didn't rape her. I believe him because I know how a lot of these young girls are, even if their mothers don't want to think so. Raging here on the ground, he's pitiful in his anger and his hurt, and he won't even look at me.

By a small woodpile Emory finds Gregory's gas can. As Tommy pulls his jeans off his crotch, I look away because I don't want to embarrass him any more than he already is, nor do I want to see that black horror Alice Jewell poured on him. I don't know but what I could shoot her myself. Tommy screams.

"Fuck! Burns, it just fucking burns."

I look, and where the black doesn't cover his skin, the gasoline is turning the flesh red. At the edges the tar is starting to dissolve and run in dirty brown trickles. I think of soap and water, of washing him when he was a baby and would get the terrible diaper rash, and between his legs would look as chafed as if it had been rubbed with steel wool. After washing him, I'd spread this A and D ointment all over his bottom and legs and just hold him on my lap until he stopped screaming. He's screaming now. I know soap and water won't take away the tar, I know he can't stand the gasoline, and I know I have to do something.

"We'll take him to the hospital," I say.

Again they both say, "No."

"You men are more stubborn than stupid. Emory, grab his shoulders."

I take his feet, and we try to jar him as little as possible carrying him to the truck, but when we raise him up to the bed, the tar cracks and tears. Tommy's screams slice my heart from end to end, and shame at what he saw cuts it the other way. Finally we get him lying on his back in the truck and covered with an old army blanket I take from Gregory's cot.

"You want to use his dope to pay for his medical care?" Emory asks me in the truck. He holds up the plastic bag. "He surely doesn't have any Blue Cross."

In the back I see Tommy bouncing, holding his hands out, palm down on the metal, trying to steady himself. More pain. I think of all the pain he suffers from dope and liquor and from the girls chasing him for dope and liquor. There's a huge rotten hunk of mad in me. It'll explode if I don't get rid of it. I grab the bag of pot and throw it out the window right into the roadside weeds.

"I guess Tommy'll have to be a welfare patient," Emory says.

"Let them bill Alice Jewell."

At the emergency entrance a man and a woman wheel out a gurney. As Emory's telling them what happened—"this crazy bitch poured driveway tar on his crotch"—the army blanket slides over Tommy. "Worse case of black balls I ever saw," the man mutters. The woman laughs. Emory laughs. The man's laughing, but they miss the gurney with Tommy, who lands kerspash on the pavement with his ankle twisted up against a cement curbing. He reaches for his toes and screams all anew from bone fractures and tar tearing at his groin.

Inside we have to wait because the nurse says they're working on two people from a car wreck. After about half an hour, I tell them Tommy was in a stretcher wreck right outside their door.

Before I know it, I'm crying and hollering. Emory's telling them to at least give the boy something for his pain and see what damage they've done to his feet. They wheel him off to x-ray, and the nurse explains they can't give him painkillers if he's full of alcohol.

I say, "He can damn well have aspirin, can't he! Besides, he hasn't been drinking. Do you think he fell into that tar?"

Then we wait another hour, but at least I don't hear Tommy so much as moaning. Emory talks about suing the hospital, though he was the one started telling the story about Tommy to the people who dropped Tommy. Not the joke about "black balls," of course, but he laughed at it. I know I don't want to stand in court and explain how Emory and I came to be at Gregory's, nor tell why I was dancing before we found Tommy. Wild Tommy. What will he do? Emory says Alice can prosecute Tommy for statutory rape and put Tommy behind bars for years, though I believe she is too much my friend to do that. What she did with the tar, she did in the heat of anger over hurt to her child. I can understand that, but I'm afraid of what Tommy will do to Alice when he heals. Ain't nobody likes to be humiliated, least of all Tommy.

Or Jim. He'll find out, even if Emory pays the hospital bill, because Tommy's mad enough to tell his father. Why Tommy has it in for Emory and not Scooter, I'll never understand. All the while Emory's sitting beside me, sliding his arm over my shoulders and patting my hand, like he's consoling me for a death and getting ready to make love both. Even if he can't make love, he's not so far from other men as he thinks. But I know about death, and this isn't it. Love? Maybe I don't know as much about love as I thought I did.

"He's broken some toes," says the doctor after introducing himself. "He's finally clean of tar, but I had to use a lifetime supply of industrial-strength degreaser. I've made a copy of my report for you to take to the police."

"Thank you," Emory says.

On the way out, we stop at the business office. Tommy sits outside in a blue canvas wheelchair. He won't look at me. When he turns inward like this, he frightens me. It's like those awful days when they evicted him from the school, before the fire. Jim could be just like that, at least he seems to be with Emory, something in the male race, I guess.

"You write 'paid in full' on the bill," says Emory to the woman at the desk, "and we'll call it square."

"Are you his father?"

"Uncle."

It doesn't matter because Tommy's of age and will have to sign any agreements or release forms himself. I'm looking in my purse for Jim's health insurance card, though naturally Tommy's not covered under Jim's policy. I hope it will get us out of here without a row.

"I'm signing nothing," Tommy says in a voice as cold as a frozen gate on bare fingers. "My lawyer will take care of this."

JIM

"Guess what surprise I got in the mail today?" Malcolm says. It don't take a genius to figure out he's being sarcastic, so I don't even shrug my shoulders. "That psychologist's check—stamped 'insufficient funds.' Can you imagine a doctor without the money to pay for a lousy truckload of gravel?"

"He's a doctor of psychology, Malcolm."

"A doctor's a doctor, ain't he? It ain't like he's a farmer or a mechanic."

I don't know why he takes me with him, for entertainment I guess, but when Malcolm pulls into the Doctor of Psychology's yard, there's the man himself running around his brand-new tennis court and wearing those little white shorts.

"My wife just can't make bank deposits on time," the Doctor of Psychology tells Malcolm. Course, having one of those wives at home, who pays only the bills she feels like, I develop a spoonful of understanding for the Doctor of Psychology. "I won't have it," the Doctor of Psychology winds up with. "You give me that check, Mr. Hurd, I'm writing you out a new one for the full amount, plus twenty-five dollars for all your trouble over this."

I see those twenty-five extra dollars light up Malcolm's eyes. And I understand this fella deserves his handle Doctor of Psychology. Malcolm tucks that check in his shirt pocket and is planning to send the Doctor of Psychology a card on his next birthday.

When we pull into Malcolm's yard, there stands this big, strapping woman in shorts and a work shirt, and she ain't come to play tennis. She's hauled up a horse trailer and come to do business. This woman ain't come to buy no picture of a donkey.

"You got that donkey in the barn?" she asks.

"He's so miserable, I penned him," Malcolm says, "right there by his house."

"House!" the woman snorts like she might be half-horse herself. "No wonder he's contrary for you."

She gets right in the pen with that donkey and looks him over and handles his equipment, and if he has anything to say about it, he chooses the wiser way and holds his tongue.

"What's your low dollar?" She wipes her hands on her shirt, moving a hefty pair of bosoms around in there. I'd guess she could hurt you with those too, if she wanted.

Malcolm says, "I advertised him for two hundred."

"I can read, you know," she snaps. "I've got five females, and I want them bred. Now, I'll lease him, or I'll give you one hundred for him right now."

Turning my back to the woman, I tell Malcolm, "Take the hundred, or else you'll be up to your armpits in donkeys."

So we load old Guitar into the horse trailer, and the tall woman, she smiles and tells Malcolm he could've got the whole two hundred if he were man enough to bargain with her. She writes out a check, which I see is on the same bank the Doctor of Psychology uses. "Malcolm," I says, "do yourself a favor, call that bank and see if this woman's husband forgot to make a deposit."

So he goes in the house, and when he comes back, he looks like he stubbed all his toes to once. I'm getting ready to drag that miserable donkey out of the horse trailer, but Malcolm says to let her go, her check is good. It's the Doctor of Psychology. The brand-new check he gave Malcolm is "insufficient funds," twenty-five-dollar bonus or no twenty-five-dollar bonus.

It gives me a laugh. And I need a laugh because I've decided that I'm moving out of the trailer and up to Gregory's. I don't need to stay with a woman who wants to play Little Egypt for the men in town.

13
thirteen

JIM

I feel like one of those old crows, those road crows you see on the turnpike, stumping along the breakdown lane looking for their piece of heaven in a chunk of roadkill. Sometimes I look real close at their faces, and I can tell what they're thinking, those old crows.

Another call comes from the IRS. Right at work, asking for "Jim." I tell Frank, "I ain't no stranger down there, you know. We're on a first-name basis." Which is good because their calling me "Mr. Hutchins" would make me dribble pee. We're not talking three hundred dollars anymore, she says. Now she tells me I owe them twenty-two hundred dollars.

I tell her I'll lie down, spread out my arms, and they can open veins on both sides.

I changed my working conditions a year or so ago, going from employee to independent contractor. Frank was contracting to me. He told me he'd sheltered three thousand dollars of my income, but he must have sheltered it in a lean-to because they found it the first time the wind blew. And it gets worse. See, the whole idea of contracting was that Frank raised my pay two dollars an hour. What I didn't figure was, he could do that because he wasn't paying any social security on my wages. I was supposed to pay it all now. There were other things Frank wasn't paying, like workmen's comp, but I didn't owe the IRS for that. The whole thing is, I got grabby. I had all those bills, and I got grabby. I didn't figure on all those taxes. Now they can put me in jail or bleed me to death.

This is the time to move Tommy and Lisa right out to Gregory's place. Gregory himself, once he's released from the New Hampshire Hospital. That way if we all pull together and pool our resources, as they say, I can get clear of some of these bills. Pauline she can have the trailer. I don't care anymore about it. Maybe she can give dancing lessons there to add to what she makes housekeeping at the motel.

There's a time when you have to give up on a thing. You've replaced tires and exhaust systems, even installed a new radiator, put in a rebuilt alternator and a water pump, changed the timing belt, and you're fooled into thinking the vehicle will run forever. Just as long as you can shell out fifty bucks here and a hundred there, you can drive that car down the highway for another year. You're feeling just as confident as one of those old road crows. Then you get the news—the transmission's shot, they can't find a used one, you're looking at a grand, fifteen hundred to get a rebuilt. There's your million-mile miracle car being dragged on its hind wheels to the junkyard. And you're pacing back and forth in some garage waiting room wondering what you're going to do next now that your car died.

Your wife entertains your brother-in-law with her body. Maybe she calls it sex therapy, and Emory pays her out of his Blue Cross policy. Right now I'd change places with one of those old road crows.

Ms. Emerson, the IRS woman, has got more hair than can be good for her. Must be everything she eats goes into making hair. She must wear heavy shoes to keep from tipping over. I don't see her feet because she doesn't stand when I come into her little office. I could be back in school, sitting in the principal's office waiting hellfire and damnation.

"You owe us a lot of money, Mr. Hutchins," Ms. Emerson begins. "With penalties and interest it amounts to over twenty-three hundred dollars."

"And you'll get it all, every penny." On the wall behind her is a child's drawing of a big sun, all yellow, with a blue sky.

"When?"

"I don't have my checkbook on me, but I'd like to work out a payment plan."

"Mr. Hutchins, we can attach your bank account, sell your property, whatever it takes to satisfy this debt." She doesn't run her hand through the forest of hair the way a lot of these young women do. It might as well just be sitting there like a brood hen.

"I don't have a bank account, and to tell you the truth, if I could figure a way to make any money out of my property, I'd sell it myself."

"You don't want to go to jail, do you, Mr. Hutchins?"

"You see I thought I could work for myself, but if I have to hire a lawyer and an accountant and pay all these extra taxes, I can't really afford it. Do you see what I mean? Not if I'm to put food on the table. I guess I could starve to death, but I don't believe my body'd bring twenty-three hundred dollars either."

"We don't expect you to die over this." A smile creases enough of her face to move her hair. I'm surprised to see it move.

"Your child make that for you?" I ask, pointing to the bright sun behind her.

"One day I said something about spending most of the day making people unhappy, and she came back fifteen minutes later with that and said, 'Here, Mommy, take this to work, and people will feel better.' "

Naturally I thought of Elizabeth, who always wanted everybody to be happy and smiling. I tell Ms. Emerson about Elizabeth's smile, warmed with her own heart's blood, and I tell her about Elizabeth's drowning. When I finish, I ask how old her little girl is.

"Courtney is eight." She turns to look at the bright, yellow sun on her wall. "I can't imagine losing her."

"No."

"Mr. Hutchins—"

"Jim."

"Jim, can you send us a hundred a month?" She starts to write something on the paper in front of her. "I'm sorry, but it will be best for you to clear this debt. We're not an agency you want to owe money to."

"I'll try that hundred. Tell Courtney she cheered up one poor fella today."

Ms. Emerson smiles, a real smile, even if it wouldn't raise your temperature more than half a degree.

TOMMY

My crotch is a brush fire. It hurts to sit, let alone walk. Sometimes I think Momma lacks the brains God gave grunt, throwing away five hundred dollars' worth of weed. That would pay for my lawyer and leave some for her and Father instead of me always taking from them like a leech. In the dust and weeds lie beer cans, plastic, sun-faded wrappers. I'm thinking wasted, like I want to be to take away this pain in my crotch, and my foot. Wasted like Mama did throwing away the weed. I'm not letting it go. I'll find it if I have to walk all the way to Gregory's. I wish I could have seen it flying out the window and marked the location, but all that filled my eyes were blue sky and pain.

If I think about my crotch, tears come again and interfere with my search. I walk like I've got a load in my pants, running me back to six years old wandering dirt roads instead of going home from school. And my toes, black and purple and swollen hard, hobble me. I could be a convict in chains, for Christ's sake. I guess you can find disgrace in anything if you look hard enough.

Disgrace is the word. When I finish with Alice Jewell, if I ever finish with her, she'll know about disgrace. I'll make her sorry she ever wrapped her hand around a pistol grip or bought a can of tar. When I get through with her, she won't want to even drive on a blacktop highway.

I've limped two miles, I'll bet. Way up high flies a hawk looking for dinner. Not a peregrine falcon. A red tail, I think. I wish I had his eyes to spot my bag. At least I'm walking on the left side of the road like an upright citizen, like we were taught in school. You watch the traffic. Don't make it difficult for drivers. They have enough to do without worrying where you are or what you'll do. Now that's who I am. I'm the guy who makes people worry where I am and what I'll do. I'll make Alice Jewell worry. And I'll satisfy her curiosity.

Across the ditch, sun shines off plastic. I step quickly and slide in a foot of muck, doing a split. My crotch is scoured with raspy pain. Nails drive into my toes.

That's it! Praise the Lord and any passing angel that led me to it. My pot. My pot of gold. I was going to give Uncle all the prof-its from the other bag, but now I'm home free. I'll get that cam-corder, then it'll be on to Alice Jewell. Oh, shit, what's this? The Ziploc held fine in the Homelite fuel tank, protecting the weed from gasoline, sealing it even from vapors, but it was no fucking defense against wild animals. Tooth and claw have shredded this.

In amongst the bad weeds is scattered my good weed. I gather most of my stash and drop it into the bag, careful it doesn't spill out the tear holes in the Ziploc.

Blue lights. Goddamn BB Eyes. And I'm holding.

At least he doesn't have his gun out.

Not to be stupid and obvious, I force the Ziploc into my pocket. Jesus Christ, does that hurt my crotch.

"Come here, Tommy," BB Eyes orders. "Just step over to the car with no fighting or fussing. I ain't risking a heart attack to chase you down. I'll just shoot you."

Maybe I should be happy it ain't Dumont because Dumont would shoot me without any running, but as soon as BB Eyes gets me to the station, they'll discover my pot. It ain't only the jail time that pisses me off, it's losing the pot I just found. I could've just dropped it on the ground. I didn't need to find it just this very second. Fat BB Eyes ain't going to risk no heart attack crossing the ditch to check out a lousy plastic bag. It's too late now. And goddamn Alice Jewell's going to miss her just reward, at least for a while. Something always delays a man on a righteous mission. Fate fucks the fella looking for his due.

"I can't hurry, BB Eyes. I'm bearing a skinless crotch and a frac-tured foot."

"Then I guess you won't want to run either. Damn these medical problems." He smiles like ailments make us brothers. I'm think-ing it's bad enough having Emory in the family. I ain't opening the door to cops too. "You're lucky. Your girlfriend still loves you."

He tells me he investigated Alice Jewell's charge of rape on me, but Mary Beth said it never happened. She told BB Eyes she'd testify I never laid a hand on her. "You can lie all you want, I know you been dicking that girl right up to the eyeballs, only now her mother's put your pecker out of commission for a while."

"You going to charge her with assault?"

"You going to bring charges? You going to testify? Bad enough people hear you can't get into Mary Beth's pants, professional swordsman like you. What'll it do to your reputation when they hear how her mother blunted that sword of yours?"

Then he tells me I'd better stay away from Mary Beth, or else Alice will shoot me instead of just tarring my balls. Then he tells me I better not think about harming Alice herself or he'll have to arrest me and add more charges and guarantee I'll do hard time.

"And don't you so much as dream about a gun," he says, hand off his belly to waggle a finger in my face. Course I don't need a gun. Guns won't be involved at all if I can just get going on my mission, starting with selling this fine pot.

"Let's have that bag you stuffed in your pants. Must be painful stretching the cloth all around your pecker."

He's hefting the torn bag, holding a hand under it to catch any that falls out of the holes. He rattles on about there might be a pound here, enough to charge me with a class A felony, possession with intent to distribute.

"BB Eyes, I'm doing my duty as a good citizen, picking up roadside litter and helping to keep America beautiful, and you want to put me in jail."

"This pot doesn't belong to you?"

"No more than I own a twat."

"Then you won't mind if I take it down to the station."

"Be careful when you smoke it. This modern stuff has twice the THC as the pot in your toking days."

Dry, yellow gravel at the road edge reminds me again of my burning crotch. My broken toes make me walk in a perpetual stumble, every step a wince. Pain will grind at me while I'm crawling around Emory's taking his camcorder. Always something to chew at a man with a heart full of dedicated intention.

With all the money I was going to make on that pot, I should've been able to buy two camcorders and take care of the lawyer, but now I have to sell the half pound left to pay back Uncle. So here I am, cracking every scrape and burn in my crotch to hip over Emory's windowsill. I'm bound to get that camcorder, but I don't want to look at Emory's face over the barrel of a gun again. The lights go out. For a minute it's so dark I couldn't find my dick if I had to piss. The bed forms a dark shape. I can't figure how the light went out when no one flipped a switch. Maybe a circuit breaker threw?

"How do you like my new security system? Are you stealing more tapes?"

It's Emory. Naturally I can't tell whether or not he's holding a gun, but what difference does it make? With a foot aching like it's been chewed by a hedge clipper, I ain't running anywhere. "What the hell you talking about?"

"Don't bullshit me, Tommy." I can't tell how much danger is in his voice. If he broke out in a laugh right now, it wouldn't surprise me any more than if he kicked me in the balls. "You know what I think of you and vice versa."

"Did you want to shake my hand?"

"I want you to give me back my tape. You'll wind up in the New Hampshire State Prison. You could be a career criminal before you even have a career."

"I been in jail."

"You ain't been in prison."

So he's not going to shoot me, he's going to turn me over to the cops. "How much are you paying for the tape?"

"You aren't breaking into my house to replace it, are you?" The smell of sarcasm damn near chokes me.

"I ain't got it, but I can get it. A hundred bucks." You can always come down, and I figure this will give me enough money to rent a camcorder.

"Where are you getting the tape?"

"Turn on the light, Emory. We don't need to talk like cavemen, for Christ's sakes."

He won't do it. I hear a step, and he grabs my arm. There ain't no point in fighting him. Besides, Uncle says when you're doing business, never let the other fella think you're uneasy about anything. Make him think you got the world by the ass. So with Emory leading me through the dark, while my crotch stings like a model home for ants, I'm trying to stand tall on my broken toes.

"You give me fifty now, earnest money, you can pay me the other fifty when I bring you the tape." This is even better than stealing Emory's camcorder.

"Have you watched the tape?" I tell him no. He grabs the back of my neck and shakes my head until my teeth rattle. "Don't," he says. Then he gives me fifty bucks and tells me if I don't bring it or the tape back to him, he'll make my face feel worse than my crotch.

"Nice doing business with you, Emory," I tell him quietly as I limp tall out his front door.

I ain't long down the road when I run into Scooter. He gives me a ride and will share a case if I got something to contribute.

The rate on a camcorder runs thirty-nine fifty a day, leaving me a clear ten bucks over, so we end up with two cases. I wish I had picked up some acid in the city because the way things are going, I can sell nickel bags and acid and buy out Jiffy Rental and put the best lawyer in the state on retainer to handle any nuisances like BB Eyes. Maybe I could even take Emory to court and save Gregory's place.

Which reminds me, I got to get out there for the half pound of pot I hid in the can of poly. And I'll look around real good for any videotapes in case it was Gregory stole it. Maybe he hid it at Father's trailer in our old hiding place. I could use another fifty bucks. I'll watch it first. Who knows, there might be a lot more than fifty bucks in it for me. Emory gave me the first fifty awful easy.

"Hey, Tom."

Bless my balls if it isn't Mary Beth Jewell and Lisa. "How did you get out of the house?" I ask.

"I told that old bitch I hoped she'd die," MB says. She told Alice she was just jealous. Alice told her she was only trying to protect her. " 'Protect me from what?' I asked her. 'From love? Which you never had from the day you drove my father away.'"

"That's the truth," I tell MB. "Your mother's so dry, she makes the Sahara Desert look like a cold ocean."

"I told her if she didn't let me out, when I did leave, I'd never come back. I told her she couldn't watch me all the time."

"How'd she know to look for me at Gregory's? That's what I'd like to know."

"That's my fault, hon. I told her if she didn't leave me alone, I'd go live with you, and she said you didn't have a place to live, and I said, yes, you did, at your brother's."

Back at Lisa's, MB doesn't have but a couple of brewskis in her when she asks how my crotch is. She's horny as a mink. She wants to kiss it and make it better. I tell her tomorrow. We'll do it tomorrow. All day if she wants. I tell her I'm smeared with ointment against infection that I've got to leave on until tomorrow.

"I'd like to kill my mother," she says, and sticks her tongue in my ear.

"Yeah, we'll take care of old Alice Jewell tomorrow too."

There's a vibrating hum of pleasure running through the night's dark. I grab another beer. What's hurting in my crotch right now is my galloping hard-on, and it ain't lathered with any fucking ointment either. But I'll wait. They say I have no self-control, that my drinking and my dick lead me into trouble every time, but God knows when I have a purpose, I can do what I want. Tomorrow will be a fine day, a fine day all the way around.

14
fourteen

JIM

Who'd think Tommy'd be up at this hour, much less hobbling around my place looking for a videotape. "What videotape?" I ask him.

"One I loaned Gregory."

Tommy's smoking a filtered cigarette, so somewhere he's come into money. With his crowd, having the price of a pack of cigarettes or a six-pack counts for having money. Having a place to stay puts you right among the idle rich. I don't guess the IRS bothers Tommy much.

"This may surprise you," he says, "but it's X-rated. A regular dirty movie."

"And what do you want it for?" I ask him casually, like I might plan to take off an hour early so I can come home and watch my wife frolic on the TV screen instead of having to work extra to keep the IRS from throwing me into jail.

"It's Scooter's, and he wants it back."

I feel myself twitching. I ain't sure how close to approach the truth of this videotape, nor can I figure what Tommy wants with it. God doesn't have to tell me there's money involved. I know Tommy well enough for that.

"You've seen this movie?"

"No. I gave it to Gregory before he got sick."

"Gregory was sick for a long time, but he ain't the only one sick around here."

"You heard about Alice Jewell, huh?"

No stare at the horizon or glance at the dirt by his feet betrays this as a lie or shift in subject. He's getting clever as he gets older. "I told you to stay away from that girl. I guess you found out what her mother can do with a little tar."

"I'll settle Alice Jewell."

"How'd you get out of the hospital bill?"

"Emory was going to pay it, but they'll end up paying me."

"Emory?"

"Yeah, I guess Momma didn't tell you she was with him when she found me."

I want to tell him his mother worries about him. Angry as I am, I want to tell him that. But I don't. I don't mention her at all. I tell him I hope he heals fast because a bad foot and burned crotch are bound to hinder a man. Then I wish him useless good luck in finding the videotape. After he's gone, I go out to the shed and take care of the goddamn videotape. I've seen all of it I care to. I ain't real curious as to how the story comes out.

"What was that you were burning out there?" Pauline asks me when I come in. She's getting ready to leave for work, and I'm about to go myself.

"You're always harping I should get rid of some of the junk around here. Well, I've started." I don't tell her I ain't likely to be home tonight.

She holds her teacup tight and close. If she throws it, I'll haul out of here without a second thought. She can have everything right down to the peafowl and guinea hens. I'll even throw in Buffy.

"Looks like it's going to be a fine day," she says, setting her cup down and snapping shut her purse. "Maybe we could go out for a fish dinner tonight."

"With all our bills, somebody'd arrest us if they caught us eating out."

"Oh," she says, like money is just one more of my worries. "Was that Tommy you were talking to outside?"

"I was giving him some advice about women. You wouldn't want to hear it. Neither would Emory."

TOMMY

The guy at Jiffy Rental wears *Raymond* on his shirt. I peel the two twenties out of my wallet and set them on the case. "When does my time start?" I ask him, in case I should go find MB first.

"As soon as you put down two hundred dollars for deposit. Against damage."

"I don't intend to damage the machine." I grab the handle.

"No one does, but it happens. We do take checks."

"I'll go get my checkbook." Shit. Now I got to come up with two hundred bucks or hit Raymond over the head and take his goddamn camcorder. Maybe I could steal his shirt, so he could forget who he is.

PAULINE

"Pauline, I've got to speak to you."

It's Carol, and if she's not bringing bad news, she'd doing a good imitation of it. I don't ask anything. I just switch off the laundry room TV and close the washing machine door. Out of habit I guess. What could the washer hear?

"Elaine's lost her baby."

"I'm sorry."

"I'm sorry too, but Elaine's going to come back to work."

I never thought of that. Without a baby of course Elaine's coming back to work. Hours are short enough without having to split them with Elaine, and she was here first, so there's no sense trying to argue I need the money more than she does. Carol and David got their own sense of fair, and they stick by it.

"The other thing is," says Carol without looking away, "we have to give you notice."

"Yes?" I say, not sure what she's getting at, though I have a feeling of dread like dark water flowing over me.

"Come fall, when business slows up, we're going to keep Elaine on full-time."

"Is this about that fifty dollars?" I snap. "I don't know why you don't—"

"Elaine's been with us longer." She tells me that she and David discussed it last night, trying to figure out the fairest way to decide who should work full-time, and came up with seniority as the most objective.

I open the dryer, knowing full well the sheets aren't finished, then start the machine spinning again. "Maybe both of us can work part-time?"

"Why, Pauline, you were the one who wanted to work full-time in the first place." That was true, and I had made a big point of it when Elaine said she was going to stay home with her baby.

"But she doesn't have a family—"

"Neither do you. Now, you've got a couple of weeks to find something to do, full-time."

It's that damn fifty dollars, I know it is. Why am I still being punished? Poor Elizabeth, and Lisa sick with something, and Tommy near mutilated by Alice, who's supposed to be my friend, and now my job, not just part-time, but all of it gone. I'm losing things so fast it's a wonder I can keep myself upright in the world.

Is it because of Emory?

TOMMY

I've spent more of Emory's money for oregano. Cutting the pot is a stupid thing to do if you're going to be in the business, Uncle told me. After all, in a small town most of your customers are going to be repeat. It's not like you have a steady supply of new buyers. But this is a one-shot deal for me. I wouldn't even be in it except I want to pay the lawyer myself. I won't have Momma taking it from Emory anymore. And the IRS has got its hooks so deep into Father, they're taxing his farts. A judicious mixture of oregano will double my profit. If I had the whole pound, I'd have five hundred extra, enough to buy airbrushing equipment. I'd like that. I really would. But I'm not selling another pound. This is a one-shot deal, in and out.

Oregano and Ziplocs come to ten bucks, plus four bucks for a blank videotape, plus ten bucks for a taxi ride out to Gregory's road. I ain't lazy, but with my red-raw crotch and purple toes, I walk like an old man with a hernia, and I want to get this pot sold, so I can rent the camcorder, so I can make this video before I'm too old to make it. I limp all the way down Gregory's crude road, and who's staring me right in the face but Emory.

"Glad you brought the tape," he says.

He yanks the bag out of my hand and rips it open as easily as gutting a fish. Ziplocs, oregano, and videotape fall like bad rain on his feet. "That ain't it," he says, pointing at the blank tape still wrapped in cellophane.

"Not unless they're recording on them through the box."

"You're going to make a copy!" he shouts like he's just discovered God or something. Right then and there he sets his bootheel into that blank videotape, stomping it like you would a caterpillar.

"Come on." He yanks my arm a good one. "Let's get the tape."

"It ain't in there," I tell him, but he drags me inside and makes me search while he watches. My crotch feels like a million ant bites, and my foot feels like a mink's got my toe. One thing for sure, I don't need Emory confiscating my pot. I open up Gregory's trunk, turn over the cooking pan, upend the old mattress. I don't want Emory to figure I'm avoiding the poly can, so I rattle it.

"Bring that can here," he says, just like the screw that'd make you peel off your socks during strip search and tell you it was his job and he was a professional and he was going to do it right. Emory hefts the can, then figures they don't make a tape that'd fit in there. He hefts it again, dancing it in his hands, then heaves it back in the corner. "Get up in those rafters."

He makes me run my hand along the top of every rafter, collecting more splinters than I ever got cutting stove lengths.

"It ain't here, Emory. I could've saved you sweat and me splinters."

He grabs and twists my shirt. "I want that tape or I want my fifty bucks, you got that?" He shoves me away, and then he lights a cigarette and asks me what the hell I'm doing here.

"Gregory stole your tape." I figure Gregory is safe from whatever revenge Emory might want to take. Putting it off on Gregory ain't going to harm him.

"What were you doing with that blank tape?"

"I'm going to leave it place of yours, so as not to upset Gregory when he comes out of the hospital." It's a shitty lie, but I ain't got a good one handy.

"It's the wrong brand."

"Gregory wouldn't notice."

"The tape or my fifty bucks. Tonight."

As soon as he's gone, I'm outside scooping up the Ziplocs and oregano, sorting out as much dirt as I can. Twigs and leaves don't matter so much, but dirt's obvious. And it don't burn. It takes me longer to walk to town than it does to sell the nickel bags. Then I'm standing at the Jiffy Rental counter with two hundred and thirty-nine fifty resting in front of me while I pick out my camcorder.

"You got a tripod fits this?" I ask.

Naturally they do, for another seven-fifty, but the camcorder deposit will cover any damage problem. Besides, I'm standing here with practically three hundred left over. What do I care?

"Driver's license," he says.

The printer is spitting out this long form in duplicate, and the asshole is asking me for a license. "DMV's got it. They're going to bronze it for me."

"No license, no rental."

"What?"

"Company policy."

"I got the money!"

"You're out of luck."

"Jesus fucking Christ." I walk before I deck the clerk. My crotch tears me with pain.

"Mr. Hutchins."

I could kill him. I could fucking kill him.

"Your money, Mr. Hutchins. You've left your money on our counter."

JIM

I just parked this minivan out back, and now the owner says she won't budge. All I need is for Frank to bill me for destroying a customer's vehicle. Sure enough, the van won't move. All I did was change the radiator and back it out into this space. Now it won't start.

"I'll check if there are any service bulletins on it," I tell the owner, which is as good a stall as I can come up with right now.

Wham!

It's a hell of a noise, and the first thing I can think of is earthquake. *Wham! Crash!* It ain't no earthquake, though the thuds and bangs shake the ground. Glass is breaking, metal's tearing in shrieks. It's Frank's Aged Rentals. Someone's playing demo derby in his lot. There's an old LTD and a Chevy Caprice ramming into those cars like they want to put all Frank's prized Aged Rentals right out of their misery.

Out of the back comes Frank himself, screaming as loud as those car crashes. And out of that LTD comes Lisa, and she's laughing and running with that goddamned Scooter Holler, who's just jumped from the Caprice before it rolls into a little Cavalier. I don't need no Breathalyzer to tell me their BAC is way over legal. Still, I'm thinking, Run! Goddamnit, run! Legal or not, she is my daughter.

"Ain't that Lisa?" Frank asks me, his voice hoarse from screeching. If he kept a gun at the garage, like he does during deer season, I swear he'd've killed them both. "And Scooter Holler? Now what the fuck did I ever do to those two?"

I don't guess this is the right time to remind him he did evict Lisa out of her place. No, he's probably not looking for that kind of answer at all because Frank is one of the guys who's always convinced that everything he does is reasonable and right, and anyone who disagrees, why, they're unreasonable and wrong. I suppose it makes it easier for him to live with himself, but it also makes it hard for him to understand anybody else. He don't understand Kari or Gary and they're his family.

"It's a mess, all right," I tell him. I figure it'll be a couple of hours of wrecker work disentangling those cars and figuring which ones to send to the junkyard. Course he got those wrecks cheap at the auction. I don't see any customers' cars out there. I do wish I had a nice big wrecker that'd allow me to disentangle the smashed and rammed and running wild members of my family. That's what I wish.

"I'm going to have to file charges on her, Jim. I just don't understand the girl."

"I know you don't, but it don't help any. It don't amount to day-old spit."

It takes me an hour working on this goddamn minivan to figure out the computer box is gone. The brain must have blown the minute I backed it into this space. At least it ain't nothing I did or didn't do, but it makes me think the brain's gone right out of the Hutchins clan. Soon's I replace the computer box, I'm heading home for some supplies, then right up to Gregory's. I think I'll include a six-pack on my list.

TOMMY

Buying this goddamn camcorder takes just about every cent I've got. Not counting the money for the lawyer, I barely had enough left over to buy a blank tape, to say nothing of a tripod. No tripod, which is going to complicate things, but what I really have to remember is the refund policy—sales slip, original packaging, and the merchandise.

"We got the three no's policy," says the salesclerk. "*No* questions, *no* hassles, *no* bull."

No ride, that's my policy. Lugging this thing three miles from the shopping center ain't my idea of paradise. When I get to Lisa's, both her and Scooter are passed out, so I take the keys to Scooter's truck. Then I pick up MB and head for Gregory's.

It'd be easier if I had someone to operate the camera, but MB won't go for that. It'd be a lot easier if I didn't have to drag all this packing around, but I need it to return the camera. Then I get my money back. Then I can pay Uncle back. It ain't my practice to extend credit, Uncle said, but seeing's you're family, I'll make an exception. Just don't you make me sorry. And don't give any away. In this business you have no friends. Remember that. Not even yourself.

At least I'll have enough to pay him back when I return the camera for my refund. I guess I'll have to give Emory back his fifty, unless I can figure out what the hell tape he's talking about. Gregory probably knows. Gregory probably took it when he was at Emory's. But it ain't at Gregory's. I'll have to pay Gregory a little visit at the New Hampshire State Hospital. Father says he's better. Let's see if he's better enough to make sense of the videotape Emory wants so bad.

"Tom?" MB's been sitting so quiet I'll bet she's been thinking as fast as me. She just better not be thinking of backing out, not now. "How're you going to do it?"

"I'll set the camera up on the table there, and we'll—"

"I mean there's no electricity there, is there? Didn't you tell me your brother had no electricity? Did you buy a battery for the camera? Is it charged?"

"You *really* want to do this." I run my hand on her thigh and run my tongue along her neck.

"Don't you run off the road," she says, slapping my hand back on the wheel. "The cops would love to catch you driving without a license again."

"Gregory had an outlet installed on a utility pole, but I'll need to pick up an extension cord."

"You'd better because I ain't doing this outdoors."

It takes me twenty minutes to drive over to the trailer, hoping every minute Momma ain't home and BB Eyes ain't prowling the town roads, then it takes me another twenty minutes to find the hundred-foot, red extension cord. It's way out in the back shed, right beside a pile of ashes and a half-melted videotape case. The label's burned right off, but it makes me wonder. Twenty more minutes, MB's gone through just about every cigarette we've got, and we reach Gregory's place. Thank God the extension cord stretches all the way into the house. So I turn her on, put in the blank tape, and we're ready for the show.

JIM

I can't fathom what the hell I did with my extension cord. I know I had it out here in the barn, and now here it is—gone. It looks like someone poked around Pauline's sex tape. Fucking bitch. Exactly right, fucking like a dog in heat, can't stay away from it. No wonder Tommy's all the time tripping over his dick. Poor bastard's got it in his blood, a curse right from his mother.

I slam an empty bottle down on the burned tape just like you'd crack the skull of some bastard attacking you in the dark. The jagged shreds of glass dare me to mash my face right down to them and kiss that filthy videotape. This beer goes to my head faster even than when I was a kid sneaking whiskey into the movies with Emory. Part of a quart he'd stole from home. I remember I was still drunk when I got home, my face flushed.

Then, oh, Jesus, did I puke and pray to God never to let liquor pass my lips again.

When I quit the last time, I prayed too, but I tried to be more sensible about it. I didn't want to die drunk. Now, it don't seem like such a bad idea.

Extension cord or no, I'm heading for Gregory's. I've got a grocery bag full of underwear and socks, and I've loaded three gallon jugs of water into the cab, so I guess I'm set.

I've got bills to pay. The town will take the property. Unless Emory pays the taxes. I suppose he can do that, just as he can sit and watch Pauline dance. Whatever impotence he had is long over. Just something to make people feel sorry for him after Helen died. After he killed her, because he pushed her down those stairs, whether he meant to or not. I guess Pauline didn't suffer any big guilt lying to cover up for him.

Blue lights.

"What is it, BB Eyes, you find another pair of panties on my property?" I finish off my beer and pitch it on the floor.

"How many of those have you had?" He points to the suitcase on the seat.

"Been so long since I bought beer," I tell him, "I didn't know how much I could save buying in bulk."

"Been so long you didn't know they changed the law. No open containers allowed now."

"BB Eyes, what's the chance of reopening the case of my sister's death. Really getting deep into it? Investigating Emory like he ought to be investigated?"

"Jim—"

"Be a bigger feather in your cap than catching the panty pervert."

"Jim, you aren't driving far, are you?"

"Out to Gregory's." I invite him to come out when he goes off duty. "We'll down a few."

"Don't you down any more until you get that truck in Gregory's yard. I'm going to have enough trouble with Lisa, but I won't go over there until she sleeps it off. Then maybe she'll be civil, or as near to it as she ever gets."

Off I drive, laughing and opening another beer. Fuck BB Eyes, I'm nearly to Gregory's gate anyways. It's open. I wonder who's down here now.

Just before reaching the yard, I cut the engine. The motor tick-ticks metal contractions while I drain the rest of my beer, letting the cool liquid bring that old warm feeling from my gut to my face to the top of my head. God, it can feel good to be alone for a while without my crazy family throwing carpet tacks in front of my wheels. Even the IRS can't call me out here.

But I'm not alone. There right in front of Gregory's place sits Scooter's truck. Jesus Christ, some brand of kick-me must have entered the Hutchins line a while back. God knows we all got it.

And look at this, my extension cord, running from post to front door, my name printed in extra-big black letters right at the plug. What in hell is that son of a bitch stealing my cord for? What's he doing in there? It's a cinch he ain't making coffee. I yank the plug straight out from that receptacle. I'll close down whatever operation that prick's got going.

"Hey!" It don't sound like Scooter. "Stick that back in."

Unsteady my feet may be, but my legs are running across the yard, up the steps, right into the place because the door ain't latched, to allow the cord to come in. And running right across the room is Mary Beth Jewell, stripped naked, hiding her face instead of her jouncing tits, her hairy pussy, her tight little ass. But Tommy is not running.

"For Christ's sake, Father," he says, pulling his pants up over his still stiff dick. "I told you to plug it back in." Out the door he runs, off to the utility pole.

Mary Beth, back to me, slides into her clothes. "Want me to holler 'rape' for you while you're busy dressing?" I ask her. She's too busy to even answer.

Back in runs Tommy and pops out a tape from a video camera I hadn't noticed sitting on the table. So that's what the cord's for.

"Out!" I yell. "Get out of here! Goddamn it all to hell, get out, and leave me the fuck alone."

Last week I saw a TV special about giant pandas that explained how they're a solitary animal. They live way up in the Chinese puckerbrush, and all they do is eat bamboo and once in a while get together to make baby pandas. They don't travel in herds. They don't sit around yakking about the other pandas over the hill or worry about what they've got or run off with their wives. They just keep to themselves and go about the business of eating. They eat about thirty pounds of bamboo a day, which is no small accomplishment when you think of it. So there you go, eat all day, leave the other pandas alone, it ain't a bad life really. These giant pandas are dying out. There ain't enough bamboo stands, and poachers are killing them to sell for rugs or something. I say it's a goddamn shame because I say those pandas could teach us a thing or two. I'll bet that's something old Fesmire and I might even agree on. Now ain't that something.

I crack a beer and open the door and head for my truck. Parking it around back will let me see anyone driving in before they see me.

I'm going to have to buy one of those multiple-outlet strips for my electricity here. I should have thought of that. I'll plug in a coffeepot, a hot plate, a TV, and a clock. No, screw the clock. There's a clock in the truck. Clock enough. And a fridge? No, I'll just use ice like Gregory did. The boy wa'n't altogether crazy. No one can say he was altogether crazy. When he gets out, he can come live here with me, and so can Lisa and her children. Gregory likes her children. Only she won't be able to drink and smash up cars like that. Jesus Christ. Of course, if Gregory's here to play with the kids like he does, turning into a regular pony for all the rides he gives them, why, Lisa won't be so quick to turn her hand to drink.

I grab a fresh beer. I forgot to bring any food out here. I'll just make up for it in beer. Pauline says there's calories in beer. When I started cooking, she said that's because you've quit drinking and found your appetite. It ain't buried under all that booze.

I wanted to have Tommy here too, but now I don't think so. He'd be dragging home snakes every night. And videotaping them. What the hell does he need videotapes of Mary Beth Jewell for? He sure as hell ain't any impotent pup. He ain't any Emory. He's got a dick on him like a divining rod for Christ's sake. I ought to smash this camera to hell. I'd like to smash every fucking video camera in the state to hell. I'm going to drink this beer, then I'm going to smash that camera into so many parts there won't be numbers high enough to count the parts.

I'm moving my hairy paws through the stiff shoots. Though snow crunches under my feet, the sun beats hot on my face. My sixth finger presses the bamboo in clumps. My teeth crunch the clumps, but my feet are cold. Something I haven't done. I've taken off my boots. I haven't pulled up the blanket. The blanket is under the video camera. I forgot to smash the video camera. It's too late now.

I'm smashed. Not dreaming now. Something is smashing things. Outside, some giant panda, growling. The roof tears. The sky shines through the roof. A rafter hits the table and smashes it. Another bite out of the roof. The sky shows, moon, and blurry stars, and the panda's giant arm, yellow. The fingers all together, and I run out the back door and watch the walls collapse into Gregory's house and smash Tommy's video camera all to pieces.

"You trying to kill me, you fucker? I thought you'd get around to killing again."

"I didn't know you were in there," says Emory, stepping out of the Case backhoe he's destroyed Gregory's place with. "If I wanted to kill you, I'd just shoot you."

Gregory's house creaks and cracks in a pile of broken wood.

"Why didn't you just burn it?"

"That's what I'm planning on doing next."

15

fifteen

PAULINE

Emory says he'll pay Gregory for the lumber and building materials in his cabin when Gregory comes home, which shows the size of Emory's heart. *He* was always bighearted, which I believe caused his sex problems after Helen died, and is also why I could never believe he deliberately pushed her down those stairs, as if he could cold-bloodedly kill her for money. That's the envy in people, that money, because a sight of money can twist what people see. That's what Pa used to say, and I've seen enough right in my very own house to say he's right. I've seen worry over money twist Jim until he's just as tight as knotted twine.

Gregory's place was tearing at the boy. His land, his house, and fighting with Emory and hating me for even talking to Emory, and calling me his sworn enemy, as if I wasn't the mother who raised him and cared for him and loved him every minute of his natural life. Maybe because I've had to put so much of my heart into Tommy, Gregory got to thinking I cared less for him, but it's never been so. I love them all. God, I love poor Elizabeth up there at the cemetery, how could I not love Gregory, living and walking the face of the earth?

Course none of them remember what day it is, not even Jim, wherever he is, drinking somewhere or pulled into some rest area to sleep it off. I can't blame Emory for not knowing the day. After all, it ain't a day he'd remember, but the others should because they were there.

I've got the cake and candles and the party hat sitting right here on the seat beside me, and I even remembered to bring a lighter and to buy new film for my Instamatic. They were selling packs of small hats, but I paid a little more money to get this big one, red with gold swirls around it. Fancy, like Elizabeth always wanted, pretty, just as pretty as can be, the cake's decorated with red and white unicorns all around the edge, and naturally, her name. It's a small cake, and her name covers right across the top in gold on the blue frosting, which cost me eight dollars. Next year I may not be able to spare the money.

It's all I can do to load myself up with cake and camera and lighter and party hat. It's dark, and the gate's closed. I walk slow because my back's hurting from all those beds and bathrooms I cleaned and made yesterday, but I'd walk slow anyways because I'm not going to trip here in the dark and drop my cake.

Safely at the grave, I set down the cake and light the candles. I only put on twelve because she'll always be turning twelve, so I never get any more than twelve candles. Then I set the red and gold party hat on the doll's head, pulling the elastic down around her chin. When the camera shows ready, back I step to snap a picture.

"Hold it."

I turn into the glare of a high-powered flashlight. Shielding my eyes, I ask who it is.

"What are you doing, Mrs. Hutchinson? It's after dark. Don't you know the cemetery closes at dark. Don't you know you can't be in here?"

"Sergeant Dumont. It's Hutchins."

"Right."

"It's my daughter's birthday. Little Elizabeth."

He gulps like I hit him right in his hairy Adam's apple. Then he turns the flashlight onto the Cabbage Patch doll, plays the light up to the hat, and gulps again. "What are you doing?"

"It's a little party for Elizabeth," I tell him. "Elizabeth was always a party girl."

"I never heard of such a thing." His flashlight beam bounces from headstone to cake to me.

"You have children, Sergeant Dumont?"

"I've got kids."

"Good. Please shine your light on the headstone. The flash on this Instamatic is a little weak." I snap a couple of pictures, then move farther back to get the grave, the cake, and the doll all in the same shot. Last Halloween I took three really good pictures of the doll with its costume on, a fairy princess.

"Mrs. Hutchins."

"I usually wait until the candles burn down a little. Then I blow them out, take my things, and go. I don't leave behind any litter or any fire danger."

"Mrs. Hutchins," he says. "Mrs. Jewell, Alice, asked me to find you. She's my tenant, you see, and—"

"I know that." I wish I had a high-powered flashlight right now to shine in his eyes while I tell him what else I know about him and his tenant, Mrs. Alice Jewell.

"She'd like to talk with you."

"We used to be friends."

"She wants to show you something. If you agree to look at it, it can keep Tommy out of jail. Mrs. Hutchins, I realize this is a bad time, but if I were you, I'd see her."

"Tommy's going to jail anyway."

"Mrs. Hutchins, in jail the inmates have a code." He looks away, then turns off his flashlight. "They get a guy in there for a sex crime, like a rape, they call him a skinner, and they hate him." He says the inmates torment and even beat these skinners. "They have their ways. Sometimes it's through the food, sometimes other ways."

I agree to see Alice because we were friends, and to help Tommy stay out of jail I'll do what I have to. I'm thinking I've brought cake and a party hat to my daughter's grave, and Alice used a gun and a bucket of tar to take care of her daughter. Slob, the first thing I think when I walk into Alice's apartment. All the time I've known Alice, I never thought such things, but now all I see is mess. I hope she doesn't expect me to show her any sympathy because I've got no sympathy.

"Look, Pauline," she says, "we're both mothers, mothers who want to protect their children. I've only got Mary Beth—"

"You think I love mine any less because I've got four? And I've got one at the cemetery, so don't talk to me about protecting children."

"Pauline, let's watch a little TV while we talk."

A TV is in the room, a big one. There's lots of machines under the TV, making me wonder how many times a month Sergeant Dumont goes in and out this door to collect his rent. She pushes buttons on her clicker, and the TV comes to life.

"Now my daughter's not of age, and your Tommy is, which makes for a problem."

On the TV is her daughter, pushing her hair away from her face. Half these young girls spend their time growing and teasing and poufing up their hair, then they're always at it to get it out of their face. Mary Beth's not a pretty girl, small nose and heavy eyebrows that grow too close together. Tommy's not just taken by looks, I know that.

"Mary Beth's in love with Tommy," I say. "She won't go to any court against him."

Mary Beth's unbuttoning her blouse. I don't know why, it's a crazy idea, but I think she's trying out for something, like cheer-leading or auditioning for a play. When she unsnaps her bra, I know it isn't anything to do with school.

"There are other ways to go to court, Pauline. And there are other charges besides rape."

On Mary Beth's breast is a tattoo, a drawing it takes me a minute to figure out. It's a man, holding her breast and running a long tongue to her nipple. "I think you have to be of age to get a tattoo," I say.

"Not if Tommy does it for free. I guess he must be quite the artist."

I'm thinking her daughter's no innocent babe to have that drawing on her chest, and I don't think Tommy forced it on her. Mary Beth is smiling now, a big smile as she unbuttons her jeans and slides out of them, leaving her standing there in nothing but her black panties. I guess nobody'll have to steal them. She'll gladly give them away. She steps back, and the camera moves like it's pointing to a simple single bed. Only then do I realize this is Gregory's place.

"When did you get this tape?" I ask.

"Last night. It was a gift."

Mary Beth's a fleshy girl, fleshy breasts, fleshy belly, fleshy hips and thighs. By the time she's forty she'll be fat, and there won't be anybody calling her fleshy. There won't be anybody calling her at all, unless it's the landlord for his rent.

Someone's coming from behind the camera. It's Tommy. He puts his hands behind Mary Beth's neck and pulls her to him for a big kiss, a French kiss with their mouths open and their tongues wagging against each other.

"Tommy gave me the tape." Alice lights a cigarette, and by the sloppy way she pulls it from her mouth, I can tell she's been drinking, drinking a lot. "He's not as smart as he thinks he is."

Tommy's hopping on one foot, pulling off his jeans. His underwear is stained, not dirty but stained from the ointments they put on him at the hospital. Mary Beth reaches to pull off his T-shirt and knocks him off-balance. "Shit," he says. The camera's tilted, looking up at the rafters I guess. It's dark. "Shit," he says again. The camera comes back to the bed, and Tommy, naked except for his socks, comes back into the picture. His crotch, all dark red and hairless, looks like one of those funny baboons with the bright-colored behinds.

"I know what happens next," I say. "I don't have to watch it to find out how the story ends."

Hands move over each other's bodies. "Ooh!" Tommy screams. Mary Beth must have got to some part that doesn't feel so good, from her mother's tarring and the hospital's degreasing.

"That was my favorite scene," Alice says. "Leave if you want to, but if you do, I'll turn this over to BB Eyes to prosecute Tommy. I don't think there's any doubt that is Tommy Hutchins and not some other guy who looks like Tommy and has a red crotch."

My fingers grip the sofa's cloth so tight my wedding band's standing up from my finger. I wonder when she vacuumed this couch last. The dust lies in layers on it. It has mixed with my sweat and turned my hand dirty.

"How about a nice long suck?" Tommy asks, though he's looking more at the camera than at Mary Beth.

"I love to suck your big hard dick," Mary Beth says. She too looks more at the camera than at Tommy.

A grunt comes out of Alice, and she takes a big drag from her cigarette. "Nice talk for a young girl," she says. "She never used that language before she started running with Tommy."

"I don't think he's that fast a teacher."

Tommy's lying on his back. Gently, more gently than I would've guessed the girl could find, Mary Beth lifts his penis into her mouth. It isn't big and hard yet, so she fits most of the length of it inside her mouth.

"Don't turn away, Pauline. The deal is you watch this, all of it, or Tommy will be rubbing that thing on a jail-bed mattress."

I didn't know I had turned away. What was I looking at? The doorway out to the kitchen where a pizza box covers the table like a cheap decoration.

Tommy's hard now. Just the head is in Mary Beth's mouth. "Suck harder," he says, this time to her, not the camera. There must not be anyone running the camera because it doesn't move, like get closer, the way they did in the X-rated movie Emory showed me. I don't need close-ups to make this worse.

Mary Beth pulls her face away, licks her lips, and says to the camera, "Ummm, good."

"He rehearsed her," Alice says. "The son of a bitch rehearsed her."

Mary Beth sets her face over Tommy's crotch, careful not to put any pressure on his tender flesh. His skin looks like old cat food, horrible to think, but it does, even if he is my son. Mary Beth sticks her tongue out and licks Tommy's testicles. She doesn't touch them with her hands. Tommy has reached around to grab Mary Beth's breasts and rub her nipple between his finger and thumb.

"Yeah," she says. "I love that."

There's a moldy smell from this couch, not animal hair, but unwashed people, old sweat, maybe worse. I wonder if this is where Alice pays her rent. I wonder if Mary Beth learned her tricks watching from the other room.

Tommy turns restless. Off the bed he walks into the camera, tells Mary Beth to lie down, then the camera moves towards her face in a jerky motion that turns my stomach. He straddles Mary Beth and slides his penis between her fat breasts.

I look at Alice. She's not watching the television. She's watching me, and she points a finger at the screen but says nothing, like the teachers in grade school, so sure of their power, they didn't have to speak. Woe to you if they spoke. Woe to Tommy if I don't watch this disgusting movie.

Just the tip of his penis is in her mouth now. She's sucking and licking as fast as she can. She keeps her eyes open. Not at the camera, just open, like she might be washing the dishes. It shocks me, this girl, bold as a March wind, keeps sucking his penis with her eyes wide open.

When Tommy shoots off, she still doesn't close her eyes. Cream spurts in her wide open mouth, on her tongue, runs down her chin, onto her cheeks. She licks her lips, her eyes still open.

"Look, Ma," she says, "no hands."

From beside him Tommy takes his underpants and wipes the cream off Mary Beth's face.

"When I put my head on my pillow," Alice tells me, "that's what my face touched, those filthy underpants, wrapped on that tape. MB knows there's no light in the bedroom. She did that deliberately."

"I guess you shouldn't have taped them to his face," I say, because Alice acts like she's got no part in this at all.

"There are laws, Pauline. There are laws—"

"Yes, there are!" I'm standing, and I'm shouting now. "But you didn't go to the law. You went to a gun and a can of tar. And as for your darling daughter, I didn't see any gun to her head."

"She's a child."

"Alice Jewell, don't you for a single breath's time think I like this thing. Mary Beth is not a girl I'd pick for Tommy, not if all the others had hooves."

"Good." She presses her clicker and plucks the tape out of her VCR. "Here's your tape. Keep Tommy away from Mary Beth."

If shameless has a name, it's Mary Beth Jewell, and she's got her hooks set so deep into Tommy, he thinks he's pulling his own strings.

TOMMY

It ain't bad enough Uncle calls me at Lisa's to sell me another pound and, by the way, ask for his five hundred for the first pound. I got to walk all the way out here on a bad foot and a burning crotch to see Gregory's place tumbled to the ground. Scooter's pissed off because I used his truck and caught a rock in the rear wheel well racing out of Gregory's road. You Hutchinses can't do anything right, he grumbled, still hungover from yesterday. Nothing except fuck. He looked at Lisa when he said that. Then she punched his face, cut his lip. You can't say that about me, she said. I'm a mother. Then she licked the blood off his lip. Moodiest woman I know, my sister. I'm in a mood now. Gregory's place lies in wreckage all over my camcorder. The camcorder I've got to return. I'm sure the original packing material is stove all to hell and the camera itself may not be good for much other than packing material. I don't know why I can't get one simple plan to work without someone coming along to fuck it up.

Father, of course, wouldn't have the brains to take the thing with him when he left because he's so damn trusting. He thinks I'm the only thief in town. Nor did I murder my wife and steal his, like a certain brother-in-law he knows. No, Father can only see the problems and troubles I cause him, the ones up close, without noticing how Emory and Frank Reed and God knows how many others who aren't even related to him are dicking him over.

It looks like there's a tunnel right here. After all, the place didn't collapse flat and level, so maybe the camcorder's sitting in there just as cherry as fresh paint. I find Father's red extension cord, something to follow through this trash to locate my treasure. Maybe fate's going to stop farting in my face for a while.

I wish I could've seen Alice Jewell's face when she watched that video—when she saw MB's face with my cum on her. That's the only downside of that deal—I didn't get to see old Alice's reaction. Otherwise, it went slicker than pussy juice, no weapons, no threats, no violence, and MB laid those cum-soaked underpants of mine right on her mother's pillow. Alice better worry about what will happen if I really get serious.

Right here the extension cord ducks under and runs through this other tunnel. It don't look like I can heave these rafters off or even slide them over, so I guess I'm going to have to turn cave explorer. Hell, no one could ever say this boy don't have balls, even if they have been tarred black and scoured red.

This ain't no easy crawl. Whatever Gregory nailed, he hammered it home well and true, so I can't just shove and push my way through here. It's more by way of a slither that I make any progress. Course all along my leg hurts and my crotch burns. I must be getting used to it, like it's part of my permanent condition in life. Right by this big carrying timber runs the extension cord, diving down into the rubble. Pushing along with my good leg, I slide as close to that timber as I can get.

God, it's dark in here. No place to turn around. I'll have to crab out, dragging the camcorder as I go, no not dragging, carrying as best I can because I don't need to put any more damage onto what it already has. I hope it's just nested in there. If it fell and then the table tipped over above it, the camera might have been protected. Lucky thing the place wasn't flattened into the ground.

Shoving and pushing, I've muscled my way at least another body length into the hole. I can't see a goddamned thing. Just following the extension cord keeps me going. Goddamnit. I've reached the end of the cord. Maybe Father did take the camcorder. But why didn't he take his precious extension cord too? No, the plug must have pulled out when the house collapsed. I just hope it didn't rip out the back of the camera.

I'm moving blind now, no light, no extension cord to guide me. I've got to find it. I'm in tight now. Boards and beams hem me like a goat-tight fence. I'm scrunching my shoulders and squeezing my chest to wiggle through. Behind me I hear wood shifting, creaking, and cracking, even falling, though nothing's going to fall far enough to hurt me. I hear something else. A motor. Jesus Christ, here it is!

I feel that hard, black plastic, like my fingers feel the black even in the dark. No crack, no breaks, just smooth black plastic and its cord. I'll bet there ain't a thing wrong with it. Once again effort and guts have saved my ass.

The noise is an engine, truck engine, idling. I hear the door open and slam. The engine's still idling. It ain't Father. He always shuts his off. Besides, his never sounds so smooth. Nothing Father does is smooth.

"Hello!" It's Emory Holler. "Anybody in there?" He laughs like he thinks he's witty. Why the hell is he here? I suppose he's the one that knocked Gregory's house down, so now he's out viewing his work. Seeing there's no naked women around to entertain him, he won't stay long, unless Momma is stripping up on the truck bed.

I'll just lie here until he goes. I don't need him bothering me about that fucking fifty dollars or trying to take away the camcorder. I've got my hand right on it ready to pull it along with me as soon as he leaves.

What's that smell? Smells like gasoline for Christ's sakes. Shit, it's diesel, and it's burning. The asshole's torched the place. Jamming backward, I make a couple of feet and stop. If I go out there, Emory's going to take away the camcorder. I'll have to drag it with me until I can just jump up and run. With this bum foot I won't run very fast, but if he don't see the camera, he won't chase me anyways. He don't care that much about his fifty bucks.

Smoke from the diesel seeps into my space. I won't be able to stay here much longer without heaving up a lung. Emory'd find me easy enough then. My best bet lies in ramming right back, jumping up free of this junk, and making a run for it right across the yard to the woods.

I'm moving as fast as I can without hollering or dislodging boards. Finding the tunnel with my feet ain't easy. I'm baffled with choices, while concentrating on dragging the camcorder out. Jesus. A board carrying what's got to be a tenpenny spike has jabbed right into my ass. If I'm snagged on the son of a bitch, I'll just about have the meat. My burned crotch is screaming for a lukewarm bath.

Wriggling ain't getting me nowhere but dug with that spike.

The flames are getting closer because I hear the wood cracking. Trust Gregory to use seasoned lumber when he built. If I stay here much longer, that's what I'll be—seasoned lumber. I go forward. It works. Going forward freed me from that spike so I can crawl backwards again. Ain't that fucking amazing.

I'll be out of here in a minute, which is a good thing because the heat is cooking me now. The fire must be close. The tunnel should turn up here. Only it doesn't. It doesn't turn anywhere. It's blocked. Now I remember the sounds of shifting wood, boards which must have tumbled into my passageway. Passageway no more. Now it's a close-ended tunnel. Now it's a goddamn tomb.

I'm thrashing what little I can, but not a stick moves. I ain't careful about noise or drawing attention to myself now. The only thing I'm careful about is the camcorder. I fucking hurt all over.

"Help!" I'm yelling as loud as I can. "Help!"

"What the hell?" Emory says.

"Over here!" I scream. I shove up on those boards to make a volcano of wood for him to find me. "Here! Here!" The fire's burning my goddamn feet. I can't breathe.

He clomps across the boards. I reach for the camcorder. He's almost here. Crack! A board snaps, the pile gives way. I feel his foot on my hand, see daylight. He grabs my hand and pulls me up out of the wood and spikes, and as I rise, he sinks a little, his boots squashing down on my camcorder. The case cracks and splits.

He drags me off the ruins, and I hobble away from the fire.

"You all right?" he asks. He's lighting a cigarette and offering me one, which I turn down. I see all the smoke I want to see as my camcorder melts in the middle of Gregory's house.

"I'm okay."

"What the hell were you doing in there, you stupid fuck?"

I'm picking goddamn splinters out of my hands and trying to think how I'm going to come up with five hundred bucks for

Uncle without giving him the lawyer's money. Just when you think things have screwed you six ways to Sunday, they find a seventh way. I yank a splinter out from under my thumbnail. Emory's looking at me like I owe him an answer. Which I don't.

"Digging in there for more pot. Weren't you?" I nod my head because I'm not going to explain about the video. "It's supposed to be a recreational drug, but the only recreation you're going to get is growing flowers out of your chest."

Fuck you, I think, but I don't say it because I got enough troubles.

Here comes the cruiser, lights aflashing, and BB Eyes pushing his fat body out onto solid ground. "I saw the fire and wondered," he says to Emory. I figure he's going to bust him for arson, and I'm smiling when he turns to me. "Tommy, you're under arrest. You know I've got to cuff you."

LISA

It ain't bad enough I've got this killer headache, I've got to drag the kids over to Frank Reed's garage so he can bitch me out for smashing up his rental cars. Father says if I don't come, Reed'll have me in the jail, which is a nice way to invite somebody, I think, but Father just said, Bring the kids, and the first words out of your mouth better be "I'm sorry."

"I'm sorry," I tell Reed. That geeky son of his, Gary, stands there with his hands in his back pockets. Only piece of ass he ever gets, that's what Scooter says about Gary.

"To protect myself and my insurance, I've had to file charges," Reed says. He don't fool around with any "nice day" or "cute kids," the way Father does. "I'll be happy to drop them if you make restitution." We're standing in his store full of auto parts in front of his garage full of work, and he expects me to pay him?

"Look, I was drunk, Mr. Reed. I don't get a lot of fun out of life, so when I drink, I drink too much. I didn't set out to damage your property. I thought those cars were just junkers waiting to be hauled off. I was surprised that any of them ran. I do apologize."

It seems Scooter and my uncle will pay for half the damage, but, of course, my father hasn't got money like Emory, so Frank Reed is asking me for it.

"Prosecuting ain't something he wants to do," says Gary. He is a whiny little creep. His nose still looks like shit from where Tommy decked him.

"I won't be able to pay anything if I'm in jail," I say.

"Oh, they won't keep you in jail," Reed says, "only I've got to file charges or my insurance company won't pay."

The kids fuss because they're edgy here. If Father would pick one of them up or give them something to play with, they'd settle, but he acts more like a stranger than their grandfather. On most days the kids give him a "Hi, Grampy!" and he wrings out a smile to wipe the tears off half a dozen babies.

"I guess you'll have to prosecute," I tell Reed, "because I don't have any money at the end of the month. Most of what I get on the third of the month is gone on the fourth for bills."

Back at the apartment I call Fesmire because I've got to get the money somehow. He sends me twenty-five a week for the kids and gives me a twenty here and there. Of course that's under the table so the welfare won't reduce their payments. Every penny you got, they want to take something away. It's a wonder they don't come down to confiscate the kids' Christmas presents.

"Where am I going to get that kind of money, Lisa?"

"You could sell your boat."

"False economy. False economy all around. Then I'd have to buy fish instead of getting it for free. Why I'd eat the value of that boat in no time. You might as well tell me to sell my gun."

"I'm in a fix here, Leo."

"That you are, but you hold tight, and I'll be down to see what I can do. Course I'll lose a day's pay doing it."

He won't even tell me where he's working. He says he shifts jobs a lot, says I'd spend all his money just trying to reach him at his work, and then maybe even lose him the job because it's one of those occupations where they don't allow personal calls. Very professional, he says, they've got a sign right by the telephone says NO PERSONAL CALLS DURING BUSINESS HOURS.

Shaking. Rattled. I'm being shaken. My eyeballs clang in my head. "No wonder you got no money," Leo says, "sleeping naked on the couch in the middle of the day."

"It's suppertime."

"I see that. I see the children out there getting supper while you lie in here."

"Aren't you proud that your children can take care of themselves? Didn't you always preach at me about self-sufficiency?"

"I love the two that are mine. The other one ain't my responsibility."

"You prick!"

"It's my prick, and I know where it's been and done, and what it ain't done." He lights his pipe and sits his skinny self in the stuffed chair. "Put some clothes on, and we'll talk about my children."

Stretched out there on my chair with his pipe going, he does stink. After I came back here, Father told me he could always smell Fesmire. Hot clothes and no baths, I said. I must have gotten used to it. Father said, You shouldn't've gotten used to him starving you and knocking you around. That ain't hot clothes or no baths or not believing in this or that. That's meanness. You shouldn't get used to meanness. And I shed myself of it, not taking anything from anybody since, only now Father doesn't feel sorry for me or proud of me. He just treats me like a car that he can't fix.

Along with his smell Leo's got his meanness back. He'll take Rebecca and Seth home with him. That's his solution to my financial problems. Alison, not being a Fesmire, will stay with me, allowing me to still collect AFDC, and I can visit Rebecca and Seth every other weekend. It's all very sensible the way he's worked it out.

"Where's the money I'm supposed to pay Frank Reed for his goddamned cars?"

"That's another matter. Yes, that's not to do with me and my children."

"Goddamn you, Leo, it'll have to do with you and your children if I have to go to jail!" Headache or not, I'm standing now, and I'll have satisfaction, or I'll be throwing things.

"Indeed it will if you go to jail," he says, standing himself and pointing the stem of his pipe at me, "because then I'll file a petition to have you declared an unfit mother. Then I won't be suggesting Rebecca and Seth live with me. Then they'll take your fatherless Alison away too, so when you get out of jail, you'll wish you had a boat to go fishing in."

"I ain't like you, Leo. I ain't afraid of work. And if you try to take my kids, I ain't afraid—" I kick, as high and as quick as I can. I connect. He's turned, though, so I get his thigh. He has my foot. Jesus Christ! He yanks me off the floor and grabs my other ankle. I sock him in the crotch. Bang, he slams my head to the floor. The blood runs to my brain so I can hardly keep my eyes open.

I don't see him leave the room. I barely hear the car pull away on the street, so I don't know who brought him down here unless he threw his principles to the wild animals and got a driver's license. Bet he didn't. Bet he's got some bitch with a license and a car. That's why he wants the kids so he can cash in on their support, now that he's got a mommy for them, a cunt that'll baby-sit. I'll tear his balls off before I let him take my kids and give them to another woman. And the bitch better watch her ass too.

It takes me most of an hour on the telephone to locate Scooter, but I tell him to hustle his truck over here. I load the kids and their pj's and their sleepy toys in the cab, and we ride up to the trailer. Nearly to the trailer because Scooter still won't chance parking on Father's land. Say what you want about Scooter, when he's sober, he's as conservative as an old man peering just over the steering wheel.

"I guess he won't be taking the kids," Father says after I tell him about Leo's visit. "Where does Fesmire get such ideas anyway? He must watch channels no one else receives."

"He's got a girlfriend," I say. "She's giving him ideas."

Momma asks if the kids have eaten. She leads them down to the end of the trailer to put their sleepy toys in her bedroom.

"Give me Gregory's shotgun," I tell Father. "I won't sleep if I don't have some way to defend myself."

"It ain't right, Lisa," Father says, and though I'm not sure what he means, I just wait. He gets me that shotgun but no shells for it. "This ought to do it. Fesmire ain't going to risk getting shot over money. I can smell that in him."

"Make more sense for you to stay here," Momma says. I shake my head. "Or I could get you a unit at the motel for a couple of nights?"

"I ain't letting no man run me out of my home," I say.

After he drives me home, Scooter wants to come in, but I'm not interested in sex tonight. I do three shots of vodka to quiet the sawing in my head. Something else is wrong too. I check all the screens, lock the back door, lay the shotgun next to me on my bed. I know what it is. Out of the closet comes the room refresher. Spray deodorizes the room. Droplets fill the living room air until it feels like it's raining. Finally, I rid the place of Leo's smell. Then, all lights out, I lie into dreams.

People are skinny. Everybody's skinny. Their faces flow in the neon-crayon lines, bright colors, primary colors, plus pink and lime, like we were all dipped in sherbet. Father says, Out here, he doesn't smell, he smiles. Leo, gliding along the ground without bending his knees, smiles silently. He doesn't have to speak. Only Gregory wears different colors, gray and faded blues. From a hospital bed he waves to me. He's not smiling. He's not silent. He calls to me, yells my name, orders me to come here. Come here! he's yelling. Come here!

I can't tell where we are except I know we're outside. Even the trees wear these daring colors, ringlets of red and green and blue hang from their branches. Sitting in the sky are the kids, each on a different cloud. They're so far up I can't see the expressions on their faces.

Here, here, sounds again, only it's not Gregory, not yelling, not loud, more like whispering.

Breathing.

Real breathing. In my room. I open my eyes as quietly as I can. My head clears of colors. Everything in my room is dark, except for the breathing. Leo. He's looking for the kids, only he won't find them. For once I'm smarter than Mr. Leo Fesmire. I've got the gun. The bureau drawer slides open. What the hell is he looking for?

I keep my eyes on his dark form and reach for the shotgun. It's not here! I had it right beside me. Did he take it before I woke up? I pat the bed for it.

"What the hell?" It's not Leo.

He's on me. His hands pull my shirt up over my face and hold it there. My arms are caught. I can't see. I can hardly breathe. His mouth is on my tits. Tonguing, biting, pain runs from my nipple to my navel in a string. Tearing pain. I jam my knee in his crotch. Not hard enough. He rolls to the side. One hand holds the T-shirt and locks my arms. Grabbing with the other, he yanks at my panties. His fingers are in my slit, jamming hard to get inside my pussy.

"You bastard!" I yell. "You son of a bitch! Help!"

"Shut up, and I won't hurt you."

It's Gary Reed. He's not whining now, but it's his voice.

"Help!"

Slap. It's an open-hand slap, stinging through my shirt, snapping my face over. My nose runs blood. "Shut up."

I wait. He's not messing with my tits now. Out comes his dick. I can feel it warm and soft on my leg. He digs his fingers into my crotch again. Dry, rough, it burns.

"Lick it," I tell him.

He moves his head down to my cunt. His arm, still holding the shirt and trapping my arms, stretches across my chest and neck. He's losing leverage. I feel his mouth against my skin. I slam my knee against his chin and roll off the bed. I pick up the shotgun from the floor and click on my light.

There he stands, Gary Reed, little dick hanging out his fly and blood coming over his lip.

"I'll kill you!" I yell.

He moves toward the door.

"I'll shoot you!" I yell.

As if he knows the gun is empty, he turns to me. "You wouldn't shoot anybody."

I swing the barrel and lam his arm near his elbow. Something cracks. "Get out now."

He holds his arm. "I'll get you, Lisa."

I follow him right out the door and lock it after him. I guess since his father owns the building, getting a key didn't take Gary a lot of trouble. Back in the bedroom, I see my underwear all messed up in the bureau drawer. Then I know what the hell he was doing here.

16

sixteen

JIM

Things could be worse. I could be sleeping in the truck. But with no place to go and grandchildren to protect, I went back to the trailer. I didn't slink, and I didn't swagger either. I don't keep my pride like old Fesmire. No, sir. Poverty washes the starch right out of my principles.

At least Frank Reed ain't going to prosecute Lisa no more, though he says the insurance company will still want their money.

"Everybody wants their money, Frank," I tell him. "I want my money, only the IRS won't let me have it."

"It wouldn't be fair to make Scooter make restitution for his half of those rental cars and let Lisa get away without paying a cent."

"Why? Did your boy try to rape Scooter too?" If it's one thing I'm champion at, it's having trouble with kids, so I don't feel all cold and harsh reminding him about Gary. He won't be the first kid in town to go to jail, only his name ain't Hutchins. Frank must figure if you're not a Hutchins, then you're deserving of an extra glass of human kindness.

"He's pathetic," Frank tells me for maybe the twelfth time today. "Stealing underwear. He didn't even think Lisa was home. He thought she'd gone to your place. She just scared him is all, otherwise he'd never touched her."

"And what scared him when he planted those panties up to my place? He damn near landed me in jail."

He says Gary was probably trying to get back at Tommy for breaking his nose. Gary thought Tommy had moved back to the trailer after he got out of jail.

"He seems to make a lot of mistakes about where people live, don't he?" I say. "I'd like to punch him out myself if I knew where to find him."

"I told BB Eyes, and I'm telling you, I don't know where he is."

"Just don't think the cops are the only ones looking for him."

Right now I'm glad Tommy's back in jail because if he were out, he'd be rashing up and down the countryside wanting a club for Gary Reed. And right about now Gary Reed's turned dangerous for the first time in his life and might end up shooting Tommy on sight. I told Emory just exactly that so he wouldn't listen to any pleas from Pauline to put up Tommy's bail. I told him the boy's blood would be on his hands if Tommy got out and got shot. I told him he had enough of my family's blood on his hands already. Now that was harsh, but I can't say I feel like treating Emory like a baby bunny lately. And I ain't the only one. When Gregory gets out, he might want to take a 'dozer to Emory's place.

I'm thinking of that big D7 'dozer up to Malcolm's place. I've got to head up there to check on the bees. Malcolm bought these fancy, docile Italian bees to pollinate his trees and produce honey. He's spent enough money on those docile bees to give each one a dollar and send him to the store to buy a pound of honey.

I get done with them, I've got to feed the trout. Once upon a time there was a nice little swamp beside Malcolm's place, the kind of swamp that minds its own business and does nobody any harm, which is just the kind of swamp a rich man like Malcolm's got to attack and turn into a trout pond.

It's quite a sight all right. All summer adults won't swim in it because of the bloodsuckers. Come winter it freezes over to a nice skating pond, only Malcolm won't even put a pair of skates next to his feet. He won't tell me how much this pond cost. He has done all right by the trout. They've prospered. He's never caught a one of them, nor has anybody else.

When I throw the food into that pond, the water just boils with fish. There are so many of them, I'll bet he's up nights naming them.

"Jim," he says, "BB Eyes says he can't find Gary. He says Lisa's demanding twenty-four-hour police protection from Gary. Maybe you ought to go down there."

"I can't give her no twenty-four-hour protection. I can't even protect myself."

"And another thing, get rid of Gregory's shotgun. Give it to BB Eyes or sell it or do something with it before one of you Hutchinses kills someone with it."

But when I get to Lisa's, I see it's too late because Gregory's shotgun rests right in Gregory's lap, and the only thing I'm wondering about is why the box of shells is here too.

"Momma dropped them off when she left the children," Lisa tells me, "on her way to work."

"You're looking spruce, Gregory," I tell him.

He's cleaner and fatter than when he left. I haven't seen him for a month. "They tell me I'm all right," he says. "I told them I didn't ever want another one of them headaches as long as I live."

So he takes his pills regularly. His "meds," he calls them, patting the bulge in his pants pocket.

"Doesn't Gregory look good?" Lisa says.

"He looks fit as a billy goat in the spring." I wonder when he's going to bring up about my kneecapping him. I also wonder has he slid any shells into that goddamn shotgun. "Looks like he's fit to tackle any man-sized job they put in his way."

"I got a chance at Tommy's old job," he says, "cutting and splitting cordwood. But Tommy's got to say it's okay first."

"Tommy ain't going to care," says Lisa. "Tommy ain't going to care about any job for a couple months." I'm waving at her to shut up.

"Tommy's got to say it's okay," Gregory says again.

"I'll take care of that shotgun for you," I tell him, but as I reach for it, up he stands and presses the gun to his chest like it was his very own child. The kneecapping could be playing in his mind right now, turning me into the latest of his sworn enemies. His eyes, calm blue, tell me no more than the dark end of the shotgun barrel.

"It's mine. I'll be responsible for it."

"Let's take it out to the trailer," I say. "You going to stay there, ain't you?"

Course it's going to be crowded, what with our room used and Elizabeth's room locked up, the third room where Lisa's kids sleep when they come up ain't much more than a double closet. Ain't even got a bed in it.

"Maybe Momma could make some shepherd's pie," he says. "I ain't eaten a shepherd's pie since the skies fell."

"Sure she will, Gregory," Lisa says. "Or I'll make it if she can't."

"I like hers. I'm used to hers." Gregory's talking calm like it was just roads and weather with no sworn enemies and voices from the radio. I don't like this "skies fell" business, but at least he ain't waving his gun around and threatening anybody. I'd like to get him out of here because if there's to be a fracas, it oughtn't be in front of Lisa's kids. God knows they've seen enough in the fracas department.

"Let's get up to the trailer and stow your gun away," I say. "You ain't going to split no firewood with that."

"Lisa said she was glad I came because she was afraid," Gregory says. "I been protecting her. I wouldn't let anyone hurt the children. Anyone who'd want to hurt the children—or Lisa either— why, I'd stop them."

There ain't a bit of fury on his face or in his voice, and don't that scare me even more than if there was. "BB Eyes is handling it," I tell him. "This is his job now."

"I don't get into nothing with the police. I don't break any laws."

"Leo's coming down," Lisa says. "I called him this morning, and he said he'd be down as soon as he could. You just go along with Father, Gregory. I'll be all right. BB Eyes said he'd check the place for any sign of Gary."

"Gary should have his eyes ripped out," Gregory says. "He pretended to be a friend of mine."

The bitterness in his words make my eyes burn.

TOMMY

I must be a popular guy the way the cops snap my pictures at every stop. First at the local station, and then out here at Webster County with the trick mirror. When I ask the screw would he like to take another one for his mother, he tells me he can start writing me up anytime.

"Hutchins," he says, "you been here before. That means you carry an additional charge now."

"What's that?" I ask as he wipes my hand for fingerprinting.

"Stupidity. They should've charged you with stupidity."

I tell him all the stuff from DOB to social security number. When he asks for my driver's license number, I laugh. I tell him I'm a nonsmoker.

"Since when?" he asks.

There's no smoking at County, so I figure they'll watch me a little less if they think I quit. "For my kid. I didn't want to smoke around my boy."

I'm tired, and I'm hungry. If he doesn't hurry up, I'll miss dinner at four and have to lie on a goddamn bunk listening to TV until eleven with my stomach providing music for the stupid show. I can't sleep with all the noise from the pod, and I'll be having a goddamn nicotine fit at the same time. The screw hands me the property sheet to sign, listing all my stuff BB Eyes sent up, watch and wallet and lighter, and holds it halfway between us, like a shank he might stab me with.

"I ain't illiterate," I tell him. "I can sign my name."

"What're you carrying a lighter for if you don't smoke?"

"My girlfriend smokes. And I'm a gentleman."

I'm in the tank while the screw goes out for a smoke or whatever the hell he's doing. You always know which screws smoke because you can smell it on them. They like to get close to you so you can suffer. I drink out of the faucet and piss into the toilet. Both sink and bowl are stainless steel, a little dull gleam to shock the eyes and make you feel you're in an up-to-date, sterile, medical-type facility. Course it's easier to clean. I know that. I've cleaned the son of a bitch after some bastard heaved and shit all over the place, even the concrete slab they call a bed. But I ain't drunk, so they don't leave me here long.

A different screw, Correctional Officer Cross, tells me to strip. Standing there, tall, lean, real military, and holding my papers, he looks like a real Boy Scout. "Don't you want to bring in a female officer?" I ask. "Got a girlfriend or a wife on the staff?"

"Mr. Hutchins, how would it be if the other inmates learned you were charged with sexual assault on a minor?"

"The guys can smell bullshit." I'm charged with assault and selling because one kid got mostly oregano and turned me in.

"You could be charged with a sex crime. People think you should be. You don't want to spend your time here in segregation, and you certainly wouldn't want us to release you into the general population. Not if they think you're a skinner."

"I can take care of myself." I hand him my shirt, which he goes through by turning it inside out.

"Against one or two, maybe." He looks through my boots, then shakes my jeans. When I peel off my underpants, he takes a breath. "I heard about that." He points at my crotch.

"Don't laugh."

"Do you hear me laughing, Mr. Hutchins?"

He runs his hands through my hair. I raise my arms so he can scan my pits. Then I have to squat and cough, so if I'm packing, the stuff will shoot out my ass. What happens is I fall over. When he tells me to stand, I stumble.

"They hurt my foot." I tell him about the hospital.

"Can you stand in a shower? I want the nurse to give you a good physical."

"You afraid I'll sue you?"

"I'll tell you something, Mr. Hutchins, you ought to sue somebody, only it's not us."

The nurse is good. I'll give her credit. She's smart and she's quick. We're through the questions about suicide and hepatitis and tuberculosis faster than I can chug a beer. She's checked my charred crotch and decided the hospital did as well as they could to prevent infection and minimize damage.

"But they didn't do well by you on these toes," she says. "Look at this swelling. They could have at least bandaged them and given you something for the pain. Of course it never should have happened in the first place."

I guess I'd gotten used to the pain and the hobbling, but when I see the purple mess at the end of my foot, I understand why Officer Cross said I should sue somebody. Course right now I can barely afford a lawyer to get me out of this charge, much less go suing a goddamn hospital.

The nurse gives me a cane, tells me to keep my weight off that foot and elevate it whenever I can.

Officer Cross is finishing up when an inmate brings me my prison clothes. I check carefully—a set of blues, three sets of whites, and so on—because being plus or minus so much as a pair of socks can land you in front of the Disciplinary Board and lose you good time.

I'm initialing my T.H. beside the items and about to ask for my bra when the inmate whispers to me, "Your uncle must still love you. He wants you to know you're in his memory for five hundred."

"I know."

"He don't want you to forget."

"I'll take care of it."

"Things can go real mean, here, Tommy."

Officer Cross interrupts. "What's all this jabbering?"

The inmate pulls a torn sock out of my whites. "Defective sock, Officer Cross." He gives me a shit-eating grin. "Wouldn't want Mr. Hutchins charged with destruction of county property."

I want to swing on him, but I remember—loss of privileges. I'll be down to one visiting day a week, and that will be noncontact.

They won't even let me hold Aaron. "Thanks," I tell the inmate. "I owe you one."

Officer Cross takes me to the Pre-Trial pod, and I stow my stuff in my cell. My cellmate, a guy named LaRoux waiting on a burglary trial, says he's heard of me because everybody talks about that tattoo gun I made out of the Walkman and the ballpoint.

"Clever," he says. "They say you're real clever."

"I wa'n't clever enough. They found it and took away all my good time."

"I heard someone ratted on you."

"No one rats here, LaRoux."

Next to his bunk stands a pyramid of Coke cans. Very artistic. The top ones are empty. One by one I set them on his bed as I dismantle the pyramid. The bottom row has heavy cans. I figure the middle one, and I'm right. A good job though, the flip top lies flat and solid against the aluminum top. The can weighs in at close to a legal twelve ounces. There's even a little motion inside in the can when I tilt it. Gently I press on the edge of the top and push the cut lid off. Inside is a toilet paper core surrounded by melted wax and holding cigarettes.

"LaRoux, we're P-T, we got no good time to lose, so they'll take away everything else." I sniff the cigarettes. The tobacco sets my heart ticking. "I ain't going to lose visits with my boy. Don't you ever light up in here. Even if I'm out in the dayroom."

"You better not rat on me."

"I won't need to," I say, rebuilding his pyramid. "Will I?"

GREGORY

At the trailer Father shoves the shotgun away. He says neither one of us needs it. They'll be telling tales about us Hutchinses long after we're gone, I guess, so he wants to work it so the tales ring right.

"You can use it whenever you want," I tell Father. The lines in his face wave and wobble, like they're out of focus. "I don't care how much you use it."

"That's what worries me. I don't either."

It's crowded in the trailer with Lisa's children using one room sometimes and Elizabeth's room all sealed up. I don't want to sleep on the sofa all out in the open like I had to sleep in the open at the hospital. It edges the ease out of me. Father's uneasy, unsteady almost, the way he walks, flitting from foot to foot and going nowhere.

"We could open up Elizabeth's room," he says. "Maybe it's time we did that anyway."

"No." I couldn't sleep in there. I've heard enough voices and had headaches enough to last my lifetime. Sleeping in Elizabeth's room would be like going to the graveyard by myself. I'll only go to the graveyard with someone. I promised the doctor never to attend on Elizabeth's grave alone. Always have another person to protect me from visits from the voices. Just to keep you comfortable, Gregory, he said. Everybody wants to feel comfortable. That doesn't make you weird.

"I'd feel more comfortable if I had a little place of my own," I tell Father.

"Gregory, your place—"

"I know I can't have that place anymore, but maybe I could set up a little camper." There's an old tagalong up to Malcolm Hurd's that he doesn't use anymore. Stove up inside, I think, but I bet I could fix it up to be comfortable and cozy. I ask Father.

"Hell, Malcolm'd give you that just to have it off his property. You wouldn't have to pay for that."

"Can we go see my property now? I feel comfortable with

you with me." But when we step outside, there's Uncle Emory.

Father says to me, "Already it's a good thing we set your shotgun aside."

Emory moves uneasy, like Father did in the trailer. Maybe he didn't expect to find anybody to home. There's a bristling tone just short of barking in the talk between him and Father. Fight flickers in Father like the false dawn that danced on my windows at the hospital, teasing and testing through tree branches, saying, not breakfast, not yet, still yesterday, stay in bed. They'll stick you with sick if you leap up for coffee. I collected my coffee, but regular, like regular people now, not with half the sugar bowl. Now, I'm not sick. I just have to take my meds, the pink pills with the hole like a yoke.

"So what did you come to steal this time?" Father asks Emory. His voice slashes viciously. I hope Buffy doesn't hear him and begin to bark.

"She danced, Jim," Emory answers, aggravation ankle deep in his words. "That's all there is to it. You know I can't get it up."

"Had my way, you wouldn't even be able to find it. Now don't hand me a line of shit. I've seen that fucking video."

"So, you've got it. I wasted fifty dollars on that worthless Tommy—"

"I stole your video," I tell Emory. Some things I don't remember, but I remember that I should be honest. I was always honest. Honesty never brought me the horrors. The doctor told me nobody could've helped me getting the horrors. "I remember taking it. It's at my place. We'll go out there, and I'll give it back to you. I'm not a thief or a liar."

Father and Emory are looking at me like I've changed color. My words have weaved a peace between them for a minute so they look at me and wonder about what I've said. I wish I could bring peace always, even if it took more than just saying something, because I'm willing to work. I could help Lisa so that Fesmire would favor the children, if I had to work with Fesmire. It wouldn't matter to me. I don't have any enemies anymore.

"You're the second person I'd like to shoot," Father tells Emory, "but I'd take you first if I can't find that goddamned Gary Reed."

"I can help you out with your taxes," Emory says. "I'll give you—"

"You ain't turning me into a whore!" Father yells. "I ain't sucking your cock for rent money."

"Nobody's sucking my cock," Emory says. "I guess you got a right to be jealous, but you watched the videotape. You know—"

Father slugs him, a roundhouse right. He's using his feet, kicking Emory's head, his back, as Emory scrambles. Emory grabs Father's foot and tips him right over. Emory's up and running. I'm screaming I don't know what, screaming words to weave peace.

"Hold him, Gregory," Emory says, ducking around his truck.

"I'll kill you!" Father shouts. He runs into the trailer.

I'm still screaming peace words when Father runs out of the trailer with my shotgun and raises it against Emory, who's ducking into his cab. Emory's still ducking and turning the ignition, waiting for that diesel to fire up, while I'm watching Father aim the shotgun. I'm not screaming now. I rush Father to force the shotgun away. Emory's engine starts. Father squeezes the trigger. The hammer falls. Click. Emory's tires kick up gravel as he grinds out onto the road.

"Next time I'll have shells in it," Father says. "And more in my pocket for that goddamn rapist, Gary Reed."

"Who'd he rape?" I know Lisa beat him up for a burglar, but she won't get in trouble for it because he tried to touch her and steal her things. "Did Emory rape Momma? Is that why you're trying to shoot him?"

"Gregory, did you watch that videotape you took from Emory's?"

I remember watching a videotape, lots of dirty stuff, as bad as what Tommy told me was on fuck films. "Bad," I tell Father. "Lots of bad stuff." But I stop because I see twisting turns of lines on his forehead and temples. I don't want to make Father feel bad. I know he's already twice troubled, angered up to his armpits. He might shoot Emory or Gary with my shotgun, and they would put him in prison. They've just jailed Tommy. We should drive to my place, where it's always pleasant.

"All right, Gregory, let's go."

I want to take Dog, but Father says he's not around, he ran away. The ride is beautiful. The trees show full leaf, some starting to turn, red on the swamp sumac, yellow on the puny poplars. My gate gapes wide open, inviting everybody in to my friendly familiar place. I feel like I'm bouncing on a blanket, riding down the road I cut through the woods myself. Starting tomorrow I'll be cutting trees again, cutting up cordwood, working outdoors, taking care of my tools, and working to keep people warm. Helping others and making my own living, that's what makes me feel fine. The doctor agreed with me. He said, More people ought to listen to your ideas, Gregory, and the world would be a better place. But I told him I don't preach. I told him to look at what happened to me. That wasn't your idea, the doctor said, that was the chemicals in your brain. Like a bad mix of oil and gas in a chain saw? I asked him. That's about right, he said, too much oil for your old two-cycle.

Can't I just see the blue smoke roar out of the muffler when there's too much oil in the fuel? But that's easily adjusted. Just like my meds, I guess. Now I take two a day, like aspirin. They're the size of aspirin, only I take one at a time. One hundred in a bottle, two a day means I have almost two months' worth.

Around the bend I'll see the place, but I won't want it because

I know I don't own it. I can't live there anymore. I can't really call it mine. But I built it, and I'm proud of how it stands sturdy and tight, holding against wind or rain or snow to keep you warm and dry.

Father's not talking. We take the turn, and there's my house—gone.

"He's going to bulldoze the ashes later," Father says, "if I don't kill him first."

"It's gone." Emory didn't even save the wood, just burned everything and let my place go up into the empty air. What did I think, to cart it off on a flatbed and set it up in Father's backyard? But just to turn it into smoke and ashes. Naturally, Emory wouldn't have moved into it. Nor would Scooter. All my work, the boards I cut and nailed, smoke and ashes. It's gone. When he bulldozes it, there'll be only a clearing here. Even that will go. First ferns and blackberries, then milkweed, preparing for the hardwoods.

"Gregory, what are you doing?"

I'm scuffing dirt, trying to see if the weeds have started. "Did you want to look for that videotape?" I ask Father.

"I took the tape. I burned it."

"I wish Emory hadn't burned my house."

"I shouldn't've brought you here, Gregory."

"I know."

LISA

You never know how things can change. Here's Leo with a license and driving a truck he claims is his. And even if he won't claim Alison as his, he takes her and Rebecca, Seth, and me up to the jail so I can visit Tommy. I wanted to stop for Aaron, but Leo said he didn't want to fuss with Penny and listen to her ask us for money. I suppose he's right about that because it's for sure that woman was named accurately. For herself. No matter what she says, it's always for herself. So here we are, without Aaron, but at least Tommy will have a visit his first full day in jail.

Leo says maybe I should leave the kids in the truck because Tommy might feel bad seeing the three of them and not being able to see Aaron. I hadn't thought of it that way. Tommy is nearly as good to my children as Gregory is, though nobody is as crazy over them as Gregory is. God knows I don't want to load Tommy's tray with more sand to eat. The poor guy's got a double heaping as it is.

Course right away they smell the tobacco smoke on me. I'm not in the entrance three steps before they're telling me to store my purse and to be sure I'm not carrying any tobacco products inside the jail.

"You can be barred from visiting anyone in this facility, Mrs. Fesmire," says the guard, "if you bring in any tobacco products."

"I've been here before," I tell her. It don't pay to wise off to these people. I've told Tommy that before, and I tell him again.

"I'll try to do my time the easy way for once," he says. His hand starts across the table to pat my hand, but he stops and just grins that handsome boy grin of his. He knows the COs watch every touch for the passing of cigarettes or drugs. "If I got to serve a sentence here, I want to get on work to give Aaron support. And on work I can smoke."

I take my change to the tonic machines and buy us each a Coke. Even then I feel the hot eyes of the guards on me. I know they watch the others sitting at these long, foldaway tables like some church coffee klatch. Course you can tell quickly enough this isn't a church the way the men touch their visitors over and over with their eyes, and never with their hands, except to say hello and good-bye. With all the tension in this room, you'd think you could hear the nicotine fits boiling over in each and every prisoner, but there's enough joy in seeing wives and girl-friends and kids that it stifles that monkey.

I ask Tommy if he's going to get a public defender.

He sips his Coke, looking almost dainty compared to the way he chugs a beer. "I want a regular lawyer. And I got another legal matter to take up. A lawsuit."

"Who you suing?"

"The hospital. It could be enough money to set your pulse rate up a notch or two."

I think maybe that could give him hope, and that hope and the fear he'll lose Aaron if he does hard time might keep him to the easy way. But he says he can't afford a lawyer and pay Uncle back both.

"Tommy, Tommy," I say, my hand reaching as automatically as did his. I switch mine to the Coke and take a big swallow. "You need a little legal education."

I explain to him that when you use a lawyer to sue somebody, they work on a contingency basis. You don't have to pay anything ahead of time. And most cases like his are settled out of court, meaning no trial and not much waiting, as long as he doesn't get greedy. With luck maybe we could find a lawyer who would take on the criminal work too without demanding a retainer. Tommy belts back a healthy slug of Coke and asks me if I'm sure.

"I didn't live all those years with Leo and not learn about law-suits."

"How much do you think I can get?"

"That's what I mean about greedy," I tell him, but I have to help him hold on to the hope I've stuck him with. "It's always in the thousands, I can tell you that. Enough to pay for a good lawyer, pay back Uncle, and support Aaron."

"You know I heard about Gary Reed." His voice goes down a notch to that raspy, mean tone. "He lands in here, he won't need no lawyer."

"Don't be stupid, Tommy," I tell him. "You sure were stupid with that videotape."

"I got Alice, though, didn't I? I got that goddamn bitch." When I tell him Momma has seen it because Alice made her watch it as a condition of giving it to her, Tommy snaps his Coke can on the table. Before he can say anything, the guard looms behind him.

"It slipped," I say.

"No trouble, Mr. Hutchins," the guard says. "You know what it means."

"Just didn't want to spill my Coke," Tommy tells her. "I've made enough messes lately."

When the guard moves away, Tommy asks me to bring MB next time I visit. "Aaron for sure," I say. "MB not."

"I want to see her."

"You can't fuck her in here." Sometimes Tommy lacks the common sense of a toad.

"I love her."

I guess he does. I'm sure he does. But he loved Penny, and look what that's got him. Love hasn't been too good for Hutchinses, if you figure in Leo and me, and whatever the hell is going on between Momma and Father. Now that's not good, with Father acting stranger and stranger, chasing people away from my place when what he really wants to do is chase Uncle Emory away from Momma. How often in this family we don't do what we want to do, or else it takes us so long to get around to it, that we spoil it and hurt ourselves in the process.

"You know how much trouble you'll be in if MB comes here?" I ask him. "You seem to forget, Tommy, MB's not a legal adult."

"She can forge her mother's permission."

"Great, Tommy, that's what they call contributing to the delinquency of a minor. Aren't you already charged with that? Or is it child endangerment?"

"So what's another charge?"

"It's one they could prove. It'd be one they wouldn't need MB's testimony for. You're goddamn lucky Alice gave Momma that tape."

"Momma shouldn't have had to watch that." I see him swallow his temper. I see the shame too. "How much of my money will the lawyer take on this—what is it, contingency?—deal?"

"A third, a quarter, something like that. It's a lot, but at least the lawyer's working for you, do you see what I mean? The more you get, the more she or he gets. It makes them work harder. When's the last time you had somebody working for you?"

He tips back his Coke, letting it all run down his throat in a stream. "MB. She worked for me for free. Worked on me big time. Make sure you bring her here next visit."

Outside, I'm ready to tell Leo what a romantic fool my brother is, but I don't see Leo. I don't even see his truck.

"Mommy?"

It's Alison, coming from beside the building where the prison staff smoke their cigarettes. I take one out of my purse. I don't see Leo or Rebecca or Seth. "Where's everybody?"

"Mommy, here." Alison hands me a folded piece of white paper, with ACE AUTO SUPPLY printed across the top. "They went in Daddy's truck. He told me to wait here and give this to you."

Talk about child endangerment! Did Leo get some sudden craving for a *strong* cup of coffee? *Lisa*, he wrote at the top of the paper. No *Dear*, just *Lisa*. Then, in coarse printing, a solid block of words showing the old Leo, the Fesmire Father always smelled.

> I told you your behavior, drinking, and partying worries me. It
> sets a bad example for our children, especially Rebecca. She

worries about you more than she should have to. At her
young age she seems more the mother than you do. Drug use
always leads to the abuse of the children. I wonder if that is
where my money is going. You know that is against my principles, strictly. I have worried that one of the many "friends"
you have in and out of your apartment would hurt or abuse
the children. I have worried that one of them might even try
to sell the children sexually to get drug money. Such things do
happen. I know you would never do such things or deliberately hurt the children, but you do neglect them. You're not
always in control of yourself or of your "friends." Now I find
out even you are in danger from these people. One of them
tried to rape you. And you keep a gun in the house, you are in
such danger. What kind of environment is this to bring our
children up in? What if Seth at his young age had to shoot
one of your attackers? Where are your principles? You used to
think of such things. Now, I'm afraid you no longer do. I can-
not trust you to be the good mother our children need and
deserve, the good mother you were when you lived with me.
Until you can show me you can raise them by good principles,
I will take care of Rebecca and Seth and raise them as they
should be raised, according to right principles. I hope you
contact the other one's father, so that he can take responsibility for her. Although she is not mine, I believe she should be
raised by right principles too.

Leo

No *Sincerely*, no *Love*, just *Leo*, then a P.S.

P.S. I have told your girl Alison not to call me Daddy. It is
against my principles to fool children. I do not answer her

when she calls me Daddy. This is another example of your
failure to be a responsible mother.

Nowhere does he call me "unfit." He knows that's a legal term.
I wonder if he knows the legalities of kidnapping children? I wonder how sly the son of a bitch will feel when I shove the shotgun
up his ass.

"What do you say, Alison? You want to hear your daddy
respond? I don't care if he isn't your goddamn daddy, I'll make
him respond. You may as well learn early to use every weapon you
got on a man because the bastards will use all of theirs on you." A
long drag on my cigarette stops my spew of words, but in my mind
I see Leo die.

"Mommy?" I look at Alison; whose ever child she is, she's
mine. And so are Rebecca and Seth. "We don't have a ride," she
says.

17
seventeen

JIM

"I'm not going to see you put on the street, Jim." Malcolm's nervous enough to bum a cigarette from me, though he smokes it with a scowl. "Are you three years back?"

He knows I am, else the town wouldn't be ready to foreclose on its lien. Course if I pay the town taxes, the IRS will want to put me in jail, which might be a better deal for me than landing on the street. Tommy says the food ain't bad, and you can always get bread and peanut butter. Course if I am to go to jail, I'd rather it was for putting Emory Holler out of my misery.

"That's my problem, Malcolm, and I'll try to work it out or work it off. If I can't, I'll let you know." I've taken money from Malcolm before, but not this time I won't. "What I really want is that old camper trailer you got sitting out back."

"You running away?"

"For Gregory. So he can have a place of his own to live, but still be on my property."

"The town's property."

"He can buy it at auction. Or from the IRS."

"Can't see why he shouldn't have the camper. It's awful ratty though. Let me see about getting it fixed up before he takes it." Malcolm likes this. I can tell by the way he squares his shoulders and sets the cigarette in the center of his mouth to take a good, strong pull that he likes this. Give Malcolm the chance to spend some big money, it eats away the rust in his soul.

"Gregory'd fix it up himself," I say. I jostle Gregory because he's been standing here quiet as if he were waiting to be hung. "Gregory, won't you like to put your mark on it?"

"I got to give you money for it," Gregory tells Malcolm, "and get a bill of sale. I don't mean to be a stinker about the business only I just saw what Emory did to my place because I didn't have a bill of sale. He had the right to bulldoze it, no matter that it had my mark all over it. I got to ride on top of the road now. I can't be trying to drive underneath it."

"One of these days I'll put Emory underneath his bulldozer, then we'll see about rights and bills of sale," I say.

"I'll give you a fair price for the camper, Malcolm," Gregory says. I see he wants to shush my talk about Emory. "You tell me what it's worth."

"He's going to give it to you," I say. "Wait until you see the inside of it. You may think Malcolm's getting the better of the bargain."

"A dollar, Gregory," Malcolm says, "and I'll have my lawyer draw up a bill of sale for you." He pitches the cigarette at my feet. "Jesus, Christ, Jim, don't you understand what he wants? What the hell will happen to the camper sitting at your place if the town does claim your property?"

"I ain't taking your money, Malcolm," I tell him. "Why don't you smoke another one of my cigarettes to calm your mind."

"It ain't the point!" Malcolm shouts. "It ain't the money, it's—"

"Let's look at the camper," Gregory says. I know he wants to duck a row.

"Why don't you take another one of my cigarettes," I tell Malcolm. "Wa'n't that one any good?"

Gregory looks to me to come inspect the camper with him, but I'm in no mood. I'll just fight with Malcolm, and Gregory'll have to top off his meds. I say I'll see what I can find to pull that camper over to our place because my truck don't have a tow.

"Mine does," Malcolm says, like he ain't heard a thing I've said.

"Yes, but your wires are all cross-rigged," I tell him. "The camper won't plug into your pigtail." Course I don't care if it'd light up like Christmas, I just want to get out of here. "And if I find Gary Reed, I'll kill him too."

On the way to the garage I stop for the shotgun and the shells, and I load one in the chamber and three in the magazine because I don't intend to break his arm or kneecap him. I intend to gut-shoot him and blow away his cock and balls in the process.

"Of course I'm going to kill him," I tell Frank Reed when I've got up in his tow truck with the motor running and the tank full of gas. "You'd do the same if it was Tommy raped your daughter."

Fuming and fussing drive him back and forth under my window, but I've got the truck in gear and can be on the road before he touches the door handle. "It ain't legal, and it ain't right," he says, "and just riding around with that gun will wind you in more trouble."

"Trouble to me ain't no worse than earwax."

"Gary didn't rape her, Jim."

"He didn't get it in her, that's all." I've heard enough of that shit to wonder if that's the coming kick. All these so-called impotent bastards getting their kicks doing weird shit with their cocks still soft. They think it gives 'em special fucking privileges. Assholes with money they didn't earn, like Gary and Emory. Maybe it's money makes your dick go soft.

"I'm calling BB Eyes," he says.

"Gary's dangerous. I got a right to shoot him on sight. Maybe you just want to fire me? Or would that make you look bad after you screwed me with the IRS and your boy raped Lisa?"

Enough talk. Let him call BB Eyes. Let him get his own gun and come looking for me. It ain't like I give a shit. I drive right to Frank's house, figuring BB Eyes might not have searched there real well. After all, if rich Frank Reed gives his word he ain't seen the boy, then Gary must not be there. And maybe he doesn't care about catching Gary as much as he ought to. After all, Gary didn't stick it in, and she did break his arm. A broken arm trades about even for raping a Hutchins. Maybe he figures Gary even got the short shitty end. He should have come out like Emory and not had anything broken, just throw down a little money, which he misses about as much as I miss the spit from my mouth.

"Jim!" Kari says.

She's wrapping a fuzzy bathrobe around her body, as surprised at seeing me in the middle of her kitchen as I am seeing her. "Where's your brother?" I ask her.

She's moving back toward the door to the dining room, her hands searching behind her like she's blind. "What are doing with the gun?"

"I'm going to gut-shoot Gary. Keep it fair so that he puts in some time suffering like he made Lisa suffer. I want him to hurt. That's fair, ain't it?"

"I don't know, Jim. I'm not up on my religion the way I should be. Anyway, Gary's not here."

Now Kari's always had a voice loud enough to call home the cows, but it seems to me she's calling cows from the neighbor's pasture now. All in a rush I push past her and into the dining room, but I don't see Gary. Maybe he's downstairs. Frank fixed up his whole basement into bedrooms and a den. Kari grabs my arm. I swing hard enough to knock her away. "Don't fuck with me!"

"No, Jim. I don't think shooting him is fair. I mean, I don't think it comes out." She's rubbing her elbow where it banged into the table.

"I'm sorry, Kari. I didn't mean to hurt you." I hate that if you go after a prick like Gary you end up hurting somebody else. Now with Emory, I don't care if I run over Scooter too. I can't figure how Scooter and Tommy are still buddies. Even Lisa tags after Scooter. "I'm going to search this house. If you want to tell me where he is, it'll be easier. If you don't, I'll find him anyway."

I'm in a rush now, running down the hall of bedrooms, looking under beds, poking the gun into clothes closets, whipping open the sliding glass shower door. I move so fast even God couldn't slip past me. At the hall's end is a trapdoor in the ceiling. A light fixture nearly edges it, making the contraption hard to spot. I grab the rechargeable flashlight stuck in the wall socket, then yank open the trapdoor. Down unfolds the neatest set of steps you ever saw.

"You go up there ahead of me," I tell her.

"There are bats up there, Jim."

"Let's just make sure your brother ain't one of them."

The attic ain't much more than a crawl space with a little light streaking in from the grille vents. Frank must have been awful disappointed he couldn't put in half a dozen bedrooms.

"There's one!" Kari says, and drives her hand right to my wrist so that the flashlight beam bounces across the stringers. There ain't just one but there's twenty, hanging upside down. I move the gun away from Kari, but I guess she really is scared of the bats and not trying to interfere with me. "Sometimes they get down into the house and scare the shit out of me." Her hand still grips mine, like I might be keeping her from falling.

Crawling over these joists with flashlight in one hand and shotgun in the other doesn't appeal to me right now. One slip and I'd be down through insulation and wallboard and land with the gun up my ass. If Gary's grabbed himself a gun, I could be the one who gets his balls blown away. I'm holding the gun, and I don't intend to be the fool here.

"New plan," I say. "I'm going back down. You stay put until you tell me where your brother is."

"Don't, Jim." I've got to yank my hand out of her grasp, and I lose the flashlight. It smacks to the floor. "Oh, Jesus, you're going to leave me in the dark with these bats."

"Just until you tell me."

"Oh, Jesus! Oh, fuck!"

Course those bats won't hurt her. They won't even leave their roosts. From the hallway I push up the folding staircase. She's screaming. She keeps that up, she'll roust them bats good, and they'll fly around a bit. Her screams tear into me. You'd think those bats had tore off her bathrobe and were nibbling right into her flesh. This ain't right, goddamnit. It ain't right.

"Where is he?" I shout. Her only answer is to scream louder. As I yank down the stairs, I realize I'm yelling too. I stop and say, "Come down from there, Kari."

She's down in the hall, shaking, and I'm up in the attic shaking. For a wonder the bats ain't moved. *Blam!* I let loose a shot, and pump another shell in the chamber and blast away again. Red, green, and gold fill the air. There's probably bat guts too, at least they'll find some next Christmas when they put up the decorations. A couple of bats fly around screaming at the other end.

There's a tall box down there. I hope to finish off the remaining bats and Gary Reed in one shot. *Blam!* No bat, no Gary, but Frank will be looking to buy a new Christmas tree come next December.

"I'm sorry," Kari says when I get back down. "I didn't know myself how scared I am of those things."

"At least I killed some of them for you."

She grabs me and hugs me. I don't know what the hell is going on. It's like she forgot I made her stay up there with her fears, which was wrong of me. I admit it. It was wrong. But she's not trying to take the gun, and she's not trying to hurt me, like she has every right in the world to do. Jesus himself would be riled at what I done to her.

"It ain't fair," she says. She's shaking from holding back tears.

"I'm sorry. It was a stupid thing to do."

She shakes a last shudder out of her and says, "It isn't fair for you to shoot Gary and go to jail for it." She talks in her foghorn voice now, saying she didn't go to work today because she couldn't bear the shame of it. I tell her I've had a semi-load of shame and embarrassment both from members of my family.

"I know," she says. "You don't deserve that either." She keeps talking about how things aren't fair, and her brother's nasty and hurtful, and even though people thought he was a pukey pussy, he's miserable worse.

Then she unties her robe so it opens. I was right. She is naked. "Make love to me, Jim. That'll be fair."

I push her away and see her tits sway. I expect her to cover up, give up this nonsense, like she's hopped over to hysterical without crying.

"No. I got to find Gary."

"Fuck me." she says. "Your wife's doing the nasty with Emory

Holler. Gary tried to rape Lisa. It would be fair, if you're looking for fair. And you won't go to jail."

I don't think I've ever heard her giggle. When we kissed before, I was drunk, a couple of years ago at the Christmas party. Her lips tasted good. I was surprised at how sexy she was. It's been a while since I've held a woman who wanted to be sexy for me. It's been a long while. Pauline hasn't gone out of her way to dance for me. A naked body in front of me asking, Would you rather shoot my brother and go to prison for the rest of your life or make love to me and get even with everybody? My fingers grip the gun to the point of ache. Pinpricks of pain stab my joints. Arthritis? I'm getting old. I'd rather fight than fuck?

"Come in my room, Jim. I've wanted to do this for a long time." She runs her hand up the back of my head, fingers through my hair. It's very sexy.

My rush through the house searching for Gary didn't give me much chance to look around. There's a whole electronic setup in her bedroom, from TV and VCR to stereo to God knows what. And, for a wonder, a computer. I know she does all the inventory control for the store on the office computer, but what the hell has she got one of the damn things in her bedroom for?

"Games," she says. "I love to play games. I'm good too, better than most guys. Better than my twerpy brother."

"Why'd Gary steal underwear?" I'm sitting on her bed with her lying behind me, rubbing my neck and shoulders. It doesn't feel as good as it should. "Was that some game he was playing?"

She doesn't answer me but goes on rubbing, massaging my back. She sits up, and I can feel her breasts against me as she kneads my body. "You're very tight. Strong too."

"Is Gary a pervert?"

"I told him to stop years ago when I caught him taking my

underwear." She quits rubbing my back. "You know how sick that made me feel, my own brother jerking off in my panties!"

She had known all along that he was the underwear thief. "Did he try to rape you?"

"I never thought he could get it up for a flesh-and-blood woman. I never thought he could hurt anybody. He's sick, but I thought he was just a wimpy, pukey fuck."

She stops, shudders, goes to rubbing my back again. I lay the shotgun on the floor. She knew all along, and she protected him. Didn't tell anyone. She sure didn't tell her father. Frank would've locked the bastard up, particularly if he found out about Kari's underwear. If she thinks he's such a disgusting puke, why did she protect him? Because he's her brother, he's family, and not by marriage either. Not like my disgusting puke of a brother-in-law Emory Holler. If Helen hadn't married him—

"Too many clothes, Jim," she says, untucking my shirt from my pants and running her hands under it. "I like the feel of your skin."

Now her bare breasts touch my bare back. Is she still protecting her brother? Protecting him and hating him at the same time? Does she think she can fuck me out of shooting him? What makes her think I won't just fuck her and shoot him anyway? Because that wouldn't be fair? Does she know me that well?

Maybe she's just been waiting to fuck me. Her brother's just an excuse. Keep thinking that, you'll raise two swelled heads.

A door closes. The stupid bastard couldn't even do that right. I grab the gun and rush to the hallway. There he is, Gary fucking Reed. I'm going to shoot him. I'm not going to talk to him. I'm going to gut-shoot the son of a bitch, just low enough to ruin his fucking equipment and leave him to lie here in his pain.

"Jim," he says. Just like that, like he can call my name and I'll stop. Like I'll listen to him because he's Gary Reed, and he's paying attention to and even following along so I'll end up doing what he says. He can start with my name like a prayer, and just like God, I'll drop all my plans so I can satisfy him. He don't know God don't enter into this deal. This one didn't require holy vows or prayers, the only righteousness lies in this shotgun that's going to shoot heaven's flame into Gary Reed's crotch.

"Jim." He doesn't move. Does he think he can stop time and me with a word? Like everybody can do what they fucking want to, and I can't do anything about it? I got the answer to his goddamn prayers right here. It's coming down the hammer lane.

I poke the gun forward to level it at his guts. *Blam!*

He's falling and he's running. Kari's climbing all over me. She must have jumped me just before I fired. White shreds of wallboard hang in the hole I blew in the wall. Naked flesh is all over me. Gary is running.

"Jim!" she shouts. "He's not worth it."

I push her down and I fire, but the well is empty. He's out the door. I pull shells out of my pocket. She's on me yanking, pulling the gun to her body.

"Fuck me, Jim."

His truck starts, peels out.

"I'll kill him," I say.

GREGORY

Father's hauled Malcolm's camper up here, taken off with my shotgun, and told me not to worry. Whenever anybody says that to me, I know I'll have to wrestle snakes and box with bears to keep the worry out of my mind. Why don't they just say it straight? Don't go out to kill Leo Fesmire. There, that says it straight. Besides, Father took my shotgun with him, so he knows

I don't have a weapon, I don't have money to buy a weapon, and I ain't a thief like Tommy to steal a weapon.

This camper is quite a mess, but nothing I can't handle. Not like trying not to worry because Fesmire has taken Rebecca and Seth back up to his place and left Lisa and Alison standing outside the county jail without a ride. Poor Lisa didn't know if she even had so much as a dime to call me to come get her. She told me she'd rather walk the eight miles than walk ten feet back into that jail and ask to borrow a dime, but as luck would have it, one of the officers started talking to Alison, asking why she was waiting, and Lisa told him that miserable drone Fesmire had driven off without her while she was in visiting Tommy. The officer said he knew Tommy, and he gave Lisa the money for the call. Don't worry about it, he said, from what I hear, your brother's going to be a rich man.

Tommy's never going to be a rich man because he doesn't keep a job long enough before he's drunk or in jail. Even when he's working, he's spending like he's already a rich man. All it ends up with is Father and Momma paying to bail him out, paying his lawyers, paying his fines. And he never pays them back. How he hopes to raise Aaron is beyond me. Lisa says he's going to raise Aaron. He thinks Penny'll give Aaron up. Tommy can't even pay for himself; how's he going to pay for Aaron?

Lisa said I could get credit or a credit card to buy new furniture for the camper, but that's foreign to me. That's foreign to the way I want to live. Credit invites worry right into your life. As soon as I finish with this brush and bucket, the camper'll look a hundred percent better. Just to have my own place again makes up for the sag in the sofa bed. And I don't think it will take much tinkering to fix the little propane stove, though I won't drink so much coffee as I used to.

And not go to the cemetery alone. I remember that.

Father's gone with my gun. And I'm not supposed to worry about that either.

It takes me nearly three hours to wash the walls and floors, but there ain't a bit of grime or a bug left when I'm done. I wish I could clean the ceiling too, but it's that porous tile that becomes a sponge in water. I'll have to ask Lisa how to clean it. She's just about the cleanest person I know. Ever since she left Fesmire, she won't permit a speck of dirt to live. It ain't healthy for children to be in filth. They fail to thrive, she says. Something she learned from a community person up there living with Fesmire because he made sure she used every one of the community resources.

That's what makes Fesmire a rich man even if he doesn't make much money. He can rely on all these community resources, which make him a good living without his having to put in too many days working. I ain't smart enough for that. Tommy's smart until he battles booze. They always keep him from making money.

I'm on my way to wealth.

Don't spend. That's my secret. The doctor asked me, How will you live, Gregory? Simple, I told him, spend less than I make. I work hard, and I don't need much. But, he said, you must take care of yourself, not just keep up with your medication and avoid conflict, but give yourself some pleasure. Don't be too parsimonious. Parsimonious? I asked. Like parsnip? He laughed. Stingy, he said, don't be too stingy with yourself.

Like parsnips, you got to get them just right to be sweet, otherwise they're bitter or hollow, taste like old newspaper. Frost helps them. A little cold is good for the soul. Lisa says I'm so used to cold my heart must be on gas heat, and I told her maybe that's why Fesmire has to stay bundled up because his heart's flame went out. Only I guess it hasn't since he's got a girlfriend and kidnapped the kids, unless he needs them to warm him like extra layers of wool.

I'm careful never to get too cold because it's so hard to warm up again in winter weather. And I'll be careful not to be too parsimonious, so I'll buy my jelly doughnuts or a Milky Way to lift up my life. And still I'll save for my own piece of land, and maybe a new dog if I can't find Dog. I won't have to buy a new dog because Lisa always sees "Free to Good Home Dogs," and Malcolm has more dogs than a breeder, but I'd have to spend money to feed him and get him his shots. I wouldn't be too parsimonious with a new dog.

And not go to the cemetery alone.

I'm going to the trailer alone.

I get my Milky Way from my truck, brew up a cup of coffee, and treat myself to a sit-down, sweet break. No one is here. Momma's at work, and Father's—I wonder. The fish Malcolm gave him swim around in the tank like they were looking for something. I'd feed them only Father said you can kill them by giving them too much food. That's what Malcolm nearly did. Father said just to watch them, not to feed them or try to pet them, so I'll let them swim around looking for something that's not in their tank. I think Father's looking for something, maybe like these fish in the tank, only they don't have shotguns.

The Milky Way goes sticky, sweet gooey in my mouth. I take a swallow of coffee to wash it down. I'm supposed to feel good, and I do. I enjoy this. Gregory, the doctor said, let yourself enjoy things. Just if you find yourself obsessing about things, whether it's coffee or work, whatever it is, I want you to call me right away. And don't go to the cemetery alone, I said. Right, he said. I'm sure you won't forget that.

And now I want to go there.

I can find Father, and he'll go with me. He'll help me not to worry by going with me to the cemetery. He'll see I can go to Eliz-abeth's grave and not go gravy in the brain. If I can't find Father, I won't go to the cemetery by myself. I'll drive up to Fesmire's and ask him for the children and take them with me to see Elizabeth's grave. Just like I'm their uncle, she's their aunt.

I stop at the police station to talk with BB Eyes about Dog.

"Gregory," he says, putting his hands out like he wants me to inspect them. I had to do that at the hospital, stick out my hands and spread my fingers for the aides to inspect. "I've got an attempted rape case. Gary's running around loose. Half the town is ready to kill him, the other half is scared as turkeys at Thanks-giving time." He puts his inspected hands on my shoulders. "I'm sure you understand I haven't been able to focus on finding your pet. But I haven't forgotten. I'm just as much a dog lover as you are."

I tell him I might get a new dog.

"If I was you, I'd hold off on the new dog. Good idea to hold off. Do you know where your father is?"

"No, but I know he's got my shotgun."

"Jesus Christ, Frank Reed told me he had a gun, and I thought he was just aggravating me. Jesus Christ."

He's out of his chair and moving fast for a fat man. If he can motivate like this, there's no need for the town to worry him about his weight. "If you find Father," I yell to BB Eyes as he runs outside, "tell him I want to take him to the cemetery."

"Oh, Jesus Christ!" BB Eyes yells, but he keeps on running.

TOMMY

I'm not in jail two days, don't have time to talk to my lawyer even, and I'm written up. I can't take it after a while. It's that goddamn crud Brusseau that I punched on my last tour of duty here. Been any other screw, he'd've let me go.

"Do you waive your right to twenty-four-hour notification?" asks Officer Cross.

He's the tough, buttoned-up guy, real by-the-book military, but he's fair. He don't hold grudges. "Sure," I say. "I won't give you any hassles about procedures." What the hell, I can't have a lawyer, and it ain't like I need time to gather evidence, talk to witnesses, and prepare a defense.

"You're charged with smoking, which is a class one, major violation," Cross says. "How do you plead?"

"Not guilty."

Cross looks at the other guy on the D Board, a middle-aged man who's in charge of security. He slips on glasses to read Brusseau's write-up. I figure Cross pressed him for this job so there'd be a board instead of just one guy making the ruling. As far as I can see, Cross makes the decisions anyway.

"Officer Brusseau says he came into your room from the pod and saw you with a cigarette," Cross says. I was proud that I didn't slug Brusseau and lucky there were three other guys who saw I didn't hit him. I didn't even dis him, except in my mind, the dinkless bug fucker.

"That's not the way it happened, sir."

Looking at each of them in turn, right in the face like I know to do, I tell them what happened. I get to the part where "one of the guys" (course I'm not going to name my roommate) has lit up and someone yells, "Sixty-five," so my roomie flicks his butt on my bed. Cross, following everything I say and even taking notes, interrupts me.

"How'd he light it?"

I figure this is no big secret and doesn't mark my roommate nor set me in the rats' circle, so I tell Cross about shorting the Walkman AC adapters. "You know, just cross the wires, and you get a spark."

"You smoke, Hutchins?" the other guy asks.

"On the outside, not in here."

"Hard thing to quit, smoking," he says, like I don't know this. "Most guys can't quit even in jail."

"They tell me I'm a hard guy," I say, pitching this to Cross, who I figure likes toughness. "I'm trying to make it work for me."

"So how did you end up with the cigarette?" Cross asks.

"It was still smoldering." Smoldering, hell, it was still burning. "I brushed it to the floor and stepped on it. I didn't want a fire."

"You weren't smoking it?" the other guy asks. "You were that close to it and not smoking it? You hold your breath so you couldn't smell it?"

"If you look at the report, you'll see Officer Brusseau didn't see me smoking or holding a cigarette. He found it under my bed."

Cross sees that's right and says technically Brusseau should have written me up for possession of contraband, still a class one violation, but not as stiff a penalty if they believe it wasn't my cigarette. "Did Officer Brusseau tell you he was going to write you up?"

"Yes, sir."

"In front of the other inmates?"

"Yes, sir."

"And the one who was smoking the cigarette didn't say anything? None of them stood up for you?" I just shake my head. "Aren't they your buddies?"

"No, sir."

"They were in your room."

"They're jail buddies. They're not real friends." What's more important to me is these guys don't call me a skinner. Selling drugs, alcohol to minors, those are nothing. Burglary, assault, hell, you can walk a little taller with those under your belt. But if they name you a skinner, you got to ask for protective custody or fight every son of a bitch in the jail. On PC you can't work, get no privileges, no gym, no nothing.

"You're acting more reasonably this time, Tom," Cross says. "What's different?"

"I want to keep my boy, my little boy, Aaron. His mother's a bitch, excuse the language, and I don't want to lose him to her. And I got a chance to pick up some money. I am going to sue the hospital."

"I'm going back to CO Brusseau," Cross says. "Maybe he'll rewrite the charges. Maybe he'll drop them. As far as I can see, you should have been written up for stupidity."

"I guess that's right, sir." Sure's a hell of a way to tell you they don't hate you, calling you stupid. Course that's the way it is with these authority guys. You got to admit and show you're inferior before they'll help you. It's like saying you're sorry. "If I'm going to be here, I'd like to protect my good time, get on work release, get out as soon as I can. And I don't want to sit on the tier all day. I'm not lazy. I need the money for my boy."

"I thought some lawyer was going to make you rich," the other guy says. They like to needle you to see if they can pop your boil.

"I know that's not certain, sir," I tell him, straight in his face. "I can't depend on that until I cash the check. And even so, I need money now for my boy, and I want to see my boy more than once a week while I'm here."

Cross shuffles the reports together. He's ready to call this one a win for himself. "How's the tobacco coming in?" he asks.

That question goes right where the hair is short and curly. I look quick to the door, wondering who might be outside listening. The next write-up for the D Board? One of the guys from the laundry next door? A sweeper leaning on his broom?

"I couldn't get into that," I say.

Cross looks at the papers in front of him like he might have to reexamine Brusseau's report. It's a calculated look. "You're asking something from us, aren't you?"

"Well, not if it comes to that." I may be throwing it all away right here. The guy before me was written up for saying, "She can suck my dick," not *to*, but *about* the administrator, and they gave him five days lockup for Christ sakes. He told me he didn't think he could get in trouble for disrespect if the person wasn't there. How could I dis her when she wasn't even there? he asked.

Cross is still looking at me like I'm going to say something else. He's got that wrong. I'm not even going to deny knowing how the tobacco comes in. I just look him in the face. Fucking place is just like school. Don't smoke. Don't pass notes. Go stand in the corner. Detention. Only here, they don't throw you out. He knows how it comes in. The guys on work release pack it in. Or the guys working over at the County Home have pickup places from friends on the outside. What he wants are names.

"We'll notify you of the results by the end of the day," Cross says.

PAULINE

I'm trying to open this damn videotape and destroy it before Carol comes down here with some other piece of bad news, like they're going to report me to the police for stealing that guest's fifty dollars. I know there's some spring or something to press that releases the cover. Even little Elizabeth could open one of those movies and inspect it with her curious eyes while she sat on the couch. Naturally, all her movies were family movies, a far cry from this thing Tommy made with Mary Beth, which he shouldn't have done, and he surely knew better than give it to Alice. That was wrong. I guess she is my friend, or she'd've given it to Dumont, though how she can bear to sleep with that turd is beyond me.

This doorlike thing lifts. I pry, pull, yank that damn black plastic, tape spinning the wheel as it unspools, tangles of black tape on the floor. Stupid, putting their bodies on tape like that. I don't even like touching this disgusting tape. I spray it with Speedball and jam it into a garbage bag, gone forever.

Rejection, that's what I told Jim he was feeling, rejection, and I told him it wasn't worth killing somebody over and going to prison for. Him, who couldn't stop yakking at me when Tommy got sent to jail. At the one hand he acts as if he doesn't care what happens to the children, then if one of them is seen so much as picking their nose, he has a fit over it. It's embarrassing, he told me. Then he was talking about me and Emory. It ain't rejection, for Christ's sake, he says, it's embarrassing to have everybody know how you run over there to that murdering pervert every chance you get and don't even have the consideration to be careful. I wonder you ain't pregnant.

He thinks I ought to be ashamed, only he won't say it.

There's a truck still parked in front of cabin three, just a single man who only registered for one night, and it's way past checkout time. Twice already I've knocked on the door, but no answer, not a sound, not even the television. I go back to the laundry room, give that garbage bag with the tape a kick, and start folding. Elaine will be back soon, which will turn me poorer and ruin all the schemes I had of making it on my own. Course Emory says anytime I need money, he's got more than a kid with measles has got spots. They don't get that anymore, I told him, they get vaccinated for it now. But if I were to take to living off Emory's money, I know what that'd make me.

I yank open that garbage bag, set it up here in the sink, and pour bleach right on that tangled tape. What the Speedball didn't take off, the bleach will clean up.

When he's not mad, Jim says he's discouraged, and he acts like discouragement sicced him like a rabid dog. He can't seem to understand that the face of man is marked for discouragement. When Elizabeth died, he never could see how discouragement struck me in the face and grief kicked me in the heart. I ain't saying he didn't love Elizabeth because I know he was hurt too, but he couldn't see my discouragement and how it became my daily bread. All he could think to do was to lock Elizabeth's room as if that would keep the thief from stealing my heart.

I walk upstairs to the office for one last check of the man in number three. Sure enough, one night. Signed in with a funny name, Greed, R. Greed. I never heard that name before, and I'm sure if it were mine, I'd change it. Anyway, Mr. R. Greed paid for one night, which is now up.

I push the cart over to number three, take out the master key, and knock loud enough to shake the door. I don't want any surprises today, like a naked man. I knock again but still no answer. The chain lock's not hooked, so I push right in and announce myself.

No one's here. It doesn't look like anybody'd even stayed here, and I wonder if R. Greed left his truck outside and went off with somebody. There's no suitcase, nothing hanging in the closet. I always double-check the closet because I found a suit for Jim in a closet once, the one he wore for our anniversary and for Elizabeth's funeral. Otherwise I don't know what he would've put on. R. Greed didn't take a shower, didn't use the sink as far as I can tell; I wonder if he so much as walked into the place. At least there won't be much to clean.

A scrap of paper on the bureau I crumple and shove in my

pocket. No sense in changing the wastebasket liner because there's nothing in it, nothing in the room to throw away. David should give the guy half his money back. Here's something, a glass is gone from the setup tray, no plastic wrap, no glass. Maybe he mixed a drink and went out the door, and he wouldn't be the first man to do that, or woman either. Probably a good thing I don't drink, otherwise this could be me, mix a drink and wander off. Jim tried it, only he didn't wander too far.

I quick spray the bathroom because I wouldn't feel right if I didn't. Even if R. Greed didn't use the place, he was in here, and the next people have a right to a fresh bathroom, and I'm being paid to clean the unit, whether he dirtied it or not.

Here it is, the used glass with the plastic wrap at the bottom of the bathroom wastebasket, so I pull the liner and pitch that toward the door. While the disinfectant's working, I'll decide if I have to change everything on the bed. It doesn't even look sat on, much less slept in. I check under it.

"Gary Reed!" I yell. "Get out from under that bed!"

I back right to the open door because no matter how much of a twink Lisa says Gary is, he's still a rapist. Not a peep out of him. Imagine, sleeping under the bed, like he can hide there. R. Greed—my sakes, he didn't stretch his mind too much coming up with that name. I don't know why I didn't recognize his truck because I've seen it often enough parked down there to the garage.

I hit the 911 on the cordless to tell the police I've found their wanted man right here at the motel. I expect any minute for Gary to roll right from under that bed. I'm talking in a loud enough voice so even if he's sound asleep, Gary's got to know what I'm doing here.

I bend down to look across the carpet at him, but he's not moving, not a bit. As I slide along the floor toward him, everything seems so quiet that my own breaths sound like a giant panting. My heart's beating pots and pans.

"Gary? The police are coming to arrest you."

I nudge him, and he sort of sludges, like Jell-O that's set too long and got the skim on it.

"Gary?"

I touch his arm, which is cold. His face holds a gray cast, like old cigarette ashes.

I take the scrap of paper from my pocket. It says:

> I'm so ashamed. I thought I was safe, but I got greedy. Greedy.
> Rotten Greedy. I'm so ashamed. Please forgive me.
>
> Gary Reed

"You coward!" I yell. I push him again and watch his body roll sludgy then settle. "You can rape, but you can't live with it. I don't forgive you, you creep!"

My throat's hurting. Here I am screaming like a ninny at a dead man, dead boy, because no matter now old Gary grew to be, he was never going to turn man, not on this earth anyway. Maybe that's why he stole all that underwear, because there wasn't the man in him to make love to a woman. One thing you can say for Tommy, he's a man, and he gets into man troubles. Course fooling around with Mary Beth Jewell is dumb, but he does that because he thinks a grown woman won't have him. That damn Penny did that to him, fixed his mind good, so he thinks he's too useless for a woman, and he's got to fool with these girls. After what I saw on that videotape, I'd claim Alice ain't harboring any Little Miss Muffin there to her home. That girl eats the curds and the whey and the spider too, with no shame at all.

Shame, he wrote, like Jim talking about shame, like Alice, I guess. Or embarrassment. But it runs deeper than embarrassment. Or else she wouldn't have shown me the tape, Gary wouldn't have killed himself. Jim wouldn't—

I'm not going to think about that right now, not now. I hope the police get here soon because being in the same room with Gary's body makes me think too much about death, all the kinds of death. Elizabeth. She was dead so long before she died. Jim said he knew she died in the cow pond, but Gregory had worked so hard, and the EMTs worked on her, so I had to believe she was still alive. Only she wasn't. Your heart can beat right through your death. I believe Elizabeth was in heaven, right from the cow pond.

But I died too.

And I died to Jim's shame. Everything's fallen on him from Gregory to Lisa to Tommy to—

I look under the bed again. There's no gun, no knife, no blood. I could never shoot myself. Disfiguring yourself like that, turning your God-given body into a bloody mess revolts me. Gary must have taken something, pills or poison or something. His face shows no pain, nothing, just as plain and sad as the cold, dirty ashtray Jim leaves overnight on the kitchen table. The next morning I empty it, rinse it out, wipe it dry, and set it back on the table. Meaningless. As meaningless as—

I can feel it like a hand running up my leg.

"Don't move!"

I'm pushed to the floor, carpet biting my cheek.

"Everybody, hands behind your head!"

It's a different voice. I swivel my head and see two policemen, one a state trooper, holding their guns. The trooper has a shotgun or rifle.

"He's under the bed," I tell them. "He ain't going to escape."

LISA

Who'd've thought Gregory'd be driving me up to Leo's to get back my children? I know he's always disapproved of Leo, disapproved of me too for that matter, at least of my drinking. He lumps me and Tommy together in the drunk sack, as identical as two lumpy potatoes. But here he is, old Gregory, calm as a cat, wheeling his truck up the highway at a steady fifty-five miles an hour.

The funny thing is, Father said that Gregory would want to avoid all conflicts.

"I don't want you to hurt Leo," I say. "I already hurt Gary Reed. I guess I can take care of that kind of business myself." Not that I'd dare swing on Leo because he's got ways about him that would keep me from hitting even if I knew he was stone dead. But shooting him is a different matter. If he doesn't give my children back, I will shoot him.

"Where's your shotgun now, Gregory?"

"Father's got it." He glances at the speedometer to assure himself of the purity of his legal speed. "I think he wants to shoot somebody."

"Gary Reed?"

"I don't know. Probably."

He switches his eyes to Alison, like he wants to shut off all conversation about hurt before the child. On the steering wheel his knuckles gleam a little white. Clean and unskun for a change, his big hands look almost artificial. Strong hands, soft heart, that's Gregory, that's my brother. Only Father said when Gregory came at him, he thought Gregory would murder and mutilate him right there on the spot. Maybe Father exaggerated to get Gregory put away. Or to salve his guilt for kneecapping his own son with a shovel. I could never do that, hit one of my children.

Just strong words from my mouth wilts them. If I find Leo hitting either one of them, I'll shoot him if I have to chase Father from one end of New Hampshire to the other to get the shotgun.

Slowly Gregory takes his hand off the steering wheel, passes it in front of Alison, and grips me, covering most of my wrist and hand. "Fesmire's not going to keep Rebecca and Seth," he says, that low rumble Father calls Gregory's growl. "Don't you worry."

Of course now I worry. Nothing pushes my worry button worse than someone saying not to worry because it always means there's more wrong than they're willing to say. Even Gregory, slow and moderate as Father claims he is, can slide things under his plate. Just because we're not armed going up here doesn't mean Leo won't bring out his squirrel rifle or his shotgun. I don't think I'll ever as long as I live forget him blowing away the children's stuffed toys that day Father came up for us. Or forgive him for it, either.

If Gregory gets into a fight with Leo and Leo shoots him, I don't know what I'll do. I should've just found Father and had him drive me up. My hand is shaking so bad I can barely hold the cigarette still.

"Maybe we shouldn't go, Gregory."

"It's not right, Lisa. Fesmire will understand that."

Gregory doesn't see how Leo always twists what's right until he's sitting on God's right hand and God is whispering in his ear. It's like no matter what you say, Leo manipulates the figures so they add up in his favor. Why Gregory thinks he can outargue a professional like Leo is beyond me.

"If there's any trouble, we'll come straight home," I tell Gregory. "I'll get a lawyer to handle this."

"Like Tommy?"

He looks at me like I've sinned or something. Then he sees a little restaurant, pulls into the lot, and asks Alison would she like ice cream, pie, or pie and ice cream. It doesn't take that little dessert hawk long to decide, so while she's wolfing down a slab of blueberry with vanilla, Gregory's drinking two cups of coffee, gulp by gulp, and I'm smoking my umpteenth cigarette of the day. My stomach's not right at all, which will keep me up half the night. I know it will. And I haven't even started looking for a lawyer for Tommy.

When we get to Leo's, there's a sign on the tree by the mailbox:

Leo Fesmire Does Not Live Here

"I wonder who put that up?" I ask.

"Whoever bought the place," Gregory says. "They didn't want it shot up by people looking for Fesmire."

Which is what we do for the next half hour. Down at the store where I used to call on their telephone the woman spits. She's sitting outside by the door, and when I ask her if she knows where Leo is living, she spits. I ask her if she remembers who I am, and she spits again.

"I'm Lisa Fesmire, and—"

"I know who you are. About Fesmire I don't know. I don't want to know." She spits again. My mouth's going dry watching her. "I'm surprised you want to know. If it's money you're after, you'd be better off gathering up that." Her toe points to the dirt her spit has wet.

"Never mind," says Gregory, "I know where we can find out."

And he does too. The post office. They've forwarded his mail to a rural box number, and the route driver has just come back to the office. He reels off a set of hard lefts and soft rights, but Gregory stays with him. He's so confident he asks the mail carrier if Leo was home.

"Waiting for his mail about an hour ago," the man says.

Then we leave town, turning onto gravel roads with no signs and probably no names to put on the signs. Gregory's turning hard and soft, not bothering to ask if I think this is right, and after we've left the last human habitation a mile behind, he pulls up beside a giant pine and says Leo's is just around the turn.

"How'd you know he'd leave a forwarding address?" I ask him.

"He depends on mail. Checks."

"You want me to go talk to him?"

"I want you to stay in the truck."

This new girlfriend of his ain't rich. I see that as soon as we round the bend and I'm looking at what must've been a hunting camp. At least the rooflines look straight and the shingles have silvered up, so I'll say someone built it right if not big. Leo's boat lies in the front yard.

Gregory is out of the truck and gives me a quick look, half warning, half smile, before he shuts the door. I think how few smiles I've seen on Gregory in the past year. His big, empty hands swinging, he strides up to the house, but before he can knock, Leo comes out. My window is open so I can hear fine. Besides, they're not whispering.

"Your sister's not a right woman," Leo says. "She doesn't provide a good environment for my children to grow up in, and I'm sworn to see to it that my children do grow up in a good environment. I see what's become of the Hutchins clan."

He's not armed. I know he sometimes straps a hunting knife to his belt, but he's naked of that too today.

"We don't need to stand out here calling names," says Gregory, that half smile playing on his face. "You and Lisa had children together. I think you can raise them together."

"I'm in love here, Gregory. I won't break the bonds of true love to go back with Lisa. Breaking bonds and vows is her way, not mine."

That smile grows right across Gregory's face. "You can cooperate on raising them. I'll transport them back and forth, seeing as how she lacks a car."

I want to jump right out of the truck and scream, No, he can't have my kids, can't drag them up here with some new woman to call Momma. He can't take just the two and leave Alison behind.

"She's had her chance," says Leo, "and she's made a mess of her life."

"Something wrong with Rebecca or Seth?" Gregory asks, the smile gone as fast as light in the cellar. "You show me right now what's wrong with either one of them kids."

"Not now there isn't, but in the future—"

Leo's fumbling for words, like he's lost a set of keys.

Gregory grips him between shoulder and neck, a hard grip I can tell. "I want you and Lisa to agree about raising the kids. I'll see that you get to see them regular. But you got to remember something."

Leo backs out of Gregory's grip. "Yeah?"

Gregory reaches, pulls Leo back to him, and whispers in his ear. Leo looks like the skin's been ripped right off his face. His eyes go glassy.

"Yes," he says. "That's so. I hadn't ever thought of that."

Riding back in the crowded truck, I ask Gregory what he said to Leo.

"You know," Gregory tells me, "I got to buy one of those trucks with the jump seats to hold all these children."

"Gregory, what did you whisper?"

The full smile runs right across his face. "I told him that since I'm certified crazy, that I'm not responsible for what I do. I can get away with damn near anything. That makes me richer than him even."

18
eighteen

JIM

An embolism in his brain," BB Eyes says. "It blew up like the Hindenburg."

Which means Malcolm didn't feel a thing. Just sat down to his dinner—he still called his noon meal "dinner"—and his heart blew his brains out. Dead right there at the table with Bernice left wondering what kind of broil was starting now, face down in his dinner. Hell of a thing when the best you can say of a man is "He didn't feel a thing." BB Eyes calls it "a good death."

"I got to get over there," I tell BB Eyes. My tears lock somewhere behind my face. Must be the lines are plugged. My eyes feel dry. Everything in my system clots and clogs.

"Bernice left for her sister's." BB Eyes is rooting in his shirt pocket for a candy bar, but I see it's perfectly empty. "She's having him cremated."

"I got to tell his bees."

"Have you gone completely fucking crazy?"

"If you don't tell bees gently about their owner's death, they'll abandon their hives, just leave the place."

"You believe that shit?" He pulls a candy bar out of the cruiser and peels the wrapper like you'd skin a banana.

"Malcolm did. Out of respect for him—"

"And out of respect for him, you stay away from manhunting." Bits of chocolate and sugary goo roam around his teeth and he issues me my orders. "Things settle out, I'll return your shotgun."

"Give it to Gregory. Rightfully, it belongs to him."

"You just remember, Jim, Malcolm wouldn't want you to wind up in jail." Then he's off.

And so am I, highballing right down to Malcolm's place. BB Eyes is dead right that Malcolm would puke right up on my plans. There ain't no dispute there at all. But Malcolm ain't around now to hire me, pay my taxes, buy gravestones, or give me advice. And he ain't never going to be around to do any of them things. There's only one woolly-assed cutter around to take care of Jim Hutchins, and he goes by the same name. Course Malcolm *is* going to help me out here, more than he would were he stomping back and forth in his yard telling me what a goddamn fool I am.

I out my keys and walk right through the house to that gun case we set up, and I pick out a nice pump-action twelve gauge, a hell of a lot nicer than Gregory or I together could ever afford.

Then I stroll up to the hives and yell as loud as I can, "Malcolm is dead."

I hope that shocks all that stinging tribe so they move clear out of the state of New Hampshire and don't venture north of the Massachusetts line as long as they live. And to make me really happy, that don't have to be too very long.

When Lisa divorced Fesmire, the official paper drawn up by her lawyer started off, "Now comes Lisa." Now I'm ready. You can write me up. Now comes Jim. I ain't using lawyers, and I ain't going to court. I ain't even drinking. I've had my head shoved up my ass, and now I've come up for air.

Now comes Jim.

With a shotgun. My dead friend's shotgun because I couldn't scratch up enough cash to buy even shells, let alone the gun. Now, ain't that pitiful?

I've called after Pauline. She ain't to home. Not that that should surprise me, only I know her shift at the motel is long over, and it don't take that long to drive here. I've called Lisa, who naturally hasn't seen her mother all day. She's babbling on about how wonderful Gregory was to rescue her children and set Fesmire straight. And I said, Yes, it takes somebody crazy to fix things around here because they're the only ones can see things in their true right. You got to be crazy to see the light flash where the timing mark should be on the flywheel. It's the crazies that got a vision of the top dead center of this spinning life.

I call Emory. He is to home. At least his voice answers the telephone. I hear enough of it before I hang up to identify it was definitely Emory Holler. A voice full of sawdust. An old doll's head, with a painted smile, who killed my sister and fucks my wife. The sawdust in his voice is as much disguise as his phony claim of impotence. As if he feels guilty over Helen's death. Or anything else for that matter.

Pauline feels no guilt. She makes it like I'm at fault. Okay. I'll be at fault. I'm on my way over to Emory's right now to act dumb and be at fault. And I ain't feeling guilty or impotent, I can tell you that right in plain English.

Now comes Jim.

I drive out to poor Gregory's smashed-up, burned-out place, another wreckage Emory don't feel guilty over. I could drive straight down the road like any other citizen because I ain't no criminal like Gary Reed or Emory. I got every right to heist myself on the public road, as Fesmire would claim, only I got an idea BB Eyes might have a lookout for me, like I'm as crazy as Gregory. Hell, if I were as crazy as Gregory, I'd've seen the whole situation clear right from firing up time, and I'd've brought it right to a screeching halt. Including young Gary Reed, stopped him before he graduated from jerking off in stolen panties to trying to get inside the wrapper.

Hell, if I were crazy enough, I might have stopped Emory from killing Helen.

Maybe I could've slowed Malcolm down enough so he wouldn't have overrevved his heart motor into seizing.

Now comes Jim.

Trudging through these woods with Malcolm's shotgun on my shoulder, I look like any other poaching hunter. Just keep the Fish and Game up to full employment. And I ain't wearing safety orange. There's another law I'm breaking. And I don't have a hunting license this year, not for any Fesmire-fancy reason, but only because they're not giving them away. And the game I'm after is out of season. So I guess they can get me on three counts. I'm as wild-assed as Malcolm on a drunken bash, only I'm sober as a cold chisel.

Rat-tat-tat.

I swear someone's operating machinery right out here in the woods. It's loud enough to hurt my ears. Maybe Emory's bought a jackhammer to play with. *Bam-a-da-bam-a-da, bam, bam,* reverberates through the whole woods. I pull the shotgun from my shoulder and switch off the safety. There shouldn't be anybody else out here. After all, doesn't Emory own everything in sight and then some? Come to think of it, that means anything I shoot or destroy belongs to Emory.

Bam-bam-bam-bam-bam.

Off to the right and not far off either. Look out because now comes Jim.

I'm quiet. It's hard not to be quiet with that pounding racket unless I were to fire off this gun. More to the right. *Bam! Bam! Bam!* and I'm almost on it. Slopes lead down to a little ravine with a clearing, a couple of tall, dead trees, and the biggest woodpecker I've ever seen. You could shish kebab a roast on his bill.

Pileated. That's what he is. A pileated woodpecker. I never hoped to see one. Damn rare, I'd say. Naturally, it'd be here on Emory's property that I'd see the only one of my life. It isn't a tough shot. *Bam, bam, bam,* shouting out of that hollow tree. Well, shit, I can't shoot him. I didn't really expect I could. He almost makes me laugh. He can be my mascot, like Malcolm and his pets, his donkeys, his bees. Like Pauline is for Emory. Yeah, my mascot, a goofy, fucking woodpecker.

So I'm back on the hunt for Emory. I ain't no meat hunter, nor trophy hunter either. We're talking survival hunting here, testing whether or not I'm fit to survive. Now comes Jim.

There it is, Emory's house, and the garage he uses to play mechanic with his truck and RV and whatever other toys he feels like buying. Like Malcolm, collecting and making pets out of everything, only Malcolm's had a heart beating in him so soft it must have had threads of rebar in it to keep from falling right through to his feet, and a soul to father most any living thing, especially if it'd make him joyful mad. But Emory's always looking for amusement, like a kid always saying there's nothing to do. His heart's so light it must flit around his insides like a jay, nothing can claim him. I wonder how he'd like it if I burned and bull-dozed his castle of amusement, his palace of possessions?

Does he count Pauline in his inventory or just among his amusements?

The sun shines down through the trees casting shadows on his back lawn. He's got a big Gravely tractor to mow this. I wonder Emory don't hire it out, but I guess it amuses him to ride around cutting grass and thinking who he can fuck next.

I take no precautions. I stomp right over his yard, wishing he had a flower bed or vegetable garden I could kick around. I don't need to take precautions. I'm carrying a loaded gun. Now comes Jim.

"Emory, you bastard!"

I know he's got guns in the house. I know if he comes out with one, I'll shoot him, right on the spot. I'll blow his fucking head right off. Jim, the goofy, fucking woodpecker.

"Emory, you bastard! Where's my wife?"

I'll blow holes in every wall of his castle. I'll blow so many holes the goddamn walls will tumble down.

He's probably in there with the music turned up, watching her do a strip dance for him. Tilted back in his leather recliner, smoking a cigarette, drinking a fucking beer, and nursing his goddamn impotent hard-on.

"Emory!"

Blam. I take out the big bay window in the ell between house and garage. Glass and wood fill the air and float like cheap jewelry to the ground. Helen wanted to put a little greenhouse here, but she didn't live long enough. Now it's an open-air greenhouse. Emory'll be the envy of the whole goddamn town.

Here he comes. Only he ain't carrying a gun. He's carrying a video camera and taping me like I was the greatest fucking show on earth. Funny cartoon, just for his amusement, he and Pauline can sit and laugh over it.

"I got you on tape, Bucko," he says. "Present for posterity and the court."

A blinking red eye on the camera mocks me. It's the same red eye that stares at Pauline naked. It's cold, burning right into my crotch. It's the tar Alice spread on Tommy's balls. I tell him to put down the camera, just lay it right on his neatly cut grass.

"We won't need any record of this," I say.

Blam.

The camera destroyed doesn't make half so pretty a picture as the bay window. I guess that figures.

"How are you going to pay for that?" Emory asks me.

"Where's Pauline?"

He laughs. "You planning to win her back with a shotgun?" He's laughing like I'm the biggest joke God planned for the year, like you can make fun of this goofy, fucking woodpecker.

"Your ass," I say. I motion him inside with the gun.

"You want me to stick my hands up, like in the movies?" Now he ain't laughing. He's turned around and is walking to the house just like I want him to. If I'd known it was this easy, I'd been pulling the trigger a lot earlier and a lot more often than this. He crunches his fancy sneakers over the broken glass toward the house, me right after him. Tendinitis chews on my elbow like it's taken on full-time work. I'm making a thorough search. I tell him to call her name as we walk. It sounds funny, kind of bland, like milky oatmeal, like your name when they call it at the medical clinic, could be a routine checkup, could be goddamn cancer of the esophagus, they call it in the same tone.

"Pauline. Pauline."

The "ine" part kind of lingers in the sawdust of his mouth like he's got a mush mouth, a lisp. He's becoming a dummy calling her name with a shotgun pointed at his back.

Malcolm didn't get a chance to call out anything, not a single claim on life.

Thick carpet all over the living room. I wonder if Emory fucked her on the floor. *Blam!* I blow away his glass-and-oak gun case. I'm liking the glass-filled air. I hope I ruined a couple of his prize weapons with that shot. It relieves some of the pain in my arm to move the gun. To fire it is a sudden, shocking joy.

"Jim." His voice shakes, and it ain't over the cabinet.

"Keep calling her name, goddamnit! You can do that, can't you?"

Again "Pauline" sounds funny. *Blam.* I blow away the leather couch. I'm sure they fucked on that.

"She ain't here," he says.

I load up the gun again. "I'll tell you what. If she ain't here, I'll kill you. How's that for a deal?"

"You can see her car ain't here." The sawdust's clogging up his words.

"I think she likes riding in your big, monster-fucking truck better than in that little shitbox Tempo we can afford."

I tell him to keep calling her as I march him down to the bedrooms. I'm choking up. Looking at that huge bed, I remember Kari Reed offering to fuck me in her bed. Here in this rich room, on this bouncing bed. Naked. I'm going to puke. Do woodpeckers puke?

"Pauline."

"Shut the fuck up!"

Why don't I shoot up this room? Why don't I shoot fucking Emory?

"Jim, for Christ's sake, what do you want?"

She ain't here. I know that. She ain't like Gary Reed, hiding in rafters or under crawl spaces. Course she could be in the garage, his fancy garage, where he keeps more of his toys. He can fill every room of his house with toys.

She ain't here either. This oversized double garage holds a lot of shit, but it doesn't hold Pauline. I even make Emory switch on the lights in the upper storage space, but sure enough, she ain't there. I take a break and light a cigarette. Even switching hands to hold the gun leaves that cord of pain still aching.

"Mind if I have a smoke?" The oatmeal's gone out of his voice.

"I don't give a fuck."

"You know, Jim, you can't make people do what you want." He shoots two streams of smoke out his nostrils like he's just said something so philosophical, he's proud of it.

"If I could pay for it, I could, only I ain't supposed to have to pay my wife. I ain't supposed to have to pay her to stop fucking you."

"She ain't fucking me. You know goddamn well I can't fuck anybody."

"You been porking me. You porked my sister to death."

He says it ain't true. What did I expect? He'll say anything now. A gun in the face takes the brag out of most everybody. It would me too, if I had any brag in me, which I ain't. Haven't had any brag for years. Just getting up in the morning is brag enough for me. I don't have to kill my wife and fuck some other man's so I can have some brag. I get to be a woodpecker, that's all my brag. I whoop out that goofy laugh.

"Jim!"

Out through the windows I see BB Eyes has arrived, blue lights spinning. I push the lock button on the door to the ell and heel the garage doors to the concrete to seal them. BB Eyes stands with his hands on his hips and hollers my name again. His gun is holstered. He looks back up the drive like he expects somebody else to come, then he heads for the house.

"Don't bother," I yell to him. "We ain't buying anything today."

"Is Emory there?"

Emory looks at me for permission, and I nod, so he yells out to BB Eyes. BB Eyes tells us to come out.

"No," I say.

"Then I'm coming in."

"You'd better bring a shop vac to suck up Emory."

"You carrying a gun?"

"You carrying your dick?"

I watch him go back to the cruiser to call on the radio. I suppose the Staties will be next and the SWAT team and the goddamn six-o'clock news. Ain't this pretty. Now, I'll be arrested, I ain't found Pauline, I'll be keeping Tommy company in jail while Pauline and Emory ball their brains out, and Gary Reed is free to go on a raping rampage. I might's well give up the whole herd.

Now comes Jim.

"You are fucked," says Emory, taking a big drag and nose-blowing the smoke.

"Douse that cigarette, and douse it good."

He's got a cutting torch sitting on the shelf. I see the tanks, and knowing Emory, I'll bet that black one is fill up to the brim. Three, four hundred dollars' worth of regulators and torches so he can play around in here. Well, I'm only going to use a couple of dollars' worth of gas. I crank open the valve. With a rushing hiss, the dead garlic scent of acetylene pours out into the garage.

"He's filling the place with gas!" Emory shouts. It's the first time I've seen him panicked. It's a fine feeling. I'm flying in the tall trees now. I break out with my woodpecker laugh.

"Don't fire a shot!" I yell to BB Eyes. "I won't even have to aim, and we'll go to kingdom come."

Up drives another cop car, not the Staties, but Sergeant Dumont. Maybe we will go out in a fireball with that asshole on the job. He takes off his dark glasses to peer into the tiny garage windows, draws his gun, and swaggers himself three steps closer. He's a lean, mean, nonsmoking professional cop, and I'd guess he's got it in mind that he's the selectmen's sweetheart, so just as soon as they can dump poor old fat BB Eyes, he'll be chief of police.

"Back off, Dumont!" I yell at him. "When this place blows, it'll take you with it."

I see BB Eyes explaining about the gas to Dumont and pointing for him to holster his gun. Dumont shakes his head, looks mean at the garage, then points out to the road where the Staties will come from. Dumont's one of those model guys who would walk right into the line of fire as long as you let him take home the flak jacket and hang it in his closet.

"How's Alice Jewell, Dumont?" I holler out. And I let him hear my laugh.

"Any spark—"

"Shut up, Emory," I tell him. If he'd just piss his pants, I could die happy. "I know what it takes to set off an explosion."

"If they shoot in here—"

"That's the point, ain't it." They ain't going to shoot, of course, and if they did, a lead bullet don't spark, but he ain't thinking that. He don't seem to know what will spark an explosion, but by God I do. "Hey, Dumont, Emory says Alice Jewell is a real good fuck!" I tell Emory I don't want Dumont feeling too sorry for him when the garage blows. "It might keep the poor fella up a night or two, might turn him temporarily impotent or something, then I'd have Alice Jewell's sexual frustration on my conscience too."

The garlic scent's taken over in here, like morning-after spaghetti sauce. Emory's garage is all acetylene. Emory starts to cough, and I think how walking into that bedroom of his started to choke me. I think how bills and kids and taxes and troubles have choked me full up. I think about Malcolm dropping his face right onto his dinner plate. Shaking a cigarette out my pack, I ask him if he wants a smoke.

"Are you nuts?" His voice carries an edge as sharp as the garlicky smell of acetylene.

Not nuts like Gregory, but wacky like the woodpecker, so I just stick it in my mouth and hope Emory'll piss his pants. He reaches out to stop me from lighting it, his hand quick, until I bring the shotgun up to his chest. That slows him down, but he still doesn't piss his pants. He doesn't even shake, though his voice keeps that fearful edge on it.

"Are you going to shoot me?"

"I won't have to. As soon as this gun goes off, the garage will explode." I break out my wacky laugh.

Am I going to shoot him? Shoot him and blow up myself, pain-stung arm and all. Now comes Jim. Now comes Jim for what? Now I really would like a smoke. I fake-draw on the cigarette in my mouth. Emory, he looks forlorn. Outside, BB Eyes and Dumont watch a car pull up the driveway. It ain't the Staties or the SWAT team or even the five-o'clock news. It's Pauline. She's out of the car and running when Dumont catches her, and BB Eyes talks to her, pointing at the garage.

The scent's powerful now. We're inside the mouth of the garlic. Both Emory and I are coughing. He's gagging. I wish he'd just wet his pants. I cough so hard my cigarette falls to the floor. Emory looks at it panicked like even that might spark an explosion.

"Jim!" Pauline yells. "Don't kill yourself."

I'm gagging too now. I open a window and stick my head out so I can breathe and talk. "Got you at a standstill, don't I, Dumont."

He's fiddling with his glasses, probably to keep his hands away from his gun. "You know, it don't matter how bad a shot I am, I can blow us all to hell. I can't miss. It don't matter a damn where I shoot. I can be good, bad, smart, or dumb, I can be any fucking thing at all. If I squeeze this trigger, boom! off we go." I laugh, the woodpecker laugh.

Pauline starts toward me. "Jim, I didn't understand about the shame."

Dumont drops his forty-dollar glasses and grabs Pauline. "Mrs. Hutchinson, you can't go there. This is a police matter, under our control. We're in charge here."

"It's Hutchins, you idiot!" she yells. She slaps his face and breaks away from him.

BB Eyes says, "Dumont, we ain't in charge of squat here. Jim's in control. Let the woman go talk to him less you got a better idea."

"The only idea Dumont's got is being chief," I say.

Pauline walks over to the open window. I tell Emory to hunker in the corner. The air will be better down low, and I won't have to think about him trying any Tarzan moves in case he decides to impress his ladylove.

I expect her to try to talk me out of the garage, but she's telling me about finding Gary Reed under the motel bed. There he was, dead. "Jim, he scared the wits right out of me. Then I read the note he left."

She says it turned her scared for me. It's all mixed up with shame and grief for Elizabeth and—

"Don't you think I grieved for her?" I ask. "She's my daughter too, you know."

"It didn't seem you could act like it." Her lip's quivering like a wet flower. For the first time I can hear sorrow instead of mad when she talks to me.

"It was all burden," I tell her. "The load of it kept my heart from popping right out onto the ground."

"You'd never go to her grave with me." Tears leak right down her cheeks, not tears for Elizabeth now. "Like you couldn't be bothered. Or you were ashamed of me."

"I thought you wanted to be alone. I tried to keep things going so you could tend to her. Only when you turned to Emory—"

"See, he wasn't connected to Elizabeth."

"And I was."

"I'm sorry."

Mad and sad and shame and blame all wrap together in my stomach, where I can hold them or spit them up. "Got so I couldn't laugh."

"There's enough grief to go twice around," she says.

Malcolm makes me tear up, lips quiver, stomach suck in gasps. Lines clear. I hear Emory gagging. He still hasn't pissed his pants, but I tell him to turn off the gas anyway. I don't know what's going to happen, but I ain't going to die in Emory Holler's fucking garage. As he twists the valves, he says he didn't kill Helen and he didn't screw Pauline. He mumbles some, but Pauline hears him.

"Of course he didn't," she says. "Don't you think he's got enough grief too?"

"Let's get out of here," I say. I punch the garage door lift, and Emory and I walk out. Pauline grabs my hand.

Grief and hatred and shame hunker down. They ain't going to leave peaceful. They've got all used to living in me like a comfortable suburban housing development, but it's eviction time. I bulldozer them out with my woodpecker laugh. I squeeze Pauline's hand.

"It's hard to speak," she says. "Some words dry your throat right up and stick there before they reach your mouth."

"We're out of practice, maybe."

"It ain't only practice. Practice cuts both ways." She squeezes my hand back but doesn't say any more.

"Cut through practice and history and grief too," I say. I out again with my woodpecker laugh.

"I love you," she says.

Tears wash away my woodpecker laugh. Next thing I know Dumont's got his gun right in my ear and yanks Malcolm's shotgun away from me. He tosses it to BB Eyes. "Now, we know who's in charge. Lie down with your hands behind you."

Even though BB Eyes is telling him it ain't necessary, I lie down because with a do-it-yourself asshole like Dumont you don't want to make him too nervous. All to once my arm stops hurting.

"I'm going to show you something," says Dumont. "You think you're so goddamn smart you had us stymied, but we could've taken you out anytime with no danger to Mr. Holler or his property." He aims his magnum at the open garage door.

"Don't," says BB Eyes, but of course he ain't fleet of foot. I'm on the ground. Emory and Pauline just stare at Dumont like watching a man stick his bare hand in a beehive.

Blam!

The bullet flies through the empty air, then strikes the tools on the workbench. You don't hardly see the spark because there's a hell of a fireball that frickle-fries everything in that garage and singes the hair of us poor fools watching from outside.

"Nice shot, Dumont," I say.

Acknowledgments

My thanks to the following experts for showing me the ropes and letting me hang by them:

Jim Gallagher
Joe Gasiecki
George Albee
Earle Scott
Randy Dunham
Fred Fenton
Robert Kimball

Jack White
Bob Wicklund
Jim McGonigle
Tim Deal
Charles Murray
Wayne Sargent
Doug Giles

My thanks to the following writers and critical readers for their suggestions and encouragement:

Acknowledgments

Bill Bozzone	David Bradt
Tricia Bauer	Lois Bradt
Leon Forrest	Don Kimball
Tom Williams	Arlene Mullen
Donald Hall	Madge Rand
Bob Begiebing	Wesley McNair

Part of this novel was written with the support of a National Endowment for the Arts fellowship, for which I am grateful.